THE
THIEF LORD

A compelling tale, rich in ingenious twists, with a setting and
cast that will linger in readers' memories.
SCHOOL LIBRARY JOURNAL

[A] radiant novel...Today's young readers will probably love
this book as they love the Harry Potter series, for its zany plot
and well-defined characters ... splendid.
THE NEW YORK TIMES BOOK REVIEW

A darn good yarn ...the charming tale of a band of urchin-
thieves, a magical carousel and two orphaned brothers.
NEWSWEEK

[An] exquisitely told tale of adventure and intrigue.
Display[s] the kind of zest that makes you inhale a book in
as few sittings as possible.
USA TODAY

A European best-seller ... Funke's deft exploration of a
timeless theme ... the longing of kids to grow up and of
grown-ups to relive their youth ... should engage both
young and old.
PEOPLE

Wholly original. SLATE

Will satisfy readers whose hearts have been touched
by the loyalty and courage of the two brothers.
THE HORN BOOK

The Venetian setting is ripe for mystery, and the city's alleys
and canals ratchet up the suspense in the chase scenes.
PUBLISHERS WEEKLY

From the Chicken House

I was caught up in *THE THIEF LORD* straightaway – lost
immediately in the alleys and canals of Venice. It was as
if I was in the very best of films, with Prosper and Bo and
all their friends.
Cornelia Funke weaves the most marvellous storyteller's
magic and makes this *your* adventure. Through every
twist and turn, each page will catch your imagination in
new ways: sad, serious, exciting or fantastical!
Don't worry, I won't spoil the end – but I can't wait to
read the beginning of her next book!

Barry Cunningham
Publisher
The Chicken House

THE
THIEF LORD

CORNELIA FUNKE

The
Chicken HOUSE

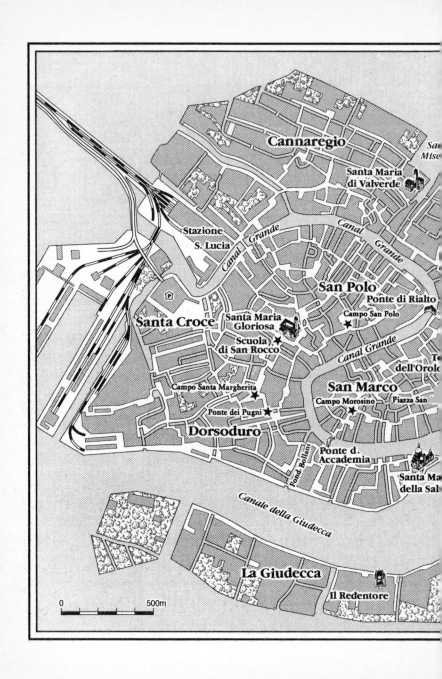

VENICE

San Michele

SS. Giovanni e Paolo

★ Calle del Paradiso

San Marco
Palazzo
Ducale (Doge's Palace)
Riva degli Schiavoni

Arsenale

Castello

Canale di S. Marco

San Giorgio
Maggiore

TO ROLF – AND TO BOB HOSKINS,
WHO LOOKS EXACTLY LIKE VICTOR

First published in Germany by Cecilie Dressler Verlag Hamburg 2000
Original Text © Cornelia Funke 2000
English Translation © Oliver Latsch 2002

The Publishers would like to thank Christine Kidney, Vivien Brett,
Ali Evans and Rachel Hickman for their help with this edition.
And a special thank you to Clara Bagenal George who first told us
about Cornelia Funke and her books.

This edition published in Great Britain in 2003
The Chicken House
2 Palmer Street
Frome, Somerset BA11 1DF
United Kingdom
www.doublecluck.com

PB ISBN 1 903434 77 7
HB ISBN 1 903434 70 X

Cover illustration © Christian Birmingham 2002
Inside illustration © Cornelia Funke
Map © Lothar Meier 2000
Cover design by Alison Withey
Designed and typeset by Dorchester Typesetting Group Ltd
Printed and bound in Great Britain

British Library Cataloguing in Publication data available.

1 Victor's New Clients

It was autumn in Venice when Victor first heard of Prosper and Bo. The canals, gleaming in the sun, dappled the ancient brickwork with gold. But the wind was blowing ice-cold air from the sea, reminding the Venetians that winter was approaching. Even the air in the alleyways tasted of snow, and only the wings of the carved angels and dragons high up on the rooftops felt any real warmth from the pale sun.

The house in which Victor lived and worked stood close to a canal; so close, in fact, that the water lapped against its walls. At night, he sometimes dreamt that the house was sinking into the waves, and that the sea would wash away the causeway that Venice clings to, breaking the thin thread that binds the city to Italy's mainland. In his dream the sea would sweep the lagoon away too, swallowing everything – the houses, the bridges, the churches, the palaces, and the people who had built so boldly on its surface.

For the time being, however, the city still stood firmly on its wooden legs. Victor leaned against his window and looked out through the dusty glass. Surely no other place on earth was more proud of its beauty than Venice, and as he watched its spires and domes, each caught the sun as if trying to out-shine one another. Whistling a tune, Victor turned away from the window and walked over to his large mirror. Just the weather for trying out his new disguise, he thought, as the sun warmed the back of his sturdy neck. He had bought this new treasure only the previous day: an enormous moustache, so dark and bushy that it would have made any self-respecting walrus extremely jealous. He stuck it carefully under his nose and stood on his toes to make himself taller. He turned to the left, to the right, and became so engrossed in his reflection that he only heard the footsteps on the stairs when they stopped outside his door.

Clients. Blast! Why were they bothering him now of all times?

With a deep sigh he sat behind his desk. He heard voices whispering outside his door. They were probably admiring his nameplate, Victor thought, a handsome black shiny sign with his name engraved in gold letters.

Victor Getz
Private Detective
Investigations of Any Kind

It was written in three languages – after all, he often had clients from abroad. Next to the sign was a knocker – a lion's head with a brass ring in its mouth, which Victor had polished just that morning.

What are they waiting for? he thought, tapping his fingers on the armrest of his chair. '*Avanti!*' He called out, '*Come in!*'

The door opened. A man and a woman stepped into

10

Victor's office, which also doubled as his living room. They looked around warily, taking in the cacti, the beard and moustache collection, the coat stand bursting with Victor's caps, hats and wigs, the huge street map of Venice on the wall, and the winged lion that served as a paperweight on Victor's desk.

'Do you speak English?' asked the woman, although her Italian sounded quite fluent.

'Of course!' Victor answered, gesturing towards the chairs in front of his desk. 'English is my mother tongue. What can I do for you?'

They both sat down hesitantly. The man folded his arms and looked rather sullen, the woman stared at Victor's walrus moustache.

'Oh, that's just for camouflage,' he explained, pulling the moustache from his lip. 'Quite a necessity in my line of work. Well, what can I do for you? Anything lost or stolen, any pet run away?'

Without saying a word, the woman reached into her bag. She had ash-blonde hair and a pointed nose. Her mouth didn't look as if smiling was its favourite activity. The man was a giant, at least two full heads taller than Victor. His nose was peeling from sunburn and his eyes were small and dull. Doesn't look like he can take a joke either, Victor thought, as he committed the two faces to memory. He could never remember a phone number, but he never forgot a face.

'*This* is what we've lost,' said the woman as she pushed the photograph across the desk. Her English was even better than her Italian.

Two boys looked out at Victor from the photograph. One was small and blonde, with a broad smile on his face; the other was older, dark-haired and more serious looking. He had

11

his arm around the younger boy's shoulder, as if he wanted to protect him from all that was evil in the world.

'Children?' Victor looked up in surprise. 'I've tracked down a lot of things in my time – suitcases, dogs, a couple of escaped lizards, and some husbands – but you are the first clients to come to me because they've lost their children, Mr and Mrs... ?' He looked at them inquisitively.

'Hartlieb,' the woman answered. 'Esther and Max Hartlieb.'

'And they are *not* our children,' her husband stated firmly, which immediately earnt him an angry look from his pointy-nosed wife.

'Prosper and Boniface are my late sister's sons,' she explained. 'She raised the boys on her own. Prosper has just turned twelve, and Bo is five.'

'Prosper and Boniface,' murmured Victor. 'Unusual names. Doesn't Prosper mean "the lucky one"?'

Esther Hartlieb arched her eyebrows. 'Does it? Well, one thing's for sure, they're very strange names, and that's putting it mildly. My late sister had a fondness for anything peculiar. When she died three months ago, my husband and I applied for custody of Bo since we sadly don't have any children of our own. But we couldn't possibly have taken on his older brother as well. Any reasonable person could see that. But Prosper got very upset, acting like a lunatic, accusing us of stealing his brother – although we would have allowed him to visit Bo once a month.' Her pale face grew even paler.

'They ran away more than eight weeks ago,' Max Hartlieb continued, 'from their grandfather's house in Hamburg, where they were staying at the time. Prosper's quite capable of talking his brother into any foolish scheme, and everything we have found out so far indicates that he has brought him here, to Venice.'

'From Hamburg to Venice?' Victor raised his eyebrows. 'That's a long way for two children to travel on their own. Have you contacted the police here?'

'Of course we have,' hissed Esther Hartlieb. 'They were no help at all. Surely it can't be that hard to find two children, who are all alone—'

But her husband cut her off. 'Sadly, I have to return home on urgent business. We would therefore like to put you in charge of the search for the boys, Mr Getz. The concierge at our hotel recommended you.'

'How nice of him,' Victor mumbled. He fiddled with the false moustache. The thing looked like a dead mouse lying next to the phone. 'But what makes you so sure they've come to Venice? Surely they didn't come just to ride on the gondolas...'

'It's their mother's fault!' Mrs Harltieb pursed her lips and glanced out through Victor's dirty window. Outside on the balcony, the wind was ruffling the feathers of a pigeon. 'My sister kept telling the boys about this city. She told them stories about winged lions, a golden cathedral, and about angels and dragons perched on top of the buildings. She told them that water nymphs came ashore for walks at night up the little steps on the edges of the canals.' She shook her head angrily. 'My sister could talk about these things in a way that she almost made me believe her. It was Venice this, Venice that, nothing but Venice! Bo drew winged lions all the time and Prosper simply drank in every word his mother said. He probably thought that if they could make it to Venice, he and Bo would land right in the middle of fairyland. What an idea!' She wrinkled her nose and cast a contemptuous look through the window at the crumbling plaster of the neighbouring houses.

Mr Hartlieb adjusted his tie. 'It has cost us a lot of money to trace the boys this far, Mr Getz,' he said, 'and I can assure you that they are here. Somewhere…'

'…in this filth!' Mrs Hartlieb finished her husband's sentence for him.

'Well, at least there aren't any cars here to run them over,' Victor said under his breath. He looked up at the street map on his wall and stared at the maze of lanes and canals that made Venice so unique. Then turning back to look at his desk, deep in thought, he started scratching doodles on to its surface with his letter opener.

Mr Hartlieb cleared his throat. 'Mr Getz … will you take the case on?'

Victor looked once more at the photograph of the two very different faces – the tall, serious boy and the carefree smile of the younger one. And then he nodded. 'Yes, I'll take it,' he said. 'I will find them. They look a little too young to be coping on their own. Tell me, did you ever run away as children?'

'For heaven's sake, of course I didn't!' Esther Hartlieb looked flabbergasted. Her husband just shook his head as if it was the strangest thing he'd ever heard.

'Well, I did.' Victor wedged the photograph under the winged lion. 'But I was by myself. I didn't have a brother, big or small, to look after me… Well, leave me your address and telephone number, and let's talk about my fee.'

As the Hartliebs struggled back down the narrow staircase, Victor stepped on to the balcony. A cold wind whipped at his face, bearing the salty tang of the nearby sea. Shivering, he leaned against the balustrade and watched the Hartliebs step on to a bridge a few houses further down the canal. It was a pretty bridge, but the couple seemed not to take any notice of it. They rushed across it sullenly, without even a glance at the scrawny dog barking at them from a passing barge. And – of course – they didn't spit into the canal, like Victor always did.

'Well, who says you have to like your clients,' the detective muttered to himself. He leaned over a cardboard box on the floor of the balcony, out of which the heads of two tortoises were peeking. 'Parents like that are still better than no parents at all, right? What do you think? Don't tortoises have parents?'

Victor looked through the balustrade at the canal below, and at the houses, whose stony feet were washed by the water day in, day out. He had lived in Venice for more than fifteen years and he still didn't know all the city's nooks and crannies – but then again no one did. The job wouldn't be easy, particularly if the boys didn't want to be found. There were so many hiding places, and so many narrow alleys with names no one could remember – some of them with no names at all. Boarded-up churches, deserted houses … the whole city was one huge invitation to play hide-and-seek.

Well, I've always liked playing hide-and-seek, thought Victor, and so far I've found everyone I've ever looked for. The two boys had already been coping alone for eight weeks. Eight weeks! When *he* had run away from home he had only managed to cope with his freedom for one afternoon. At dusk, he had slunk back home, feeling sad and sorry for himself.

The tortoises nibbled at the lettuce leaf Victor was holding out to them. 'I think I'd better take you inside tonight,' he

15

said. 'This wind tastes of winter.'

Lando and Paula looked at him through their lashless eyes. He sometimes got them mixed up but they didn't seem to mind. He had found them one day at the fish market, where he had gone in search of a client's Persian cat. Once Victor had managed to fish the pedigree cat out of a barrel full of stinking sardines and stowed her in a scratch-safe box, he had discovered the two tortoises. They had been meandering between all the human feet, completely oblivious to the world. When Victor picked them up they quickly retreated into their shells.

'Where shall I start?' Victor wondered. 'In the orphanages? The hospitals? They're such sad places. But maybe I don't need to begin there – the Hartliebs have probably done that already.' He leaned over the balcony and spat into the dark canal.

Bo and Prosper. Nice names, he thought, even if they are a little unusual.

2 *Three Children*

The Hartliebs had been right: Prosper and Bo had indeed managed to get to Venice. They had travelled a long way, squatting in rattling trains, hiding from conductors and nosy old ladies. They had locked themselves into stinking toilets, slept in dark corners, squeezed tightly together, hungry, tired and frozen. But they had done it, and they were still together.

At exactly the same time their Aunt Esther was sitting down on a chair in front of Victor Getz's desk, the two boys were standing in a doorway just a few steps from the Rialto bridge. The cold wind blew in their faces – there was no doubt about it, the warm days were gone.

Esther had been wrong about one thing: Prosper and Bo were not alone. There was a girl with them. She was slender and had brown hair, which she wore in a long, thin plait that went right down to her hips and looked like a long sting. It had given her her nickname: Hornet. She never answered to anything else.

The girl was frowning as she stared at a crumpled piece of paper. People pushed past her, ramming their full shopping bags into her back. 'I think we've got everything,' she said in a quiet, slightly hoarse voice. Prosper had liked that voice as soon as he'd heard Hornet speak, even before he'd been able to understand much of what she was saying. At first he remembered just the few words of Italian that his mother had taught him alongside her stories of Venice, but he'd had to learn fast. 'Now there's just the batteries for Mosca. Where can we get those?'

Prosper pushed his fringe out of his face. 'There's a hardware store back in that side alley,' he said. He saw that Bo was hunching his shoulders up against the cold, so he turned up his brother's collar. The children pushed back into the crowd. It was market day at the Rialto and the narrow alleys were even more crowded than usual. Men and women, young and old, were squashed between the stalls, most of them laden with bags and parcels, everyone trying to squeeze past each other. There were old ladies, who had probably never left the city, weaving their way around the tourists. The air smelled of fish, autumn flowers and dried mushrooms.

'Hornet?' Bo reached for her hand and gave her his sweetest smile. 'Will you buy me one of those little cakes over there?'

Hornet pinched his cheek affectionately and shook her head. 'No!' she said firmly, pulling him along.

The hardware store Prosper had discovered was tiny. In its window, between coffee machines and toasters, stood a few toys. Bo gazed at them, his mouth open. 'But I'm hungry,' he moaned, pressing his hands against the glass.

'You're always hungry,' Prosper smiled. He opened the door and stayed with Bo near the entrance while Hornet walked up to the counter.

The girl addressed an elderly lady who had her back turned to the counter and was dusting some radios. '*Scusi*, I need batteries. Two. For a small radio.'

The lady packed the batteries in a paper bag and pushed a handful of sweets across the counter. 'What a sweet boy,' she said, winking at Bo. 'Fair as an angel. Is he your brother?'

Hornet shook her head, 'No, they're my cousins. They're just visiting.'

Prosper pushed Bo behind his back, but the boy slipped through his brother's arms and snatched the sweets from the counter. '*Grazie!*' he said. He smiled at the old lady and hopped back to Prosper.

The lady smiled. '*Un vero angelo!*' She put Hornet's money in the till. 'But his mother should darn his trousers and dress him in warmer clothes. The winter is coming. Didn't you hear the wind in the chimneys today?'

'We'll tell her,' Hornet stuffed the batteries into her full shopping bag. 'Have a nice day, *Signora*.'

'*Angelo*, huh!' Prosper shook his head as they elbowed their way back into the crowd. 'How come they all fall for you, Bo?'

His little brother just stuck his tongue out at him and skipped ahead. The two older children had to struggle to keep up with him as he nimbly wove his way through all the legs and bodies.

'Not so fast, Bo!' Prosper shouted after him.

Hornet just laughed. 'Leave him!' she said. 'We won't lose him. See? He's right there.'

Bo pulled a face. He tried to hop around an orange he'd seen on the ground, but he stumbled and crashed into a group of Japanese tourists. Startled, he scrambled up again, only to start smiling as soon as he saw that two of the women were pointing their cameras at him. But before they could take their pictures, Prosper was already dragging his brother away by the collar.

'How often do I have to tell you not to let yourself get photographed?' he hissed at him.

Bo pulled away from Prosper's hand and skipped over an empty cigarette pack. 'But they were Japanese! Aunt Esther won't look at Japanese photographs, will she? And *you* said she was going to adopt another boy anyway.'

Prosper nodded and mumbled, 'Yes.' But he couldn't help looking around as if he expected his aunt to be lurking in the crowd, just waiting for her chance to grab Bo.

Hornet noticed the look on Prosper's face. 'You're thinking about your aunt again, aren't you?' she whispered, although Bo had wandered out of earshot again. 'Forget her! She's not looking for you any more. And even if she is, then she wouldn't be looking here, would she?'

Prosper shrugged. He cast an uneasy glance at a couple of women passing by. 'Probably not,' he murmured.

But Hornet insisted: 'Definitely not! So stop worrying!'

Prosper agreed, although he knew he wouldn't be able to stop. Every night, while Bo slept as soundly as a kitten, Prosper dreamt of Esther. Upright, nervous, hairspray-sticky Esther.

'Hey, Prop!' Bo suddenly stopped in front of them again. He held a full wallet up towards Prosper. 'Look what I found!'

Prosper snatched the wallet from his brother's hand and pulled him into a dark arcade away from the crowd.

'Where did you get that, Bo?'

Hornet had followed them behind a pile of old crates. A couple of pigeons were pecking at bits of squashed fruit on the ground.

Bo stuck out his lower lip defiantly, sulkily holding onto Hornet's arm. 'I found it! I told you! A big bald man dropped it out of his pocket. He didn't even notice it. And then I found it!'

Prosper sighed.

Since they had begun to fend for themselves, Prosper had learnt how to steal. Only food at first, but then money, too. He hated it. He always got scared and his fingers started to tremble every time. Bo, however, thought it was an exciting game. Prosper had forbidden his brother to steal anything and he told him off very harshly every time he caught him. He certainly didn't want to give Esther a chance to say that he had turned his little brother into a thief.

'Calm down, Prop,' Hornet said, giving Bo a cuddle. 'He told you he didn't steal it, and the man is long gone. At least have a look and see how much is in it.'

Reluctantly, Prosper opened the wallet.

The visitors who came to Venice to see the palaces and churches were always losing things. Mostly just bottles of water or the cheap carnival masks that you could buy on any street corner. But every now and then the strap of a camera would snap, or a handful of change would fall out of someone's pocket – and sometimes even a wallet like this! Prosper leafed through the compartments but there were only a few 1000 Lire notes tucked in between crumpled receipts, restaurant bills, and used Vaporetto tickets.

'Well, it would have been nice.' Hornet couldn't hide her disappointment as Prosper threw the wallet into an empty crate. 'Our cash-tin is nearly empty. Let's hope the Thief Lord can fill it up again tonight.'

'Of course he will!' Bo looked at Hornet as if she had

doubted that the earth was round. 'And one day I'm going to help him! I'm going to be a big thief. Scipio will teach me!'

'Over my dead body,' Prosper grumbled, pushing Bo back into the alley.

'It's OK,' Hornet whispered to Prosper. Bo was trotting ahead of them, looking deeply insulted. 'You don't really think Scipio is going take him along on a raid, do you?'

Prosper shook his head but he was still worried. Keeping an eye on Bo was difficult. Ever since they had run away from their grandfather's house, Prosper had asked himself at least three times a day whether he had been right to take his little brother with him. On that night, eight weeks ago, Bo had trailed alongside him with sleepy eyes. He had held on to his big brother's hand all the way to the station.

Getting to Venice had been easier than Prosper had expected. But it was already autumn when they arrived in the city, and the air had not been as warm and gentle as Prosper had imagined it would be. A damp wind had greeted them as they climbed down the steps from the station, blowing right through their thin clothes. All they had with them was a small bag and a backpack. Prosper's pocket money hadn't lasted long, and after the second night Bo had already started coughing so badly that Prosper had taken him by the hand to go and find a policeman. He had been determined to use the few bits of Italian he had learnt from his mother, and to say, '*Scusi*, we have run away from home, but my brother is sick. Could you call my aunt so she can come and pick him up?'

He had been desperate.

And then Hornet had appeared.

She had taken them to her hiding place, where they'd met Riccio and Mosca, and had given them dry clothes and something hot to eat. Then she had explained to Prosper that they could forget about stealing and being cold, as from now on Scipio, the Thief Lord, would look after them, just like he looked after Hornet and her friends.

'The others are probably waiting for us.' Hornet's voice startled Prosper out of his thoughts and for a moment he was confused by the smells of coffee, and sweet pastries, that wafted at him from the houses.

Their home had smelt very different.

'I bet we'll still have to tidy up,' said Bo. 'Scipio doesn't like it when the hideout is untidy.'

'You can talk,' Prosper mocked. 'Who spilt the bucket full of canal water yesterday?'

'And he always leaves out some cheese for the mice.' Hornet giggled as Bo gave her a shove with his elbow. Even though he knows the Thief Lord hates nothing more than mouse droppings. It's too bad that the wonderful hideout he's found for us is full of them – and that it's so difficult to keep the place warm. Perhaps something less grand would have been more practical, but of course our Thief Lord won't have it any other way.'

'The Star-Palace,' Bo corrected her. He ran after the other two as they turned into a less crowded alley. 'Scipio says it's called the Star-Palace!'

Hornet rolled her eyes. 'Watch it,' she whispered to Prosper, 'soon Bo won't listen to you at all any more – only to what Scipio tells him.'

'And what can I do about it?' Prosper replied sulkily.

Prosper knew perfectly well that it was only thanks to Scipio that they didn't have to sleep on the street any more, especially now when in the evenings a cold mist hung over the alleys and canals. Scipio's raids paid for their pasta and their fresh fruit. Scipio had brought the shoes that were keeping Bo's feet warm, even though they were a bit big for him. Scipio made sure they could eat without having to always steal for it. Scipio had given them a home again – a home without Esther. But, still, Scipio was a thief.

The alleys they walked through became narrower. It was quiet between the houses and soon they entered the hidden heart of the city, where there were hardly any strangers. Cats darted away as their footsteps rang out on the paving stones. Pigeons cooed from the roofs. The ever-present water swayed beneath the bridges, splashing against boats and wooden posts, and reflecting back the old faces of the houses. The children wandered deeper and deeper into the maze of alleys. The houses seemed to be moving in on them, watching them, as if they knew who they were.

Their hiding place was in a building that stood out from its neighbours like a child among grown-ups – low and flat between the taller houses. Boarded-up windows looked out into the alley. The walls were covered with old, yellowed film posters and the entrance was blocked off with rusty shutters. A big crooked sign hanging above the entrance said: STELLA. The cinema's neon sign hadn't been lit up for a long time. But that suited its current inhabitants just fine.

Hornet cast a careful glance up and down the alley while Prosper made sure no one was watching them from the sur-rounding windows. Then they vanished, one by one, into the narrow passageway that opened up a few steps down from the cinema's main entrance.

They were home.

3 The Star-Palace

A water rat scuttled away as the children felt their way along the narrow passage. It led to a canal, like so many of Venice's alleys and passages. Hornet, Prosper, and Bo, however, only followed it as far as a metal door set in the window-less wall to their right. Someone had painted '*Vietato Ingresso*' in clumsy letters on it – No Entry. The door had once been one of the cinema's emergency exits. Now it was the entrance to a hiding place that only six children knew anything about.

Next to the door was a cord and Prosper gave it two strong tugs. He waited for a moment and then pulled it once more. This was their sign, but it still took quite a while before something happened. Bo hopped impatiently from one foot to the other. Finally, the door opened just a crack and a suspicious voice asked: 'Password?'

'Come on, Riccio, you know we never remember the stupid password,' Prosper grumbled angrily.

Hornet stepped up to the door and hissed. 'Do you see these bags in my hands, Hedgehog? I just dragged them all the way from the Rialto market. My arms are as long as a monkey's, so open the door!'

Riccio opened the door, looking very worried. 'OK, OK. But only if Prosper doesn't tell Scipio again, like last time.'

Riccio was a scrawny boy and at least a head shorter than Prosper, although he wasn't much younger than him. At least that's what he claimed. His brown hair always stuck out from his head in every direction, earning him the nickname Riccio the Hedgehog.

'No one can remember Scipio's passwords!' Hornet muttered as she pushed past him. 'And anyway, the special ring is enough.'

'Scipio doesn't think so.' Riccio carefully pushed the bolt across the door.

'Well, then he should make up passwords we *can* remember. Can *you* remember the last one?'

Riccio scratched his spiky head. 'Hold on ... Catago ... Diddledoo ... East. Or something like that.'

Hornet rolled her eyes. Bo giggled.

Riccio walked ahead, shining the way with his torch. 'We've already started cleaning up,' he said. 'But we haven't got far. Mosca just wants to fiddle with his radio all the time. And until an hour ago we were standing in front of the Palazzo Pisani. I really don't know why Scipio had to pick such a palace of all places for his next raid. There's something going on in there nearly every night: parties, receptions, dinners – all the posh families of Venice seem to be in and out all the time. Beats me how Scipio thinks he can get *in there!*'

Prosper shrugged. So far the Thief Lord hadn't asked him and Bo to stake out one of his targets, although Bo kept begging him to. It was usually Riccio and Mosca who were sent to check out the houses Scipio planned to 'visit' at night. Scipio had a name for the two of them: he called them 'his eyes'. Hornet's task was to make sure that the money from his raids was not spent too quickly. Prosper and Bo, as the Thief Lord's most recent charges, had so far only been allowed to tag along when the loot was sold or, like today, to do some shopping. Prosper didn't mind that at all. Bo, however, would have loved to sneak with Scipio into the city's smartest houses to steal all the amazing things the Thief Lord always brought back from his raids.

'Scipio can get into any house,' Bo said, skipping along next to Riccio. Two hops on his right leg, two on the left; Bo never just walked – he ran or he bounced. 'He raided the Doge's Palace and wasn't caught. He *is* the Thief Lord.'

'Oh yes, the raid at The Doge's Palace – how can we ever forget!' Hornet grinned at Prosper. 'Even you must have heard that story a hundred times by now.'

Prosper had to smile back.

'Well, I could hear it a thousand times,' Riccio said, pushing aside a dark and musty curtain. Ahead of them lay the cinema's auditorium. It was not very old, but it was in a much worse condition than some of the city's houses that had stood for hundreds of years. Dusty wire cables stuck out from the walls where there had once been large chandeliers. The children had strung a few naked light bulbs running on batteries throughout the large room, and even in their dim light you could see the plaster coming off the ceiling. Only the front three rows of seats remained and each of those was missing a few chairs. Mice had built their nests in the soft, red upholstery. The cinema's screen was hidden behind a thick curtain embroidered with golden stars. The curtain was moth-eaten but it had kept its old splendour. The golden thread on the pale blue fabric still shimmered full of promise, and Bo had to touch the golden stars at least once every day.

Sitting on the bare floor in front of the curtain was a boy. He was fiddling with an old radio and was so engrossed in his work that he didn't notice Bo creeping up on him. Bo jumped on to his back and the boy spun around.

'Damn it, Bo!' he shouted. 'I nearly stabbed myself with the screwdriver.'

But Bo skipped away. Laughing, he climbed like a squirrel over the folding chairs. 'Just you wait, you little water rat!' Mosca roared, trying to catch Bo. 'This time I'm going to tickle you until you burst!'

Bo screamed, 'Prop, help me!' But Prosper just stood there, grinning. He didn't lift a finger, not even when Mosca tucked his little brother under his arm like a parcel. Mosca was the biggest and strongest of them all, and however much Bo kicked and struggled, Mosca wouldn't let go. Unimpressed by his wriggling, Mosca carried his prisoner over to the others.

'What do you think? Shall I tickle him, or shall I keep him prisoner here, for ever, under my arm?'

Bo screamed, 'Let me go, Mosca!'

Mosca's skin was beautifully black. Riccio always claimed he could hide like a shadow in the dark alleyways of the city.

'All right. I will pardon you this time, dwarf!' Mosca said grandly while Bo tried more and more desperately to free himself. Then, he asked,

'So, did you bring the paint for my boat?'

'No. It's too expensive. We'll buy it when Scipio brings us the new loot,' Hornet answered. She dumped the bags on a chair. 'We can't afford it at the moment.'

'But we've got enough emergency cash!' Mosca put Bo

back on his feet and crossed his arms angrily. 'What are you going to do with all that money?'

'How often do I have to tell you? The money is for bad times.' Hornet pulled Bo to her side. 'Do you think you can manage to put the things in the fridge?'

Bo nodded and dashed off, nearly falling flat on his face. He dragged the bags, one by one, through the double doors that used to open to let in the audience. Beyond the doors, in the entrance hall, was a large display cabinet that had once held drinks and ice cream. Although it didn't work any more, it was still useful for storing supplies.

While Bo carried away the heavy bags Mosca knelt down in front of his radio again. 'Too expensive!' he grumbled. 'My boat will rot away soon if I don't paint it. But you lot don't care, because you're just a bunch of landlubbers! There's always enough money for Hornet's books.'

Hornet didn't answer that. Silently, she began to collect paper and other rubbish from the floor while Prosper swept up the mouse droppings. Hornet really did have a lot of books. She had even bought some of them, but mostly they were cheap paperbacks that had been thrown away by tourists. Hornet fished them out of rubbish bins and waste-paper baskets, or she found them under the seats of Vaporetto boats or at the train station. You could hardly see her mattress behind the stacks of books.

They all had their beds close together at the back of the cinema. At night, after they had switched off the lights and blown out the last candle, the large, windowless auditorium would be flooded with such complete darkness, that it made them feel as tiny as ants – and very lost. But the sounds of each others breathing made them all feel a little safer.

Riccio's mattress was covered in old comic books and his sleeping bag was stuffed with so many cuddly toys that there was hardly any space left for him. Mosca's bed could easily be spotted by his toolbox and fishing rods, which he liked to sleep next to. Tucked under the pillow was Mosca's greatest treasure, his lucky charm. This was a brass sea horse, exactly like the ones that adorned most gondolas in the city. Mosca swore that he hadn't stolen it from a gondola but had fished it from the canal behind the cinema. 'A stolen lucky charm,' he always claimed, 'brings only bad luck. Everybody knows that.'

Bo and Prosper huddled together every night on a single mattress. Bo's collection of plastic fans was lined up neatly at the top end. There were six of them, all in pretty good shape, but Bo's favourite was still the one Prosper had found at the station on the day they arrived.

The Thief Lord never slept with his followers in the Star-Palace. No one knew where Scipio spent the nights, and he never spoke about it, although every now and then he would drop a mysterious hint about an abandoned church. Riccio had tried to follow him once, but Scipio had spotted him immediately and had been so angry that since then none of them even dared watch him leave. Their leader came and went as he pleased, and they had got used to it. He sometimes turned up three days in a row and then they wouldn't see him again for nearly a week.

But he did want to come that day – and when the Thief Lord announced a visit he always came. But you could never be sure *exactly* when Scipio would appear. As Riccio's clock showed almost eleven and Bo was nearly asleep on Prosper's lap, the children crept under their blankets and

Hornet began to read to them. She usually read to make them sleepy, to drive away their fear of the dreams that were waiting for them in the dark. That night, however, Hornet read to keep them awake until Scipio's arrival. She selected the most thrilling story from her pile of books while the others lit the candles which stood in empty bottles and jars among the mattresses. Riccio placed five brand-new candles in their only proper candlestick. They were long and slender and made from pale wax.

'Riccio?' Hornet asked when they were all lying around her, waiting for their story. 'Where did you get the candles?'

Riccio self-consciously hid his face between his soft toys. 'From the Salute Church,' he mumbled. 'There are hundreds, probably thousands lying around there. So it doesn't really matter if I take a few every now and then. Why should we spend our precious money on candles? I swear,' he grinned at Hornet, 'I always blow the Virgin Mary a kiss for each one.'

Hornet buried her face in her hands and sighed.

'Oh, go on, start reading!' Mosca said impatiently. 'No Carabinieri will ever arrest Riccio for nicking a few candles, would he?'

'They could!' mumbled Bo. He yawned and cuddled up to Prosper, who was struggling with a needle and thread over the holes in his brother's trousers. 'Because Riccio's guardian angel won't look after him if he steals things from a church. He's not allowed to.'

'Pah, rubbish! Guardian angel!' Riccio made a contemptuous face, although he did sound a little worried.

Hornet read for nearly an hour, while the night outside grew darker and all those who had filled the city with noise during the day were long in their beds. Finally the book slipped from her fingers, and her eyelids drooped. When Scipio finally arrived they were all fast asleep.

4 The Thief Lord

Prosper wasn't sure what had woken him – Riccio mumbling in his sleep or Scipio's quiet steps. As he started from his sleep, a slender figure emerged from the dark. Under the black mask that hid Scipio's eyes, Prosper could make out his pale chin. The mask's long crooked nose gave him an eerie bird-like appearance. Similar masks had once been worn by the doctors of Venice, at the time when the Black Death had raged through the city more than three hundred years ago: the Birds of Death, people called them. Smiling, The Thief Lord pulled the creepy thing from his face.

'Hi, Prop!' Scipio let the light of his torch wander over the others' sleeping faces. 'Sorry it got so late.'

Prosper pushed Bo's arm carefully from his chest and sat up. 'One day you're going to scare someone to death with that mask,' he said quietly. 'How did you sneak in here? We bolted everything really well this time.'

Scipio shrugged. He ran his slender fingers through his long raven-black hair, which he usually wore in a ponytail.

'You should know by now that I can get into any place I want to.'

Scipio, the Thief Lord.

He liked to act grown up, although he was not much older than Prosper, and a good bit smaller than Mosca – even in his high-heeled boots. These were much too big for him, but he always kept them well polished – they were black leather, as black as the strange long coat that reached down to his knees. He never went anywhere without them.

'Wake the others,' Scipio commanded in his special bossy, condescending voice, which Hornet hated so much. Prosper ignored him.

'Well you've woken me already!' Mosca grumbled behind them, yawning. He pushed himself up from among his fishing rods. 'Don't you ever sleep, Thief Lord?'

Scipio didn't answer. He strutted like a peacock through the auditorium while Hornet and Mosca woke the others.

'I see you've done some clearing up!' Scipio called out. 'Excellent. The place did rather look like a pigsty last time.'

'Hi, Scip!' Bo scrambled so quickly out of his sleeping bag that he nearly fell over his own hands. Barefoot, he ran towards Scipio. Bo was the only one who could call the Thief Lord Scip without getting an icy stare in response. 'What did you steal this time?' he asked excitedly, jumping around Scipio like a puppy. Smiling, the Thief Lord slipped a black sack from his shoulder.

'Did we check out everything properly this time?' Riccio asked humbly, crawling out from underneath his cuddly toys. 'Come on, tell us.'

'He'll start kissing his boots soon!' Hornet grumbled so quietly that only Prosper heard it. 'I for one would be happy enough if the fine gentleman didn't turn up so often in the middle of the night.' She frowned at Scipio while she squeezed her spindly legs into her boots.

'I had to change my plans at short notice!' Scipio announced, as they all assembled around him. He threw a folded newspaper towards Riccio. 'Read. Page four. At the top.'

Eagerly, Riccio knelt down on the floor and started leafing through the large pages. Mosca and Prosper leaned over his shoulders. Hornet stood a little way away and played with her plait.

'Spectacular break-in at the Palazzo Contarini,' Riccio read haltingly. 'Valuable jewellery and various works of art stolen. No trace of the perpetrators!' He raised his head in surprise. 'Contarini? But we watched the Palazzo Pisani.'

Scipio shrugged. 'So, I changed my mind. The Palazzo Pisani comes later. It won't run away, will it? And the Palazzo Contarini' – he dangled the sack in front of Riccio's face – 'had a few worthwhile things in it, too.'

He enjoyed the attentive faces around him for a moment and then sat down cross-legged in front of the starry curtain. He poured the contents of his sack on the floor in front of him. 'I've already sold the jewels,' he explained as the others stepped forward reverently. 'I had to pay off a few debts and I also needed new tools, but here, these are for you.'

On the floor, sparkling in the dim light, lay a couple of silver spoons, a medallion, a magnifying glass with a silver snake coiled around its handle, and a pair of golden tongs, set with tiny precious stones with a handle shaped like a rose.

Bo, wide eyed, leaned over Scipio's haul. Carefully, as if the treasures could crumble in his small hands, he picked up one piece after another, felt it, and put it back. 'Is it all real?' he asked, looking at Scipio.

Scipio just nodded. Pleased with himself and the world, he stretched his arms and lay down on his side. 'So what do you say? Am I the Thief Lord, or not?'

Riccio just nodded dumbfounded and even Hornet couldn't hide the fact that she was quite impressed.

'Boy, one day they are going to catch you,' Mosca murmured, staring fascinated at the serpentine magnifying glass.

'No way!' Scipio rolled onto his back and looked up at the ceiling. 'Although I have to say it was quite a close thing this time. The alarm system was not as old-fashioned as I expected and the lady of the house woke up just as I snatched the medallion from her bedside table. But I was on the roof of the house next door faster than she could climb out of her bed.' He winked at Bo who was leaning against his knee, looking at him awe-struck.

'What are these for?' Hornet asked, holding up the rose tongs. 'For pulling hair out of your nostrils?'

'Hell, no!' Scipio pushed himself up and snatched the tongs from her fingers. 'Those are sugar tongs.'

'How do you know all this stuff?' Riccio gave Scipio a look between admiration and envy. 'You grew up in an orphanage just like me, but the nuns never told me anything about sugar tongs or stuff like that.'

'Well, it's been a while since I ran away from the orphanage,' Scipio answered, brushing the dust from his black coat. 'And, furthermore, I don't just stick my nose in comics all day...'

Riccio stared at the floor in embarrassment.

'Well I don't only read comics,' said Hornet, putting her arm around Riccio's shoulder, 'and I've never heard of sugar tongs. And even if I had, I wouldn't be stupid enough to get all stuck-up about it!'

Scipio cleared his throat, avoiding Hornet's look. Finally he said more gently, 'I didn't mean it, Riccio. You can get through life perfectly well without knowing what sugar tongs are. But I can tell you, this little thing is worth quite a bit, so this time you'd better get a decent price from Barbarossa. Understood?'

'Can you also tell us how, then?' Mosca exchanged helpless glances with the others. 'We really tried last time but he's just too smart for us.'

They all looked at Scipio remorsefully. Ever since he had become their provider and their leader, it had been their job to turn the loot into money while he took care of the stealing. Scipio had told them who to go to, but he left the haggling to them. The only person in town who would do business with a gang of kids was Ernesto Barbarossa. A fat man with a red beard, Barbarossa had an antiques shop where he sold cheap trash to the tourists, but he also did secret deals with more valuable, and usually stolen, items.

'We're not all cut out for this!' Mosca continued. 'Negotiations and haggling, and so on. The redbeard just takes advantage of us.'

Scipio frowned while he fiddled with the cord of his sack.

'Prop can haggle like no one else,' Bo suddenly said. 'When we used to sell things at the flea market, he always put on this stony face and...'

'Shut up, Bo!' Prosper interrupted his little brother. His ears had turned bright red. 'Selling old toys is a little different from all this...' He nervously took the medallion out of Bo's hand.

'What's so different?' Scipio scrutinized Prosper's face as if he could read there whether Bo had been right or not.

'Well, I would be very glad if you dealt with it for us, Prop,' Mosca said.

'Yes.' Hornet shuddered. 'The redbeard gives me the creeps every time he looks at me with his little piggy eyes. I always think he's secretly laughing at us or that he's going to call the police or something. I can never wait to get out of his shop.'

Prosper scratched himself behind the ear, still looking embarrassed. 'If you think so,' he said. 'I can probably haggle quite well. But Barbarossa is crafty. I was there last time when Mosca sold him the other stuff.'

'Try it.' Scipio jumped up and hung the empty sack over his shoulder. 'I've got to go. I have another appointment to keep tonight, but I'll be back tomorrow.' He pulled the mask over his eyes. 'Sometime in the late afternoon. I want to hear what the redbeard paid you for these things here. If he offers you...' he cast a thoughtful look over his loot '...well, if he offers you less than two hundred thousand lire then just bring the stuff back for the time being.'

'Two hundred thousand!' Riccio's mouth stayed open.

'These things are definitely worth much more,' Prosper insisted.

Scipio turned around and just said, 'Probably.' He looked quite scary again, with the long, black bird nose. The naked lights cast his shadow massively on the cinema's walls. 'See you!' he said. He turned once more before vanishing through the musty curtain. 'Do we need a new code word?'

'No!' The answer came very quickly, and in perfect harmony.

'Fine. Oh yes, Bo' – Scipio turned around again – 'there's a cardboard box behind the curtain. There are two little kittens in there. Someone wanted to drown them in the canal. Look after them, will you? Good night, everybody.'

5 Barbarossa

The shop where so much of the Thief Lord's loot had been turned into money lay in a small alley not far from the Basilica San Marco. Next door to it was a *pasticceria* with pastries and cakes of all shapes and sizes in its windows.

'Come on,' Prosper grumbled at Riccio who was pressing his nose against the shop window. Reluctantly, Riccio let himself be dragged away, his head still swimming with the scent of sweet almonds.

Barbarossa's shop didn't exactly smell as nice. From the outside it didn't look any different from all the other junk shops in Venice. The glass front was painted with ornate letters: *Ernesto Barbarossa – Recordi di Venezia, Souvenirs of Venice*. In the window itself, there were vases and candlesticks, surrounded by little gondolas and glass insects, laid out on threadbare velvet drapes. Thin china plates were crammed next to piles of old books, and pictures in tarnished silver frames lay next to cheap paper masks. Barbarossa stocked whatever anyone could desire. And if something particular wasn't on show, then the redbeard would get hold of it – by crooked means if necessary.

Dozens of glass bells chimed above his head as Prosper opened the shop door. Inside, a few tourists stood among the crammed shelves, whispering as solemnly as if they were in a church. They seemed awed, either by the chandeliers that hung from the dark ceiling, or by the countless candles that burnt everywhere in their heavy holders.

With bowed heads, Prosper and Riccio pushed past the tourists. A man was holding a statuette that Mosca had sold to the redbeard two weeks before. When Prosper saw the price tag underneath its plinth he nearly knocked over a large statue in the centre of the shop.

'Do you remember how much Barbarossa paid us for that figure there?' he whispered to Riccio.

'No. You know I can't remember numbers.'

'Well, that number has now got two more zeros on the end of it,' Prosper whispered. 'Not a bad profit for the redbeard, is it?'

He stepped up to the counter and rang the bell next to the till. Riccio pulled faces at the masked lady smiling down at them from a large painting on the wall. This was his regular joke, for behind the lady's mask was a peephole through which Barbarossa kept an eye on his customers.

A few seconds later the beaded curtain behind the counter tinkled into life and Ernesto Barbarossa appeared in person. The redbeard was a very fat man but Prosper was always amazed at how nimbly he could move through his crammed shop.

'I hope you brought some decent goods this time,' the man murmured disdainfully, but the boys noticed how he stared at the bag in Prosper's hands, like a hungry cat eyeing up a fat juicy mouse.

'I think you'll be interested,' Prosper answered. Riccio said nothing. He was staring at Barbarossa's ginger beard as if he expected something to crawl out of it at any moment.

'What are you looking at, you little ferret?' the redbeard cursed.

'Oh, I, I—' Riccio began to stutter '—I was just wondering whether it was real. The colour, I mean.'

'Of course it's real! Are you saying I dye my beard?' Barbarossa growled at him. 'You gnomes get some strange ideas.' He stroked his beard with his fat, ringed fingers. Then he nodded discreetly in the direction of the couple of tourists that were still standing by the shelves, whispering to each other. 'I'll get rid of them as quickly as possible,' he muttered. 'Go ahead into my office – and don't even think of touching anything! Clear?'

Prosper and Riccio nodded. Then they disappeared behind the beaded curtain.

Barbarossa's office looked completely different from his shop. Here, there were no chandeliers, no candles, or glass insects. The windowless room was lit by a neon light and was completely bare, except for a big desk with a massive leather armchair behind it, two guest chairs, and a few high shelves stuffed with meticulously labelled boxes. A poster from the *Museo di Accademia* hung on the white wall behind the desk.

There was also an upholstered bench, placed underneath Barbarossa's peephole. Riccio climbed on to it and peered into the shop. 'You've got to see this, Prop,' he whispered. 'The redbeard is purring around those tourists like a fat tomcat. I don't think anyone has ever escaped his shop without buying something.'

'Or without paying far too much for it.' Prosper placed the bag with Scipio's loot on one of the chairs and looked around.

'He definitely dyes it,' Riccio murmured without taking his eye from the peephole. 'I've bet Hornet three comics that he does.'

Barbarossa's head was as bald as a glitter ball. His beard, however, grew thick and frizzy and was the colour of fox fur. 'I think there's a bathroom behind that door,' whispered Riccio. Have a look and see if he's got any hair dye in there!'

'If I have to.' Prosper crossed the narrow passage and put his head round another door. 'Wow! There's more marble here than in The Doge's Palace,' Riccio heard him say. 'This is just about the classiest toilet I've ever seen.'

Riccio pressed his eye against the peephole. 'Prosper, get out of there,' he called under his breath. 'The redbeard is finished with the customers – and he's locking the door!'

'He dyes it, Riccio!' Prosper called. 'The bottle's right here, next to his pongy aftershave. Eurghh, that stinks! Shall I dye a bit of toilet paper as evidence?'

'No! Get out of there!' Riccio jumped off the bench. 'Quick, he's coming back!'

The beaded curtain announced Barbarossa as he entered the office.

Prosper and Riccio were sitting in front of his desk, wearing their most innocent faces.

'I'm going to have to deduct the money for a glass beetle,' the burly redbeard announced as he let himself fall into his vast armchair. 'Your little brother,' he gave Prosper a disapproving look, 'broke it last time.'

'He did not,' Prosper protested.

'Oh yes he did,' Barbarossa replied without looking at him.

He took a pair of spectacles from his drawer. 'So, what have you got for me today? I hope it's not just fake gold and inferior silver spoons.'

With a stony face, Prosper emptied his bag onto the desk. Barbarossa leaned forward. He took the sugar tongs, the medallions, and the magnifying glass, one by one, and turned them in his podgy fingers. He inspected them from every angle, the boys watching him closely. His face showed nothing. He picked each item up, put it back down, and picked it up again, then pushed it aside, looked at it again – until the boys were scraping their feet impatiently on the floor.

Finally, Barbarossa leaned back with a sigh and put his spectacles on the desk. He stroked his beard as if he was stroking the fur of a small animal.

'Do you want to tell me what you want for them, or shall I give you my best offer?' he asked.

Prosper and Riccio exchanged a quick glance.

'Give me your offer,' came Prosper's answer. He tried to look as if he knew exactly what Scipio's loot was worth.

'My offer...' Barbarossa paused. He put his fingertips together and closed his eyes. 'Well, I admit, there are a couple of quite decent items here this time. So I'll offer you,' he opened his eyes again, 'one hundred thousand lire. And I'm still doing you a favour.'

Riccio held his breath. He imagined all the cakes he could buy for one hundred thousand lire. Mountains of cakes.

But Prosper shook his head. He looked Barbarossa straight in the eyes and said: 'No. Five hundred thousand. Or the deal is off.'

For a split second, Barbarossa couldn't hide his surprise. But he regained his composure and conjured an expression of honest outrage onto his face. 'Have you lost your mind, boy?' he bellowed. 'Here I am, making you a generous offer – far too generous – and you go and make outrageous demands. Tell the Thief Lord never again to send such impertinent kids if he wants to continue doing business with Ernesto Barbarossa!'

Riccio looked worried, but Prosper just got up and silently started putting the loot back into his bag.

Barbarossa watched him calmly. But when Prosper reached for the sugar tongs, he grabbed his hand so quickly that the boy gave a start. 'You're a smart fellow, a bit too smart for my taste. The Thief Lord and I have done good business so far and so I'll give you four hundred thousand lire for the lot. Although most of it is rubbish, I like the tongs. Tell the Thief Lord if he offers me more stuff like those we shall definitely stay in business together. Even if he insists on using such cheeky errand boys.' He looked at Prosper with a mixture of anger and respect. 'One more thing.' He cleared his throat. 'Ask the Thief Lord if he would take on a job.'

The boys looked at each other. 'A job?'

Barbarossa shuffled a few papers together. 'One of my most important clients is looking for a talented man who will – let's say – fetch something for him. Something my client wants rather badly. As far as I have gathered, the item is here, in Venice. Should be child's play for someone—' Barbarossa twisted his face into a scornful smile '—who likes to call himself the Thief Lord, shouldn't it?'

Prosper didn't answer. The redbeard had never seen Scipio and so he probably thought he was dealing with an adult. He didn't have the faintest idea that the Thief Lord was just as young as his messengers.

That didn't seem to bother Riccio, who said, 'Sure, we'll ask him.'

'Excellent.' Barbarossa leaned back in his armchair with a smug smile. He was holding the sugar tongs in his hands, tenderly stroking their curved handles. 'If he wants to take on the job, tell him to send one of you with his answer. I will then arrange a meeting with my client.' He lowered his voice. 'The payment will be very generous. My client has assured me of that.'

'As Riccio said, we'll ask him,' Prosper repeated. 'But now we would like to have our money.'

Barbarossa burst out laughing. Riccio nearly jumped out of his chair. 'Yes, yes, you will get your money,' the redbeard smirked. 'Don't worry. But get out of my office. Do you really think I would open my safe with you little thieves watching me?'

'What do you think? Will Scipio take the job?' Riccio whispered to Prosper as they leaned against the counter, waiting for Barbarossa.

'It's probably best not to tell him about it at all,' Prosper answered. He looked intently at the portrait of the masked lady.

'And why not?'

Prosper shrugged. 'Don't know. It's just a feeling. I don't trust the redbeard.'

Just then, Barbarossa heaved himself through the tinkling beaded curtain. 'There you are,' he said. He held out a thick wad of bank notes to them. 'But don't get robbed on your way home now. All those tourists out there with their cameras and bulging wallets attract thieves like flies.'

The boys ignored the old crook's grin. Prosper took the

money and looked at it, uncertain what to do.

'No, you don't need to count it,' Barbarossa said, as if he had guessed the boy's thoughts. 'It's all there. I only deducted the glass beetle your brother broke last time. Sign the receipt here. You can write, I hope?'

Prosper just scowled and scribbled his name on to the pad. He hesitated a moment over his surname and then wrote down a fake one. 'Prosper,' the redbeard paused, 'you're not from Venice, are you?'

'No,' Prosper answered shortly. He threw the empty bag over his shoulder and walked to the door. 'Come on, Riccio.'

'Let me know as soon as possible about that job!' Barbarossa shouted after them.

'Will do,' Prosper answered and pulled the shop door shut behind him.

He was determined not to mention a word of it to Scipio.

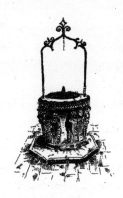

6 A Nasty Coincidence

As soon as they had left Barbarossa's shop, Riccio dragged Prosper into the *pasticceria* he had stared at so longingly before. Prosper didn't get a chance to protest and the shop assistant patiently waited for their order while Riccio bullied Prosper into changing two banknotes from Barbarossa's wad and buying a box of cakes for them all, to celebrate.

Prosper was always amazed by the great care the bakers of Venice took over wrapping their cakes. They didn't just hand them over in a plastic bag – no, they were always packed in a beautiful box and tied up with a ribbon.

Riccio, however, was decidedly unimpressed by all this effort. As soon as they were back on the street he got out is pocket knife and cut the ribbon.

'What are you doing?' Prosper cried trying to take the box off Riccio. 'I thought this was for the others as well.'

'There'll be more than enough left for them.' Riccio peered greedily into the box. 'And we deserve a treat after all that. *Madonna*, no one has ever managed to get one single lira more out of the redbeard than he wanted to pay. And now he's just given you four times what he first offered us – even I can work that out. Scipio will never let anyone else sell his loot again.'

'Well, I think those things were probably worth even

48

more.' Prosper took one of the cakes. It was dusted generously with icing sugar, which spilled down his jacket with the first bite. The tip of Riccio's nose was already covered in chocolate.

'Anyway, we can definitely use the money,' Prosper continued. 'Now we can afford a few of the things we really need, especially with winter coming. Hornet and Bo don't have warm jackets and your shoes look like you just fished them out of a canal.'

Riccio licked the chocolate from his nose and looked down at his worn trainers. 'Why? They're OK,' he said. 'But perhaps we could buy a small second-hand TV. Mosca could get it connected somehow.'

'You've got to be joking!'

Prosper stopped in front of a shop selling newspapers, postcards and toys. He and Bo hadn't brought any toys with them when they ran away, and his brother didn't even have a cuddly animal, apart from the sorry-looking lion that Riccio had given him.

'What about getting Bo those indians there?' Riccio put his sticky chin on Prosper's shoulder. 'They would go well with the cork cowboys Hornet made for him.'

Prosper frowned. He touched the money in his jacket pocket. 'No,' he said. He pushed the cake box into Riccio's hands and strode on. 'We need the money for other things.'

Riccio sighed, and walked after him. 'You know, if Scipio doesn't take Barbarossa's job,' he lowered his voice, 'then I'll do it. You heard what the baldhead said about the money. I'm not a bad thief – just a bit out of practice. And I'd share the loot with everyone. Bo could get his indians, Hornet could get some new books, and Mosca could get the paint for that boat he's been going on about so much. I'd get a little TV and you...' he gave Prosper a curious look. 'Actually, what would you want?'

'I don't need anything.' Prosper hunched his shoulders as if a cold draft had gone down his neck. He looked around uneasily. 'Just stop talking about stealing things. Have you forgotten how they nearly caught you last time?'

'Yes, yes,' Riccio said angrily. He really didn't want to remember that. He gazed after a woman with huge pearl earrings.

Prosper added: 'And you won't tell Scipio about this job, agreed?'

Riccio stopped. 'Don't be an idiot! I don't understand what's the matter with you. Of course I'll tell him! How can this be more dangerous than breaking into The Doge's Palace?' A young couple holding hands turned around and Riccio quickly lowered his voice. 'Or into the Palazzo Contarini!'

Prosper shook his head and walked on. He wasn't quite sure himself why he didn't like Barbarossa's offer. Lost in thought, he walked around two women who were arguing noisily in the middle of the street – only to walk straight into a man who had just stepped out of a bar with a slice of pizza his hand. The man was small and stocky. A piece of cheese clung to his thick walrus-moustache. He spun round, annoyed – and then stared at Prosper as if he had seen a ghost.

Prosper muttered '*Scusi*' and quickly pushed past the man and disappeared into the crowd.

'Hey, why are you running?' Riccio followed him awkwardly, nearly dropping the cake box.

Prosper looked around. 'Someone just gave me a very weird

look.' He eyed the passing crowds uneasily. The man with the walrus moustache was nowhere to be seen.

'A weird look?' Riccio shrugged. 'And? Did you recognize him?'

Prosper shook his head. He looked around once more. A couple of schoolchildren, an old man, three women with stuffed shopping bags, a group of nuns...suddenly he grabbed Riccio's arm and pulled him inside a doorway.

Riccio nearly dropped the cake box again. 'What now?'

'That man's following us.' Prosper started to run faster, keeping his hand firmly on Barbarossa's money so it wouldn't fall out of his pocket.

Riccio called after him, 'What are you talking about?'

'He's after us!' Prosper gasped. 'He was trying to hide, but I saw him.'

Riccio looked around for their pursuer but all he could see were bored faces staring into shop windows and a bunch of giggling schoolchildren.

'Prop, this is really stupid!' He caught up with Prosper and blocked his path. 'Calm down, OK? You're seeing things.'

But Prosper didn't answer.

'Come on,' he hissed. He dragged Riccio into an alley that was so narrow that Barbarossa would certainly have got stuck in it. The wind whistled past them. Riccio knew where this tiny passage led: into a labyrinth of alleys that could confuse even a Venetian. It wasn't a bad route if you wanted to lose someone. But Prosper had stopped again. He flattened himself against the wall and watched the people passing by the entrance to the passage.

'And what are you doing now?' Riccio leaned against the wall next to Prosper. He shivered and pulled the sleeves of his jumper over his hands.

'When he walks past I'll point him out to you.'

'And then?'

'If he sees us, we run.'

'Great plan!' Riccio said sarcastically. He pushed his tongue nervously into the gap in his front teeth. He had lost that tooth during a chase.

'Let's just go now,' he whispered to Prosper. 'The others are waiting for us.'

But Prosper didn't move.

The schoolchildren skipped past the alley. Then the nuns walked past. And then came the short and stocky man, with the big feet and a walrus moustache. He looked around, he stood on his toes, he craned his neck, and then he cursed.

The boys hardly dared to breathe. Finally, the man walked on.

Riccio was the first to move. 'I know him!' he hissed quietly. 'Let's get away from here before he comes back.'

Prosper stumbled after him, his heart beating like mad. Soon he had completely lost his bearings, but Riccio kept running as if he knew the way through the maze of alleys and bridges by heart. Suddenly, they stumbled back into bright sunlight. Ahead of them lay the Grand Canal. Its banks were crowded with people and its glittering surface teemed with boats.

Riccio pulled Prosper towards a *Vaporetto* stop. Soon they disappeared into the throng of people waiting for the next boat. The *Vaporetti* are the water buses of Venice – they take the Venetians to work and the tourists from one museum to the next when their feet begin to ache.

Prosper scrutinized every face passing by, but their pursuer wasn't among them. When the next *Vaporetto* finally arrived, the boys smuggled themselves on to the boat with the crowd. While the other passengers scrambled after the few remaining free seats in the roofed section of the boat, Prosper and Riccio walked up to the deck-rail and kept a close eye on the bank of the canal.

'We don't have a ticket,' Prosper whispered when the fully loaded boat cast off.

'Doesn't matter,' Riccio whispered back, 'we're getting off at the next stop anyway. But look who's standing over there.' He pointed towards the stop. 'Do you see him?'

Oh yes, Prosper saw him quite clearly. There was the man with the walrus moustache, squinting after the departing boat. Riccio gave him a hearty wave.

Prosper pulled Riccio's arm down. 'What are you doing?'

'Why? You think he's going to swim after us? No, my friend. That's the good thing about this city. If someone is after you, all you have to do is cross the canal, and the other fool's had it! Even you should know by now that there are only two bridges across the Grand Canal!'

Prosper didn't reply. The stranger had long vanished out of sight but Prosper kept staring towards the bank just in case he suddenly appeared between the elegant columns of one of the palaces, or on a hotel balcony, or even on one of the oncoming boats. Prosper was worried.

'Stop looking like that. We've lost him!' Riccio shook his friend by the shoulder until he turned round.

Prosper stared at Riccio anxiously. 'So you know who he is?'

Riccio leaned against the rail. 'Yeah – he's a detective. He works for the tourists – looking for lost handbags and wallets.

He nearly caught me with one once.' Riccio pulled his ear and grinned. 'But, he's not very fast. He gave Prosper a curious look. 'It did look, well, as if he was after you. What would a detective want with you? Is someone looking for you?'

Prosper gazed at the shore again. The *Vaporetto* steered sluggishly towards the next stop. 'There might be,' he said, without looking at Riccio. A swarm of gulls took to the air with a great noise as the boat drifted towards the jetty.

'Let's get off here,' Riccio said. They jumped off the boat while the new passengers were already pushing aboard.

'Hell! The others are probably thinking we've taken Scipio's loot and done a runner,' Riccio said as they turned their backs on the Grand Canal again. 'Our little boat trip hasn't made our way back any shorter.' He gave Prosper another quizzical look. 'Do you feel like telling me who could have put that detective on your trail? What have you done? Did you steal something?'

'Rubbish, you know I don't steal – not if I can help it.' Prosper put his hand into his jacket and, relieved, pulled it out again. Barbarossa's money was still there.

'Yeah, I know.' Riccio frowned. Then he lowered his voice. 'Is it one of those child-slave traders?'

Prosper looked shocked. 'No. Don't be silly. It's really not that bad.' He stared back at a gargoyle that was eyeing him from a stone archway. 'I think my Aunt Esther is looking for us. She's my mum's sister. She's got loads of money and no children. When my mum died she wanted to adopt Bo. They were going to send me to a boarding school. So we ran away. What was I supposed to do? He's my little brother.' Prosper stopped. 'Do you think Esther ever asked Bo whether he wanted her to be his new mum? He can't stand her. He says she smells like paint. And,' he smiled, 'that she looks like one of those china dolls she collects.'

He bent down and picked up a plastic fan from a doorstep. The handle was gone, but Bo wouldn't mind that.

'Bo thinks I can take care of everything,' he said, stuffing his find into his pocket. 'But if Hornet hadn't found us...'

'Come on, stop worrying about the snoop!' Riccio pulled him along. 'He won't find you again. Simple: we'll dye Bo's angel hair black and we'll paint your face so you look like Mosca's twin brother.'

Prosper laughed. Riccio could always make him laugh, even if he didn't feel like it. 'Do you sometimes wish you were grown up?' he asked as they crossed a bridge and looked down at its hazy reflection on the water.

Riccio shook his head with astonishment. 'No. Why? It's great being young. You don't stand out so much and your stomach fills up more quickly. You know what Scipio always says?' He jumped from the bridge onto the street. 'Children are caterpillars and adults are butterflies. No butterfly ever remembers what it felt like being a caterpillar.'

'Probably not,' Prosper sighed.

'Don't tell Bo anything about the detective, OK?'

Riccio nodded.

7 Bad luck for Victor

Once Victor realized that Prosper had got away, he kicked the nearest wooden post he could find, sprained his foot – and then hobbled home.

He kept muttering to himself most of the way. People turned their heads, but Victor didn't notice. 'Like an amateur,' he grunted. 'You just let that boy shake you off like a stupid amateur. And who was the other one? Too big to be his little brother. Damn it, damn it, and damn it again! The boy stumbles right into your arms and you let him get away. Stupid ass!' He kicked an empty cigarette packet with his sprained foot and his face twisted up in pain. 'Your own stupid fault,' he growled. 'Yes, you've only got yourself to blame. No decent detective chases after children. You could pay for tortoise feed even without this blasted job.'

Victor's foot was still hurting badly when he opened his front door. 'Well, at least now I know they're here,' he grumbled as he limped up the stairs. 'And if the big one's here then the small one will be too, that's for sure.'

Once in his flat, he pulled his shoes off and staggered on

to the balcony to feed his tortoises. His office still smelt of Esther Hartlieb's hairspray. Phew, he just couldn't get that smell out of his nose.

The boys haunted him day and night. He shouldn't have put their picture up on the wall – they were always looking at him. Where did they sleep at night? It was already getting quite cold in the evenings, as soon as the sun vanished behind the houses. And because it had rained so much the previous winter the city had flooded a dozen times. Still, Venice had lots of nooks and crannies, like an old rabbit warren. There was always some dry place for two children. Some abandoned house. Or one of the many churches. Not all of them were swarming with tourists.

'I'm going to find them,' Victor swore. 'Simple as that!'

Once his tortoises were fed, he stuffed himself with mounds of spaghetti and fried sausages. Then he applied some ointment to his aching foot and sat down at his desk to do some of the paperwork that had piled up. After all, he still had other jobs apart from searching for those boys.

Perhaps I should sit on the Piazza San Marco more often over the next few days, Victor thought, drink some coffee, feed the pigeons, and wait for them to turn up. Everyone in Venice comes to St Mark's Square at least once a day. Why shouldn't that also be true for runaway children?'

8 Scipio's Answer

When Prosper and Riccio finally returned to the Star-Palace,
Bo immediately came rushing to greet them and so, for the
time being, they did not tell the others about the detective
who had delayed them. But the long wait was quickly forgotten anyway, when Prosper pulled out the money he had wan-
gled out of the redbeard. They sat around him, lost for words,
while Riccio recounted in great detail how Prosper had coolly
held his own against Barbarossa.

'And anyway,' Riccio declared as he came to the end, 'the
fat liar does dye his beard after all. So I get three brand-new
comics from you, Hornet – you haven't forgotten our bet,
have you?'

About two hours after Prosper and Riccio's return the bell
at the entrance rang and the Thief Lord was at the front door,
just as he had promised. And, for once, he had arrived before
the moon was already high above the roofs of the city. Of
course Mosca opened the door without asking for the password and earned himself a terrible telling off. But when Bo
came running excitedly towards him, Barbarossa's wad of

money in his hands, even Scipio was silenced. He took the money with an amazed expression and counted every single note.

'Well, Scip, what do you say to that? You look as if you've seen a ghost,' Mosca teased. 'Now you can tell Hornet to buy some paint for my boat!'

'Your boat? Sure, sure, of course.' Scipio nodded absent-mindedly before turning to Prosper and Riccio. 'Was there anything Barbarossa liked especially?'

'Yes, he was really taken by the sugar-tongs', Riccio answered. 'He said you should bring him things like that more often.'

Scipio frowned. 'The sugar-tongs,' he murmured, 'yes, they were probably quite valuable.' He shook his head as if he wanted to get rid of a troublesome thought. 'Riccio,' he said, 'go and buy some olives and spicy sausage. We've got to celebrate. I haven't much time, so hurry.'

Riccio quickly stuffed two of Barbarossa's banknotes into his pocket and dashed off. When he came back, with a plastic bag full of olives, bread, pepper-red salami, and a bag of *mandorlati*, the chocolates wrapped in colourful paper that Scipio liked so much, the others had already spread the cushions and blankets in front of the curtain. Bo and Hornet had gathered all the candles they could find and their flickering light filled the cinema with dancing shadows.

'Here's to a few carefree months!' Hornet said once they had all gathered in a circle. She poured grape-juice into the red goblets Scipio had brought back from one of his previous raids. Then she raised her glass to Prosper. 'And here's to you, because you got the redbeard to part with all that money – it usually sticks to his fat fingers like chewing-gum.'

Riccio and Mosca also raised their glasses. Prosper didn't know where to look. Bo, however, leaned proudly against his big brother and put one of the kittens that Scipio had given him on his knee.

'Yes, here's to you, Prop!' Scipio said, now also raising his glass. 'Herewith I name you my chief loot-seller. However,' he fondled the wad of money with his fingers, 'I'm thinking that it might be wise to take a break after a raid like this.' For a moment he fell silent and then added, 'A thief should never become too greedy, or he'll get caught.'

'But you can't stop – not just now!' Riccio pretended not to notice Prosper's fierce warning glance. 'Barbarossa told us something interesting today.'

'And what was that?' Scipio popped an olive into his mouth and spat the stone into his hand.

'A customer of his is looking for a thief. The deal is supposed to be very good, and we're supposed to ask you whether you'd be interested.'

Scipio gave Riccio a surprised look – but remained silent.

'Sounds good, doesn't it?' Riccio stuffed a slice of the sausage into his mouth. Its spiciness made his eyes water. He quickly handed his empty glass to Hornet.

Scipio still hadn't said anything. He stroked his hair absent-mindedly and fiddled with the ribbon around his ponytail. Then he cleared his throat. 'Interesting', he said. 'A job for a thief – why not? What will I have to steal?'

'No idea.' Riccio rubbed his greasy fingers on his trouser-legs. 'Not even the redbeard knows anything about it yet. But he seems to think that the Thief Lord is just the man for the job.' Riccio grinned. 'The fatso probably imagines you're a huge guy with a stocking on his head who creeps around the pillars of The Doge's Palace like a cat. Anyway, he wants a quick answer.'

They all looked at Scipio. He just sat there and toyed with his mask. Lost in thought, he stroked its long, bent nose. It was so quiet that you could hear the crackle of the candles. 'Yes, that is indeed quite interesting,' he wondered aloud. 'Yes, why not?'

Prosper watched him uneasily. He still had the feeling that something dark and threatening was moving in on them. Trouble ... and danger...

Scipio seemed to read his mind. 'What do you think of all this, Prop?' he asked.

'Not much,' Prosper answered. 'I don't trust Barbarossa.' He could hardly say: because I don't think much of stealing. After all, he lived off Scipio being such a master of it.

Scipio nodded.

Just then Bo, of all people, let Prosper down. 'So what?' he said. He knelt next to Scipio, his eyes shiny with excitement. 'It'll be easy for you, won't it? Right, Scip?'

Scipio had to smile. He took the kitten out of Bo's arms and placed it on his lap, stroking its tiny ears.

'And I will help you!' Bo moved even closer to Scipio. 'Right, Scip? I'll come with you.'

'Bo! Stop talking such complete nonsense!' Prosper shouted at him. 'You're not going anywhere, is that clear? And you're definitely not going to do anything dangerous.'

'You bet I will!' Bo pulled a face at his brother and folded his arms defiantly.

Scipio still hadn't said anything.

Mosca smoothed out one of the colourful *mandorlati*-sweet wrappers. Riccio pushed his tongue through the gap in his teeth and kept his eyes fixed on Scipio.

'I agree with Prosper,' Hornet said breaking the silence. 'There's no reason to take any more risks. We've got enough money for now.'

Scipio examined his mask and poked a finger into one of its hollow eyes. 'I *will* take the job,' he said. 'Riccio, you will go to Barbarossa tomorrow morning and give him my reply.'

Riccio nodded. His scrawny face beamed all over. 'And this time you'll take us along, won't you?' he asked. 'Please! I'd love to see a big, fine house from the inside – just once.'

'Yes, I'd like that too.' Mosca gazed dreamily up at the curtain, which was glittering in the candlelight as if it was covered in golden spider's threads. 'I've often wondered what it must be like. I've heard that in some of the houses the floors are paved with gold and that they have real diamonds on the doorknobs.'

'Well, go to the *Scuola di San Rocco*, if you want to see things like that!' Hornet gave the boys an angry look. 'Scipio just said himself, he should take a break for a while. After all, they're probably still looking for the man who broke into the *Palazzo Contarini*. Another break-in would be madness right now. Just stupid!' She turned to Scipio. 'If Barbarossa knew that the Thief Lord hasn't got a single hair on his chin and doesn't reach up to his shoulder even in a pair of high-heeled boots, he would have never asked him anyway...'

'Oh yeah?' Scipio straightened himself up as if that would prove Hornet wrong. 'Did you know that Alexander the Great was smaller than me? He had to push a table in front of the Persian throne so he could climb on to it. I've made my decision. Tell Barbarossa that the Thief Lord will take the job. I have to go now, but I will be back tomorrow.' He started to leave, but Hornet stood in his way.

'Scipio,' she said quietly. 'Now listen. Maybe you're a better thief than all the grown-up thieves in this city, but when Barbarossa sees you in your high heels with all your grown-up playacting, he'll just laugh at you.'

The others looked at him in embarrassment. Never before had any of them dared to talk to him like that.

Scipio stood completely still and stared straight at Hornet. Then his mouth twisted into a snear. 'Well, the redbeard is not going to see me!' he said, pulling the mask over his face. 'And should he ever dare to laugh at me then I'll just spit into his moon-face and laugh right back at him, twice as loud. He is just a fat, old man. I am the Thief Lord.' With a sudden spin he turned his back on Hornet and stalked off. 'I'll be quite late tomorrow,' he called over his shoulder.

Then he was swallowed by the shadows.

9 Everybody is Small at Night

In the middle of the night, while everybody was asleep, Prosper got up. He pulled the blanket over Bo's exposed feet and fished his torch from underneath the pillows. Then he put on his jacket and crept past the others. Riccio was tossing and turning in his sleep and Mosca was holding on tight to his sea horse. One of Bo's kittens was sleeping on Hornet's pillow, its head hidden in her brown hair.

Prosper opened the door of the emergency exit and shuddered as the cold air assaulted him. It was a starlit night and the moon shimmered on the canal behind the cinema. The houses on the opposite side were dark – except for one window, where a light still shone. Someone else who can't sleep, Prosper thought. A few broad, worn steps led down to the water. They looked as if they led all the way to the bottom of the canal. Deeper and deeper, and into another world. Once he had sat by the canal with Bo and Mosca, and Bo had claimed that mermen and naiads – fairy folk – had built those steps. Mosca had asked him how they used them with their slippery fishtails. Prosper smiled as he remembered. He sat down on the topmost step and looked across the moonlit surface of the water. The canal showed the blurred reflections of the houses, just as it had done long before Prosper had been born, before his parents and even his grandparents had been born. Often, as he walked through the city, Prosper ran his fingers along the walls. The stones in Venice felt very different, everything was different from anything he had known before.

Prosper tried not to think about it. He wasn't homesick – he hadn't been for a long time, not even at night. This was his home now. The city had welcomed Bo and him like a great, gentle animal. It had hidden them in its winding alleys and had enchanted them with its exotic sounds and strange smells. It had even provided them with friends. Prosper didn't ever want to leave again. Never. He had grown so used to hearing the water smack and slurp against wood and stone.

But what if they had to run again? Just because of that man with the walrus-moustache? Prosper and Riccio still hadn't told the others about their pursuer. But they were all in danger, for if the detective got on to Prosper and Bo's trail, then he would also find the Star-Palace and the others. The others ... Mosca, who didn't want to go back to his family because they didn't even miss him; for Riccio, there was only the children's home; Hornet, who never told them anything about her old life because it just made her too sad; and – Scipio. Prosper shivered. He wrapped his arms around his knees. What if the detective also got on to the trail of the Thief Lord while he searched for Prosper and Bo? A fine thank you that would be to Scipio for taking them under his wing.

On the wet steps lay a torn *Vaporetto* ticket. Prosper let it flutter down into the canal and watched it drift out of sight.

It's no good; I have to tell them about the detective, Prosper thought. But how could he do that without Bo finding out? Bo, who felt so safe, and who believed that Esther would never follow them to Venice, because that's what his big brother had told him.

A shadow moved behind the lit window in the house opposite. Then the light went off. Prosper got up. The stone steps were cold and wet and he was freezing. He would tell the others about the walrus moustache, right now, while Bo was still asleep. Perhaps then Scipio would forget about Barbarossa's offer. But maybe – Prosper could hardly bear the thought – maybe Scipio would send him and Bo away. And what then?

Prosper returned to the cinema with a heavy heart.

'Hornet, wake up!' Prosper shook her very gently by the shoulder, but Hornet shot up so fast that the kitten rolled off her pillow like a ball. 'What is it?' she mumbled, rubbing sleep out of her eyes.

'Nothing, I just have to tell you all something.'

'In the middle of the night?'

'Yes.' Prosper went to wake Mosca, but Hornet held him back. 'Wait, tell me first, before you wake the others.'

Prosper looked across at Mosca who had crawled so deep into his blanket that only his short, frizzy hair could be seen. 'OK, Riccio knows about it anyway.'

They sat down next to each other on the folding chairs, two blankets wrapped around their shoulders. The cinema's heating, just like the lights, didn't work and the heaters that Scipio had brought them did little to drive the cold from the large auditorium.

Hornet lit two candles. 'So?' she asked, giving Prosper an expectant look.

'When Riccio and I were walking back from Barbarossa's,' Prosper tucked his chin under the blanket, 'I ran into a man. All I noticed at first was that he was staring at me in a strange way, but then I realized that he was following me. We gave him the slip – and ran towards the Grand Canal and took a *Vaporetto* to the opposite side to get away. But Riccio recognized him. He says the man is a detective. And it looks like he's after me – after me and Bo.'

'A real detective?' Hornet shook her head in disbelief. 'I thought they only existed in books and films. And Riccio's sure?'

Prosper nodded.

'Yes, but perhaps it's Riccio he's after. You know he can't stop stealing things.'

'No.' Prosper sighed and looked up towards the ceiling where the darkness hung over them like a black cloud. 'He was after me. The way he looked at me . . . he's going to find us. And my aunt and uncle will probably put me into a boarding school and I'll get to see Bo twice a month, or during the summer and at Christmas.' He felt a sudden wave of sickness clawing at his stomach. He closed his eyes, as if he could keep his fears out of his head that way, but of course it didn't work.

'That's nonsense! How is he going to find you here?' Hornet put a comforting hand on Prosper's shoulder. 'Come on, don't drive yourself crazy.'

Prosper buried his face in his hands. From the back of the auditorium, Riccio muttered something in his sleep.

Prosper pulled himself together. 'Just don't say anything to Bo, OK? Let him go on believing that we're perfectly safe here. We'll have to tell Mosca and Scipio, though. After all, you could all get into a lot of trouble if that snoop finds us here...'

'No way!' Hornet rubbed her nose. 'This is a perfect hiding place. The very best! Oh blast, I think I've caught another cold. Why can't Scipio steal a better heater for a change, instead of sugar tongs and silver spoons?'

Prosper handed his crumpled handkerchief to her and she gratefully blew her nose.

'Riccio wants to dye Bo's hair and I'm supposed to paint my face black so that the snoop won't recognize us,' Prosper said.

Hornet gave a quiet laugh. 'I think it'll be enough if I cut your hair really short, but that's quite a good idea about Bo's hair. We'll just tell him that the old ladies won't pat his head any more when his hair is black.'

'Do you think he'll believe that?'

'Well, if he doesn't, then Scipio will just have to tell him that he'll never be a famous thief with his blonde hair. Bo would fly if Scipio asked him to.'

'That's true.' Prosper smiled although he felt a small stab of jealousy.

'Scipio will just love the whole detective business.' Hornet shivered and rubbed her arms. 'He'll probably just be disappointed that the man's not after him. That would be quite an interesting job for a detective, discovering where the Thief Lord sleeps. Maybe he abseils at dawn from the *Palazzo Ducale*, after having spent the night in some cosy dungeon? Does he sleep in the old *piombi* prisons, where they let the enemies of Venice die from heat and fear, or down in the *ponti*, where they let them rot? You see, I even got a smile out of you!' Looking pleased, Hornet got up and tousled Prosper's hair. 'Tomorrow you'll get a new hair-do,' she said, 'and now stop worrying about that detective.'

Prosper nodded. 'So you don't think . . .' he asked hesitantly, 'that we should leave, Bo and I?'

'Pigeon-poo!' Hornet shook her head impatiently. 'Why should you? The police have been looking for Riccio for ever, and have we thrown him out? No. And what about Scipio? Doesn't he put us in danger, with his ever more crazy raids?' Hornet pulled Prosper from his seat. 'Come on, let's go to sleep,' she said. 'Oh dear, the noise Mosca makes with his snoring!'

Prosper undressed again and crawled underneath the blanket, next to Bo. But it took a long while before he finally fell asleep.

10 The Message

The next morning Riccio went to Barbarossa to give him the Thief Lord's answer, just like Scipio had told him.

'He accepts? Good, that will please my customer,' the redbeard said with a self-satisfied smile. 'But you will have to be patient. It won't be easy to get a message to him. He hasn't even got a telephone.'

For the next two days Riccio returned to Barbarossa's shop in vain, but on the third day the redbeard finally had the news they had been waiting for.

'My customer wants to meet you in the Basilica, the *Basilica San Marco*,' Barbarossa explained. He was standing in front of the mirror in his office, snipping away at his beard with a tiny pair of scissors. 'The Conte likes to be mysterious, but there are never any problems business-wise. He's already sold me some very nice pieces, and always at a fair price. Just don't ask him any nosy questions, understood?' He swapped the scissors for a pair of tweezers.

'The Conte?' Riccio asked, impressed. 'Does that mean he's a real count or something?'

'Indeed it does. I just hope the Thief Lord behaves accordingly.' Barbarossa looked very self-important before plucking a hair from his nostril. 'Once you meet the Conte in person you will see that there can be no doubt as to his distinguished ancestry. To this day he hasn't told me his name but my guess is he's a Vallaresso. Some members of this venerable family have not been blessed by fate. There has even been talk of a curse. Anyway.' The redbeard moved a little closer to the mirror and tugged at a particularly stubborn hair. 'Be that as it may, they are still one of the old families – well, you know, like the Correr, Vendramin, Contarini, Venier, Loredan, Barbarigo and countless others. They've ruled this city for centuries without any of us ever really knowing what was going on. Isn't that right?'

Riccio nodded respectfully. Of course he had heard all the names the redbeard had just so pompously strung out. He knew the palaces and museums that bore their names, but about the people themselves, he knew nothing.

Barbarossa took a step back and smugly inspected his reflection. 'So, as I said, just address him as Conte and he'll be pleased. The Thief Lord will probably get along fine with him. After all, your leader also likes to shroud himself in mystery. Probably quite a good idea in his line of work, right?'

Riccio nodded once more. He couldn't wait for the fat man to get back to the point so that he could deliver the news to the others. He shifted impatiently from one foot to the other. 'When? When are we supposed to meet him in the Basilica?' he asked as Barbarossa stepped up to the mirror again – this time to pluck his eyebrows.

'Tomorrow afternoon. Three o'clock sharp. The Conte will wait for you in the first confessional on the left. And don't be late. The man is always very punctual.'

'Fine,' Riccio mumbled. 'Three o'clock. Confessional. First left. Three o'clock sharp.' He turned to leave.

'Hold on, hold on, Hedgehog!' Barbarossa waved Riccio back once more. 'Tell the Thief Lord: the Conte wants to meet him in person. He can bring any companions he likes. Apes, elephants, or even his little children. But he has to come in person. The Conte wants to judge for himself before he tells him anything more about the job. After all,' his face took on a rather hurt expression, 'he hasn't even told me any more about it.'

That didn't really surprise Riccio, but the Conte's condition to meet Scipio made his heart beat faster. 'That, that…' he stammered, '…Sci…The Thief Lord won't like that at all.'

'Well,' Barbarossa shrugged his fat shoulders, 'then he won't get the job. Have a nice day, boy.'

'Same to you,' Riccio muttered, poking his tongue out at Barbarossa's back before making his uneasy way home.

11 Victor Waits

Victor sat in St. Mark's Square, surrounded by hundreds of tables and thousands of chairs, and drank his third espresso. Black, with three cubes of sugar. Difficult to stir in the tiny cup, and so expensive that he'd rather not think about it. For more than an hour he had been sitting on the cold, hard chair, scrutinizing the faces of the people passing by his table. Victor was not wearing the moustache he had worn when Prosper had stumbled into him. This time he had refrained from wearing any false whiskers at all. On his nose sat a thick pair of spectacles with plain lenses that made him look slightly dim-witted and completely harmless. He looked down at himself and felt very satisfied. Perfect – he thought – the perfect look: Victor the tourist. A baseball cap and a big camera hanging in front of his chest – this was one of his favourite disguises. As a tourist he could take as many pictures as he liked without anyone thinking anything of it. He could mingle with the big groups that stumbled off the boats and raced through town for a few hours, photographing everything that looked old with a bit of gold on its gable.

Now this is how I like my work – Victor thought as he

blinked into the low sun and stirred his coffee with a spoon that was far too small for his fingers. A large crowd of people started to swarm into the square. He eyed them patiently, one by one. But the two faces he was looking for were not among them. Well, maybe I'm relying too heavily on chance, Victor thought. He blew his nose, which had begun to feel seriously cold, and ordered another coffee from the waiter rushing past him.

Victor sighed and looked at his watch. Just before three. About time I filled my stomach with something other than coffee, he thought, and blew his icy nose again. Suddenly, he spotted six children on the far side of the square, by the tables of the café opposite. Victor noticed them because they were obviously in quite a hurry and because one of the boys, clearly their leader, wore a mask that made him look like a bird of prey. They were walking towards the Basilica. There was also a girl and a little boy, but he wasn't blonde. Victor picked up his newspaper and watched the children from behind it. The scrawny one with the spiky hair, the one who walked right behind the leader – looked familiar. But before Victor could take a closer look, the six children disappeared, swallowed by a big group of Canadian tourists with bright red backpacks. You could have filled a whole *Vaporetto* with these people. Out of the way, you backpackers, Victor grumbled to himself as he tried to crane his short neck. There. There they were again: four boys and a girl, not counting their masked leader. And there was the skinny fellow who had seemed so familiar. Damn, the hedgehog hairdo . . . of course! Victor got up. He had already paid for his four coffees. A detective always pays straight away, in case he loses a suspect due to a busy waiter. Victor sauntered towards the Basilica and picked another table nearer the children, keeping a close eye on them all the time.

Yes, that's him, Victor thought as he adjusted his fake glasses. That's the boy who was with Prosper. And that one ... 'Turn around!' Victor muttered, keeping the lens of his camera on the dark-haired boy who had now fallen behind a little. How protective he was, his arm around the little boy's shoulders. Yes, that just had to be Prosper. 'Look over here!' Victor hissed. 'Please, look this way, Prosper!'

The lady at the table to his right turned around and eyed him suspiciously. Victor gave her a coy smile. Why couldn't he stop talking to himself?

There. Finally! The dark-haired boy looked around.

'Damn it, it's him!' Victor drummed the table triumphantly. 'Prosper, the Fortunate One. Well, my dear boy, your good fortune is about to desert you, and Victor is going to have it instead. You cut your hair? I am sorry, but Victor Getz is not fooled that easily. And what about the little one, the one with your brotherly arm around his shoulder? His hair is so black, he might have fallen into a barrel of ink.'

Ink. Of course.

Victor hummed to himself while he took one picture after another of the Basilica, the winged lion, and the two brothers.

Everyone in Venice comes to St. Mark's Square at least once a day. You just have to be patient. Patience. Staying power. And luck. A whole barrel full of luck. And of course a pair of very sharp eyes.

Not much longer and Victor would have started to purr like a satisfied tomcat.

12 Meeting in the Confessional

'Move along, Bo!' Prosper urged. 'It's nearly three o'clock.'

But Bo was standing in front of the massive portal of the Basilica, looking up at the horses. Whenever he came to St. Mark's Square he stopped and tipped his head back to stare up at them. Four horses – massive golden horses – stood frozen there, stomping and neighing. Every time Bo wondered again why they hadn't jumped down yet. They looked so alive.

'Bo!'

Impatiently, Prosper dragged him along through the throngs of people, waiting eagerly at the entrance to the huge church to see the gilded walls and ceilings.

'They're angry,' said Bo, looking back.

'Who are?'

'The golden horses.'

'Angry?' Prosper frowned as he pulled him along. 'About what?'

'Because someone stole them and carried them off here,' Bo

whispered, 'Hornet told me.' He held on tight to Prosper's hand so he wouldn't lose his big brother in the crowd as they circled the Basilica. Back in the narrow alleys he wasn't usually afraid, but it was different here on the wide-open square. Bo called it the Lion Square. He knew it had a proper name really, but he called it that anyway. During the day every cobblestone here belonged to the pigeons and the tourists. But at night when the pigeons slept on the roofs and the people lay in their hotel beds, the square belonged to the horses and the winged lion that stood among the stars. Bo was certain about that.

'It is a thousand, or even a hundred years ago that they brought them here,' Bo said.

'Who?' Prosper, pushed his brother past a bride and groom who were having their picture taken in front of the Basilica.

'The horses!' Bo turned around again but he couldn't see them any more.

Scipio and the others were already standing by the lion fountain at the side entrance of the Basilica, waiting for them. Scipio had taken off his mask and was fiddling with it anxiously.

'At last!' Scipio said when Bo sat down next to him on the edge of the fountain. 'Were you looking at the horses again?'

Embarrassed, Bo stared at his feet. Hornet had bought him a new pair of shoes. They were quite big but they were really nice – and warm.

'Listen!' Scipio waved the others over to him and lowered his voice, as if he was afraid that one of the bystanders could overhear what he was about to say. 'I don't want to turn up at this meeting with my whole entourage, so this is how we are going to do it: Prosper and Mosca are coming inside with me. The others will wait here by the fountain.'

Bo and Riccio exchanged disappointed looks.

'But I don't want to wait here!' Bo's bottom lip began to tremble dangerously. Hornet stroked his hair comfortingly, but Bo pulled his head away.

'Bo's right!' Riccio called out. 'Why can't we all go? Why only Prosper and Mosca?'

Hornet answered before Scipio could say anything: 'Because we three are not good enough to be in the Thief Lord's crew! Bo is too small, you look scarcely any older than eight, and I'm a girl, which simply isn't good enough! No, we three would make you look foolish, wouldn't we, oh Thief Lord?'

Scipio pressed his lips together. Without another word he stalked off down the steps leading away from the fountain. 'Come,' he said to Mosca and Prosper. But the two boys hesitated for a moment. Only when Hornet said, 'Oh, go on,' did they follow him.

Riccio just stood there, trying to swallow tears of disappointment as he stared after the others. But Bo started sobbing so violently that Prosper came running back to him in spite of Scipio's angry glare. 'But you don't even like the Basilica!' he whispered to Bo. 'It's scary in there so don't be silly. You stay here at the fountain and look after Hornet. And don't move.'

'But that's boring,' Bo gulped, stroking the paw of one of the fountain's lions.

'Come on now, Prosper!' Scipio called angrily from the side entrance.

'See you later,' Prosper said, and then he followed Mosca and the Thief Lord into the big church.

When Prosper first took him there, Bo had called the

Basilica 'The Golden Cave'. The gilded mosaics of angels, kings, and saints, which decorated the walls and ceilings, only shone at certain times when the sunlight fell through the church windows. Right now everything was dark.

The three boys moved hesitantly down the wide centre aisle, their steps ringing out on the flagstone floor. The golden domes that arched above their heads kept their splendour hidden in the gloom, and in between the tall marble pillars that supported them the boys felt as small as insects. Instinctively, they moved closer together.

'Where are the confessionals?' Mosca whispered, looking uneasily around him. 'I haven't been in here very often. I don't like churches. They're creepy.'

'I know where they are,' Scipio replied. He pushed the mask back on to his face and led the way as purposefully as one of the Basilica's Tourist Guides. The confessionals were tucked away in one of the side aisles. The first one on the left looked no different to the others. It was a tall box made from black wood, draped with dark red curtains and with a door in the middle, which the priest used for slipping into the tiny space behind. Inside, he would sit down on a narrow bench, put his ear to a small window and listen to everyone who wanted to tell him their sins and clear their conscience.

Of course there was also a curtain on the side of the confessional to protect the sinners from curious eyes. Scipio now pushed this curtain aside, adjusting his mask one last time and clearing his throat nervously. The Thief Lord tried very hard to pretend that he was coolness itself, but Prosper and Mosca, as they followed him behind the curtain, sensed that his heart was beating just as fast as theirs.

Scipio hesitated as his eye fell on the low bench half-hidden in the darkness, but then he knelt down on it. The small window was now level with his eyes and he could be seen by whoever sat on the other side. Prosper and Mosca stood behind him like bodyguards. Scipio just knelt there, waiting.

'Perhaps he's not here yet. Shall we have a look?' Mosca whispered cautiously.

But just then someone pulled back the curtain of the small window. Two eyes, round and bright, seemingly with no pupils, gleamed through the darkness of the confessional. Prosper shuddered and only after another look did he realize that they were spectacles, reflecting the sparse light.

'One shouldn't wear a mask in a church, any more than a hat.' The uneven voice sounded like a very old man.

'One also shouldn't talk about a theft in a confessional,' Scipio answered, 'and that's what we're here for, isn't it?'

Prosper thought he could hear a small laugh. 'So you really are the Thief Lord,' the stranger said quietly. 'Well, keep your mask on if you don't want to show your face, but I can still see that you're very young.'

Scipio knelt bolt upright. 'Indeed. And you are very old, judging by your voice. Does age matter in this transaction?'

Prosper and Mosca looked quickly at each other. Scipio might have had the body of a child, but he could express himself like an adult, with a confidence that they couldn't help admiring.

'Not in the least,' the old man answered. 'You must forgive my surprise at your age. I must admit that when Barbarossa told me about the Thief Lord I did not imagine a boy of, say, twelve or thirteen years of age. But I do agree, age is of no consequence in this case. I myself had to work like an adult from the age of eight, although I was small and weak.

Nobody cared about that.'

'In my line of business a small body may be an advantage, Conte,' Scipio replied. 'If that is how I should address you.'

'You may, yes.' The man in the confessional cleared his throat. 'As Barbarossa has told you, I am looking for someone who can retrieve something for me, something I have been trying to find for many years, and which I have now finally discovered. Sadly, the item is at the moment in the possession of a stranger.' The old man cleared his throat again. His glasses now moved so close to the window that Prosper thought he could just about see the outline of a face. 'Since you call yourself the Thief Lord I assume you have already entered some of the noble houses of this city without ever being caught. Am I right?'

'Of course.' Scipio surreptitiously rubbed his aching knees. 'I have never been caught. And I have seen nearly every noble house from the inside. And without ever being invited.'

'Is that so?' Strong fingers covered with liver spots adjusted the spectacles. 'Sounds like we're in business. The house you shall visit for me is on the Campo Santa Margherita – number eleven. It belongs to a Signora Ida Spavento. It is not a particularly magnificent house but it does have a small garden, which, as you well know, is a treasure in itself in this city. I will leave behind in this confessional an envelope containing all the information you need to carry out this job. You will find a ground plan of the Casa Spavento, and a few notes on the item you are supposed to steal, as well as a photograph of it.'

'Very well.' Scipio nodded. 'That will save my assistants and I a lot of work. But let's talk about the payment.'

And again Prosper could hear the old man laugh. 'I can see

that you are a businessman. Your reward will be five million lire, payable on delivery.'

Mosca squeezed Prosper's arm so hard that it hurt. Scipio said nothing for a while and when he spoke again his voice sounded quite shaky. 'Five million,' he repeated slowly, 'sounds like a fair price.'

'I couldn't pay more even if I wanted to,' the Conte answered. 'You will see that what you are supposed to steal is of value only to me, since it is made neither of gold or silver, but of wood. So, do we have a deal?'

Scipio inhaled sharply. 'Yes,' he said, 'we have a deal. When shall we deliver the item?'

'Oh, as quickly as your skills permit. I am an old man and I would like to achieve the goal of my lifelong quest. I have no wish left in this life, except to hold in my hands what you are to steal for me.'

Longing rang through his voice. What could 'the item' be? Prosper thought. What could be so wonderful as to cause such mad desire? It was still only an object. It wasn't alive. What could be worth such a fortune?

Scipio stared thoughtfully into the dark window. 'How shall I report to you that I have been successful?' he asked. 'Barbarossa told us you're difficult to reach.'

'That is true.' Out of the darkness came quiet coughing. 'But you will find everything you need in this confessional after I have left. Once I have closed this curtain, you will count to fifty, and then you may retrieve what I have left behind for you. I also like to keep my secrets and I do not have a mask to aid me. Send me news of your success and you will receive my answer the next day at Barbarossa's. I will then tell you when you can exchange 'the item' for your reward. I'd better tell you now where we will carry out the bargain. Barbarossa is a little too fond of opening other people's letters and I would prefer to conduct this transaction without his interference. So remember this well: we will meet at the Sacca della Misericordia, a small bay to the north of the city. You can find the Sacca on any street map of Venice should it not be familiar to you. I wish you luck, Thief Lord. My heart has been longing so passionately for what you shall steal for me that it has grown quite weary.'

The Conte quickly pulled the curtain shut. Scipio got up and listened. A party of tourists shuffled past the confessional while their guide described the mosaics above their heads in a muted voice.

'Forty-eight, forty-nine, fifty!' Mosca said as soon as the tourists had moved on and the voice of the guide had faded away.

Scipio glanced at him amused. 'Well, you're certainly quick at counting,' he said and pushed the curtain aside. Carefully, one after another, they stepped into the open.

'You have a look, Prosper,' Scipio whispered, while he and Mosca shielded the confessional from view.

Prosper carefully opened the door meant only for priests and slipped inside. On the small bench underneath the window he found a sealed envelope and a basket with a woven lid. When Prosper lifted the basket he heard rustling inside. He nearly dropped it again in surprise. Scipio and Mosca looked amazed when he emerged from the confessional with his find.

'A basket? What's inside?' Mosca whispered suspiciously.

'Whatever it is, it moves.' Prosper carefully lifted the lid, but Mosca hurriedly pushed it back down. 'Wait!' he said. 'It moves? Perhaps it's a snake!'

'A snake?' Scipio teased. 'Why should the Conte give us a snake? You get these strange ideas from all those stories Hornet reads you.' He put his ear to the basket. 'Yes, there's something rustling. But I can also hear pecking sounds,' he muttered. 'Ever heard of a pecking snake?'

Scipio frowned and opened the lid just enough to peer inside. 'Well!' he said, and quickly closed the lid again. 'It's a pigeon.'

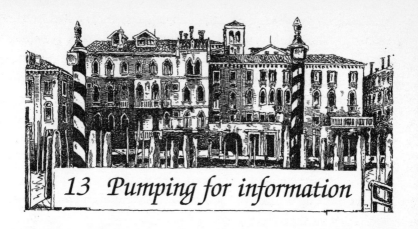

13 Pumping for information

What are they doing in the Basilica? Victor thought as he watched Prosper and Mosca vanish with Scipio through the side entrance. It seemed highly unlikely that the three boys just wanted to look at the mosaics. I hope they're not going to pick the tourists' pockets, he thought, or I'll have to hand Prosper over to the police. Not that Esther Hartlieb could care less. As far as she's concerned, it would just go to show that she'd always been right about her sister's eldest son. But if the little one was also caught thieving, that would probably be quite a blow to her.

The little one . . . Over his newspaper, Victor carefully peered towards the lion fountain. Prosper had left Bo with the girl and the little hedgehog boy. He probably trusted them or he wouldn't have left his precious little brother in their care. The girl was talking to Bo. She was obviously trying to make him laugh. The little one, however, looked pretty gloomy. As did the little hedgehog, who was staring into the water of the fountain as if he was about to drown himself in it.

What do I do now? Victor thought. He frowned and folded up his newspaper. I could grab the little one, but I would probably be lynched as a child snatcher before I had the chance to show my detective's badge. No, too many people around. Victor didn't like to admit it to himself, but there was another reason why he didn't want to take Bo. It was ridiculous, but he just couldn't do that to Prosper – to have him find his brother missing when he came out of the Basilica.

Victor shook his head and sighed. I shouldn't have taken on this case, he thought to himself. Whatever next? You can't feel pity during a game of hide-and-seek. And even less when you play tag. Stop worrying!

'Exactly!' Victor grumbled. 'I will have to get some more information first. About that gang they're hanging out with, for starters.' He pulled his baseball cap lower over his face and made sure that he hadn't finished the film in his camera. Then he strolled out into the open, just far enough for Bo to be able to see him from the lion fountain. Victor bought a bag of birdseed from one of the hawkers that stood around everywhere. He filled his pockets with seeds and scattered them with both his hands across the piazza.

'Putt, puttputtputt!' he cooed, putting on his most harmless smile. 'Come here, you winged rats and don't you dare poo on my sleeves.'

And they came. A whole flock of pigeons rose in a cloud of grey feathers and yellow beaks, fluttered towards Victor, and settled on his shoulders, arms, and even on his head, where they pecked inquisitively at his cap. This wasn't pleasant at all. Victor had to admit he was afraid of anything that flapped with a sharp beak. But how else could he attract the attention of the little boy? So Victor smiled and cooed and puttputted – and watched the children by the fountain.

The hedgehog was now sitting quite a way from the others staring at the crowds with a face like thunder. The girl had her head in a book. And Bo was bored.

'Look over here, kid!' Victor whispered while pigeons tripped all over his head. 'Go on now, look at this silly man who's playing scarecrow just for you.'

Bo pulled at his dyed hair, rubbed his nose, yawned – and then, suddenly, he discovered Victor. Victor, the pigeon roost. He cast a quick glance at the girl and checked that she was absorbed in her book. And then he slipped off the fountain.

At last! Victor sighed with relief and filled his hands with more seed. Bo strolled hesitantly towards him. He kept looking back towards the others as he pushed his way past three screaming girls who were trying to remove a couple of pigeons from their hair. Then he stood in front of Victor with his head cocked to one side.

When the pigeon on Victor's head leaned forward and pecked at the glass of his fake spectacles, Bo giggled.

'*Buongiorno*,' Victor said, chasing the cheeky bird from his head. Another pigeon immediately settled down on it.

Bo screwed his eyes together and tilted his head the other way. 'Does that hurt?'

'What?'

'Those claws, of course. And when they peck at your glasses.' The little boy's Italian sounded nearly as good as Victor's, maybe even better.

Victor shrugged, and the pigeons fluttered into the air only to settle down again immediately. 'Ah,' he replied. 'It's not so bad. And I like it when they fly around me.' What a big fat lie! But then Victor had always been good at lying, even when he was little. 'You know,' Victor said while Bo watched him intently, 'when the birds flutter around me I always imagine that I might take off at any moment and soar right up to those golden horses there.'

Bo turned around and looked at the stamping hooves above the entrance to the Basilica. 'Yes, they're brilliant! I want to sit on one of them. Hornet says they had to cut off their heads when they brought them here. I mean, when they stole them. And then they stuck them back on the wrong way round.'

'Really?' Victor had to sneeze because one of the feathers had flown up his nose. 'They look all right to me. But those are copies anyway. The real ones have been in a museum for a while now, so that the salty air doesn't eat them up. Do you like pigeons?'

'Not really,' Bo answered. 'They flap around too much. And my brother says you can get worms from touching them.' He giggled. 'Now one of them has pooed on your shoulder.'

'Vermin!' Victor threw his arms in the air so that all the pigeons scattered. 'Your brother said that? He seems to take care of you really well.'

'Yes, sometimes he looks after me a bit too much.' Bo looked up at the circling pigeons. Then he glanced back towards the lion fountain where the girl was still reading her book and the hedgehog was stirring the filthy water with his hands. Satisfied that he hadn't been missed, he looked back at Victor. 'Can I have some of those seeds?'

'Sure.' Victor put his hand in his pocket and poured some of the seeds into the little hand.

Carefully, Bo stretched out his arm – and when a pigeon perched on it immediately, he started to laugh and looked so happy that for a moment Victor forgot why he was standing there with birdseed in his hands. And then a whiff of hairspray, from a young, sour-faced woman pushing by, reminded him of the job to be done.

'What's your name?' Victor asked, picking a grey feather from his jacket. Maybe I'm wrong about them, he thought – children's faces all look alike anyway, like peas in a pod. Perhaps the ink-black hair is his real colour and perhaps the little boy genuinely came here with some friends and will go back home tonight, to his mother. His Italian was really very good.

'Me? Bo. What's yours?' Bo giggled again, as the pigeon hobbled up his arm.

'Victor,' Victor answered. Immediately, he could have slapped himself. Why, by all the devils and demons, did he tell the little one his real name? Had the pigeons pecked his last bit of sense away?

'Aren't you a bit young to be walking around alone in these crowds?' he asked nonchalantly while pouring some more seeds on to the boy's hand. 'Aren't your parents afraid that you'll get lost among all these people?'

'But my brother's here,' Bo replied. He watched in delight as a second pigeon landed on his arm. 'And my friends. Do you come from America? You talk funny. You're not a Venicer, are you?'

Victor felt his nose. It felt sore. 'No,' he answered. He adjusted his cap. 'I'm from all over the place. Where do you come from?' Victor looked across towards the fountain. The girl had raised her head and was looking around.

'From a *long* way away. But I live here now,' Bo answered. 'It's much nicer here,' he added. He was smiling at the pigeons on his arm. 'There are lions everywhere with wings and angels and dragons. They all look after Venice, Prosper says, and after us. But there's not so much danger – because there are no cars here. And that's why you can hear better – because of the water and the pigeons. And you don't have to be scared of being run over.'

'Yes, that's right.' Victor held back a smile. 'Still, you just have to be a little careful not to fall into a canal.' He turned around. 'Are those your friends over there, at the fountain?'

Bo nodded.

'I think the girl is looking for you,' Victor said. 'Why don't you give her a wave, so she doesn't worry?'

'That's Hornet.' Bo waved at her with his pigeon-free hand.

Reassured, Hornet sat down on the wall again. However, she now kept her book shut and didn't let Bo out of her sight.

Victor decided to do the pigeon-roost trick once more. That seemed the most innocent thing to do. 'I live in a hotel right by the Grand Canal,' he said while the pigeons settled down on him again. 'And you?'

'In a cinema.' Bo drew back with fright as one of the birds tried to hold on to his hair.

'In a cinema?' Victor looked at him incredulously. 'That's great. You can watch movies all day.'

'No, we can't. Mosca says the projector is gone. And most of the chairs are gone, too. And the screen is all eaten up by moths and now it's completely useless.'

'Mosca? Is that one of your friends? Do you live with your friends?'

Bo nodded proudly. 'Yes, we all live together.'

Victor looked at him closely. Was it really possible? Or was this little angel face telling him more lies? A bunch of children living alone? They certainly didn't look hungry, or as if they were sleeping under bridges. Admittedly, the knees on Bo's trousers had poorly-stitched patches on them, and he wasn't exactly wearing the cleanest of jumpers, but that wasn't unusual. And it was obvious that someone combed the little boy's hair from time to time and washed behind his ears. But maybe that was his brother?

Well, perhaps he can't tell me anymore – Victor thought. He let his arms drop again. Disappointed, the pigeons fluttered away. Victor rubbed his aching shoulders. 'What do you say,' he asked as casually as possible, 'shall we have an ice-cream over there in the café?'

Instantly, Bo became suspicious.

'I never go anywhere with strangers,' he answered haughtily and took a step back. 'Not without my big brother.'

'Of course not!' Victor said quickly. 'That's very sensible of you.'

The girl at the fountain had roused herself. She was pointing in his direction and Victor could see now that the others had returned. The masked one was carrying a basket and Prosper was looking agitated as he peered in their direction.

He can't recognize me, Victor thought, absolutely impossible. I had that walrus moustache stuck on my face before. But he still felt uncomfortable. 'I've got to go, Bo!' he said hastily as Prosper made his way towards them with a very anxious face. 'Nice of you to chat with me. I'll just take a quick picture of you, as a souvenir, OK?'

Bo smiled and posed for the camera. He still had a pigeon on his hand. As soon as Victor raised his camera Prosper quickened his pace. He was nearly running now.

Victor pressed the release, wound the film, and took another photograph. 'Thanks, kid. It was nice talking to you,' he said, ruffling Bo's ink-black hair. Yes, it was definitely dyed, no doubt about it.

Prosper was now just a few steps away. He pushed through the crowd without ever taking his eyes off Victor.

'Take care, and don't accept ice-cream from strangers!' Victor called out to Bo. Then he took a few brisk steps backwards, and slipped into the next large group wandering across the square, letting the crowd pull him away. Anybody could make himself hard to see, if he played it right. Quickly, Victor stuffed his cap into his left pocket, took off the spectacles, and pulled a small beard and a pair of sunglasses out of his right pocket. Carefully, and without rushing, he sauntered back to where the two brothers were still standing amongst a big flock of pigeons. Victor, now squeezed between five large old ladies, discreetly moved past the boys.

I won't let them shake me off again, he thought, oh no, I'm ready this time. But what if Prosper recognized him? Rubbish. How could he possibly know him again? He'd have to be a child genius to see through a Getz disguise!

'Back to work, Mr Detective,' Victor reminded himself. 'Now, let's see where these little rascals have their den.' Victor tried not to think about what he would do once he found their hiding place. Later, he thought, I'll worry about that later.

He followed the children into the maze of alleys.

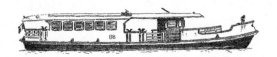

14 Premonitions

'Damn it, Bo, can't you just do as you're told for once?' Scipio scolded Bo as Prosper returned with him.

'You were gone for ages!' Bo grumbled. 'And I was bored.' He looked around but Victor the pigeon man was nowhere to be seen.

'I had him in sight all the time, Scip,' Hornet said. 'So calm down.'

'What's in the basket?' Bo poked his fingers under the lid, but Prosper pulled his arm back.

'It's a carrier pigeon, so keep your hand away from it, OK?'

'Come on, let's get back to the Star-Palace.' Scipio turned away from the big square and impatiently waved to the others to follow him. 'I haven't got much time today.'

'What about the job?' Bo called out, hopping excitedly after him. 'What do we have to steal?'

'For goodness sake, Bo!' Mosca put his hand over the boy's mouth. 'We don't know yet, OK?'

'The Conte gave us an envelope,' Prosper explained quietly

to Bo. 'But Scipio wants to open it only when we've reached the hideout.'

'And Scipio is the boss,' Riccio grumbled. His face was gloomy and his hands dug deep into his pockets, as he walked alongside the others as if far more interested in the pavement than this business with the Conte.

'And who was the Conte?' Hornet pulled Scipio's ponytail. She knew how much he hated that. 'Tell us about it, since we weren't allowed to come with you. What did he look like? Was he spooky?'

Mosca laughed. 'Spooky? No idea. We never saw him. Or did you see his face, Scip?'

Scipio shook his head.

Prosper was walking right behind him, Bo's hand firmly in his, but he kept looking over his shoulder. 'Scipio...' Prosper's voice choked with nervousness. 'You'll probably think I'm crazy but,' he looked around once more, 'the bloke on the square, the one who talked to Bo...'

'Yes?' Scipio turned around. 'What about him? He looked like a tourist to me.'

'I know, but ... on the way to the Basilica, perhaps Hornet told you about the detective who followed Riccio and me...'

Scipio frowned. 'Yes. A crazy story, if you ask me.'

'But it's true. The man just there...' Prosper desperately searched for words while Scipio just stared at him. 'I think it was him. He really did look like a tourist, but when he walked away I—'

Bo interrupted his brother: 'What detective?'

Prosper gave him a wretched look. They came to a bridge and Scipio coolly scrutinized the people pushing up the stairs behind them.

'You don't need to look as if it's the most stupid thing you've ever heard,' Riccio said. 'Victor the snoop likes to dress up. Perhaps it really was him. And—'

'The pigeon man was called Victor,' Bo interrupted him. He leaned over the balustrade.

'What?' Prosper swung Bo towards him. 'What did you just say, Bo?' A few gondolas swayed on the water. The gondoliers waited for customers at the foot of the bridge. Bo watched with fascination as they tried to chat-up the passers-by.

'I said the pigeon man's name was Victor,' Bo repeated without taking his eyes off the *gondolieri*. Then he tore away from Prosper and jumped down the steps to watch a gondolier push his boat off its mooring.

Prosper stayed on the bridge. He stood there as if rooted to the spot.

'Victor the snoop,' Riccio breathed. He stood on tip toes and peered into the crowds pushing towards the bridge. Prosper, meanwhile, turned round and ran after Bo. He pulled him away from the gondolas so violently that Bo nearly fell over. Then he vanished with him into the next alley.

'Hey, Prosper, wait!' Scipio called out before chasing after them. He caught up with them after a few metres.

'What are you doing, running off like that?' Scipio scolded, holding on to his arm. Bo freed himself from Prosper's grip and stood next to Scipio.

'Come with me!' Scipio said and without another word he pushed the two of them into the nearest souvenir shop. Riccio, Mosca and Hornet squeezed in after them.

'Act as if you're looking at something!' Scipio whispered. The shop assistant looked at them suspiciously. 'If that bloke on St Mark's Square really was that detective then it won't do any good to just run away,' he said to Prosper under his breath. 'With all those people around you'd never notice him following you!' He crouched in front of Bo and put his hands on his shoulders. 'That Victor – did he ask you any questions?' he asked. 'When you were feeding the pigeons back on the square?'

Bo crossed his arms behind his back. 'He asked me my name…'

'Did you tell him?'

Hesitantly, Bo nodded.

'What else did you tell him, Bo?' Hornet whispered.

The shop assistant looked towards them more frequently now, but luckily a party of tourists came in and kept her busy for the time being.

'I don't remember,' Bo mumbled and looked at Prosper. 'Did Esther send the detective?' His lip began to tremble.

Scipio sighed and got up again. He looked at Prosper. 'What does this detective look like?'

'But that's just it!' The tourists turned around, and Prosper immediately lowered his voice. 'This time he looked completely different! He had no beard and he wore glasses, and I could hardly see his eyes because he wore a cap. I only recognized him because he ran away. He moves his shoulders in a strange way when he walks. Like a bulldog.'

'Hmm.' Scipio felt for the Conte's envelope. It was still tucked, unopened, inside his jacket. Then he looked thoughtfully through the shop window. 'If that really was the detective,' he murmured, 'and if he really is following us, then we're leading him straight to the hideout. Unless we can get rid of him first.'

The others looked at each other uneasily. Mosca lifted the Conte's basket and peered through the lid. The pigeon was growing restless in its prison. 'It's about time we let it out of there,' Mosca whispered. 'It's probably hungry. Does anybody know what pigeons eat?'

'Ask Bo, he's just fed dozens of the creatures.' Again, Scipio felt for the envelope in his pocket. For a moment, Prosper thought he was going to open it, but to his surprise Scipio suddenly slipped out of his jacket, pulled the ribbon off his hair and took the cap off Mosca's head.

'Two can play at that game,' he said and pulled the cap over his own head. 'It's not that hard to change the way you look.' He threw his jacket at Prosper. 'You stay here, Bo. If the snoop is really after you then he's probably outside, waiting for you to come out. You just stand by the window so that he can see you through the glass. Mosca, you take the pigeon and the envelope back home.'

Mosca nodded and, with great care, placed the Conte's envelope into his trouser pocket.

'Riccio. Hornet.' Scipio waved the two of them to the door. 'We'll take a look outside. Perhaps we'll find him. What was he wearing?'

Prosper thought. 'A red jacket, light trousers, and a weird chequered jumper. He had a camera around his neck. And he had glasses and a baseball cap with something written on it. *I love Venice*, or something like that...'

'...and his watch.' Bo was nibbling his thumbnail. 'It had a moon on it.'

Scipio frowned. 'Fine. Got all that?'

Hornet, Riccio and Mosca nodded.

'Then let's go.'

97

One by one, they slipped outside. Prosper and Bo watched them through the window.

'But he was nice,' Bo mumbled.

'You never know straight away whether someone is really nice,' Prosper replied. 'And you can't tell from the way someone looks. How often do I have to tell you that?'

15 A Hiding for Victor

Victor was standing just a few metres away. Trying to look inconspicuous, he had turned his back to the shop the children had just gone into. But he was keeping an eye on the entrance by watching the reflection in the window of the shop opposite.

What are they up to in there? Victor wondered while he shifted impatiently from one foot to the other. Are they buying one of those plastic fans? Or does their leader want to buy another mask for his face? Then, Victor saw the girl step out of the shop. Hornet, Bo had called her. She glanced around, acting very casual, checking out the gondolas by the bridge, and then started towards them. Hardly a minute later the black boy left the shop. He was carrying a large basket and walked off in exactly the opposite direction. By the devil and his pestilences, what was going on now? Why were they splitting up? Well, it doesn't matter, my two suspects are still in the shop, Victor comforted himself. He adjusted his sunglasses. Next came the hedgehog. He skipped off towards the cake shop, which, a few steps away, filled the alley with its wonderful baking smells. The boy pressed his nose against the window. Perhaps all the others had to go home now to do

their homework or have lunch. Perhaps Bo's story about all
his friends living together in a cinema had just been a fantasy after all, nothing more. It made it a lot easier for Victor, of
course. The others would go home eventually, one by one,
leaving Prosper and Bo behind.

'I live in a cinema, with all my friends.' Pah! You had to
hand it to the boy, he knew how to spin a good story.
Amused, Victor looked at the reflection of his face in the
window. Hold on, who was that coming out of the shop?
Another one of those kids.

Which one was missing? The masked one. Of course. But
hadn't he looked different earlier? Victor frowned. The boy
stood in front of the shop door for a moment, looked around
with a face that gave nothing away, and then knelt down to
tie his shoelaces. He straightened himself again, blinked into
the sun, and strolled, whistling, towards the *gondolieri* who
were still out trying to net customers at the base of the
bridge. '*Gondola! Gondola!*' they called out loudly. Victor
would far rather have gone for a ride in one of those boats
than stand around here. The cushions were so soft and the
gentle rocking of the boat along the canals always made him
so wonderfully sleepy. All one could hear was the water
splashing, slurping and gurgling against the sides. And then
there was the gentle whisper of the city ... Victor closed his
eyes and sighed for a second before opening them wide with
a jolt.

'*Scusi!*' a voice said beside him.

The boy who had been looking at the gondolas was now
standing in front of him, grinning broadly. He had a very thin
face and very dark, almost black, eyes. Victor took off his sunglasses to take a closer look. Was this the boy in the mask who

had strutted like a cockerel ahead of the others across St Mark's Square?

'Can you tell me the time, please?' the boy said, staring at Victor's checked jumper.

Victor frowned as he looked at his watch. 'Four sixteen,' he grunted.

The boy nodded. 'Thank you. That's a nice watch. Does it also show the time on the moon?'

His dark eyes sparkled with laughter as he looked at Victor. What does he want from me? Victor wondered. He's definitely up to something. He cast a quick glance towards the souvenir shop and saw with relief that Prosper and Bo were still standing by the window. They were gazing at the trash on display as seriously as if it was treasure from The Doge's Palace.

'Are you English?'

'No. I'm an Eskimo, can't you tell?' Victor growled. He stroked his fake, wispy beard and sensed that it was beginning to develop a life of its own.

'An eskimo? That's interesting. They don't stray into this city too often,' the boy said before turning around and strolling away. Victor just stood there, tugging on his beard.

'Damn it!' he muttered, and turned quickly to pluck the stupid thing from his lip. Then he saw that the girl was slipping back into the shop. And even the hedgehog was no longer glued to the window of the *pasticceria*, but the boy with the black eyes was nowhere to be seen. They can't possibly have recognized me, Victor thought. Impossible. Then, to his confusion, he saw the three of them come out of the souvenir shop in perfect formation with Prosper and Bo in the middle. Not one of them glanced at him, but they all giggled and whispered and Victor had the distinct feeling that they were laughing at him. In no hurry whatsoever, they all strolled away in the direction of the Rialto.

Keeping out of sight, Victor followed them at a safe distance. But he had no practice in child-surveillance and, as he soon discovered, it was a very difficult task. They were so small, so much easier to overlook, and so quick. The alley they were walking down was very long and twisting, so it was just as well that from time to time one of the children turned and looked towards him. Victor tried to stay alert. But suddenly two large ladies stepped out of a café, laughing and arguing they blocked the alley so that Victor had to push past their large behinds. He squeezed his way free – and ran straight into the girl. The same girl who had been so engrossed in her book by the fountain. Bo had called her Hornet.

She stared at him with hostile grey eyes, and before Victor realized what she was doing she threw herself against him and flayed out at his checked jumper, screaming at the top of her voice: 'Let me go, you pig! No! I don't want to come with you! No!'

Victor was horrified. For a moment he just stood and stared down at her. Then he tried to push her away, but she wouldn't let go of his jacket and kept thrashing at his chest. The people around them turned and stared at him and the screaming girl.

'I haven't done anything!' Victor cried, appalled. 'I've done nothing! Absolutely nothing!' To his horror a dog jumped at him too, barking loudly. And in the meantime the other children disappeared into a side alley.

'Stop!' Victor yelled. 'Stop, you rotten little devils!' He

tried again to free himself from the girl but then something hit the back of his head with such force that he began to stagger. Before he knew it, the two large ladies were all over him, swinging their massive handbags at his head. Outraged, Victor bellowed back at them, holding his arms above his head, but the girl kept screaming and the ladies kept thrashing and the dog kept growling, sinking its teeth into Victor's jacket. The crowd around him grew ever more angry. They're going to tear me limb from limb, Victor thought. He couldn't believe it. He felt someone tearing a button off his jacket. Just as he was about to drop to his knees a *Carabiniere* fought his way through and pulled him up again. All around him a hundred voices shouted, simultaneously trying to explain what had caused this mayhem, and Victor realized that the girl had gone. Vanished into thin air, just like her four friends.

16 The Conte's Envelope

'We showed him all right!' Hornet said, once they were all safely back in the hideout. She had a deep scratch on her cheek and her cardigan was missing two buttons. But she was grinning from ear to ear. 'And look what *I* got in all the commotion.' Proudly, she produced Victor's wallet from underneath her jacket. She flung it over to Prosper. 'Don't get angry with me. Perhaps now you can find out more about this guy.'

Prosper murmured, 'Thanks,' and without hesitation quickly went through the wallet's various compartments. There were a few bills from some shop in San Paolo, a receipt from a supermarket, a ticket to The Doge's Palace. He threw all this carelessly to the ground. Then he held Victor's detective ID in his hands. He stared at it grimly.

Hornet looked over his shoulder. 'So he really is a detective,' she said.

Prosper nodded. He looked so desperate that she didn't know where to look. 'Come on, just forget him!' she said quietly. She slowly stretched out her hand and stroked Prosper's face. He didn't even seem to notice. He only looked up when Scipio approached them.

'What are you looking so gloomy about?' the Thief Lord said, putting his arm around Prosper's shoulder. 'We gave him the slip. Don't you want to see what's in the Conte's envelope?'

Prosper nodded and stuffed Victor's wallet into his pocket.

Scipio opened the envelope with great ceremony; he slit it open with his penknife while the others, sitting on the folding seats in front of him, watched with rapt anticipation.

'By the way, where's the pigeon, Mosca?' Scipio asked as he pulled a photograph and a folded sheet of paper from the envelope.

'Still sitting in the basket. I threw it some breadcrumbs,' Mosca answered. 'And now for goodness sake get on with it. What's that piece of paper?'

Scipio smiled. He dropped the empty envelope on the ground and unfolded the large sheet of paper. 'The house he wants me to pay a little visit to is on the Campo Santa Margherita,' he said, 'and this is the ground plan. Anyone want to see it?'

'Oh, just give it to me!' Hornet said impatiently. Scipio handed her the plan. Hornet took a quick look at it and then passed it to Mosca. Scipio meanwhile studied the photograph that had also been in the envelope. He seemed confused, as if he couldn't quite work out what he was looking at.

'What is it?' The suspense made Riccio jump up out of his seat. 'Go on, Scipio.'

'Looks like a wing,' Scipio mumbled. 'What do you think it is?'

The photograph went from one child to the other and all of them looked at it in just as much bewilderment as Scipio.

'Yes, it's a wing,' Prosper agreed after having studied it from all possible angles. 'And it seems to be made of wood, just as the Conte said.'

Scipio took the picture from his hands and stared at it.

'Five million lire for a broken wooden wing?' Mosca shook his head incredulously.

'How much?' The question came simultaneously from Hornet and Riccio.

'That's quite a lot, isn't it?' Bo asked.

Prosper nodded. 'Take another look at the envelope, Scip,' he said, 'perhaps there's something else in there to explain all this.'

Scipio nodded and picked up the envelope. He peered inside and then took out a small card, closely written on both sides.

'*The wing shown on the enclosed photograph,*' Scipio read, '*is the counterpart to the wing I am looking for. They look identical. Both are about seventy centimetres long and thirty centimetres wide. The wood was once painted white, but this will certainly have faded, and the gold on the edges of the feathers has probably also flaked off from the second wing. At the base of the wing there should be two long metal pins, each approximately two centimetres in diameter.*'

Scipio lifted his head. His face showed disappointment. He had obviously not expected the item he was supposed to steal – which had made the old man's voice quiver with longing – would be a piece of old wood!

'Perhaps the Conte has one of these beautiful carved angels,' Hornet ventured. 'You know, like they have in big churches. An angel like that is probably quite valuable, but only if it has both its wings. And he has probably somehow lost one of them.'

'I don't know.' Mosca shook his head. He went over to Scipio to have another look at the picture. 'What's that in the background?' he asked. 'It's very blurry, but it looks like a wooden horse.'

Scipio turned the card over and frowned. 'Wait, there's more. Listen: *The living quarters of the Casa Spavento, as far as I have been informed, are mostly on the first floor. The wing is probably kept there somewhere. I have had no information about any alarm systems, but it is possible that there are dogs in the house. Hurry, my friend! I will await your report with great impatience. Feed the pigeon bread and let it fly a little. Sofia is a friendly and dependable creature.'*

'Sofia. I like that name,' said Bo, peeking into the pigeon-basket.

'Yes, but you must keep your cats away from her,' Mosca teased him. 'They'll eat her whether she's got a nice name or not.'

Bo looked shocked.

'A wooden angel!' Riccio wrinkled his nose and pushed a finger into his mouth. He often had toothache, but today it was particularly bad. 'Not even a whole angel, just a wing. And that's supposed to be worth five million lire?'

Hornet leaned against the starry curtain and shrugged. 'I don't like it,' she said. 'All the secrecy – and the redbeard being part of it.'

'No, Barbarossa is just the middle man.' Scipio was staring at the photograph. 'You should have heard the Conte! He's completely crazy about this wing. It didn't sound as if this was only about the money he could get for a valuable statue.

No, there's something else behind all this. Do you still have my jacket, Prop?'

Prosper threw the jacket over to him. Scipio slipped into the long sleeves and sighed. 'Here, you'd better keep this safe. It's probably best in our money box,' he said, handing Hornet the photograph, the card, and the ground plan. 'I've got to go. I'll be out of the city for three days. Until I return you will observe the house. We have to know everything: who comes and goes, the habits of the people living there, how many visitors, when the house is empty, the best way to get in, and whether there really are any dogs there. You know, the usual stuff. Check whether the doors are marked in the right places on the ground plan. The house is supposed to have a garden, which may be useful. Oh, and Prosper' – Scipio turned to him once more – 'you and Bo had better not leave the hideout in the next few days. We've shaken off the detective for now, but you never know.' Scipio pulled the mask over his face.

As Scipio turned to leave Riccio stood in his way. 'Listen, can we help you with this job? I mean not just with the staking out, but with the robbery itself. Can't you take us with you just this once? We— we—' – Riccio stuttered with excitement – 'we could keep watch and help you carry the loot. The wing is probably quite heavy. It's not like a gold chain or a pair of sugar-tongs, which you can just stuff into a bag, is it? What … what do you say?'

Scipio listened to him impassively, his face hidden by the mask. Riccio had finished and was looking at him apprehensively, but Scipio was quiet, thinking. Then he shrugged and said: 'Fine.'

Riccio was so stunned that he just looked at Scipio open-mouthed.

'Yes, why not?' Scipio continued. 'Let's do this robbery together. Of course, only those who really want to.' He looked at Prosper, who remained silent.

'I want to do it!' Bo cried, jumping excitedly around Scipio. 'I'm really small, I can squeeze into little holes and—'

'Stop it, Bo!' Prosper's voice sounded so harsh that Bo spun around looking frightened. 'I won't take part, Scip,' Prosper answered, 'I can't do it. And I have to look after Bo. You understand that, don't you?'

Scipio nodded. 'Of course,' he said, but he sounded disappointed.

'And about that detective,' Prosper said nervously, 'I found my aunt's card in his wallet. That proves that he was after Bo and me. And Riccio was right about his name. He's called Victor Getz and he lives over in San Paolo.'

'No! He lives on the Grand Canal,' Bo said, casting a rather dark look at his brother. 'And I *will* go and steal the wing! It's not fair – you're not mummy!'

'Come on, Bo!' Hornet placed her hands on his shoulders. 'Prosper is right. A robbery is a dangerous thing. I'm not sure whether I will take part myself yet. But what makes you think the detective lives on the Grand Canal?'

'He told me. Go away!' Bo pushed her hands away and swallowed hard, trying not to cry. 'You're all horrible, really, really horrible!' Even when Mosca tried to tickle him to make him laugh, Bo pinched his hand hard.

'Hey, now listen!' Prosper, looking stern, knelt down in front of his brother and turned Bo towards him. 'You two seem to have talked quite a lot. Did you tell the detective anything else? About our hideout, for example?'

Bo bit his lip. 'No,' he grumbled without looking at

Prosper. 'I didn't!'

Prosper smiled with relief.

'Come on, Bo,' Hornet said, pulling him away. 'Help me with the pasta. I'm hungry.' Bo trailed after her with a gloomy face, stopping first to poke his tongue out at the others.

17 Victor's Trace

Victor's head hurt for three days. But what hurt more than the bumps on his skull was his injured pride. Taken for a fool by a bunch of kids! He ground his teeth every time he thought about it. The *Carabinieri* had dragged him to the police station like a common criminal. They had treated him like a child snatcher and when, full of rage, Victor wanted to show them his detective's ID, he realized that the little brats had robbed him as well.

Well, that was it! He would feel no more pity for them. Enough was enough!

While Victor cooled the lumps on his head with ice and warmed his sick tortoise with an infra-red light, he thought about nothing else except how to find that gang again. He recalled every single thing Bo had told him until one word rang in his brain as clear as the church bell chiming across the square.

Cinema. *We live in a cinema.*

What if it was true after all? What if it wasn't some childish fantasy? Victor hadn't told the police anything about Bo's strange clue, although they were now also looking for the children, since it was clear that they had stolen his wallet and that he really was a detective. But Victor didn't want the police to catch the little thieves. Oh no, I'll find them myself, he thought as he sat on the carpet, tickling his tortoises' crinkly heads. They'll soon learn that I'm not the idiot they think I am!

Oh blast! One of the tortoises was really sneezing quite worryingly. If he wasn't mistaken that was probably Paula. The vet had assured him that Paula couldn't pass her cold on to Lando, which was why Victor had left them in the same carton. He'd brought them in from the balcony, where the nights were now growing ever colder and he had even made them a house under his desk.

A cinema...

What had Bo said? Yes: the chairs were missing and the projector was gone. So it had to be a disused cinema, of course, a cinema that had been closed down and forgotten about by the owner. There weren't many cinemas in Venice. Victor opened the current telephone book as well as last year's edition, then called every cinema he could find. In most cases he was asked whether he wanted to book a ticket, but in one of them, the Fantasia, no one answered the phone. Another cinema had no address listed next to its name. This one was called the Stella and the number only appeared in the older telephone book.

The Stella and the Fantasia. Well, that gives us two possibilities, Victor thought before re-heating yesterday's risotto. Then he took the snivelling tortoise to the vet again. On the way back he took a detour to the Fantasia.

The cinema was just opening for the afternoon show when Victor arrived. There wasn't really a big crowd. The only ones in line for tickets were two children and a young couple who immediately vanished inside the dark auditorium. Victor approached the ticket booth and cleared his throat.

'Front or back?' said the lady in the booth popping a piece of chewing gum into her mouth. 'Where do you want to sit?'

'Nowhere,' Victor replied. 'But I would like to know whether you have heard of a cinema called the Stella?'

The ticket lady blew a large chewing-gum bubble with her brightly painted lips and let it pop. 'The Stella? That's been closed for a few months now.'

Victor's heart leaped. 'Yes, I thought so,' he said. He answered the ticket lady's baffled look with a satisfied smile. 'Do you happen to know the address?' He rested the box with the sick tortoise on the counter next to the register.

The ticket lady let another gum bubble pop and eyed the box curiously. 'What have you got in there?'

'A sniffy tortoise,' Victor answered. 'But she's getting better already. So, do you know the address?'

'Can I have a look?' the lady asked.

Victor sighed and pulled away the towel which kept out the cold. Paula, startled, lifted her wrinkly head and blinked a few times before hiding inside her shell.

'Cute!' the lady cooed, throwing her chewing gum into the bin. 'No, I don't know the address, but you could ask Dottor Massimo. He's the owner of this cinema and the Stella belongs to him as well. So he should know where it is, right?'

'Presumably.' Victor produced his notebook. 'And where can I find Dottor Massimo?'

'Fondamenta Bollani,' the lady answered, yawning. 'I don't know the number, but his is the biggest house around there. He's a very rich man, our owner is. He only keeps the cinemas for fun, although he still closed down the Stella.'

'Really?' Victor mumbled. He carefully placed the towel

over Paula's box again. 'Well, I may just pay Dottor Massimo a visit. Or perhaps you have his telephone number?'

The lady scribbled the number on a piece of paper, which she pushed towards Victor. 'When you talk to him,' she said, 'could you please tell him that the show was nearly sold out? Otherwise he may just close down the Fantasia as well.'

Victor looked around the empty foyer, smiling. 'I see what you mean! The queue stretches right back down the alley.' Then he went to find a phone box. The battery of his mobile had gone flat again. He should never have bought the stupid thing.

A booming voice grunted '*Pronto*' into Victor's ear.

'Am I speaking to Dottor Massimo, the owner of the old Stella cinema?' Victor asked. Paula rustled around in her box as if looking for a way out of her boring cardboard prison.

'Yes, indeed,' Dottor Massimo answered. 'Are you interested? Then do come along. Fondamenta Bollani, 233. I'm free for about another half hour.'

Then there was a loud *click* in Victor's ear. He gave the receiver a surprised look. Well, he certainly doesn't waste time, Victor thought as he squeezed himself out of the phone-box. Half an hour, and the next *vaporetto* stop was miles away. Well, it would have to be his aching feet again.

Dottor Massimo's house was not only the biggest house on the Fondamenta Bollani, it was also the most magnificent. Victor stood admiring the front of the house for a second – its ornate columns and balconies, and how the wrought-iron grilles in front of the ground-floor windows wound and intertwined, turning into the shapes of flowers and leaves.

A maid opened the door. She led Victor past the columns and into the courtyard from where a steep and impressive staircase led up to the first floor. The girl walked up the stairs so quickly that Victor hardly got a chance to look around. When he leaned over the balustrade to take another look at the fountain in the courtyard his guide turned around impatiently. 'Dottor Massimo is only free for another ten minutes,' she declared pertly.

Victor could not stop himself from asking: 'And what urgent appointment does the *dottore* have to keep?'

The girl gave Victor a surprised look as if he had just asked her about the colour of Dottor Massimo's underpants. Victor followed after her, just fast enough for him not to lose her in the labyrinth of corridors and doors. All this for an address. I should have just phoned him again.

Finally, as he had got quite out of breath and Paula had probably grown seasick in her box, the girl stopped and knocked on a door fit for a giant.

'Yes?' came the same booming voice that had barked at Victor down the telephone. Dottor Massimo was sitting behind a massive desk in a study that was bigger than Victor's whole flat. He received his visitor with a cool, appraising look.

Victor coughed politely. He felt ridiculous in this magnificent room, with his tortoise box under his arm and shoes that showed quite clearly that he did a lot of walking for a living. 'Good day to you, Dottore,' he said. 'Victor Getz. We just spoke on the phone. Unfortunately, you hung up so quickly that I didn't get a chance to explain what I wanted. I'm not exactly interested in buying your cinema, but—'

Before Victor could go on, a door opened behind him. 'Father,' a boy's voice said, 'I think the cat's sick…'

'Scipio!' Dottor Massimo's face turned purple with anger. 'Can't you see I have a visitor? How often do I have to tell you to knock? What if the gentlemen from Rome had been here already? How would it look if my son barged into our meeting because of a sick cat?'

Victor turned around and looked into a pair of frightened black eyes. 'She's really not well,' Dottor Massimo's son murmured. He quickly lowered his head, but Victor had already recognized him. His hair was tied back in a tight little ponytail and his eyes didn't look quite as arrogant as they had done on their last encounter, but there could be no doubt: this was the boy who had so innocently asked Victor the time, just before he and his friends had tricked him.

The world was full of surprises.

'She's probably unwell because she's just had kittens,' Dottor Massimo said with a bored voice. 'It's not worth calling a vet. If she dies you can always get a new one.' And then ignoring his son, the *dottore* turned to Victor again. 'Do continue, Signor…?'

'Getz,' Victor repeated. Scipio was still standing behind him, stiff and silent. 'As I said, I am not interested in buying the Stella.' Victor could see from the corner of his eye how Scipio jumped at the mention of the cinema's name. 'I'm writing an article about the city's cinemas and I would like to include the Stella. So I would like your permission to have a look around there.'

'Interesting,' the *dottore* said, glancing out of the window to where a water-taxi had just pulled up on the canal. 'Please excuse me, I believe my guests from Rome are here. Naturally you have my permission to look around the Stella. It is in the Calle del Paradiso. I'd be grateful if you'd say that it's to this city's shame that such a wonderful cinema had to be closed. Apparently we only cater for the interests of tourists these days.'

'Why was it closed down?' Victor asked.

Scipio was still standing at the door, listening intently to what Victor and his father were discussing.

'An expert from the mainland declared it unsafe!' Dottor Massimo got up from behind his desk. He went over to a cabinet and opened one its many drawers. 'Unsafe! The whole city is unsafe!' he declared arrogantly. 'Now they've ordered an extortionately expensive renovation. Where is that key? My manager brought it to me months ago.' He rummaged impatiently through the drawer. 'Scipio, come and help me, since you're just standing there like a lemon.'

Victor got the impression that Scipio had just decided to sneak away. He already had the doorknob in his hands, but when the *dottore* waved towards him, he pushed past Victor and walked, pale-faced and hesitant, towards his father.

'*Dottore!*' the maid put her head around the door. 'Your guests from Rome are waiting. Will you receive the gentlemen in the library or shall I bring them up?'

'I'll come to the library,' Dottor Massimo answered curtly. 'Scipio, will you ask Mr Getz to sign a receipt for the key? You can manage to do that, I hope? There should be a tag on the key ring with the name of the cinema.

'I know,' Scipio muttered without looking at his father.

'Do send me a copy of your article, as soon as it is published,' the *dottore* said, already striding past Victor and out of the office.

Now that he had left the room, there was a deathly silence. Scipio stood next to the open drawer and watched Victor like a mouse would watch a cat. Then he suddenly made a dash for the door.

'Hold it!' Victor called, standing in the boy's way. 'Where

are you going? To warn your friends? That won't be necessary. I don't intend to hand them over to the police, even though you did steal my wallet. I'm not even interested in the fact that you're obviously keeping a little gang in your father's dilapidated cinema. I don't care! I'm only interested in the two brothers – the ones you have taken in. Prosper and Bo.'

Scipio stared at him wordlessly. Then he whispered contemptuously: 'You rotten snoop!' before leaning forward and giving the carpet on which Victor was standing such a sharp tug that the detective lost his balance and landed with an almighty crash on his backside. He just about managed to hold on to the box with the tortoise. Quick as a flash, Scipio shot past him and ran towards the door. Victor threw himself to the side to grab hold of the boy's legs, but Scipio just jumped over him and vanished before Victor could get back on his feet.

Fuming with frustration, Victor charged after him as quickly as his short legs would carry him. But when he reached the top of the stairs, panting heavily, Scipio was already leaping down the last steps.

'Stop, you little rat!' Victor bellowed after him. His voice echoed through the huge house so loudly that two maids came running across the courtyard. 'Stop!' Victor bent over the balustrade and suddenly felt distinctly nauseous when he saw the drop below. 'I WILL FIND YOU, do you hear!'

But Scipio just pulled a face and ran out of the house.

18 Alarm!

'Well, let's go through it once more,' Mosca muttered, pouring over the ground plan the Conte had given them. 'We've seen three people entering and leaving the place so far: the fat housekeeper, her husband, and the lady with the dyed-blonde hair.

'Signora Ida Spavento,' Riccio explained. 'At first we thought the fat one was the signora and the blonde her daughter. But the man who runs the news-stand on the Campo Santa Margherita likes to talk a lot. He told me that the younger one is Ida Spavento and the fat one only looks after the house. Signora Spavento lives alone and she travels a lot. The newspaper man said she's a photographer. He showed me a magazine with pictures of Venice that she had taken. She comes and goes at different times. But the housekeeper goes home between six and seven every evening like clockwork and her husband usually arrives around midday but he never stays for long. Just as well – he looks as if he eats children for breakfast.'

'Yeah, he does!' Mosca said, grinning.

Riccio continued: 'So there's always someone in the house during the day. And the evenings,' he sighed, 'are the same. Signora Spavento obviously only likes going out during the day. But at least she goes to bed early. The light in her bedroom is out by ten o'clock at the latest.

'If that really is her bedroom,' Hornet said. She didn't sound very convinced. 'If, if, if! *If* the wing is on the first floor. *If* Signora Spavento sleeps on the second floor. *If* there really is no alarm system. There are too many 'ifs' for my liking. And what about the dogs?'

'Silly little yappers.' Riccio picked a piece of gum from the gap in his teeth. 'And they probably belong to the housekeeper. She usually takes them home with her in the evenings.'

'Usually!' Hornet rolled her eyes.

'Well, even if she doesn't,' Mosca waved his hand dismissively, 'then we'll just give them some sausages.'

'Well, aren't you the expert!' Hornet muttered. She was fiddling nervously with her plait. She had already pinched lots of things from shops, in *vaporetto* stations, in crowded alleys, but sneaking into a strange house was a completely different kettle of fish. Even if Riccio and Mosca were acting as if it was all just one big adventure for them, Hornet knew they were just as scared as she was. 'I wonder where the Conte got that ground plan,' Mosca wondered.

Riccio lifted his head. 'Wasn't that the bell?'

They all listened. Someone was ringing the bell at the emergency exit.

'That can't be Scipio – he isn't coming until tomorrow!' Hornet said. 'And he usually comes in through his secret entrance anyway.'

'I'll ask for the password,' said Prosper, jumping up. 'Bo, you stay here.' The bell kept ringing, again and again, as Prosper ran down the dark corridor towards the exit. After the incident with the detective, Mosca had drilled a spy-hole into the door, but it was already dark outside. So when Prosper pressed his eye against the hole he could hardly see anything. Rain was pelting against the entrance and someone was hammering against the metal.

'Can't you hear me? Let me in!' a voice pleaded outside. 'Won't anybody let me in, damn it!' Prosper thought he heard a sob.

'Scipio?' he asked in disbelief.

'Yes, damn it!' Prosper hastily pushed the bolt aside.

A soaked Scipio stumbled past him. 'Lock the door,' he panted, 'quick!'

Prosper, bewildered, obeyed him. 'We thought you wanted to come tomorrow,' he said. 'Why didn't you creep in your usual way?'

Scipio leaned against the wall, still panting heavily. 'You have to leave,' he gasped. 'Right away. Is everybody here?'

Prosper nodded. 'What do you mean?' he asked hoarsely. 'What do you mean, we have to leave?'

But Scipio was already running down the dark corridor. Prosper followed him, his heart beating wildly. When Scipio stumbled into the auditorium the others stared at him as if he was a stranger.

'What happened to you?' Mosca asked, astonished. 'Did you fall into a canal? And what's with the posh clothes?'

'I haven't got time to explain everything to you!' Scipio yelled. His voice cracked with excitement. 'The snoop knows you're here. Grab what you need and let's get out of here.'

The others looked at him in horror.

'Don't just stare at me!' Scipio yelled. They had never seen him like this before. 'He's going to walk through the front door at any minute. We might be able to come back here later, but please, you have to leave now.'

Nobody moved. Riccio was staring open-mouthed at Scipio. Mosca was frowning and Hornet had put her arm around Bo who looked very frightened.

Prosper was the first to react. 'Get your cats, Bo,' he said. 'And put your rain coat on. It's pouring outside.' Moving fast, he began stuffing their few belongings into a bag. The spell broken, the others started to hurry as well.

'But where are we going to go?' Riccio called out in despair. 'It's raining outside. And it's really cold. I don't understand. How did the snoop find us?'

'Shut up, Riccio!' Hornet barked at him. 'I have to think.' She took her arm off Bo's shoulders and turned to Mosca. 'You go and sit out front in the ticket booth and let us know as soon as you hear anything suspicious. He'll get held up by the rubbish we've piled up by the entrance, but not for long.'

'On my way.' Mosca quickly stuffed the ground plan under his waistband before vanishing through the big double door.

'I'll fetch the money we've got left,' Scipio mumbled, avoiding the others' eyes and went off after Mosca.

Silently, Bo placed the kittens one by one into a cardboard box. When he saw that Riccio was slumped on his mattress crying, he walked over and, awkwardly, stroked his spiky head.

'Where shall we go?' Riccio kept sobbing. 'Where, for god's sake, can we go?'

Hornet had to keep wiping tears from her face while she

packed her favourite books into a plastic bag. But then, she stopped.

'Wait a minute!' she said, turning towards the others. 'I've just had an absolutely mad idea. Do you want to hear it, or shall I shut up?'

19 Trapped

Victor felt as if he had crossed at least a hundred bridges when, finally, he turned into the alley where he hoped to find Dottor Massimo's mysterious cinema. There they were, the large neon letters. A piece of an 'L' was missing, but the name was still quite obvious: the Stella. A faded movie poster still hung in one of the display windows. Someone had drawn a heart on the grimy glass.

Breathing heavily, Victor walked up the two steps to the entrance. He tried to peer through the window, but it had been boarded up with cardboard. Well, the birds have probably all flown the coop already, Victor thought. His heart was still beating far too fast. Their leader has probably warned them.

How did the son of the rich Dottor Massimo fit in with the rest of the gang? Victor would have bet his beard collection that they were all runaways: the scrawny little hedgehog with the bad teeth, the tall dark one whose trousers were much too short, and the girl with the sorrowful mouth. They were all runaways, like the two brothers Victor was after. But what was the connection with Dottor Massimo's offspring?

'Doesn't matter!' Victor muttered. He placed the box with the tortoise in it next to the door and pulled a bunch of lock picks from his pocket. The padlock was no problem at all, but the door presented more of a challenge. When it finally sprang open a crack, Victor realized that it had been barricaded with piles of rubbish.

It'll take me hours to get through here, Victor thought, throwing his full weight against the entrance. After five attempts his shoulder started to hurt badly, but the door had at least opened far enough for him to squeeze through. With only his feeble torch for illumination, he fought through the piled-up rubbish, climbing over wedged chairs, crates and broken partitions. It was pitch black behind the boarded-up door and Victor's heart nearly stopped when, by the ticket booth, he ran slap bang into a cardboard cut-out of a man pointing a machine gun into his face.

Cursing quietly, he shoved the thing aside and crept towards the double doors that led to the cinema's auditorium. He opened the entrance carefully and listened, but he couldn't hear a sound. Just his own wheezing breath after his strenuous efforts. Of course, thought Victor, just as I thought – they've left the nest.

He took a few cautious steps into the dark auditorium. He shone the beam of his torch. Rows of seats. A curtain. It was indeed a real cinema. Curious, he aimed his light first at the walls and then up towards the ceiling. Suddenly, something fluttered towards him and a wing brushed against his face. Victor screamed and dropped his torch. He groped for it in the darkness and quickly pointed its beam at whatever was hovering above him. A pigeon. A stupid pigeon. Victor rubbed his face with his free hand, as if he could wipe away the shock.

One more fright like that and my poor heart will give out, Victor thought. He took another deep breath and moved on. This huge, gloomy auditorium was certainly a strange hiding place for a bunch of homeless children. Well, there was no other explanation: the young Mr Massimo must have brought them here, into his father's empty cinema. The curtain that concealed the screen glittered faintly when Victor's torch caught it. What if they were still hiding here? He took another step forward and his shoe hit a mattress. There was a whole mattress-camp on the floor behind the seats. There were blankets, pillows, books, comics, and even a cooker.

The torch beam fell on a teddy bear, a stuffed toy rabbit, fishing rods, a toolbox, piles of books, and a plastic sword that stuck out of a sleeping bag. He was standing in the middle of a nursery – a huge nursery!

I would have got a good hiding for painting a pirate's flag on the wall when I was a kid, Victor thought. For one short moment he had a crazy urge to lie down on one of the mattresses, to light a few of the many candles around the place, and to forget everything that had happened since his ninth birthday. But then he heard another sound.

The hair on the back of Victor's neck stood on end.

There was something there. He was sure.

Victor forgot about the mattresses and crept towards the folding seats. Could they really be foolish enough to try and play hide-and-seek with him? Did they think just because he was grown up he'd forgotten how to play?

'I'm sorry to disappoint you!' Victor said out loud. 'I've always been a first-class seeker. And when I played tag I always caught everyone, even with my short legs. His voice

126

sounded strange as it echoed through the large room. 'You can't possibly think,' he called as he shone his torch between the red chairs, 'that this could go on for ever? What do you live on? Stealing? How long is that going to last? To be honest, I don't really care. I'm only interested in two of you.'

What the devil am I talking about, Victor thought, I'm far too old to be playing hide-and-seek with a bunch of children in a pitch-black cinema.

'Hey, Victor! Come and catch me!' a voice suddenly called. It was a high, clear voice. Victor recognized it. The glittering curtain suddenly developed a bulge. 'Do you have a gun?' the voice behind the star-studded fabric asked. And then Bo's ink-dyed head popped out.

'Of course!' Victor pushed his hand underneath his jacket as if he was reaching for his revolver. 'Do you want to see it?'

Bo stepped slowly out of his hiding place. He stood there, his head cocked to one side, and looked at Victor. Where was his big brother, Prosper? Victor looked first to the left, then to the right, and finally over his shoulder, but could see nothing in the complete darkness that enveloped him.

'I'm not scared,' said Bo. 'That's probably just a plastic gun.'

'Well, well, if that's what you think.' Victor held back a grin. 'You're a real smart one.' He didn't let the boy out of his sight. But that meant he couldn't keep the row of seats in his range of vision. By the time he sensed something moving between the folding chairs, it was already too late. Suddenly, five children were all over him. They yanked him off his feet and threw him to the ground like a sack of potatoes. Then they sat on his stomach. As much as he struggled and kicked, Victor couldn't free himself. His torch had dropped to the floor and it was now rolling back and forth, flashing its light crazily around the room. Victor thought he could make out the girl who had set the ladies with the handbags on him. The same girl was now holding on to his right arm while the black boy had grabbed his left. Two other kids, probably Prosper and the hedgehog, were clinging to his legs. Right on Victor's chest, however, with his knees pressing into his sides as if the felled detective was a stubborn horse, sat Scipio, smiling mockingly.

'You little demon!' Victor shouted. 'You—'

He didn't get any further. Scipio simply wedged a rag between his captive's teeth. A wet, reeking rag that smelled of damp cat fur.

'What are you doing? Shouldn't we interrogate him first?' The black boy sounded surprised. 'We don't even know yet if he's really only after Prosper and Bo.'

'Exactly!' The hedgehog nervously pushed his tongue between his teeth. 'Let's ask him how he found us, Scipio.'

Look, he'll just tell us lies anyway,' Scipio answered. 'Tie him up.'

Hesitantly, they gathered all the ropes and belts they could find and trussed Victor up like a turkey. The only freedom he had left was to roll his eyes angrily.

'You won't hurt him, will you?' That was Bo. He leaned over Victor with a worried expression on his little face. Then he suddenly giggled. 'You look funny, Victor,' he said. 'Are you really a detective?'

'Yes he is, Bo.' Prosper pushed his little brother aside, leaned forward, and frisked Victor. 'A mobile,' he said, 'and ... look at this...' He carefully held up Victor's revolver. 'I thought he was just bluffing.'

'Give it to me. I'll hide it.' Hornet took the gun off Prosper very gingerly, as if it could explode in her hand any moment.

'See what else he's got!' Scipio commanded. He got off Victor's chest and stood over him, looking serious. 'Well, Mr Detective,' he said in a quiet, threatening voice, 'that will teach you to mess with the Thief Lord.' Then he waved at the others. 'Come on, put him in the men's toilet.'

20 A Night Visit

They put a blanket on the cold tiles for Victor, that was at least something. Locked up in an old cinema by a bunch of children!

The hours passed and Victor kept going over things in his mind: I should have known, I should have known the moment that Esther woman came into my office with her pointy nose and her yellow coat. Yellow has always been my unlucky colour.

He was trying for the twentieth time to reach his shoe, which contained a few useful tools for emergencies hidden in its heel, when the door behind him opened. It happened very quietly as if whoever was coming in wanted to keep it from everyone else. A torch was flashed into Victor's face and someone knelt down next to him on the scratchy blanket. Prosper.

Victor sighed with relief. He didn't really know why, for Prosper was not looking at him in a very friendly manner. But at least he freed him from the stinking gag. Victor spat a few times to get rid of the horrible taste. 'Did your boss give you permission to do this?' he asked. 'I bet he wanted to poison me with that rag.'

'Scipio is not our boss,' Prosper answered as he helped Victor to sit up.

'No? He acts as if he is.' With a moan, Victor leaned against the tiled wall. Every bone in his body ached. 'You're not going to untie my hands, are you?'

'Do I look like a complete idiot?'

'No. But you're probably only half as hard as you act,' Victor grunted, 'so you'll go and fetch the box I left outside the front of the cinema.'

Prosper gave him a look of deep suspicion. But he went and fetched the box. 'I didn't know that tortoises were part of a detective's equipment,' he said as he placed the carton on the floor next to Victor.

'Oh, you're a comedian too? Get her out of there. You'd better pray that she's all right or you'll be in a lot of trouble.'

'Aren't we in trouble already?' Prosper carefully lifted the tortoise off the sand that Victor had poured into the bottom of the box. 'She looks a bit parched.'

'She always looks like that,' sighed Victor. 'But she needs fresh lettuce, water, and a little walk. Go on, let her walk around a bit on the blanket.'

Prosper tried not to laugh, but he did as Victor said.

'Her name's Paula. Her husband is at this moment sitting all by himself in his box under my desk and is worried sick.' Victor moved his toes. They were tingling terribly. 'You'll have to look after him as well if you want to keep me here parcelled up like a giant sausage roll.'

Prosper couldn't help it, he had to grin. He turned his face away, but Victor had seen it. 'Anything else?'

'No.' Victor tried to shift into a more comfortable position but with no success. 'So. Let's have our little chat – that's

131

what you came in for, isn't it?'

Prosper pushed his dark hair back and listened. A quiet snore came from outside. 'That's Mosca,' Prosper said. 'He was supposed to keep watch but he's sleeping like a baby.'

'Why keep watch?' Victor stifled a yawn. 'Where would I go, wrapped up like a silkworm?'

Prosper shrugged. He placed the torch next to him on the floor and started to inspect his fingernails. 'You're after me and my brother, right?' he asked without looking at Victor. 'My aunt sent you to look for us.'

Victor shrugged. 'Your little girlfriend stole my wallet – you must have found her card in there.'

Prosper nodded. 'How did Esther find out we're in Venice?' He pressed his forehead against his pulled-up knees.

Your uncle told me that it took some time and cost a lot of money.' Victor caught himself looking at the boy sympathetically.

'You would never have found us if I hadn't run into you.'

'Maybe not. Your hideout's quite unusual.'

Prosper looked around. 'Scipio found it for us. He also makes sure we have enough money to live on. If it wasn't for him we'd be in real trouble. Riccio used to steal a lot. Mosca and Hornet were both doing quite badly too, before they met Scipio. They don't like to talk about it. Hornet found Bo and me, and Scipio took us in.' Prosper lifted his head. 'I don't know why I'm telling you this. You're a detective – you've probably found this out already, haven't you?'

Victor shook his head. 'Your friends are none of my business,' he said. 'But it's my job to make sure that you and your brother have a home again. Hasn't it occurred to you that your brother is too young to get along without parents? What happens if the Thief Lord, as he seems to like to call himself, stops looking after you? Or if the police find you here? Do you want Bo to grow up in a children's home? And what about you? Wouldn't it be easier for you to be teasing your teachers in a boarding school rather than acting the grown-up when you're only twelve?'

Prosper's face froze. 'I can look after Bo,' he retorted angrily. 'Does he look unhappy to you? I'd earn money for us if I was allowed to.'

'You'll have to do that before you know it,' Victor replied gloomily.

'Hey, where's the tortoise?' Prosper asked. He got up and opened the door to the other cubicle. He shone his torch into the narrow space. Victor heard him call, 'Come here! Where are you going? There's nothing there.'

'I think we should bring Paula's outing to an end,' Victor said when Prosper returned with the tortoise under his arm. 'She'll just get frozen feet on those tiles. That won't do her cold any good.'

'Right,' agreed Prosper. He carefully placed Paula back in her box and then squatted down on the blanket next to Victor again. 'Do you have a brother?' he asked.

Victor shook his head. 'No. I was an only child. But can't brothers and sisters sometimes be a real pain as well?'

'Maybe.' Prosper shrugged. 'Bo and I have always got on well. Well, nearly always. Oh no,' he wiped his face with his sleeve, 'now I'm going to start crying.'

Victor cleared his throat. 'Your aunt says you probably came to Venice because your mother used to tell you so much about it.'

Prosper blew his nose. 'Yeah,' he said slowly, 'she did. And

133

everything is exactly like she said it would be. When we got off the train at the station – Bo and me – we were so scared that it wasn't going to be true – the houses on stilts, the roads made of water, the lions with wings. But it's all true! "The world is full of wonders" – that's what she always told us.'

Victor closed his eyes. 'Listen, Prosper,' he said tiredly, 'perhaps I can talk to your aunt again ... so that she could take you both...'

Prosper pressed his hand against Victor's mouth.

Someone was at the door. And it wasn't Mosca. He was still snoring.

'Bo!' Prosper hissed as an ink-black head of hair popped through the door. 'What are you doing here? Go back to sleep!'

But Bo had already slipped inside to join them. 'What's happening, Prop?' he mumbled sleepily. 'Are you going to throw Victor into the canal?'

'What gave you that idea?' Prosper looked at his brother in astonishment. 'Go on, back to bed.'

Bo quietly closed the door behind him. 'I could keep watch like Mosca does!' he said, before suddenly bumping into the tortoise box.

'May I introduce you to Paula?' Victor said.

'Hello Paula,' mumbled Bo, not in the slightest bit surprised by the strange animal. He sat down on the blanket, between Prosper and Victor. He poked his finger up his nose absent-mindedly and looked intently at Victor. 'You're a very good liar.' he said. 'Are you really going to catch us and take us back to Esther? We don't belong to her, you know.'

Embarrassed, Victor stared at his shoes. 'Well, children all have to belong to somebody,' he muttered.

'Do you belong to someone?'

'That's different.'

'Because you're a grown-up?' Bo looked curiously in the box, but he could only see Paula's shell. 'Prosper already looks after me. So does Hornet. And Scipio.'

'Ah, Scipio', Victor grunted. 'Is he still here, your Scipio?'

'No, he never sleeps here.' Bo shook his head as if Victor should have known that. 'Scipio is very busy. He's very, very clever. That's why,' Bo leaned over to Victor and lowered his voice to a conspiratorial whisper, 'he got the job from the Conte. Prosper doesn't want to do it, but I—'

'Shut up, Bo!' Prosper cut him off. He jumped up and grabbed Bo's hand. 'That's none of your business,' he said to Victor. 'You said yourself that you're not interested in the others. So why all these questions about Scipio?'

'Your Thief Lord...' Victor began.

But Prosper had turned his back to him. 'Come on, Bo, it's time for you to sleep.' He pulled his little brother towards the door. But Bo resisted and snatched his hand free.

'I know!' he called. 'Victor can tell Esther that we fell off a bridge and she won't have to look for us any more because we're dead. Isn't that clever, Prop?'

'Oh really, Bo!' Prosper sighed. He pushed Bo towards the door again. 'Look, no one's going to throw Victor into the canal, but we can't let him go free either. Even if he promises not to tell anyone about us. You can't trust someone like him.'

'Someone like me? Thank you very much!' Victor called after them, but Prosper had already closed the door after him. Victor was left alone in the darkness with the cold tiles at his back. So, they won't throw me into the canal, he thought.

How very generous! Well, at least I haven't got that disgusting rag stuffed in my mouth. The tap on the basin above his head was dripping. Outside, Mosca was still snoring through his watch. Could he make Esther Hartlieb believe that the two of them had fallen off a bridge? I don't think so, yawned Victor.

And then he fell into a deep sleep.

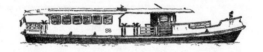

21 Baffled

'So, what are we going to do with the snoop?' Riccio asked.

Prosper had bought fresh bread for breakfast but none of them could swallow a single morsel. The only ones who had slept well were Bo – and Mosca, whose sleep had remained undisturbed until Riccio had relieved him. Hornet poured herself a third cup of coffee. Riccio was complaining. 'So, what are we going to do? I haven't slept a wink all night with that guy tied up in the toilet.'

Mosca shrugged. 'What *can* we do? We can only let him go once Scipio has found a new hideout. Scip says that with the Conte's money we could buy ourselves our own island on the lagoon, if we like.'

Riccio pulled a face. 'I don't want to live on an island! I want to stay here, in the city. Do you think I want to go on a wobbly boat every day? Yuk!'

Hornet interrupted him impatiently. 'Tell that to Scipio.' She looked at her watch. 'We're meeting him in two hours, remember?'

'I'd love to live on an island!' Mosca pushed himself up with a sigh. 'We could catch our own fish, grow vegetables…'

'Catch fish – uuugh!' Riccio wrinkled his nose. '*You* can eat them if you like. I'd *never* eat fish from the lagoon. They're all poisoned because the factories on the mainland chuck their rubbish into the sea.'

'Yeah, yeah.' Mosca pulled a face at him and got up. 'I'll take a coffee to our prisoner. Or does he only get water and mouldy bread?'

'Even that would be too good for him!' Riccio grumbled. 'Why are you all so nice to him? It's his fault we have to find a new place. This is our…' his voice faltered a little '…home. The best home we've ever had. And he spoilt it all. And now he gets a coffee as a reward?'

The others were lost for words. Riccio was right. They had all felt safe here, even though the room was scary at night, and it was already so cold that they could sometimes see their own breath. But this was their Star-Palace, their shelter from the rain, and from the dark night outside. This was their safe haven. At least that was what they had believed.

'We'll find something new,' Mosca mumbled while he poured the rest of the coffee into a mug for Victor. 'Something just as good, or even better.'

'Oh, yeah?' Riccio stared moodily at the star-embroidered curtain. 'But I don't want to find something better! Why don't we just chuck him into the canal? Then we wouldn't have to worry. I mean, why was he snooping around here anyway?'

'Riccio!' Hornet looked at him in horror.

'It's true!' Riccio's voice grew shrill. He had tears in his eyes. 'We're going to lose our Star-Palace, just because of that

– that – creep! We'll never find another hide-out like this! I don't care *what* Scipio says about an island and lots of money. It's all rotten!

The others said nothing. None of them knew what to say. Finally, Mosca murmured: 'It's probably going to be really cold in here once winter comes anyway.'

'So what? It's not going to be as cold in here as it is outside, is it?' Riccio sobbed. He buried his face in his arms.

'Hey, Riccio. It'll be OK!' Hornet said. She sat down next to him and put her arm around him. 'At least we'll stay together, right?' But Riccio just pushed her away.

Prosper hadn't said anything all this time. But now he cleared his throat. 'You won't have to throw the snoop into the canal just to stay here,' he said haltingly. 'If Bo and I leave he won't have any reason to come here again. This is all our fault and so we're going to go. We'll have to anyway, now that our aunt knows we're in Venice.'

Bo looked at his brother, his mouth open wide. Hornet turned towards him and stared at him in disbelief. 'Rubbish!' she shouted. Where are you going to go? We all belong together. Your problems are our problems.'

'Exactly!' Mosca nodded. 'Your problems are our problems. Right, Riccio?' He shoved his elbow into his friend's side, but Riccio said nothing.

'You're staying here and the snoop stays in the men's toilet,' Hornet continued. 'And we'll steal the wooden wing, take it to the Conte, and with his five million we'll make ourselves a cosy life on one of the islands. Anyone can get used to riding in boats. I hope!' she added quickly. Hornet got just as seasick as Riccio.

'Then we'll have to feed the tortoise-husband,' Bo said. 'So he doesn't die.'

'The tortoise-husband?' Mosca nearly choked on his cold coffee.

'He lives under Victor's desk,' Prosper mumbled. He was playing absentmindedly with Bo's plastic fans. 'His wife is in a box in the toilet with Victor. You have to be careful not to step on her when you go in there.'

Mosca's eyes nearly popped out of his head.

'There, you see?' Riccio shouted. 'Who ever heard of kidnappers looking after the pets of their prisoners? Have you ever seen a movie where the gangster goes to feed his victim's tortoise or cat?'

'We're not gangsters!' Hornet cut in. 'And that's why we won't let innocent tortoises starve. Go on, Mosca, take Victor his coffee.'

22 The Casa Spavento

Prosper joined Riccio and Hornet when they left to meet Scipio at the Campo Santa Margherita.

He hadn't left the hideout for more than two days because of Victor and now he longed for some fresh air. Mosca eagerly agreed to stay behind with their prisoner. He still felt guilty because he slept through his watch. Bo wanted to look after the lonely tortoise, probably because he really didn't want to walk all the way to the Campo Santa Margherita either.

It really was quite a long way. The square was in Dorsoduro, the southernmost quarter of Venice, on the other side of the Grand Canal. The houses there might not have been as magnificent or graceful as on some of the other squares in the city, but many had been standing for more than five hundred years. It had some small shops, cafés, restaurants, a fish-market every morning, and in the centre was the newspaper stand where Riccio had gained all his information about Ida Spavento. The Campanile Santa Margherita was guarded by a dragon. Riccio claimed that once, a long time ago, bear and bull-baiting fights used to take place right there at its feet, just like on the Campo San Polo towards the north of the city.

The square, which was usually very busy, was almost deserted when the three children entered it. It was a cold and rainy day. The chairs in front of the cafés were empty and a couple of women pushed their prams past the wet tables. A few old men sat on the benches underneath the bare trees, looking dourly towards the blank grey sky overhead.

The house, the target for their night-time visit had seen better days. It certainly didn't look the kind of place that would contain a treasure that was worth five million lire. The garden could only be reached through a dark, covered alley, which at first glance looked little more than a black hole between the Casa Spavento and the neighbouring house.

Riccio had already explored the alley with Mosca. They had even climbed the wall that surrounded the garden. From there they had looked down on winter-bare flowerbeds and gravel paths.

Riccio had wanted Scipio to have a look too. And so they waited. But Scipio didn't come. At first Riccio, Prosper and Hornet waited patiently at the news-stand. Dogs sniffed them, cats crept past them, stalking the fat pigeons, women laden with heavy shopping bags shuffled across the wet pavement. But still Scipio didn't appear.

'Strange!' Hornet said. She was shivering and moving from one foot to the other to keep warm. 'He's never been late for a set-up meeting before.'

'Hey, look there!' Riccio grabbed Hornet by the arm. 'That's Ida Spavento's housekeeper, coming back with the shopping.'

A fat lady waddled across the square, the leashes of three

dogs in one hand and two overstuffed shopping bags in the other. The dogs yapped at everyone who came near their little snouts. The big lady had to keep pulling them to heel.

'Here's a piece of good luck!' Riccio whispered.

'I don't like those dogs,' Hornet breathed. 'What if they're still in the house when we go in? They're small, but big enough to bite.'

'We can take care of them.' Riccio smoothed his shaggy hair, and gave the others a wink. 'Wait here.'

'What are you doing?' Hornet whispered. 'Don't be stupid.'

But Riccio was already sauntering across the square, whistling. He seemed to be looking everywhere except at Ida Spavento's housekeeper who was obviously struggling to keep up with her dogs.

'Mind out!' she shouted.

But Riccio paid her no attention. Just as she steered past him, he stepped right in her way. There was no chance for her to avoid him. They collided. The stuffed bags landed on the square and the dogs ran yapping after the apples and cabbages rolling over the wet cobbles.

Hornet whispered to Prosper: 'My goodness, what's the hedgehog doing?' Riccio was running eagerly after the cabbages while the *signora*, cursing loudly, bent over to pick up the apples.

Now they could hear the fat lady cursing: 'What the devil were you thinking, running into me like that?'

'*Scusi!*' Riccio gave her a smile so broad that it showed off all his rotten teeth. 'I'm just looking for the dentist, Dr Spavento. Is that his house there?'

'Don't be ridiculous!' the large lady snapped at him. 'There's no dentist in there. Mind you, you look like you need

143

one badly. That's the house of Signora Ida Spavento. Now get out of my way before I throw one of these cabbages at you.'

'I'm terribly sorry, Signora.' Riccio suddenly looked so downtrodden that even Prosper and Hornet nearly fell for it. 'May I help you with those bags?'

'Well, now look at that. A real gentleman!' The lady tucked a grey strand of hair out of her face. She was already looking slightly more favourably at Riccio. But then she frowned again. 'Hold on. You don't think you're going to earn something out of this, you little rascal?'

Riccio looked sincerely hurt and shook his head vigorously. 'No way, Signora!'

'All right, then, I might just take you up on your offer.' Signora Spavento's housekeeper passed Riccio the shopping bags and wrapped the dog leash tightly around her plump wrist. 'It's not every day a real gentleman crosses my path.'

Prosper and Hornet walked after them, keeping a safe distance. They saw Riccio vanish into Ida Spavento's house, but before he went he turned and flashed them a triumphant smile.

It took a long time for Riccio to come out again. But finally he stood in the entrance like a little lord at peace with himself and the entire world. He was holding a gigantic ice-cream cone that he had received for his labours. He casually pulled the door shut before making his way towards Prosper and Hornet.

'No bars on the inside!' he whispered to them importantly. 'Not even a second lock. Signora Spavento is definitely not afraid of burglars.'

'Was she at home?' Prosper asked him, looking up at the balcony above the entrance.

'I didn't see her.' Riccio let Hornet lick his ice-cream. 'But the kitchen is exactly where it's marked on the ground plan. I took the bags there for Mrs Podgy, the housekeeper. So it's probably also true that the main bedroom is in the attic. I tell you, if Signora Ida Spavento really does go to bed early then this job is going to be easier than stealing candles from a church.'

'Yeah, just don't get too excited!' Hornet warned. She looked uneasily at the windows .

'Wait. It gets even better!' Riccio chuckled. 'There's a door that's not on the plan, going straight from the kitchen into the garden. And – wait for this – that one doesn't have any bars either. Signora Spavento's really quite careless, isn't she?'

'You're forgetting the dogs again,' Hornet replied. 'What if they don't belong to the housekeeper? And what if they don't like your sausages?'

'Bah! All dogs like sausages. Right, Prop?'

Prosper nodded and looked at his watch. 'It's nearly one o'clock,' he whispered, 'and Scipio still isn't here. I hope nothing's happened.'

They waited for another half-hour. Then, feeling very anxious, they made their way to their prisoner's flat to feed his deserted tortoise.

'I don't get it,' Riccio said as they stood in front of Victor's house. 'What could have happened to Scipio?'

As they struggled up the steep staircase to Victor's office. Hornet panted: 'It's probably nothing. He's often late when we arrange to meet at the hideout.' But she looked just as worried as the other two.

Victor's tortoise-husband really looked quite lonely. He hardly poked his head out of his shell when Prosper and

Hornet bent over his box. Only when Prosper offered him a lettuce leaf did his wrinkly neck come out.

Riccio ignored the tortoise. He still thought it was ridiculous to look after a prisoner's pets. Instead, he tried out one of Victor's disguises in front of the mirror. 'Hey, look at this, Prop!' he called as he stuck the walrus moustache under his nose. 'Didn't he have this on his face when you ran into him?'

'Maybe,' Prosper answered. He was investigating Victor's desk. Underneath the paperweight lion was a picture of the two tortoises and next to the typewriter was a pile of densely written notes and an apple with one bite taken out of it.

'And how do I look now?' Riccio asked, stroking a full reddish beard.

'Like a gnome,' Hornet answered. She pulled a book from the shelf where Victor kept his well-thumbed crime novels. Then she made herself comfortable on one of the visitors' chairs and settled down to read. Prosper perched on Victor's armchair and rifled through the drawers in his desk. There was nothing interesting, only bits of paper, paperclips, a stamp-pad, scissors, keys, postcards, and three different bags of sweets.

Prosper closed all the drawers. 'Have you seen any files? He's got to have files on his cases.'

'Nope. I bet he became a detective because he likes dressing up. He hasn't got any files.' Riccio stuck some bushy eyebrows over his eyes, popped a hat on his head and tried to look dignified. 'Do you think I'll look like this one day when I'm older?'

'He's got to write things down somewhere.'

Prosper had just discovered Victor's only filing cabinet when the phone rang. Hornet didn't even lift her head. 'Let it ring,' she smiled, 'it's not going to be for us, is it?'

Ten minutes later the phone rang again, just as Prosper discovered a transparent folder with a photograph of him and his brother. Mesmerized, he stared at the picture.

Hornet looked up from her book. 'What is it?'

'Just a photo. Of Bo and me. My mum took it on my eleventh birthday.'

The phone rang once more and then fell silent again. 'What did the snoop write down about you?' Hornet asked.

Prosper put the picture in his jacket and pushed Victor's notes across to her. 'I can't make it out.'

'Let's see.' Hornet put her book aside and leaned over the desk. 'Well, he doesn't seem to like your aunt either. I think it says "weasel-face" and he's called your uncle "the wardrobe". *Not interested in the older one,*' she read, '*probably because he doesn't look like a teddy bear any more.*' Hornet smiled at Prosper. 'No, you definitely don't. He's really not that stupid, our snoop.' The phone rang again. 'Good heavens! I would never have thought he had so many customers.' She grabbed the receiver. '*Pronto!*' she said in a low voice. 'Victor Getz's office. How can I help you?'

Riccio had to squeeze his fist into his mouth to stop himself from bursting out laughing. But Prosper watched Hornet with a worried expression on his face.

'What was your name?' Hornet gave Prosper a startled sign. 'Hartlieb?'

Prosper jumped as if someone had hit him in the face. Hornet pressed a button on the telephone and Esther's voice shrilled through Victor's office. She didn't talk too fast, and her Italian was very good: '*...have been trying for days to reach Mr Getz. He told me he was on the boys' trail. He even told me* *he would send me a picture he took of the two of them on St Mark's Square...'*

Hornet gave Prosper a surprised look. 'I know nothing about that,' she stuttered. 'That, eh, may well have been a misunderstanding. He received some new information yesterday. Brand new. Mr Getz now believes that the boys are no longer here, I mean, in Venice. Hello?'

There was silence at the other end.

The three children in Victor's office hardly dared breathe.

'Well, that's all very interesting,' Esther's shrill voice replied, *'but I would really rather receive that information from Mr Getz himself. Please put me through.'*

'He, he—' Hornet began to stutter, in her panic she forgot to lower her voice. 'He's not here. I'm just his secretary. He's out on another case.'

'Who are you?' Esther's voice now began to sound irritated. *'I didn't know Mr Getz even had a secretary.'*

'Of course he has!' Hornet sounded truly offended. 'I don't know what gave you that idea. And Mr Getz will only tell you what *I've* just told you. At the moment he's out. Perhaps you could try again in a week's time.'

'Now listen, whoever you are.' Esther's voice cut through the air like a knife. *'I've already left a message for Mr Getz on the answering machine, but it can't do any harm to leave it a second time. My husband will be back in Venice on business in two days' time. I will meet Mr Getz on Tuesday in the Hotel Sandwirth, three o'clock sharp! Good day.'* Then there was a sharp click on the line.

Hornet replaced the receiver, looking miserable. 'I don't think I did very well,' she sighed.

'We've got to go,' said Prosper. He put the files back where he found them. Hornet gave him an anxious look. But then she ran over to Victor's shelf and stuffed a few books under her pullover.

'Wouldn't it be great if someone really nice was after you like that?' Riccio pushed his tongue into his tooth-gap. 'Some nice filthy-rich uncle or grandfather, just like in the stories Hornet reads to us.'

'Esther is rich,' Prosper said.

'Really?' Riccio stuffed Victor's beards into a backpack. He took the fake nose as well. 'Could you ask her if she'd take me instead of Bo? I'm not much bigger than him and I don't ask for much. Just as long as she doesn't hit me too often.'

'She wouldn't do that,' Prosper said as he looked through the drawers one last time. 'What photograph was she talking about? Blast, I knew he had photographed Bo feeding the pigeons. Riccio, take the camera. Maybe the picture's still in there.'

Riccio hung the camera around his neck and stood once more in front of Victor's mirror. '*Buongiorno*, Signora Esther!' he said, smiling and tightly closing his mouth so that no one could see his bad teeth. 'Would you like to be my mother? I hear you don't hit children and you have lots of money.'

'Forget it!' Hornet said to him as she looked over his shoulder. 'Prosper's aunt wants a little teddy bear and not a hedgehog with bad teeth. Come on, let's get out of here. We'll take the tortoise with us since the snoop is our prisoner.'

'Maybe Scipio has already turned up at the hideout!' Riccio said hopefully as they pulled Victor's door shut.

'Perhaps,' Prosper replied.

But none of them really believed it.

23 Quarrels

Bo opened the door for them when they arrived back at the hideout.

'Where's Mosca?' Prosper asked him. 'I told you not to come to the door!'

'I had to. Mosca's busy,' Bo answered. 'Victor's showing him how to repair his radio.' Then he skipped away, whistling to himself.

When Prosper, Hornet and Riccio reached the auditorium they found the door to the men's toilet was wide open. They could hear Mosca laughing.

'I don't believe it!' Riccio shouted. He planted himself in the open door. 'What on earth are you up to, Mosca? Is that your idea of keeping watch? Who said you could untie him?'

Mosca turned around in surprise. He was kneeling next to Victor on the blanket and was just passing him a screwdriver from the toolbox. 'Calm down, Riccio. He gave me his word of honour that he wouldn't run away,' he said. 'Victor knows a lot about radios and I think he can fix it.'

'To hell with your radio!' Riccio shouted. 'And to hell with his word of honour. He's going to be tied up again right now.'

'Listen, hedgehog.' Victor struggled to get up on his stiff legs. 'No one sends my word of honour to hell, understood? You can always trust Victor Getz's promise one hundred per cent.'

'Exactly.' Bo stood in front of Victor as if he wanted to protect him. 'He's our friend now.'

'Friend?' Riccio gasped for air. 'Have you gone completely mad, you silly baby? He's our prisoner, our enemy.'

'Stop it Riccio!' Hornet interrupted. 'The ropes are stupid. We may as well just lock him in. He's a bit too fat to climb out of the toilet window anyway, don't you think?'

Riccio didn't answer. He folded his arms and looked angry. 'We'll see what Scipio has to say about this!' he grumbled. 'Maybe you'll listen to *him*.'

'If he turns up,' said Prosper.

'What? I thought you were going to meet him.' Mosca got to his feet.

'We waited for two hours by the news-stand,' Hornet replied, 'but he never came.'

'Well, well.' Victor knelt down in front of the radio again. 'Well, well, well. But I hope you didn't forget my tortoise.'

'No, we even brought him with us.' Prosper looked at him. 'What was that *well, well, well* supposed to mean?'

Victor shrugged and tightened another screw.

'Spit it out!' Riccio barked at him. 'Or your tortoise has just had its last meal.'

Victor turned around very slowly. 'Aren't you a charming little fellow!' he growled. 'How much do you really know about your leader?'

Hornet opened her mouth, but Victor held up his hand. 'Yes, I know, he's not really your leader. I got that. But that

151

wasn't the question. So, once more: how much do you know about him?'

The children looked at each other.

'What should we know about him?' Mosca leaned against the tiled wall. 'None of us talk much about the past. Scipio grew up in an orphanage, just like Riccio. He did tell us about it once. He ran away when he was eight and since then he's been looking after himself. He lived with an old thief for a while who taught him everything he needed to survive. When the old man died, Scipio stole the smartest gondola from the Grand Canal and laid the old thief in it. Then he let him drift out on to the lagoon. Since then he's been by himself.'

'And goes by the name of Thief Lord,' Victor said. 'So he lives by stealing things. Which means you do too...'

'As if we'd tell you that!' Riccio said coldly. 'And what if we do? You could never catch Scipio, even if you tried a hundred times. No one can match him. Barbarossa gave us four hundred thousand lire for his last loot. What do you say to that?'

Mosca punched his elbow into Riccio's side, but it was too late.

'Barbarossa, that old scoundrel. Well, well.' Victor said under his breath. 'So you know him too. You know what? I bet my tortoises that I can tell you where Scipio stole those things.'

Riccio squinted at him suspiciously. 'So? It was in all the newspapers, that's no big deal.' Mosca gave him another shove, but Riccio was far too worked up to notice.

'In the newspapers?' Victor lifted his eyebrows. 'Oh, you probably mean the break-in at the Palazzo Contarini?' He laughed. ' Did Scipio tell you he did that?'

'What's that supposed to mean?' Riccio clenched his fists. He looked like he wanted to attack Victor, but Hornet held him back.

'It means,' Victor answered calmly, 'that your Scipio may be a clever fellow and quite a crafty liar, but he's definitely not who you think he is.'

Losing his temper, Riccio freed himself from Hornet's grip. Prosper managed to get hold of him again, but only after he had punched Victor on the nose.

'Stop it, Riccio!' Prosper shouted. He had Riccio in a head-lock. 'Let him finish. And you,' he barked at Victor, 'can stop talking in riddles. Or I'll let go of Riccio.'

'What a threat!' Victor grumbled. 'Bo, please hand me your handkerchief.'

Bo quickly pulled a grubby rag out of his pocket.

'Fine, let's talk straight,' Victor agreed, wiping his stinging nose. At least it wasn't bleeding. 'How did you meet Scipio?' Without looking at the children's baffled faces, he gathered a few screws and threw them into Mosca's toolbox.

Riccio had turned bright red.

'Go on, tell him,' Mosca said.

'I stole something off him,' Riccio muttered. 'OK, I tried to steal something, and he caught me. So I threatened him with my friends and he let me go on the condition that I took him to meet my gang.'

'Back then we were living in the basement of an old house,' Mosca explained. 'Riccio, Hornet and me. It was over in Castello. You can always find a place there. No one wants to live there any more. It was awful: wet and cold and we were always ill and we never had enough to eat.'

'You may as well say it straight: we were in deep trouble,'

153

Riccio interrupted him impatiently. "You can't live in a rat hole like this", is what Scipio said. And so he brought us here, to the Star-Palace. He picked the lock of the emergency exit and told us to barricade the front entrance. And since then we've been doing quite well. Until you turned up.'

'OK, I get it. Victor the spoilsport.' Victor looked at Prosper. 'And when Hornet picked up you and Bo,' he said to him, 'the Thief Lord just fed the two of you as well.'

'Scip brought us coats and blankets. And he even gave me these.' Bo sat down next to Victor and held up one of his kittens. Lost in thought, Victor began to tickle it behind the ears until it started to purr and lick his fingers with its rough tongue.

'Why did you say Scipio was a liar?' Hornet asked.

'Forget what I said.' Victor patted Bo's black hair. 'Just tell me one more thing. Bo told me you were going to come into a lot of money soon. You're not planning to do something stupid, are you?'

'Bo, why can't you just keep your big mouth shut for once?' Riccio tore himself away from Prosper, but he quickly caught him again.

'Hey, Riccio, don't you talk to my little brother like that, understand?'

'Then you keep a better eye on him!' Riccio pushed away Prosper's hands. 'Or he'll blab about everything!'

'Bo, you're not to tell him any more, OK?' Prosper said without letting Riccio out of his sight.

But Bo gave his brother a defiant look and whispered into Victor's ear: 'We're going to break into a house with Scipio. But we're only going to steal some silly wooden wing.'

'Bo!' Hornet shouted.

'You want to break in somewhere?' Victor was back on his feet immediately. 'Are you crazy? You want to end up in the orphanage?' He stood in front of Prosper and looked down at him angrily. 'Is that how you look after your little brother? Teaching him how to creep into strange houses?'

'That's not true!' Prosper grew quite pale. 'Bo's not coming with us.'

'I am!' Bo shouted.

'You're not!' Prosper barked back.

'Stop it!' Riccio shouted, pointing at Victor with trembling fingers. 'It's all his fault. Everything was all right, until he started snooping around here. And now we're all fighting with each other and we need a new hideout.'

'You don't need a new hideout!' Victor boomed. 'Goddamnit! I am NOT going to tell on you! But that may well change if you're going ahead with that burglary. Is that clear? What's going to happen to the little one if the *Carabinieri* catch you all? Housebreaking is a bit different from stealing cameras and handbags.'

'Scipio knows what he's doing. The Thief Lord doesn't steal handbags.' Riccio's voice cracked. 'So you can just stop being horrible about him, you blown-up toad!'

Victor gasped. 'Blown-up toad? Thief Lord? I'll tell *you* something!' He made a threatening step towards Riccio. Mosca and Hornet moved protectively between them, but Victor just pushed them away. 'You've fallen for the biggest toad who ever lived. Why don't you take a little trip to the Fondamenta Bollani number 223. That's where you'll learn the truth about the Thief Lord. Everything you'd want to know, or maybe wouldn't want to know.'

'Fondamenta Bollani?' Riccio bit his lip. 'What's this? A

trick?'

'As if!' Victor turned his back and crouched down next to the dismantled radio again. 'Don't forget to lock up your prisoner before you leave now, will you?' he said over his shoulder. 'I'll just carry on repairing this thing now.'

24 Young Master Massimo

Nobody wanted to stay behind in the cinema, not even Riccio, although during the entire journey he kept declaring how horrible he thought it was that they were spying on Scipio. Mosca had locked Victor back in the toilet before they had left. Now they were standing in front of the address Victor had given them: Fondamenta Bollani 223.

They hadn't expected such a grand house. Shyly, they looked up at the high-arched windows. They all felt small, grubby and worthless. Slowly, keeping close together, they walked towards the entrance.

'We can't just ring the bell!' Hornet whispered.

'Someone has to!' Mosca hissed back. 'If we just stand around we'll never find out what the snoop meant.'

Nobody moved.

'I'll say it again: Scipio'll go ballistic if he finds out we're spying on him,' Riccio whispered. He looked uneasily at the golden nameplate next to the entrance. It said *Massimo* in elaborate letters.

'We'll let Bo ring!' Hornet proposed. 'Bo's the least notice-able, isn't he?'

'No, I'll do it!' Prosper pushed Bo behind him and quickly pressed the golden button. Twice. He could hear the bell resound through the whole house. The others hid on either side of the entrance. So when a girl in a white apron opened the door, she saw only Prosper, with Bo smiling timidly at her from behind him.

'*Buonasera, Signora*', Prosper said. 'Do you happen to know a boy called Scipio?'

The girl frowned. 'What is this? Some stupid prank? What do you want with him?' She eyed Prosper from head to dusty shoe. His trousers were definitely not as immaculate as her whiter-than-white apron and there were some pigeon droppings on his jumper.

'So, it's true?' Prosper's tongue suddenly felt too big for his mouth. 'He lives here? Scipio?'

The girl's face became even more hostile. 'I think I'd better call Dottor Massimo,' she said. But at that moment Bo poked his head out from behind Prosper.

'I'm sure Scipio would like to see us,' he said. 'We were supposed to play today.'

'Play?' The girl still looked unconvinced, but when Bo smiled at her she almost managed a smile herself. Without another word, she opened the big door. Prosper hesitated for a second, but Bo shot across the threshold. Prosper caught a glimpse of a nervous looking Hornet before following him in.

The maid led the two boys through a dark entrance hall into the courtyard. Bo immediately made for the big staircase, but the girl gently held him back and pointed towards a stone bench at the bottom of the stairs. Then she turned without so much as another look, walked up the stairs, and vanished behind the balustrade on the first floor.

'Perhaps this is a different Scipio!' Bo whispered to Prosper. 'Or he sneaked in here so he can rob the house later on.'

'Maybe,' Prosper murmured unconvinced. He looked around uneasily while Bo ran towards the fountain in the middle of the courtyard.

Ten minutes can be a long time when you're waiting with a beating heart for something you don't understand, something you don't really want to know. Bo didn't seem particularly bothered by the whole thing. He was quite happy to touch the lions' heads by the fountain and to dip his hands into the cold water. But Prosper felt terrible. He felt betrayed. Deceived. What was Scipio doing in this house? Who was he really?

When Scipio finally appeared at the top of the stairs Prosper stared at him as if he'd seen a ghost. Scipio stared back. His face was pale and strangely unfamiliar. Then as he started down the stairs with slow and heavy steps, Bo ran towards him.

'Hey, Scip!' he called, stopping at the bottom of the flight. But Scipio didn't answer. He hesitated and looked at Prosper, who glared back at him until Scipio lowered his head. As he lifted it again to say something, a man appeared at the balustrade. He was tall and thin and had the same dark eyes as Scipio.

'What are you still doing here?' he said with a bored voice. 'Don't you have coaching today?' He glanced briefly at Prosper and Bo.

'In an hour,' Scipio replied without looking up at his father. His voice sounded completely different, as if he wasn't sure he'd find the right words. He even seemed smaller to Prosper, but that may have been because of the huge house or because he wasn't wearing his high-heeled boots. He was dressed like one of the rich kids Prosper had sometimes seen in smart restaurants, sitting stiffly and eating with a knife and fork without spilling anything.

'What are you doing, just standing around there?' Scipio's father waved his hand at them impatiently as if the three children were nothing but annoying birds polluting his house. 'Take your friends to your room. You know the courtyard is not a playground.'

'They're leaving,' Scipio answered in a small voice. 'They just wanted to bring me something.'

But his father had already turned away. The three boys watched in silence as he disappeared behind another door. 'Is that your dad, Scip?' Bo whispered incredulously. 'Have you got a mum as well?'

Scipio didn't seem to know where to look. He fiddled with his silk waistcoat. Then he nodded. 'Yes, but she travels a lot.' He looked Prosper in the eyes – but immediately turned away. 'Don't stare at me like that. I can explain everything. I would have told you soon anyway.'

'You may as well explain it to everybody right now,' Prosper answered. He took Scipio's arm. 'The others are waiting outside.' He wanted to lead the Thief Lord towards the door, but Scipio pulled away and stopped at the bottom of the stairs.

'That snoop ratted on me, didn't he?'

'If you hadn't lied to us there wouldn't have been anything to rat about,' Prosper replied. 'Come on.'

'You heard my father, I've got a lesson!' Scipio's voice now sounded defiant. 'I'll explain it all to you later. Tonight. I can get away tonight. My father's going away. And about the break-in – everything stays as planned. We do it tomorrow night. Did you check out the house like I told you?'

'Stop it, Scip!' Prosper shouted 'I bet you've never stolen anything in your whole life.' He saw Scipio cast a worried look upstairs. 'All the loot was probably taken from this house, wasn't it?' Prosper asked lowering his voice. 'What were you thinking, taking on the Conte's job? You've never broken in anywhere. And I bet that when you turn up at the hideout you probably just let yourself in with a key through some door we don't know about. Thief Lord! My god, we were so stupid.' Prosper looked at Scipio scornfully, but inside he felt numb with sadness and disappointment. Bo held on to his hand. Scipio still couldn't meet his eyes.

'Come on!' Prosper said once more. 'Come out and talk to the others.' He turned around, but Scipio stood still.

'No,' he said, 'I'll explain everything later. I haven't got time now.' Scipio turned and ran up the stairs so quickly he nearly stumbled. He didn't look back.

Mosca, Riccio and Hornet were still standing next to the entrance when Prosper came out with Bo. They were all leaning against the wall, shivering and looking depressed.

'See!' Riccio called out when Prosper and Bo came out of the house alone. 'It wasn't our Scipio, was it?' He couldn't hide his relief, but then he suddenly looked alarmed. 'But wait a minute, I can't believe we've been so stupid – we've got to get back to the hideout. Don't you understand? All this has been a trick to get us out of the cinema so that the snoop could escape.

'Why don't you just shut up for a second, Riccio?' Hornet was looking as Prosper. 'Well?'

'Victor didn't lie to us,' Prosper said. 'Let's get away from here.' Before the others could say anything he marched off towards the nearest bridge.

'Hey, wait!' Mosca called after him, but Prosper walked so fast that the others only managed to catch up with him on the other side of the canal. He stopped by the entrance to a restaurant and leaned against the wall.

'What happened?' Hornet asked when she reached him. 'You look like death warmed up.'

Prosper closed his eyes so that the others wouldn't see his tears. He felt Bo's short fingers stroking his hand very softly. 'Don't you understand? I told you: the snoop didn't lie,' he cried. 'The only one who lied was Scipio. He lives in that palace. Bo and I saw his father. They have a maid and a courtyard with a fountain. Thief Lord! Runaway from the orphanage! All his mysterious "I can cope on my own" and his "I don't need adults" – they're all lies. He must have really had a laugh at us. "Hey, let's play street-kid for a while, that sounds fun!" And we fell for it.' Prosper wiped his nose on his sleeve.

'But the loot...' Mosca's voice sounded very faint.

'Oh yeah, the loot.' Prosper laughed out loud. 'He probably stole those things from his parents. Thief Lord? – Liar Lord, more like.'

Riccio stood frozen like someone who'd just been knocked on the head. 'He was there? You saw him?'

Prosper nodded. 'He was there. But he was too afraid to come out.' Bo pushed his head under Hornet's arm.

The others didn't say a word. Hornet looked over at the Casa Massimo, standing on the opposite bank, its grandeur reflected on the canal. There was light in some of the windows, although it was still early in the afternoon. It was a grey, dark day.

'It's not that bad, Prop,' said Bo looking at his brother with big, worried eyes. 'It's not that bad.'

Hornet mumbled: 'Let's go home.'

Nobody said a word on the way back.

25 A Word of Honour

It hadn't been hard to pick the lock of the men's toilet. Mosca had taken the toolbox away from Victor before he left, but the detective always had a bit of wire and some other useful items in the hollow heel of one of his shoes. He had already reached the foyer with his two tortoise boxes when he decided he couldn't leave without a few farewell words. He couldn't find any paper, so he wrote his message on the white-washed wall with a felt-tip pen.

Pay Attention! This is Victor's Promise. The Hartliebs will not hear anything from me – not unless I hear about any strange break-ins over the next few weeks. See you later. You can count on it.

Victor

When he had finished, Victor took a step back and looked at his handiwork. I must be completely crazy, he thought as he read his own words. Then he thought about searching for his gun and his wallet. But where should he look? What if the gang walked in on him?

I'll just go home, Victor decided. Every single bone in his

body ached from the night spent on the cold tiles.

Out in the alley a few women were gossiping. They fell silent when they saw Victor come out of the abandoned cinema, but he greeted them as if there was absolutely nothing strange about him being there. As they watched, he carefully closed the boarded-up door and went home with his tortoises.

26 The Break-In

'Now, would you believe this?' Riccio shouted when they discovered the empty toilet and Victor's scrawls on the wall. 'We'll have to catch him again right away.'

'Oh yes? And how?' asked Mosca. On the blanket, was the radio. Assembled. Perfect. Mosca sat down next to it and started to fiddle with the buttons. The others were still standing in front of Victor's scribbled message.

'Well, we have to believe him, we've got no choice,' Hornet said. 'Or do you want to go looking for a new hideout right now, Riccio?' she asked. 'And what about the break-in and the deal with the Conte? Do you want to forget about all that just because the snoop has told us to?'

'No, I don't,' said Riccio. 'He'll only find out about the break-in once it's done. And by then we'll be long gone with our money. Somewhere.'

Riccio stared at Victor's scrawl. Then he turned abruptly and vanished into the auditorium.

Hornet wanted to follow him, but Prosper held her back. 'Hold on,' he said, 'do you still want to steal the wing? Don't you get it? Scipio has never done a break-in in his life!'

'Who's talking about Scipio?' Hornet crossed her arms. 'We'll do it without Scipio. The Conte won't care who gets the wing for him. And once we've got the five million, we won't need anyone. No adults, and definitely no Thief Lord. Maybe we should do it tonight. The sooner the better. What do you think? Are you with us?'

'And what about Bo?' Prosper shook his head. 'No. If you really want to risk your neck, that's fine. I wish you luck. But I won't do it. My aunt's coming to Venice in two days' time. By then Bo and I will have left the city. I'll try to sneak us on to a ship or an aeroplane – anything that'll get us away from here. Other people have done it before. It was in the paper a few days ago.'

'Yes, and I could kick myself for reading it to you. Don't you understand?' Hornet's voice sounded angry, but there were also tears in her eyes. 'That's even more crazy than sneaking into some house. We all belong together now, you and Bo, Riccio, Mosca and me. We're sort of a family now and…'

'Hey guys, come here!' Mosca shouted from the men's toilet. 'I think that snoop really did repair my radio. Even the cassette's working again.'

But Prosper and Hornet didn't react.

'Think about it!' Hornet said. Her voice sounded so anxious that Prosper almost had second thoughts. 'Please!' Then she ran after Riccio.

Dinner was cancelled. None of them was hungry and one by one they settled down into a troubled sleep. Prosper dreamt he was with Bo, back in the train that had brought them to Venice. They were looking for a seat, but whenever Prosper opened the door to a compartment, Esther was already sitting there. Suddenly, Victor stood in front of them. Prosper turned around and yanked open the nearest door he could find. But behind it was nothing but darkness. Black, limitless darkness. Before he could draw back he had already fallen into it. And Bo was no longer with him.

Prosper woke up suddenly. He was drenched in sweat. Around him was nothing but the cold dark night. Prosper felt for the torch that he always kept next to his mattress and switched it on. Hornet's mattress was empty. She was gone – and so was Bo! Prosper jumped up. He ran to Riccio's mattress and pulled open the sleeping bag. Nothing but grubby cuddly toys. Mosca's blanket was thrown in a heap just covering his old radio.

They were gone. All gone. With Bo.

Prosper guessed immediately where they would be. He ran to the cupboard that held everything Mosca had collected for the break-in: a rope, the ground plans, the sausages for the dogs, shoe polish to blacken their faces – all had vanished.

But why did they take Bo? Prosper wondered in desperation while he got dressed. How could Hornet have allowed it?

The moon hung high above the city as Prosper rushed out of the cinema. The alleys lay empty and grey wisps of fog floated eerily over the canal.

Prosper ran. His steps rang out loudly on the pavement, adding to his fears. He had to catch up with the others before they climbed over the wall, before they broke into the house. His head was full of images of policemen carrying off a struggling Bo, taking away Hornet and Mosca, dragging away Riccio by his hedgehog hair.

The Accademia Bridge was extremely slippery in the fog. High above the Grand Canal Prosper fell and grazed his knee.

He fought for breath and continued his long journey on shaking legs. Soon, there was only one more alley to go through before he'd be stumbling into the Campo Santa Margherita. The house of Ida Spavento was on the right, nearly at the opposite end of the square. None of the windows were lit. Prosper ran up to the door and listened. Nothing. Of course not. The entrance to the alley that led to the garden looked very scary.

After a few steps through the pitch-black darkness the way became lighter. The garden wall of the Casa Spavento rose between the closely built houses in front of him. There was a dark shape sitting on top of it. As soon he saw it, Prosper felt both angry and relieved at the same time.

The figure on the wall looked down at him. Despite the blackened face he recognized Hornet immediately.

'Where's Bo?' Prosper gasped. 'Why did you take him with you? Bring him back here right now!'

'Calm down!' Hornet hissed back. 'We didn't bring him along. He followed us, and then he threatened to wake up the whole Campo Santa Margherita if we didn't help him over the wall. What else could we have done? You know how stubborn he can be.'

'Is he inside?' Prosper nearly choked on his fears.

'Catch!' Hornet threw him the rope she'd been rolling up. Prosper automatically tied it around his wrist and climbed up. The wall was high and rough and he cut his hands on the jagged stones. Once he'd reached the top, Hornet quietly gathered up the rope and helped him to lower himself into the garden. His mouth was dry with fear as he finally reached the ground again. Hornet threw him the end of the rope and then she jumped down herself.

The dry leaves crackled underneath their feet as they crept towards the house. Mosca and Riccio had already started working on the kitchen door. Riccio had blackened his face like Hornet. Bo hid behind Mosca's back when he saw Prosper approaching.

'I should have left you with Esther!' Prosper hissed angrily at his little brother.

'I'm taking you away right now, come on.' He tried to pull Bo from behind Mosca's back, but Bo slipped away.

'No, I'm staying!' he shouted – so loudly that Mosca immediately pressed his hand over Bo's mouth. Riccio and Hornet looked anxiously towards the top-floor windows. They stayed dark. 'Just leave him, Prosper, please!' Hornet whispered. 'It'll be OK.'

Mosca slowly took his hand off Bo's mouth. 'Don't do that again, please?' he breathed. 'I thought I was going to die.'

'Are the dogs here?' Prosper asked.

Hornet shook her head. 'At least we haven't heard them yet,' she whispered.

Riccio knelt down again in front of the kitchen door. Mosca shone his torch on to the lock.

Hornet bent towards Prosper, who was leaning against the wall and staring up at the moon. 'You don't have to come inside,' she whispered. 'I'll look after Bo.'

'If Bo goes, I go,' Prosper answered.

Riccio said a quick prayer, and pushed the door open.

They were greeted by all the sounds of a strange house. A clock ticked. A fridge hummed. They crept on, full of curiosity and shame.

'Shut the door!' Mosca called softly.

Hornet let the beam of her torch wander across the walls.

There was nothing terribly special about Ida Spavento's kitchen. Pots and pans, spice jars, an espresso pot, a large table, a few chairs...

'Should we leave someone here as a guard?' Riccio asked quietly.

'What for?' Hornet opened the door to the hall and listened. 'The police aren't going to come over the garden wall. You go first,' she whispered to Mosca.

Mosca nodded and slipped through the door.

The door led into a narrow corridor, just as it was on the ground plan. After a few metres they came to a staircase. On the wall next to it hung masks, looking ghostly in the flickering light of the torches. One of the masks looked just like the one Scipio always wore.

The staircase led to another door. Mosca opened it a crack and listened. Then he waved the others into another corridor that was a bit wider than the one on the ground floor. Two lights on the ceiling gave off a dim light. A radiator gurgled somewhere, but otherwise there was complete silence. Mosca put a warning finger to his lips as they passed the stairs that led to the second floor. They all cast worried glances up the narrow stairs.

'Perhaps there's nobody at home,' Hornet whispered hopefully. The house felt deserted, with all its dark and empty rooms. The first two doors led to a bathroom and a tiny cupboard, Mosca remembered from the ground plan they'd got from the Conte.

'Now this is where it gets more interesting,' he whispered as they stood in front of the third door. 'This should be the living room. Perhaps Ida Spavento has put her wing above the couch.' He was just about to reach for the doorknob when someone opened the door from the inside.

Mosca recoiled so quickly that he stumbled into the others. But it wasn't Ida Spavento standing in the open door. It was Scipio.

This was the Scipio they knew. He was wearing the mask and the high-heeled boots, the black coat and his black leather gloves.

Riccio stared at him in astonishment, but Mosca's face was rigid. 'What are you doing here?' he hissed at Scipio.

'What are *you* doing here?' Scipio spat back. 'This is *my* job.'

'Oh, shut up!' Mosca shoved Scipio in the chest. 'You lying piece of garbage! You've had a great time, stringing us along, haven't you? The Thief Lord! Well, this may be quite an adventure for you, but we need the money. And that's why we're going to deliver the wing to the Conte. Is it in there?'

Scipio shrugged.

Mosca pushed him roughly aside and disappeared into the room.

'How did you get in here?' Riccio grumbled at Scipio.

'It wasn't hard – otherwise how would *you* have done it?' came Scipio's sharp answer. 'And I'm telling you: I will give the wing to the Conte. You'll get your share as usual, but now leave!'

'You leave!' Mosca appeared behind him again. 'Or we'll tell your father that his fine son likes to creep into other people's houses at night!' His voice had grown so loud that Hornet pushed between them.

'Stop it!' she whispered. 'Have you forgotten where we are?'

'You can't take anything to the Conte, Thief Lord,' Riccio hissed at Scipio. 'You can't even send him a message, because we have the pigeon.'

Scipio pressed his lips together. He had completely forgotten about the pigeon.

'Come on,' Mosca urged, without looking at Scipio. 'Let's keep looking. Prosper, you and I will take the left door and – Riccio and Hornet – you take the right.'

'And keep out of our way, Thief Lord!' Riccio added.

Scipio didn't answer. He stood there, motionless, and looked after them. Mosca, Riccio and Hornet had already disappeared behind the doors when Prosper turned back.

'You'd better go home, Scip,' he said quietly. 'The others are really angry.'

'Yeah,' Bo mumbled uncertainly, looking nervously at Scipio.

'And you?' Scipio asked. But when Prosper didn't answer immediately, he turned abruptly and ran up the next flight of stairs.

'Look at this!' Mosca pointed as Prosper pushed Bo through the open door. 'It says *Laboratorio* on the plan and I wondered what that was supposed to mean. It's a photographer's dark room! With all the mod cons!' He admiringly let his torchlight wander through the room.

'Scip's gone upstairs,' Prosper said.

'What?' Mosca looked surprised. He whirled around as Hornet and Riccio walked through the door.

'The wing's not in the dining room either,' Hornet whispered. 'How about in here?'

'Scipio's gone upstairs,' Mosca told them. 'We have to go after him.'

'Upstairs?' Riccio ran his fingers through his spiky hair. That's what they had all been afraid of: having to go to the second floor, where the owner of the house was sleeping in blissful ignorance of her night-time visitors.

'The wing's *got* to be upstairs,' Mosca whispered.

Suddenly the little room was filled with red light.

The children turned around in surprise. Someone was standing in the doorway. A woman in a thick winter coat, holding a hunting rifle under one arm.

'I do beg your pardon,' Signora Ida Spavento said, pointing the gun at Riccio, who was standing closest to her. 'I don't quite recall having invited you.'

'Please! Please don't shoot,' Riccio stuttered. He held up his hands. Bo had already vanished behind Prosper and Hornet.

'Oh, I don't really intend to shoot,' Ida Spavento said, 'but you will understand that I had to fetch the old gun when I heard you whispering. So, I decide to go out for once, and when I come back, what do I find? A gang of little thieves with torches, creeping around my house. You should be grateful I didn't call the police.'

'Please! Don't call the police!' Hornet whispered. 'Please don't.'

'Well, perhaps I won't. You don't really look terribly dangerous.' Ida Spavento lowered her gun, took a pack of cigarettes from her pocket and put one between her lips. 'Were you after my cameras? You could get those much more easily out there on the streets.'

'No, we ... didn't want to steal anything valuable, Signora,' Hornet said haltingly. 'Really, we didn't.'

'No? What, then?'

'The w-wing,' Riccio stammered, 'and it's only m-made of wood.' He was still holding up his hands even though the barrel of the gun was pointing down at his feet.

'The wing?' Ida Spavento placed the rifle against the wall.

With a relieved sigh, Riccio put down his hands. Bo now dared to come out from behind Prosper's back.

Ida Spavento looked at him with a frown. 'Well, well, here's another one. How old are you? Five? Six?'

'Five,' Bo mumbled, looking at her suspiciously.

'Five. Heavens above! You're really very young for a bunch of thieves.' Ida Spavento leaned against the doorframe and looked at them one by one. 'What am I going to do with you now? You break into my house. You try to rob me... What do you know about the wing? '

'So you have it?' Riccio looked at her with big eyes.

'And what did you want to do with it?'

'Someone asked us to steal it,' Mosca muttered.

Ida Spavento looked at him in astonishment. 'Asked you? Who?'

'We're not going to tell you!' said a voice behind her.

Ida Spavento spun around. Before she knew what was happening, Scipio had grabbed her rifle and was pointing the barrel at her.

'Scipio, what are you doing?' Hornet called out, scared. 'Give that gun back!'

'I have the wing!' Scipio said, still holding the rifle. 'It was up in the bedroom. Now let's get out of here.'

'Scipio? Who's that now?' Ida Spavento trod her cigarette out on the floor and crossed her arms. 'My house seems to be swarming with uninvited guests tonight. That's an interesting mask you're wearing, my dear. I have a very similar one, but I don't often wear it for break-ins. And now put that gun down.'

Scipio took a step backwards.

'There are a lot of mysterious stories associated with this

wing. Did your client tell you about them?'

Scipio ignored her. 'If you're not going to come with me,' he called to the others, 'then I'll go alone. And I won't share the money with you.'

The rifle shook in his hands.

'Are you coming now or not?' he called once more.

At that moment Ida Spavento stepped forward, grabbed the barrel, and yanked the rifle out of Scipio's hands. 'That's enough!' she said. 'That thing doesn't work anyway. And now give me back my wing.'

Scipio had wrapped the wing in a blanket as soon as he'd heard voices.

'We would have got away with it!' he complained as he placed it on the floor in front of the Signora. 'If those dumb-heads hadn't just stood around like statues.'

'Just shut up,' Mosca shouted. 'You've completely lost it! Waving a gun around like that!'

'I was never going to shoot!' Scipio shouted back. 'I just wanted us to get the money. I would have given all of it to you. You said yourself how much you need it.'

'The money? Of course!' Ida Spavento knelt down and unfolded the blanket. 'How much did your client offer you for my wing?'

'A lot,' Hornet answered.

She stepped forward hesitantly and stood beside Ida. The wing's white paint was faded and cracked, just like the wing in the Conte's photograph. This one, however, still showed sprinklings of gold.

'Tell me his name.' Ida Spavento replaced the cover and got up with the wing in her arms. Its tip still poking out of the wrapping. 'You tell me his name and I'll tell you why he wants to pay so much money for a piece of wood.'

'We don't know his name,' Riccio answered.

'He calls himself the Conte.' The words slipped out of Mosca's mouth, he didn't know why. Scipio shot him a dark look. 'What are you staring at, Thief Lord?' Mosca shouted at him. 'Why shouldn't we tell her?'

'*Thief Lord?*' Ida Spavento raised her eyebrows. She gave Scipio a glance full of mockery and gentle amusement. 'Anyway, I need a coffee. I suppose you lot can't wait to get out of my house, right?'

She looked at the children enquiringly.

Nobody answered. Only Hornet shook her head.

'Fine! Then you can keep me company,' Ida Spavento said. 'If you want, I'll tell you a story. A story about a lost wing, and a mysterious merry-go-round. You may stay too,' she said as she walked past Scipio, 'but maybe the Thief Lord has more important appointments to keep?'

27 An Old Story

Scipio decided to come with them to Ida Spavento's kitchen, but he kept his distance. He lounged against the doorpost as the others gathered around the big table. The wing lay in front of them on the colourful tablecloth.

'It looks beautiful,' Hornet said as she carefully stroked the wood. 'It's the wing of an angel, isn't it?'

'Angel? Oh no.' Ida Spavento took the espresso pot from the stove, the coffee still gurgling as she put it on the table. 'This is a lion's wing.'

'A lion?' Riccio looked at her in disbelief.

Ida Spavento nodded. 'Indeed.' She put her hand in her coat pocket and pulled out her cigarettes. Then she fetched sugar and a cup for herself. She got some juice and some glasses for the children. There was one for Scipio too, but he stayed by the door. At least he had taken off his mask.

'So, what about the story?' Mosca asked as he poured himself some juice.

'I'm coming to that!' Ida Spavento threw her coat over the back of her chair. She took a sip of coffee and then reached for a cigarette.

'Can I try one?' Riccio asked.

Ida looked surprised. 'Of course not. It's an unhealthy habit.'

'Why do you smoke, then?'

She sighed. 'I'm trying to quit. But let's get to the story.' She leaned back. 'Have you ever heard about the merry-go-round of the Merciful Sisters?'

The children shook their heads.

'Doesn't the orphanage in the south of the city also belong to the Merciful Sisters?,' Riccio asked.

'Exactly!' Ida stirred some more sugar into her coffee. 'About one hundred and fifty years ago – so the legend says – a rich merchant gave a very valuable gift to the orphanage: he had a merry-go-round built in the courtyard. It had five beautiful wooden figures on it. There's still a picture of them above the door to the orphanage. In it, a unicorn, a sea horse, a merman, his mermaid, and a winged lion do their rounds beneath a colourful wooden canopy. Back then some wicked tongues claimed that the rich man wanted to relieve his conscience because he himself had once brought the unwanted child of his daughter to the orphanage. Others, however, disputed that and said he was simply a warm-hearted man who wanted to share his wealth with the poor orphaned children. Whatever the case, soon everyone in Venice was talking about the amazing roundabout – and that's saying something in a city with as many wonders as this one. The rumour soon spread that, because of that roundabout, magical things were happening behind the orphanage's walls.

'Magical things?' Riccio looked at Ida Spavento wide-eyed, just the way he looked at Hornet when she read to them...

Ida nodded. 'Yes, very strange things. People said that a few turns on the roundabout of the Merciful Sisters made adults out of children and children out of adults.'

For a few moments there was complete silence. Then Mosca laughed out loud: 'And how's that supposed to work?'

Ida shrugged. 'I wouldn't know. I'm just telling you what I heard.'

Scipio detached himself from the doorframe to come and sit on the edge of the table next to Prosper and Bo.

'What's the wing got to do with the roundabout?' he asked.

'I was just coming to that,' Ida replied. She poured Bo some more juice. 'The sisters and the orphans weren't to enjoy their present for long, as it turned out. After only a few weeks, the roundabout was stolen. The sisters had taken the children on a day trip to Burano and when they returned they found the gate had been forced open and the roundabout taken. It was never seen again. However, in their hurry, the thieves had left something behind...'

'The lion's wing,' Bo whispered.

'Precisely.' Ida Spavento nodded. 'It lay unnoticed in the courtyard until one of the sisters discovered it. No one really believed her when she claimed it was a piece of the original roundabout. So she kept it, and after her death it ended up in the loft of the orphanage. And that's where I found it many, many years later.'

'What were you doing up there?' Mosca asked.

Ida extinguished her cigarette. 'I used to play up there by the dovecots,' she said. 'They're very old. They date back to when people still used pigeons to send their letters. That used to be quite popular in Venice. Whenever rich Venetians moved to the mainland during the summer, they'd use pigeons to send their messages into town. I used to play a game where I imagined that someone was keeping me prisoner up there and that I would send my pigeons for help. And that's how, one day, I found the wing, in the middle of all the pigeon droppings. One of the sisters, who knew the old story, guessed where it had come from and told me about the roundabout. When she realized how much I loved the story she gave the wing to me.'

'You played in the orphanage?' Scipio eyed her suspiciously. 'What were you doing there?'

Ida stroked her hair back. 'I lived there,' she answered. 'I was there for more than ten years. They weren't exactly my happiest ten years, but I still visit some of the sisters from time to time.'

Hornet looked at Ida as if she was seeing her face for the first time, suddenly recognising another lonely child. Then she reached into her jacket and produced the photograph the Conte had left for them. She pushed it towards Ida. 'Behind the wing there – don't you think that looks like the head of a unicorn?'

Ida Spavento bent over the photograph. 'Where did you get this?' she asked. 'From your client?'

Scipio stepped over to the kitchen window. It was still dark outside. 'The roundabout can turn you into an adult?' he asked.

'Yes, after a few turns on it. It's strange story, don't you think?' Ida placed her cup in the sink. 'But your client could probably tell you more about it than I can. I think he must know where the roundabout of the Merciful Sisters is now. Why else would he have asked you to steal my wing? It probably doesn't work without the lion's second wing.'

'He's quite old,' said Prosper. 'He can't have much time left to get the roundabout to work its magic.'

'You know, Signora...' Mosca ran his finger over the wing. The wood felt quite rough...if this wing really belongs to the lion on the roundabout, then you don't have much use for it. So you might as well give it to us, right?'

Ida Spavento smiled. 'I might, might I?' She opened the door to the garden to let in some cold night air. She stood there for quite a while, her back to the children. Then she suddenly turned around. 'How about a little deal?' she asked. 'I let you have the wing so you can take it to the Conte and he can pay you for it, and in return...'

Riccio muttered: 'Here comes the catch!'

'In return,' Ida Spavento continued, 'we will follow the Conte when he disappears with the wing. Perhaps we can find the roundabout of the Merciful Sisters. I'm saying *we*, because I will be coming with you. That's the deal.' She looked eagerly at her visitors. 'So, what do you say? I won't ask for any share in your reward. I already make more money than I can spend with my photographs. I'd love to see the roundabout just once. Go on, please say yes!'

The children didn't look very enthusiastic.

'I'm not sure ... the Conte's pretty odd,' Mosca murmured. 'What if he catches us? I think he could get quite nasty.'

'But doesn't this photo make you curious?' Ida closed the door again and went back to her chair. 'Don't you want to see the roundabout? It's supposed to be very beautiful.'

Mosca still wasn't convinced. 'The lion on St. Mark's Square is beautiful too. Why don't you just look at that?'

Scipio stood up. He could hardly ignore the others' hostile glares, but he tried his best. 'I think we should take her offer,' he said. 'It's very fair. We get our money, and even if the Conte realizes we're following him we can always out run him.'

'I keep hearing *we*,' Mosca growled. '*We* are finished, you lying toad. You don't belong with us any more. You never belonged with us, even when you pretended you did.'

'Yeah, you just go back to that posh house you live in!' Riccio sneered. 'Us *real* orphans don't want to play with the Thief Lord any more.'

Scipio stood still and bit his lip. Hornet looked miserably at the table, and Bo pushed his head under Prosper's arm as if he wanted to hide.

'Could someone explain to me what's going on here?' Ida Spavento asked. When nobody answered she went to the sink and washed her espresso pot.

Suddenly Scipio said: 'I'm not going back.' He sounded choked up. 'I will never ever go back home. That's it. I don't need them. If that roundabout really exists then I'll be on it faster than the Conte, and I'll only get off when I'm at least a good head taller than him and with a beard on my chin. If you don't want to take the deal then I'll do it alone. I'm going to find that roundabout so nobody can treat me like a stupid pet animal ever again!

After Scipio's outburst the kitchen fell so silent they could all hear the mewing of cats outside in the garden.

'I also think we should accept Signora Spavento's offer,' Hornet said into the silence. 'We should make peace until we've handed the wing to the Conte and received the money. We all have enough on our minds without making each

183

other's lives more difficult.' She looked at Prosper and Bo. 'Now, anyone against the agreement?'

Nobody moved.

'Then that's decided,' said Hornet. 'Signora Spavento, you've got yourself a deal.'

28 Scipio, the Liar

Another grey morning was already dawning when the children left Ida Spavento's house. Scipio joined the others, not saying a word, although it wasn't as if Riccio and Mosca even tried to talk to him on the way back to the hide-out. From time to time Riccio gave Scipio such a threatening look that Prosper decided to walk between the two of them. They had left the wing with Ida Spavento. She wanted to bring it with her when they met the Conte.

Bo was so sleepy that Prosper had to carry him on his back half the way home. Of course as soon as they reached the cinema, he was wide awake again, so they let him catch the Conte's messenger pigeon.

Happily, he stood underneath the basket and filled one hand with seeds. Then he held it up in the air, just like Victor had shown him on St Mark's Square. The pigeon jerked its head around and peered down at the boy, and finally flew on to his hand. Bo giggled and hunched up his shoulders as the bird walked down his arm. Then, while the pigeon pecked eagerly at the seeds in his hand, Bo carefully carried it to the emergency exit.

'Take her to the canal before you let her go, Bo!' Mosca whispered, holding the door open for him.

It was now light and very cold. When Bo stepped outside, the pigeon ruffled up its feathers and blinked, bewildered in the light. She kept her wings folded as long as Bo was still in the narrow alley. As soon as they reached the canal and the wind uncurled her wings, she pushed herself off from Bo's hand and took to the air. She rose high into the morning sky and flew faster and faster until she disappeared behind the chimneys.

'When were we supposed to collect the Conte's reply from Barbarossa?' Prosper asked as they hurried back into the cinema, shivering. 'The day after we sent our message? She can't be flying far then.'

'Pigeons can fly hundreds of kilometres in one day,' Scipio answered. 'This evening she could easily be in Paris or London.' When he noticed Hornet looking at him with irritation, he quickly added: 'I read that somewhere.' This wasn't his usual arrogant tone. Today he sounded timid and almost apologetic.

'The Conte's not very likely to live in Paris,' Riccio said scornfully. 'But who cares? The pigeon is on its way and you'd better go home now.'

Scipio gave a start. He cast a pleading look at Prosper, who avoided his eyes. Prosper had not forgotten how Scipio acted when the others had been waiting in front of his grand house. Maybe Scipio guessed his thoughts because he turned away again. He didn't seem sure where else he could look for help. Bo pretended he hadn't noticed the tense atmosphere and carried on feeding his kittens.

Hornet bowed her head. 'Riccio is right, Scip,' she said. 'You have to go back. We can't afford to have your father turning the whole city upside down because his son has run-away. I mean, how long would it take him to think of his old cinema? He'd have half the police force of Venice out here in no time. We're in enough trouble as it is.'

Scipio's face froze. Prosper could see the old Scipio return-ing, the stubborn, arrogant Scipio who would fight to get his way. 'I see,' he said. 'You're not going to throw out Prosper and Bo, even though it's completely their fault the detective came sneaking round here in the first place. But I – *I'm* not allowed to stay. *I* showed you this place. *I* gave you money and warm clothes. I even brought you the mattresses – and I nearly drowned in Mosca's rotten boat doing it. When it got cold, I brought you blankets and heaters. Do you think it was easy to steal all those things from my parents?'

'Of course it was easy.' Mosca gave Scipio a look of utter contempt. 'They probably suspected the maid, or the cook, or another of your thousands of servants.'

Scipio didn't answer that. He just turned bright red.

'Bingo!' Riccio exclaimed. 'Got it in one.'

'Do you mean they suspected someone else?' Hornet asked Scipio in astonishment.

Scipio buttoned his jacket right up to his neck. 'My nanny.'

'And? Did you at least defend her?'

'How?' Scipio returned Hornet's angry glance. 'You don't know my father. If he ever caught me stealing just a single one of his cufflinks, he'd make me walk around with a big sign around my neck saying: *I'm a rotten little thief*!'

Bo, despite his efforts not to listen to them, had heard it all. 'Did they lock her up? Like, in a real prison?'

'Of course not!' Scipio shrugged. 'They couldn't prove it. She was sacked, that's all. If I hadn't taken those damn sugar-tongs they would never have noticed anything. I took most of the stuff from rooms that are never used anyway. So now I don't have a nanny any more.' The others looked at Scipio as if he had snakes growing out of his head.

'Jeez, Scip!' Mosca muttered.

'I only did it for you!' Scipio shouted. 'Have you forgotten how you used to live before I looked after you?'

'Get lost!' Riccio shouted back at him: He gave Scipio a fierce shove in the chest. 'We can do without you. We want nothing to do with you. We should never have let you back in here again.'

'You shouldn't have let *me* in here?' Scipio was now screaming so loudly that Bo put his hands over his ears. 'Who do you think you are? All this belongs to my father!'

'Oh, sure!' Riccio yelled back. 'Why don't you tell him about us then, you little toad?'

Scipio went for him. The two of them got so entangled that Hornet and Prosper needed Mosca's help to separate them.

When Bo saw that Riccio's nose was bleeding, he let out such an anguished sob that the others rushed to comfort him.

Hornet was there first. She wrapped her arms around Bo and gently stroked his hair, which was already growing blonde at the roots. 'Go home, Scip,' she said sadly. 'We'll let you know when we're meeting the Conte. Perhaps we'll have a message by tomorrow afternoon. One of us will go to Barbarossa right after breakfast.'

'You what?' Riccio pushed Mosca away just as he was trying to wipe the blood from his face. 'You want to tell Scipio? Why?'

'Stop it Riccio!' Prosper interrupted angrily. 'I've seen Scipio's father. You wouldn't dare to steal even a single spoon off him, let alone tell him about it.'

Riccio just sniffed and pressed the back of his hand against his nose.

Scipio mumbled, 'Thanks, Prop.' His cheeks were striped raw from Riccio's fingernails. 'And you *will* let me know, right?'

Prosper nodded.

But Scipio still hesitated. 'The detective...'

'...has done a runner,' Mosca finished.

'We have his word of honour that he won't tell on us,' Bo said.

Scipio shrugged. 'If you say so.' He walked slowly past the rows of red chairs, running his fingers along the red velvet and looking intently at the embroidered stars on the curtain. He walked very slowly, as if he was waiting for the others to call him back. But nobody did, not even Bo.

He's scared, Prosper thought, as he looked after Scipio. Scared to go home.

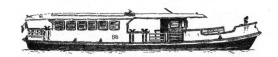

29 Another Visit

Barbarossa's shop was empty when Prosper pushed open its door the next morning. The bells above the door jangled madly and Bo, fascinated, stopped in the doorway to stare at them. Hornet pulled him into the shop. It had grown very cold overnight.

'Signor Barbarossa?' Hornet called, looking closely at the painting above the counter. She also knew all about the red-beard's peephole.

'Si, si, pazienza! Patience!' they heard him call in a bad-tempered voice.

Barbarossa poked his head through the curtain in front of his office door. His eyes were bloodshot and he was blowing his nose into a huge handkerchief. 'Oh, you brought the little one. Take care he doesn't break anything. What have you done to his angel-hair?'

With an impatient gesture he waved the children into his office.

'Winter! What the hell is winter doing here already? Has the whole world gone crazy?' he muttered as he dragged himself back to his desk. 'This city's already hard to bear in the summer, but the winter can bring even the healthiest man to the edge of his grave. But I forget who I'm talking to. You wouldn't understand. Children don't feel the chill. They skip around in the puddles and don't even get a cold.' Barbarossa slumped into his chair with the sigh of a mortally ill man. 'Sore throat, headache, a constantly runny nose!' he moaned. 'I feel like a human tap.' He wrapped his scarf even tighter around his fat neck and peered at his visitors over his handkerchief. 'No bag, no backpack? Is The Thief Lord's loot today small enough for your pockets?'

Bo reached out his hand and touched a small tin drummer on Barbarossa's desk.

'Get your sticky hands off, that's valuable,' the redbeard barked, tossing a cough-sweet at Bo.

'We're not here to sell anything,' Hornet said. 'The Conte said he would leave a letter for us with you.' Bo had unwrapped the cough-sweet and was sniffing it suspiciously.

'Ah yes, the Conte's letter.' Barbarossa blew his nose once more, then stuffed his handkerchief back into his waistcoat pocket. The waistcoat was embroidered with tiny golden gondolas. 'His sister, the Contessa, left it here yesterday. He himself only comes to town very rarely.' The redbeard popped another lozenge into his mouth and with another sigh he opened the top drawer of his desk. 'There you are!' Keeping a very straight face, he held out the envelope to Hornet. The envelope was blank – no address and no sender. When Hornet reached for it, Barbarossa snatched it back.

'We're all friends here,' he purred in a low conspiratorial voice, 'tell me what you had to steal for the Conte. The Thief Lord obviously completed his task in a satisfactory manner, am I right?'

'Perhaps,' Prosper answered vaguely, before pulling the envelope from Barbarossa's fingers.

'Hey!' The redbeard slammed his fists on the desk and pushed himself up. 'Aren't you a cocky one. Did nobody ever teach you to treat adults with respect?' A violent sneezing fit threw him back into his chair.

Prosper didn't answer. He silently put the envelope into the inside pocket of his jacket. Bo spat the sweet into his hand and banged it on to Barbarossa's desk. 'Here, you can have it back, because you shouted at my brother,' he said.

Incredulous, Barbarossa stared at the sticky sweet.

Hornet bent over the desk with her friendliest smile. 'How about you, Signor Barbarossa? Did nobody ever teach *you* how to behave in front of children?'

The redbeard had to cough so violently that his face actually turned redder than his nose. 'All right! By the lion of San Marco, you lot are very touchy!' He spat into his handkerchief. 'Well, why don't we play a little quiz? I'll start.' He leaned over his desk. 'Is what the Conte wants so badly made of gold?'

'No!' Bo answered, shaking his head with a broad grin.

'Really?' Barbarossa frowned. 'Silver?'

'Wrong! Wrong!' Bo skipped from one foot to the other. 'Guess again!'

But before the redbeard could venture another guess Prosper had already pushed his brother through the curtain. Hornet followed them.

'Copper?' Barbarossa called after them. 'No, wait! It's a painting! A sculpture!'

Prosper opened the shop door. 'Out you go, Bo,' he said, but Bo stopped once more. 'All wrong!' he shouted into the shop. 'It's made of huuuuge diamonds. And pearls!'

'You don't say!' Barbarossa was through the curtain like a shot. 'Describe it, boy.'

Hornet hauled Bo through the door. Outside, she suddenly stopped.

Snowflakes whirled through the alley. They fell so thickly from the off-white sky that Bo squeezed his eyes shut. Suddenly everything was grey and white – as if someone had erased all the colours of the city while they were in the shop.

'It's a chain. Or a ring?' Barbarossa excitedly poked his head through the shop door. 'Why don't I take you all for a nice tea over there in the cake shop, hmm? What do you say?'

But the children just wandered off without paying him anymore attention. They only had eyes for the snow. The cold flakes settled on their faces and their hair. Bo gleefully licked one off his nose. He stretched his arms wide as if he wanted to catch them all. Hornet just looked up at the sky, blinking. It hadn't snowed in Venice for years. The people they passed looked just as enchanted as the children. Even the shop assistants stepped into the street to look up at the sky.

Prosper, Hornet and Bo stopped on one of the bridges and bent over the stone parapet to watch how the grey water swallowed the snowflakes. The snow gently covered the surrounding buildings, the red roofs, the black trellises on the balconies as well as the leaves of the autumn flowers in their pots.

Prosper could feel the snow in his hair, wet and cold. He remembered a far-away time, and an almost forgotten place. He remembered a hand gently wiping snow from his hair. He stood there, between Hornet and his little brother, and lost himself in this memory for a few precious moments. He realized to his amazement that remembering didn't hurt so much any more. Perhaps it was Bo and Hornet standing by his side, warm and familiar.

'Prop?' Hornet put her arm around his shoulder. 'Everything all right?'

Prosper shook the snow from his hair and nodded.

'Let's open the envelope,' Hornet said. 'I want to know when we'll finally get to see the Conte.'

'How do you know he'll come himself?' Prosper pulled the envelope from his jacket. It was sealed, just like the one in the confessional. But this seal looked strange. As if someone had daubed it with red paint.

Hornet took it from Prosper's hand. 'Someone has already opened it!' She looked at Prosper. 'Barbarossa!'

'Doesn't matter,' replied Prosper. 'That's why the Conte already told us the meeting place in the confessional. He knew the redbeard would open the message. He seems to know him rather well.'

Hornet carefully cut open the envelope with her penknife. The Conte's message was just a few words.

> *At the arranged place*
> *on the water*
> *look out for a red lantern*
> *on Tuesday night, 1 a.m.*

'Tomorrow!' Prosper shook his head. 'One o'clock. That's late.' He put the message back in his pocket and ruffled Bo's hair. 'That was quite good, about those diamonds and pearls. Did you see Barbarossa's eyes?'

Bo giggled and licked another snowflake off his hand.

But Hornet glanced over the parapet, looking worried. 'On

the water?' she asked. 'What does he mean? Are we doing the swap on the water?'

'No problem,' Prosper answered. 'Mosca's boat is big enough for us all.'

'OK,' said Hornet, 'but I still don't like it. I can't swim very well and Riccio gets sick from just looking at a boat.'

'Don't you like boats?' Prosper teased, pulling Hornet's plait. 'But you were born here. I thought all Venetians love boats.'

'Well, you thought wrong,' Hornet answered curtly. She turned her back to the canal. 'Let's go, the others are waiting for us.'

The snow seemed to make the city quieter than usual. Hornet and Prosper walked silently next to each other. Bo skipped ahead, humming gently to himself.

'I don't want Bo to come along to the handing-over,' he whispered to Hornet.

'I can understand that,' she whispered back, 'but how are you going to tell him without him bursting our ear-drums?'

'I don't know,' Prosper muttered.

'I've got an idea.' Hornet said. 'One that will get me out of the boat trip too. I just won't get to see the Conte.'

195

30 Hopeless Lies

Victor was late. He'd been sick for two whole days and had only just managed to drag himself out of bed, reluctantly, for his dreaded meeting with the Hartliebs. It was already three o'clock when he finally stepped into the noble lobby of the Hotel Gabrielli Sandwirth. He'd last been there just a month before. He had been following someone, wearing a full black beard and a rather horrendous pair of glasses. He had hardly recognized himself in the mirror. Today he wore his own face, which always gave him the strange sensation of being smaller.

'*Buonasera,*' he said as he approached the reception. A head appeared from behind a massive flower arrangement. '*Buonasera,*' the receptionist said, 'what can I do for you?'

'My name is Victor Getz. I have an appointment with the Hartliebs,' Victor gave an apologetic smile, 'for which I am rather late. Could you please check if they are still in their room?'

'Of course.' The lady tucked a strand of black hair behind her ear. 'What do you think of the snow?' she asked.

She let the word *snow* melt on her tongue like a delicious creamy chocolate. Victor smiled as he noticed how her eyes kept straying towards the large windows and the snowflakes, which drifted past slowly.

'Hello, Signora Hartlieb,' she said into the telephone, 'there's a Signor Getz here to see you.'

The Hartliebs had no time for the snow. Outside their window, San Giorgio Maggiore seemed to be floating on the lagoon as if it had just surfaced there. The view was so beautiful that Victor felt his heart ache. Esther and her husband, however, stood side by side with their backs to the window and only had eyes for him, uneasily Victor folded his hands behind his back.

Why hadn't he at least put on a moustache? That would have made lying so much easier. But the children had stolen all his wonderful beards.

'I'm glad you received my message, after my conversation with your rather unpleasant secretary I had my doubts as to your being in Venice at all.'

'I hardly ever leave the city,' Victor answered. 'I miss it too much as soon as I try to leave.'

'Really!' Esther's eyebrows moved up and down as rapidly as a bouncing ball.

Amazing, Victor thought – I could never do that.

'So, please, Signor Getz,' Mr Hartlieb was still as big as a wardrobe and nearly as white as the snowflakes drifting past outside, 'could you tell us about your investigations.'

'My investigations, yes.' Victor nervously bobbed up and down. 'My findings are sadly quite clear. The little boy is no longer in the city, nor is his brother.'

The Hartliebs exchanged a quick glance.

'Your secretary already hinted at something like that,' Max Hartlieb said, 'but—'

'My secretary?' Victor interrupted him, but then he remembered just in time that Hornet, Prosper and Riccio had been in his office to feed his tortoise. 'My secretary, of course!' He shrugged apologetically. 'You must know, I was already hot on their heels. The photo I sent you proves that. At that time, sadly, I was unable to catch the two of them. Too many people around, you must understand. I did find out, however, that your nephews had joined a gang of young thieves. And one of them, I'm afraid, recognized me. I caught him stealing a handbag some time ago. Well, that rascal probably convinced your nephews that Venice was no longer safe for them. Much to my regret, I have learned...' He cleared his throat. Why did lying always give him such a lump in his throat? 'Hmhm, I have learned that the boys sneaked on to one of the large ferries that stop here regularly. From your window you have a good view of the moorings.'

Confused, the Hartliebs turned around and looked down at the quay, where a large flock of tourists was crowding on to an excursion boat. 'But,' Esther Hartlieb looked so disappointed that Victor almost felt sorry for her, 'where, for heaven's sake, was the boat going?'

'Corfu,' Victor answered. How calmly he said that, despite that lump in his throat.

'Corfu!' Esther Hartlieb looked at her husband hopelessly, as if he had to save her from drowning.

'Well, I can't be completely certain,' Victor continued. 'After all, when you're sneaking on to a ship you don't appear on the passenger list. I did, however, show the boys' picture to some of the crew, and they definitely recognized them.

They just couldn't agree on which day exactly they were on board.'

Max Hartlieb hugged his wife reassuringly. She let it happen, but stayed as stiff as a mannequin. She was still looking at Victor. For a second, he had the feeling that his lies were painted bright red on his forehead.

'It's not possible!' Esther Hartlieb said, detaching herself from her husband. 'I told you it was no coincidence that Prosper came to Venice. The city reminds him of his mother. I can't believe he'd just leave.'

'He probably got on that boat because he realized this place wasn't as wonderful as it sounded in his mother's stories,' her husband ventured.

'And that, even if Venice does look like heaven, she wasn't here to greet him,' Victor said thoughtfully, looking out of the window.

'No! No! No!' Esther Hartlieb shook her head violently. 'Rubbish! I have a feeling he's still here. And if Prosper is still here, then so is Bo.'

'I've had copies made of the photograph you sent us,' she continued. 'It arrived shortly after we spoke to your secretary and I had posters made from it. We're offering quite a substantial reward. I know you have already tried to dissuade us from using these means to search for the boys, and I do admit that a reward draws out the riff-raff. But I will have those posters put up by every canal, every bar, every café and every museum. I will find Bo, before he dies of pneumonia or consumption in this infernal city. He has to be protected from his selfish brother.'

Victor just shook his head wearily. 'Has it still not occurred to you?' he asked impatiently. 'The two of them only ran away because you wanted to separate Bo from his brother.'

'How dare you use that tone with me?' Esther Hartlieb shouted.

'The two of them are very close!' Victor shouted back. 'Can't you understand that?'

'We'll get Bo a dog,' Max Hartlieb answered calmly. 'And then you'll see how quickly he forgets his big brother.'

Victor stared at Mr Hartlieb as if he had just unbuttoned his shirt and shown him an empty heart. 'Please answer me one question,' Victor said. 'Do you actually like children?'

Max Hartlieb frowned. 'Children in general? No, not really. They're so fidgety and loud, and often quite dirty.'

Victor stared down at his shoes again.

'And,' Max Hartlieb continued, 'they have no idea of what's really important.'

Victor nodded. 'Well,' he said slowly, 'it must be a miracle, then, that such useless creatures grow up into into something as great and reasonable as you, don't you think?'

With that he turned and walked out of the room and down the long hotel corridor. In the lift, Victor's heart pounded wildly though he had no idea why. The lady at the reception smiled at him as he walked through the lobby. Then she looked outside again, where the snow was still falling as darkness fell.

The jetty in front of the hotel was empty. Only two warmly dressed figures were waiting for the next *vaporetto*. At first Victor went to buy a ticket as well, but then he decided to walk. He needed time to think, and a walk would calm his restless heart. At least he hoped it would. He trudged through the wind. He walked past The Doge's Palace, which was already illuminated by its pink lamps, and then stomped through the twilight across the deserted St Mark's Square.

I have to warn the boys, Victor thought, while the wind threw icy needles at his face. I have to tell them what's happening. Shall I go now? I don't even have a hat, and it's quite far to the cinema. I'll go tomorrow morning. Bad news never sounds quite so bad in the light of day. Wearily, he made his way home. When he reached his front door he remembered that he was supposed to be following someone for a new client that night. Sighing, he walked up the stairs. There was still time for a cup of coffee.

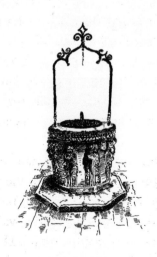

31 No Bo

The Sacca della Misericordia pokes into the maze of Venice's alleys. It looks as if the sea has taken a bite out of the city and swallowed it.

It was quarter to one in the morning when Mosca moored his boat at the last bridge before the bay. Riccio jumped ashore and tied the boat to one of the wooden stakes sticking out of the water. Behind them lay a seemingly endless trip through canals Prosper had never seen before. He had only been to the northernmost part of the city once before. The houses here were just as old if not quite as magnificent as those in the centre.

There was just the three of them in the boat: Mosca, Riccio and Prosper.

Hornet had given Bo hot milk and honey after dinner and he emptied two whole mugs without becoming suspicious. Then she had settled down with him on her mattress, her arm wrapped around him, and she had read from his favourite book, *The Lion the Witch, and the Wardrobe*. During the third chapter, Bo had already nestled his head against Hornet's chest and begun snoring softly. On cue, Prosper had quietly

crept away with Riccio and Mosca. Hornet had bravely tried
not to look too worried as she waved them goodbye.

'Can you hear anything?' Riccio peered into the night.
Some of the windows were still lit and their glow reflected on
the water's surface. The snow looked strange in the moonlight, like icing sugar on a model city. Prosper gazed down the
canal. Ida Spavento had wanted to come in her own boat, and
she was supposed to be picking Scipio up on the way.

'I think I can hear something!' Riccio climbed deftly back
into the boat. Mosca wedged an oar against the wooden pier
to stop the boat rocking.

'About time they turned up!' Prosper whispered, looking at
his watch. 'Who knows how long the Conte's going to wait
for us if we're late.'

By now the sounds of an engine came quite clearly through
the night and soon a boat drifted towards them. The boat was
much wider and heavier than Mosca's. It had a black finish,
just like a gondola. Behind the wheel sat a giant of a man and
behind him, hardly recognizable under the shawl wrapped
round her head, was Ida Spavento. Scipio was sitting by her
side.

'At last!' Mosca called out quietly as the boat came alongside his. 'Riccio, cast off!'

Scowling in Scipio's direction, Riccio jumped back aboard.

'Sorry, Giaco lost the way,' Ida said. 'And the Thief Lord
was also not very punctual.' She got up and carefully handed
a heavy parcel to Prosper: the lion wing, wrapped in a blanket and tied up with a leather strap.

'My father had some of his business partners over,' Scipio
defended himself. 'It wasn't easy to sneak out of the house.'

'Wouldn't have been such a great loss if you'd missed it

anyway,' replied Riccio.

Prosper sat down at the stern of the boat, holding on tightly to the wing.

'It's probably best if you wait with your boat over there, where the canal flows into the bay,' Mosca instructed Ida. 'If you drift out any further the Conte might see you and the whole deal could be off.'

Ida nodded. Her face was pale with excitement. 'I had to leave my camera at home. The flash would have given us away. But these' – she pulled a pair of binoculars from her coat – 'may come in handy. And if I may make a suggestion,' she eyed Mosca's boat, 'then we should use my boat to follow the Conte – should he sail out on to the lagoon after the transfer.'

'On to the lagoon?' Riccio's mouth dropped wide open in horror.

'Of course!' Ida whispered. 'He'd never keep the roundabout secret in this city. But there are lots of islands out there on the lagoon where nobody ever goes.'

Prosper and Riccio looked at each other. Out on the lagoon in the middle of the night ... they didn't like the sound of that.

But Mosca just shrugged. He felt at home on the water, especially in the dark when everything was still and silent. 'Fine by me!' he said. 'My boat's OK for fishing, but it's not up to a chase. And who knows what kind of boat the Conte's got? As soon as we see him heading for the lagoon we will row back to you as quickly as possible and then follow him in your motorboat.'

'That's how we'll do it.' Ida blew into her cold hands. 'How wonderful! I haven't done anything this crazy in a long

time!' she sighed. 'A real adventure! If only it wasn't so cold.'
She shivered and wrapped her coat around herself even
tighter.

'What about him?' Riccio nodded towards Ida's boatman.
'Is he going to come with us?' He and Mosca had immediately recognized the man: it was the husband of Ida
Spavento's housekeeper. As usual, he looked bad tempered
and hadn't yet said a word.

'Giaco?' Ida lifted her eyebrows. 'He has to come. He's
much better with the boat than I am. And he's very discreet.'

Giaco winked at Mosca and spat into the water.

'Enough talk!' Mosca picked up the oars. 'We've got to go.'

'Scipio's got to come in our boat,' Prosper interjected. 'The
Conte negotiated with him. He'll be suspicious if he's not with
us.'

Riccio pursed his lips, but he said nothing as Scipio
climbed on board. The bell of Santa Maria di Valverde was
just chiming one o'clock as they rowed out into the Sacca della
Misericordia. There were just a few lights glimmering on the
surface of the water. Ida's boat stayed behind like a shadow,
hardly more than a black speck against the dark outline of the
shore.

32 The Island

The Conte was already waiting.

His boat lay not far from the bay's western shore. It was a sailing boat. The navigation lights shone brightly across the water and a red lantern had been placed, clearly visible, on the stern.

'A sailing boat!' Mosca whispered as they rowed towards it. 'Ida was right. He came from one of the islands.'

'No doubt about it.' Scipio put on his mask. 'But the wind's in our favour. We'll easily follow him with the motor-boat.'

'Out on to the lagoon?' Riccio moaned. 'Oh Lord! Lord! Lord!'

Prosper said nothing. He held on to the wing. The cold wind had died down and Mosca's boat glided smoothly across the water. But Riccio clung miserably to the side, terrified that the boat might capsize if he only so much as looked at the black water beneath him.

The Conte was standing at the stern of his boat. He was wearing a large, grey coat. He didn't look as frail as Prosper had imagined him from their encounter in the confessional. His hair was white but he was very erect and he still appeared to be quite a strong man. There was someone standing behind the Conte, smaller than him, dressed in black from head to toe, their face hidden beneath a hood. When Mosca rowed alongside, the second figure cast a line with a hook towards Prosper to keep the boats from drifting apart.

'*Salve!*' the Conte called out towards them in a rough voice. 'I presume you are just as cold as we are, so let us complete this transaction as quickly as possible.'

'Fine. Here's the wing.' Prosper handed Scipio the parcel and he in turn carefully offered it to the Conte. The narrow boat rocked underneath Scipio's feet and he nearly stumbled. The Conte quickly leaned forward as if he feared that what he had been searching for all this time could still be lost for ever.

'That's it!' Prosper heard him whisper. The old man reverently stroked the painted wood underneath the blanket. 'Morosina, just look at it!' He impatiently waved at his companion, who had been hidden behind the mast all this time. The figure went up to him and pushed back the hood. To their surprise, the boys saw it was a woman. She was not much younger than the Conte and she wore her hair in a tight bun. 'Yes, that's it,' Prosper heard her say. 'Let's give them their reward.'

'You deal with it,' the Conte said, wrapping the blanket around the wing.

Silently, the woman handed Scipio an old bag. 'Take this,' she said, 'and use the money to find yourself another occupation. How old are you? Eleven? Twelve?'

'With this kind of money I can be as grown up as I want to be,' Scipio answered. He took the bag and put it on the floor between him and Mosca.

'Did you hear that, Renzo?' The woman leaned against the

deck rail and eyed Scipio with puzzled amusement. 'He wants to be grown up. How different dreams can be!'

'Nature will soon grant your wish,' the Conte replied. He was wrapping the wing in a tarpaulin. 'We wish the opposite to be true. Do you want to count the money, Thief Lord?'

Scipio put the bag on Mosca's lap and opened it.

'Wow!' Mosca whispered. He took a bundle of banknotes and began to count them with an expression of utter disbelief. Even Riccio forgot his fear of the water and got up. However, as the boat began to rock, he hurriedly sat down again. 'Has anyone ever seen so much money?' he wondered.

Scipio held a note in front of his torch, counted the wad, and then he gave Mosca a satisfied nod.

'Seems to be all there,' he called up to the Conte and his companion.

The grey-haired lady bowed her head and said: *'Buon ritorno!'*

The Conte stood next to her. Prosper threw him the rope and the Conte caught it. 'Safe return – and the best of luck for the future,' he said. Then he pushed off.

Prosper and Mosca took the oars and pulled away from the Conte's boat. The mouth of the canal where Ida was waiting for them seemed very far away. Prosper could see quite clearly that behind them the Conte had already pointed the bow of his boat towards where the Sacca della Misericordia opened into the lagoon.

But Scipio had been right. The wind was on their side. It barely rippled the water and when they reached Ida's boat they could still make out the Conte's sails.

'Go on, tell me: how did it go?' Ida asked impatiently as soon as the four of them had climbed aboard. 'I could only see that he's got a sailing boat, but you were too far out.'

'Everything's sorted. We've got the money and he's got the wing.' Scipio wedged the bag with the money between his legs. 'There was a woman with him. And you were right: they're sailing out to the lagoon.'

'I thought so!' Ida gave Giaco a sign, but he had already started the engine and soon they were heading out into the bay.

'He's turned off the red lantern,' Mosca shouted above the din of the engine, 'but I can still see the boat.'

Giaco grumbled something unintelligible. He held his course as if there was nothing easier than to follow a strange boat in the moonlight.

'Have you counted the money?' Ida asked.

'Sort of,' Scipio answered. 'There's definitely a lot of it.'

'Can I have a look through your binoculars?' Mosca asked.

Ida handed them to him and wrapped her scarf tighter around her head.

'He's making very slow progress, but he'll be out of the bay soon,' said Mosca.

'Don't get too close, Giaco!' Ida called forward.

'Don't worry, Signora,'

They left the city behind. Soon there was nothing but water and darkness around them. Even though it felt as if they were the only people on the lagoon, they knew they couldn't be. They kept seeing lights appear and disappear in the blackness – green and red navigation lights, just as on Ida's boat.

But even if the Conte had seen their boat, why would he suspect they were following him? After all, he had already paid them.

Prosper looked across the water nervously. He and Bo had

never been out here, although the others had told them a lot about the lagoon and its islands. Little specks of land hemmed with reeds. Here were the ruins of long-abandoned villages and fortresses, and the fruit and vegetable fields that supplied the city. Some were home to the monasteries and hospitals where the city's sick used to be brought.

The silent Giaco deftly steered the boat past the *bricole* – the wooden posts that poked out of the water everywhere. Their sides were painted white to mark the route around the shallows. But they were quite hard to see in the moonlight.

At one point, Mosca whispered: 'That's San Michele!'

They slowly cruised past the walls that surround the island where, for hundreds of years, the Venetians have buried their dead. As soon as he had passed this cemetery island, the Conte set a north-easterly course. They left Murano – the glassmakers' island – behind them and cruised on, deeper into the maze of islands and grassy islets.

Prosper felt as if the boat was going to sail on for ever. He just hoped that Bo would still be asleep when they got back. Bo would kick up a diabolical fuss if he found out that the others were meeting the Conte, and that Hornet had lulled him to sleep with hot milk and a book so they could sneak away.

'Let me have a look, Mosca.' Riccio reached for the binoculars. 'How far is that man going to sail? If we go on like this we'll soon be in Burano, and as stiff as deep-frozen chickens.'

They went on and on through the darkness. They could all feel themselves getting sleepy, despite the cold. Then Mosca suddenly whistled through his teeth. He knelt down to get a better look. 'I think he's heaving to!' he whispered breathlessly. 'There! He's sailing towards that island. I have no idea which one it is. Do you recognize it, Signora?'

Ida Spavento took the glasses and peered through them. Prosper looked over her shoulder. Even without the binoculars he could make out two lanterns on the shore, a high wall, and further back, through a tangle of black branches, the outline of a house.

'*Madonna*, I think I know which island this is!' Ida sounded startled. 'Giaco, don't go any closer! Switch off the engine. And the lights.'

As the engine died down everything was suddenly very still. Prosper felt like an invisible animal lurking in the dark. He heard the water slapping against the hull and Mosca breathing next to him. And there were voices drifting across the water.

'Yes, that's the one!' Ida whispered. 'Isola Segreta, the Secret Isle. There are some really spooky stories about this place. The Valaresso, one of the oldest families of Venice, used to have an estate here, but that was a long time ago. I thought the family had moved away years ago and that the island was deserted. It seems I was wrong.'

'Isola Segreta?' Mosca stared at the distant lights. 'That's the island where nobody ever goes.'

'That's right. It's not easy to find a boatman who will bring you there,' Ida answered, not taking the binoculars from her eyes. 'The island's supposed to be bewitched. Terrible things happen there. So that's where the roundabout of the Merciful Sisters has ended up, is it?'

'Listen!' Riccio whispered.

The baying of dogs sounded across the water. Loud and threatening.

'That sounds like two dogs!' Mosca whispered. 'Big ones.'

'Haven't you seen enough yet, Signora?' Riccio's voice sounded shrill. 'We've followed the Conte all the way to this damned island. That was our deal. So please tell that silent man there to take us home.'

But Ida didn't answer. She was still watching the island through her binoculars. 'They're going ashore,' she said quietly. 'Ah, so that's what your Conte looks like. From what you said I always imagined him to be older. And there next to him,' she lowered her voice even more, 'is the woman Scipio told me about. Who are they? Are there still Valaresso on that island?'

Mosca, Prosper and Scipio were staring at the island just as intently as Ida. Only Riccio was sitting nervously next to the bag with the money. He had fixed his eyes on Giaco's broad back, as if that could reassure him.

'There's a jetty,' Scipio whispered, 'and steps leading up the shore towards a gate in the wall.'

'Who's that on the wall?' Mosca grabbed Prosper's arm. 'I see two white figures.'

'Those are statues,' Ida said soothingly. 'Stone angels. Now they're opening the gate. Wow, those dogs are big.'

Even without binoculars the boys could see them. They were huge white mastiffs, as big as calves. Suddenly, as if they had caught a strange scent, they turned to face the water and began to bark so noisily and angrily that Ida jumped and dropped her binoculars. Prosper tried to grab them, but they slipped through his fingers and landed in the water with a loud splash.

The sound cut through the night like a gunshot.

Riccio pressed his hands against his ears while all the others ducked. Only Giaco remained steadily behind the wheel. 'They've heard us, Signora!' he said calmly. 'They're looking over here.'

'Oh my god! Ida shouted.' Keep your heads down. You too, Giaco! I think she has a gun!'

'Oh no!' Mosca moaned, pulling his jacket over his head.

Riccio had curled up on the floor with the moneybag. 'But we all glow in the dark like moon cheese. I told you this was a stupid idea. I said we should turn around.'

'Riccio, shut up!' Scipio yelled at him.

The mastiffs were barking ever more furiously. A woman's voice could also be heard now, clearly angry – and then a shot. When he saw the flash of the gun, Prosper ducked and pulled Scipio down with him. Riccio began to sob.

'Giaco!' Ida's voice sounded sharp. 'Turn around. Now!'

Without a word, Giaco started the engine.

'But what about the roundabout?' Scipio wanted to get up, but Prosper pulled him down again.

'The roundabout can't bring back the dead!' Ida shouted. 'More speed, Giaco! And you, Thief Lord, keep your head down!'

The engine roared and the water splashed into the boat, as Giaco left the Isola Segreta behind them. Soon it grew smaller and smaller, until it was swallowed by the night.

'That was close!' Ida said while she tried to pull her scarf back over her ears. 'I'm sorry I talked you into this madness. Giaco, why didn't you stop me?'

'Nobody can stop you, Signora!' Giaco answered without even turning around.

'Doesn't matter,' said Mosca. 'At least we've got the money.'

Scipio, however, just stared with a bleak expression at the

foaming path left behind by the boat.

'Come on, just forget about it,' Prosper said, giving him a nudge. 'I would've liked to see the roundabout as well, but it really doesn't matter.'

'It's there!' Scipio looked at him. 'I'm sure it's there.'

'If you say so,' Riccio threw in, 'but why don't we count our money.' Since Prosper and Scipio made no move to help, Mosca and Riccio got to work. They were still counting as the lights of the city began to glitter across the water.

Only when Giaco steered the boat back into the Sacca della Misericordia did they finally zip up the bag. 'Seems to be all there,' said Mosca. 'More or less. All these notes are difficult to count.'

'Good.' Ida sighed. 'Then I'll drop you by your boat. I do hope you have a warm place to sleep. Say "hello" to the little one from me, Prosper – and the girl too. I...' She wanted to say more, but Riccio interrupted her as if he had to say something fast, before it burnt his lips. 'Scipio's going somewhere else. Perhaps you can take him home.'

Prosper hung his head in embarrassment. Mosca played intently with the buckles of the bag and avoided Scipio's eyes.

'Of course.' Ida turned to Scipio. 'The ceasefire is over. Do you want to go back to the Accademia Bridge where I picked you up, Thief Lord?'

Scipio shook his head. 'Fondamenta Bollani,' he said quietly. 'If that's OK.'

We're not together any more, Prosper thought sadly. He tried to recall the anger, the disappointment he had felt when he had first discovered that Scipio had lied to them. But all he could see now was Scipio's pale face, his look of misery and the tight lips – probably holding back the tears.

Ida seemed to sense all this tension. 'Fine! Giaco, first to the boat and then to the Fondamenta Bollani!' she said quickly.

The snow started to fall again as they entered the canal where they had left Mosca's boat. It was a light snow. Tiny snowflakes drifted across the water. Ida got one of them in her eye and started to blink. 'Now the wing's gone,' she said, 'I'll probably be staring at the blank wall above my bed all night. I'll be asking myself whether it has really returned to the lion's back, and who the mysterious Conte and the grey-haired woman really are.' She tightened her coat around herself. 'It's safer to think about these things in a warm bed.'

Mosca's boat was swaying gently in the water right where they had left it. A cat had settled on the wooden bench. She jumped ashore as soon as she heard the motorboat approaching.

'Buonanotte!' Ida said, as Prosper, Riccio and Mosca climbed aboard their own boat. 'Come and visit me sometime. Don't wait until you're all grown up and I don't recognize you any more. And if you ever need any help, let me know. Don't tell me – you're rich now, but you never know.'

'Thanks!' Mosca mumbled. He pushed the bag under his arm. 'That's really nice. Really!'

The two of them were already climbing aboard when Prosper turned to Scipio again. The Thief Lord sat there, his face averted, staring up at the dark houses. 'You can come and pick up your share any time, Scip,' Prosper said.

For a moment, he thought Scipio wouldn't answer. But then he looked up. 'I will,' he said, 'say hello to Bo and Hornet from me.' Then he turned and left.

33 Just a Note

'Brrr, it's freezing!' Riccio whispered when they finally stood in front of the cinema's emergency exit. He groped for the string next to the door, but then he paused, startled. 'Hey, look at that! The door's not locked.' With his foot he carefully pushed it open.

'Maybe Hornet was afraid the bell wouldn't wake her up,' Mosca said.

The other two nodded, but were still uneasy as they felt their way down the dark corridor.

The auditorium was so silent that they could hear Bo's kittens playing around in the dark.

'What's the matter?' Mosca whispered, 'Hornet's forgotten to put out the candles. Remember how she freaked out the last time that happened.'

'She was probably too scared to get up in case Bo woke up – imagine the fuss he would have made.'

Riccio crept up to Hornet's mattress. It was the one farthest to the left, right by the wall. 'They're not here.'

'What do you mean?' Prosper stumbled over to the mat-

216

tress he shared with Bo. Nothing but crumpled blankets and pillows. No Bo.

'They're hiding!' Mosca said. 'Hey, Hornet, Bo!' he called. 'Come out now. We're not in the mood for playing. You can't imagine how cold it is outside. We just want to get into our blankets.'

'That's right!' Riccio shouted. 'But first you can have a look at the piles of money we've brought with us. What do you say?'

There was no answer. Not a giggle or a rustle. Prosper remembered the unlocked door. He felt like someone was slowly squeezing the breath out of him.

Riccio knelt down by Hornet's mattress. 'There's a note.'

Prosper yanked the piece of paper from Riccio's fingers.

Concerned, Mosca leaned over his shoulder. 'What does it say?'

'It's hard to read. She must have been in a real hurry.' Prosper shook his head in despair. The writing swam in front of his eyes.

> *Someone at the door.*
> *Maybe police.*
> *Meet you at the emergency meeting point.*
> *Hornet*

Prosper stared at the note.

'Damn! I knew it. Why didn't you listen to me?' Riccio kicked down the book piles, one by one. 'How could you trust that snoop? He betrayed us.'

Prosper lifted his head. Riccio was right. Only Victor could have given away the Star-Palace. Without another word,

217

Prosper stuffed Hornet's note into his pocket and started rummaging like mad through the pillows.

'What are you looking for?' Mosca asked him. Prosper didn't answer. When he got up again, he had a gun in his hand. The gun he had taken out of Victor's pocket.

'Put that thing away, Prop!' Mosca stepped in his way. 'We don't know for sure whether he ratted on us.'

'Who else could it have been?' Prosper put the gun in his jacket and pushed past Mosca. 'I'm going. He'll definitely tell us whether it was him or not, once he's got his own gun in his face.'

'Easy!' Mosca tried to hold him back. 'First we're going to the meeting point.'

'And where's that?' Prosper was shaking all over. He felt as if his legs were going to give way at any moment.

'It's the Book Man, on the Campo Morosini.'

Prosper nodded. 'Fine, let's go! What are you waiting for?'

'But what are we going to do with the money?' Riccio asked 'And our things. They're no longer safe here.'

'We'll take the money,' Mosca answered impatiently. 'We can get the other stuff later. There's nothing valuable here. And maybe it's all been a false alarm anyway.'

Mosca hid the money they had left from their last deal with Barbarossa under his jacket while Riccio took the Conte's bag. They looked around once more, not sure whether they would ever come back. Then they put out all the candles and left the cinema.

They ran nearly all the way to the Campo Morosini. In the streets the first shops were already opening although the sky was still pitch black. Big barges, bringing food into the city, pushed their way through the canals. The garbage boats collected the previous day's rubbish. The city was waking up, but the boys hardly took any notice. They ran through the dark alleys, imagining a thousand things that could have happened to Bo and Hornet, and the closer they got to the Campo Morosini, the more horrible those images became. They reached the monument, all panting heavily. The statue showed a man with a pile of books behind him, his name was Nicolò Tommaseo, but everyone in the city just called him the Book Man.

Hornet wasn't there. Nor was Bo.

Prosper turned round and started running again. 'Prop!' Mosca called after him while Riccio was still holding his aching side. 'The snoop's place is miles away. Are you going to run the whole way?'

But Prosper didn't even look back.

'Come on!' Mosca dragged the still panting Riccio with him. 'We've got to keep up, before he does anything stupid.'

34 Father and Son

Scipio had asked Ida to drop him off about two bridges before his father's house. He wanted to walk the last few steps along the snowy bank of the canal. The cold air gave him the feeling of being strong and free – as long as he didn't think of the others, or of the big house that would soon make him feel small and feeble again. Scipio scraped patterns into the snow with his heels. Then he crouched down to draw a wing with his fingers. When he lifted his head he saw the police boat. It was moored just a few steps away from his parents' house.

Scipio stood up. Thoughts raced around in his head. Did this have something to do with the Conte?

'No!' he whispered, trying to calm himself. He could hardly manage to get the key into the lock. Opening the door as quietly as possible he saw a light was burning between the columns as usual. The courtyard lay empty in front of him. Holding his breath, Scipio crept towards the stairs. He was a master creeper. This time, however, his efforts were in vain.

His foot had barely touched the first stair, when he suddenly heard voices from above. He lifted his head guiltily – and stopped dead. Two policemen were coming down the stairs, with Hornet. She looked small and helpless between the two huge officers.

His father was standing upstairs by the balustrade. He frowned as his eyes fell on Scipio.

'Gentlemen!' boomed the voice Scipio loved to imitate because it sounded so much more impressive than his own. 'As you can see, the matter seems to have resolved itself. My son has decided to come home after all, even if it is at a highly inappropriate time. But it proves he had nothing to do with those children hiding in the Stella.'

Scipio bit his lip and looked up at Hornet. She slowed down as she noticed him.

'Do you know this boy?' one of the policemen asked. He had an unfriendly narrow black moustache. 'Go on, speak.' But Hornet just shook her head.

'Where are you taking her?' Scipio was startled by the sound of his own voice, high and shrill.

The policeman with the moustache laughed while the other one grabbed Hornet's arm. 'So, you think you have to protect her? You're a little gentleman! Don't worry, we didn't take her away from anybody. She's a naughty girl who doesn't even want to tell us her name. We came here because we thought your father might learn something from her about your disappearance.'

'Our maid called me away from my reception, completely hysterical, Scipio!' Dottor Massimo called down at him. 'Because she didn't find you in your bed at midnight. And just as I got here the police called to tell me that they had found a gang of street kids in the Stella. You know, the cinema I had to close down? Of course, I immediately explained to the gentlemen here that your disappearance had nothing to do with this. And what childish fancy drove you out of the house in the middle of the night? Were you running after some stray cat again?'

Scipio didn't answer. He desperately tried not to look up at Hornet. She looked so sad and lost. This was not the Hornet who had driven him mad with her teasing.

'I just wanted to have a look at the snow,' Scipio finally muttered.

'Ah, the snow! It drives everybody mad, not just the children,' the moustachioed policeman said with a wink at Scipio. His colleague was already dragging Hornet down the stairs.

'Let me go, I can walk by myself!' Hornet spat at him. She jumped down the last step and pushed past Scipio with her head down. 'Bo is with his aunt!' she whispered.

'Hey, what's the hurry?' the policeman barked, grabbing her by the scruff of her collar.

'*Buonanotte, Dottor Massimo!*' the *Carabinieri* called out as they left. Hornet didn't turn around again.

Scipio slowly walked up the stairs. He heard the entrance door slam shut.

His father looked at him in silence.

Who had given away the secret of the Star-Palace? What about Prosper, Riccio and Mosca? Why was Bo with his aunt? Scipio's mind was racing.

'So, where did you really go?' His father scrutinized him from head to toe. Scipio was afraid his father could read his mind. He was probably asking himself yet again what he had done to deserve this strange creature he called his son. He wasn't as big as him, as interesting, as disciplined, controlled, dependable or reasonable. He wasn't like him at all.

'I told you,' Scipio answered. 'I just wanted to look at the snow. And I ran after a cat. Mine is luckily feeling better;

she's eating again.'

'Just as well I didn't call the vet.' Dottor Massimo frowned. 'Of course, all this running around in the middle of the night will have consequences.' His voice was calm. He never raised his voice, even when he was angry. 'The maid is going to lock your door in future. At least, as long as that silly snow is causing you to behave even more childishly than usual. Is that understood?'

Scipio didn't reply.

'God, how I hate that stubborn face! If you only knew how stupid you look.' Scipio's father turned abruptly. 'I have to do something about that cinema,' he said, walking away. 'Abandoned children, probably all little thieves. At least the police seem to think so. Why didn't that journalist tell me anything about it? Getz was his name, or something.'

'The girl looked quite nice. And if the children don't have a home, why shouldn't they live in your cinema? It's empty anyway,' said Scipio.

'My word, children sometimes say the oddest things. So it's empty. Do you think that's reason enough to let all the tramps in the city squat there?'

'But what's going to happen to them now?' Scipio felt himself getting hot. Then cold. Terribly cold. 'You saw the girl. Can't you take pity on her?'

'No.' His father looked surprised. 'What's that girl to you? You usually only show that much concern for cats. Are you sure you don't know her?'

'No.' Scipio heard his voice getting louder. He couldn't help himself. 'For god's sake, no!' he shouted. 'Do I have to know her to feel sorry for her? Can't you just help her? I thought you were such an important man in this city.'

'Go to bed, Scipio,' his father answered, yawning behind his hand. 'My lord, what a completely ruined evening.'

'P-please!' Scipio stammered. Tears welled up in his eyes, no matter how hard he tried to wipe them away. 'Please, Father, don't you know somebody who would take in a girl like that? She hasn't done anything wrong. She's just all alone.'

'Go to bed, Scipio,' his father cut him off. 'I think you looked at the moon too much out there. Soon you're going to start living by your horoscope, just like your mother.'

'It's got nothing to do with the moon!' Scipio was screaming now. 'You have no idea!'

But his father was already closing the bedroom door behind him.

And so Scipio stood there and cried.

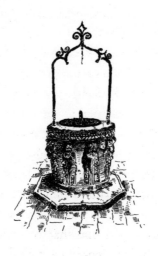

35 Visitors for Victor

A terrible night lay behind Victor. The man he'd been following had gone from one bar to another until two o'clock in the morning. When he vanished into a house Victor had to stand around outside until dawn, the snow falling on him relentlessly. Victor felt as if he was made of ice from the knees downwards, nothing but solid ice.

'I'll have a bath first,' he mumbled as he crossed the bridge close to his house. 'With water hot enough to boil an egg.'

Yawning, he searched his coat pocket for his keys. Perhaps he should find another job. The waiters in the cafés on St Mark's Square had to run around just as much, but at least they were home by midnight at the latest. And what about museum guides – why couldn't he be a museum guide? They went home even earlier. He was so sleepy that it was only as they were about to leap at him that he noticed the three small figures crouched by the entrance to his flat. They looked scared, but then one of them poked a gun in his face. It was his gun.

225

'Hey, what are you doing?' he tried a soothing voice, while the three of them dragged him over to the door.

'Open up, Victor!' Prosper hissed without moving the gun. But Victor just pushed the barrel out of his face and fished the keys out of his pocket.

'Would you be so kind as to explain to me what this fuss is all about?' he grumbled as he unlocked the door. 'If this is some new game then I have to tell you that I'm a bit too old to find it amusing.'

'Bo and Hornet have disappeared,' Mosca said breathlessly. 'And Prosper thinks you told the police about our hideout. Riccio thinks so too.'

'Either the police, or my aunt,' Prosper added. His face was deathly pale, but his eyes seemed to plead with Victor to tell him that it wasn't true.

'Have you forgotten? I gave you my word!' Victor quickly wrangled the gun from Prosper's icy hand. 'Can't you trust anyone any more? Now come inside, before we become a tourist attraction.'

They all trundled after him up the stairs.

'I always knew it wasn't you,' Mosca said as Victor ushered them into his flat. 'But Prosper...'

'Prosper can't think clearly at the moment,' Victor completed the sentence. 'That's quite understandable if his brother really has disappeared. But tell me: how could that happen? Were they on their own?'

They sat down in the tiny kitchen. Victor brewed some coffee and gave the boys some olives while they told him what had happened since he had freed himself from their toilet prison.

Once they had finished telling him their story, Victor said:

'You're lucky I already know you lot. Otherwise I wouldn't have believed a single word you've just told me. You break into someone's house and then make a deal with the owner. With her approval you sell the loot and then you go for a cruise on the lagoon to find a mysterious merry-go-round. I'd love to have a word with that crazy Signora Spavento. To take a bunch of kids to the Isola Segreta. I mean, really!'

'How could we have known that the Conte lived on *that* island of all places,' Mosca murmured meekly.

'Doesn't matter!' Victor frowned and rubbed his tired eyes. 'What's in that bag? Your reward?'

Mosca nodded.

'Show him the money,' Prosper said to him. 'He won't steal it.'

Mosca hesitated, but then he put the bag on Victor's kitchen table. When he opened it, Victor whistled quietly through his teeth. 'And you've just run half-way across the city with that?' he muttered. He took one of the wads. 'You've got some nerve!'

He pulled out a banknote, inspected it closely, then held it in front of the kitchen light. 'Hold on!' he said. 'Someone's taken you for a ride. This money's not real.'

The boys were dumbfounded. 'Fake money?' Riccio yanked the note from Victor's hand and looked at it. 'I can't see anything. Looks real to me.'

'Well, it isn't,' Victor answered. He reached into the bag and took another wad from it. 'It's all counterfeit,' he assert-ed. 'And it's not even a good forgery. Looks like someone made them with a colour-copier. I'm sorry.' He threw the money back and sighed. The boys looked shocked.

'All for nothing,' Riccio muttered. 'The break-in, the trip

across the lagoon. We nearly got shot, and for what? A pile of counterfeit money. Damn it!' He swiped the bag off the table. The wads of cash scattered all over Victor's kitchen floor.

'And now Hornet and Bo are gone as well!' Mosca buried his face in his hands.

'Exactly!' Victor gathered the money from the floor and stuffed it back into the bag. 'And that's what we should be working on right now. Where are Bo and the girl?' He got up with a deep sigh and walked across into his office. The three boys, pale as ghosts, followed him.

'The answer machine is blinking,' Mosca observed as they all stood in front of the desk.

'One day I'll throw that machine off the balcony,' Victor complained. He pressed *play*.

Prosper immediately recognized the voice. He would have known Esther's voice even if he had heard her announcing train times at Venice's main station.

'Signor Getz, this is Esther Hartlieb. Your case has resolved itself today. We finally managed to find our nephew with the help of an old lady who had seen our poster. Apparently Bo had been hiding for weeks in some dilapidated cinema, together with some girl who didn't want to give us her name. The police are taking care of her. As far as Bo is concerned, he is rather confused and quite thin. He hasn't said anything about his brother's whereabouts yet. Who knows, perhaps he's just as angry with him as I am. We can talk about your fee in the next few days. We'll be in the Sandwirth until the beginning of next week. Please call before you come. Goodbye.'

Prosper stood completely still, as if he had just been turned to stone. Victor didn't know what to say. He would have liked to say something to cheer the boy up. But he couldn't think of anything.

'What old lady?' Riccio asked with a small voice. 'Damn it! Who could that be?'

'Since yesterday, Prosper's aunt has been distributing posters all over Venice,' Victor explained, 'with a picture of Prosper and Bo.' He chose not to tell them who had taken that photograph. 'There was also something on it about a generous reward. Haven't you seen them?'

The boys shook their heads.

'Well, that old lady obviously did,' Victor concluded. 'Maybe she lives near the cinema. She could have seen you sneaking in and out of there. Perhaps she even thought she was doing a good deed when she called the poor boy's aunt.'

Prosper still hadn't moved. He was looking out at Victor's balcony. It had grown quite light by now, but the sky was grey and cloudy. 'Esther is never going to let go of Bo,' he whispered. 'Never.' He gave Victor a look of utter desperation. 'Where is the Sandwirth?'

Victor wasn't sure he should tell him, but Mosca made that decision for him. 'On the Riva degli Schiavoni,' he answered, 'but what do you want there? You'd better come back to the hideout with us. We have to get our stuff before the police turn up again. Perhaps in the meantime Victor can find out where the police have taken Hornet.' He looked enquiringly at Victor.

The detective nodded. 'Sure. A few phone calls will do it. Just give me her real name.'

Riccio looked stunned. 'We don't know it.'

'There's a name written in some of her books,' Prosper said

229

tonelessly. 'Caterina Grimani. But that won't do any good. They probably took her to some home, and you'll never get her out of there again. Just like Bo.'

'Prosper,' Victor got up and went over to him, 'come on, it's not the end of the world.'

'It is.' Prosper opened the door. 'I need to be alone right now.'

'Wait!' said Riccio desperately. 'We could take our stuff to Ida Spavento for the time being. She told us she would help, remember? Well, she's probably not expecting us to turn up quite so soon, but we could at least give it a try.'

'You try,' said Prosper. 'I don't care anymore.' Then he pulled the door closed behind him.

36 The Refuge

Riccio rang the bell and the housekeeper opened the door. His spiky head was hidden behind the huge box he was carrying.

'Don't I know you?' the lady grumbled suspiciously, pushing up her spectacles.

'Right!' Riccio gave her his broadest grin. 'But this time I'm not here to see you, but Ida Spavento.'

'Is that so?' The housekeeper crossed her arms in front of her enormous bosom. 'That's Signora Spavento to you, you rascal. And may I ask what you want from her?'

'This should be interesting,' smiled Victor, who was standing behind Riccio with an even bigger box. All the children's belongings had fitted into just three cardboard cartons. Mosca was carrying the third. The two kittens poked their heads out of Victor's coat pockets.

'Tell her that Riccio and Mosca are here. She'll know who we are.' Riccio said.

'Riccio and Mosca? That's only two.' The big lady scrutinized Victor. 'And is he your father?'

'...their uncle,' Victor answered. 'Could you please call

Signora Spavento, before this box falls on my feet? It's really quite heavy.'

The housekeeper gave him such a stern look that Victor immediately felt like a little boy. But in the end, off she went. When she returned she opened the door wordlessly and waved the three of them inside.

Victor was curious about Ida Spavento. 'She's a bit weird,' Riccio had told him, 'and she smokes like a chimney. But she's quite nice really.'

Victor wasn't too sure about that. Going out on the lagoon with three children in the middle of the night to follow a mysterious man who had sent those little thieves into her house in the first place – no, that didn't really sound nice to Victor. Crazy, maybe. But nice? No.

But when he saw Ida kneeling on her living room carpet, wearing a jumper that was far too large for her, he liked her. However much he wanted not to.

Ida was leaning over a line-up of photographs. She was pushing them around, swapping them, and sorting some of them out. 'Well, isn't this a nice surprise!' she said as Victor and the boys entered. 'I didn't expect a visit from you lot quite so soon. What's in those boxes, and where did you suddenly get an uncle from?' She pushed the photographs together and got up.

Oh dear, Victor thought, she's wearing gondola-earrings.

'We're in a lot of trouble, Ida,' said Mosca. He put down his carton. Sighing, Riccio did the same.

'Are the fat lady's dogs here?' Riccio asked. 'Because Victor has got some kittens in his coat.'

'You mean Lucia's dogs? No, we locked them out in the garden because they ate my chocolates.' Ida frowned as she looked at the boys. 'What kind of trouble? What's happened?'

'Someone told the police about our hideout!' Mosca answered. 'And the *Carabinieri* have taken Hornet and Bo, Prosper is desperate, because...'

'Hold on.' Ida put her photos on a little table. 'I'm still not quite with it this morning. Let me see if I've got this right: you had a hideout, and the police have found it. Were they searching for you? I mean, because of the thefts?'

'No!' Mosca cried. 'Because of Bo. His aunt's looking for him. But Bo wants to stay with Prosper. So they both ran away. And we took them in. And it was all OK until last night, but now someone has given our hideout away and Victor has found out that Bo has been taken by his aunt and the police have taken Hornet to the home of the Merciful Sisters and...'

'... *and* the Conte gave us fake money,' Riccio reached into his jacket and held up a wad of cash. 'It's all fake.'

Ida sank into the second best chair. 'Oh, my lord!' she muttered.

Victor couldn't hold back any longer. 'These children were in enough trouble already, Signora Spavento,' he said firmly, 'and you've made it even worse! You had to drag them into this hare-brained adventure of yours. A night-time trip to the Isola Segreta...'

'Victor, shut up', Mosca interrupted.

Ida had turned bright red under her dyed blonde hair. 'You told your uncle everything?' she asked fiercely. 'I thought we were friends...'

'He's not our uncle!' Riccio burst out. 'Victor's a detective. He wanted to come with us. And he helped us get our things. And he's found out that the *Carabinieri* have taken Hornet to the Merciful Sisters.'

'Hornet. That's the girl who was here with you, right?' Ida fiddled with her earrings. 'You know, I didn't quite understand that thing about Bo and the aunt. Maybe you'll have to explain it to me again when I'm a bit more awake. But as for Hornet – we should be able to do something about that.'

Ida got up and fished one of the kittens out of Victor's coat pocket. She carefully placed it on her shoulder and turned to Victor again.

'Fine. What shall we do?' She looked as if she expected an answer from him.

Confused, Victor returned her gaze. 'What? Us?' he stammered. '*We* can't do anything. Although we could perhaps stop Prosper from jumping into the lagoon. It's just not good enough leaving a bunch of children to look after themselves.'

'Putting them in an orphanage doesn't usually do them a lot of good either!' Ida frowned impatiently. 'These children need help. Or do you think this whole mess is going to clear up by itself, Signor…?'

'It's Victor,' said Riccio. 'You may also call him Signor Getz.'

Victor gave him an irritated look.

'I should have kept you all here when you turned up in the middle of the night!' Ida said. 'But I thought you were doing fine by yourselves. What nonsense! I just like to believe in fairy tales. I'll make it up to you. Lucia will give you something to eat and then you can take your things upstairs. I have a spare room in the attic. Now, what are we going to do about Prosper and the little one? Can't we do something?'

'We definitely can't get to Bo,' Victor answered sadly, 'his aunt has got custody. But we should keep an eye on his brother. He did look rather desperate the last time we saw him. Riccio, do you think you could find Prosper, even if he's not at the Hotel Sandwirth?'

Riccio nodded. 'I'll find him,' he said. 'And then I'll bring him here.'

'Fine.' Ida nodded. 'That sounds better already. Mosca,' she turned to him, 'I don't know what your quarrel with Scipio is about, but I think you should call him and tell him what happened last night. Let him know that you're here now. Can you do that?'

Mosca nodded, unenthusiastically. 'D'you think I should tell him about the fake money as well?' he asked.

Ida shrugged. 'He'll have to find out some time, right? And now to us', she stubbed her finger against Victor's chest, 'how about us two getting moving and trying to get that girl out of the orphanage, Victor or Signor Getz, which do you prefer?'

'Victor's fine,' he grumbled. 'But what makes you think it's going to be that easy?'

Ida put the kitten on the floor and gave him a wry smile. 'Well, I do have a few connections,' she said, 'but you don't have to come along if you don't want to. It's just that on occasions like this two adults tend to look a bit more impressive.'

Victor looked shiftily at his shoes. 'I had some trouble with the Merciful Sisters once,' he mumbled. 'I was looking for a burglar who liked to dress up as a nun and, unfortunately, I caught a real one instead. We've never been on good terms since then.'

Mosca and Riccio nudged each other, grinning. Ida, however, just gave Victor a long old-fashioned look.

'We could disguise ourselves,' she suggested. 'I have a wardrobe with some props I sometimes use for my photographs. There are also some suits in there. A couple of them are even from the nineteenth century – old enough for you?'

'I'd prefer the twenty-first,' Victor grinned.

Ida smiled. 'I even have some false beards!' she said. 'A whole collection.'

'Really?' Victor looked at Riccio. 'Mine were stolen recently, but luckily I recovered them today.'

Riccio blushed and turned to the window.

Victor followed Ida to a small room on the ground floor that contained nothing but two enormous walk-in wardrobes. While he chose a suit, he thought to himself: quite astounding that she should also have a collection of false beards.

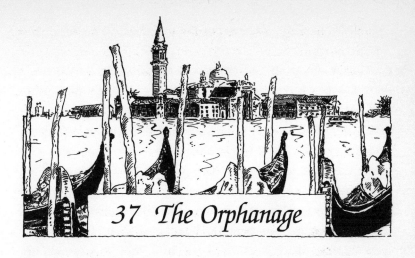

37 The Orphanage

Hornet was sitting on her allotted bed. She looked at the bare white walls that surrounded her. For the hundredth time, she closed her eyes so she could see another room in her mind's eye, one with a curtain full of stars, and a mattress surrounded by books that whispered their stories to her at night. She recalled the voices: Mosca's, Riccio's – always a bit excited, Scipio's, Prosper's – and Bo's voice, the only one higher than hers. Hornet felt the cold white sheets and imagined that she was holding Bo's little round hand, so warm...

It probably wasn't colder in the orphanage than it had been in the cinema, it was warmer more likely, but Hornet felt chilled to her bones. And to her heart. Was Bo better off with his aunt? And what about the others?

Hornet felt her stomach grumble. She hadn't eaten anything since the police had brought her here. Neither the breakfast the sisters had brought her, nor the lunch. Lunch was quite early here. The other children were still down in the dining hall. The smell of food wafted right up to the bedrooms. How much better it had smelled when Mosca made spaghetti, even if he always put too much salt in the water and let the sauce burn.

Hornet stood up and crossed to the window, so she could look down into the courtyard. A couple of pigeons were pecking between the stones. They could fly away any time, just like that. Then Hornet saw two adults walk through the gate: a woman with a black hat and a bearded man. The sister with the loud voice was leading them towards the main building. Had they come here to adopt a child? They probably wanted a small one, a baby if possible. The little ones had a good chance of finding new parents. The others would have to wait, year by year, days, weeks, months, until they were grown up. It took so long to grow up.

Hornet pressed her cheek against the cold glass. Although the sisters had kept asking her, she hadn't told them her real name. She definitely didn't want to stay here, but she also didn't want to go home. If, like Riccio, you didn't have parents, it was easy to imagine how wonderful they might have been. But what if you had parents and they weren't wonderful at all? No, she wouldn't tell them her name. Ever.

The door opened. The sister with the loud voice poked her head into the room. 'Caterina?'

Hornet jumped. How did she know her name?

'Ah, so that really seems to be your name. Fine, come with me. There's someone who wants to see you!'

'Who is it?' Hornet asked. She wasn't sure whether she should be happy or afraid.

'Why didn't you tell us who your godmother is?' the sister scolded as she walked Hornet down the bare corridor. 'Such a famous lady. You probably don't know how much she has done for the orphanage.'

Famous? Godmother? Hornet was now completely confused. She had a godmother? The sister seemed to be very excited. She kept fiddling with her glasses – they had thick lenses that made her eyes look enormous.

'Come on now, Caterina!' The sister impatiently pulled Hornet along. 'How much longer do you want to make her wait?'

Hornet wanted to shout out: Who? What's going on? But she swallowed the words as soon as she saw Ida. She almost didn't recognise her at all in that hat. And who was the man next to her?

'It seems that you were right, Signora Spavento!' the sister boomed loudly. 'The name of our anonymous girl really is Caterina. So this is your goddaughter?'

Hornet suddenly felt as light as air. She wanted to run to Ida and hug her, hide underneath her wide coat and never come out. But she was afraid to spoil it, and so she just smiled shyly and walked hesitantly towards Ida and her strange companion.

'Yes, that's her. *Cara!* Sweetheart!' Ida spread her arms and held her so tightly that Hornet felt all the warmth return to her heart.

'Hello Hornet,' the strange man at Ida's side whispered. Hornet looked up into his face with surprise – and now she recognized him too: Victor, the snoop, with a new beard! Bo's friend Victor. Her friend now, too.

'This is my lawyer, *cara*,' Ida explained after she had let go of Hornet.

Hornet mumbled '*Buongiorno*' and smiled at Victor.

'Why do you always take your parents' little quarrels so

seriously, *cara?*' Ida asked. She sighed deeply, as if she had already had to talk to Hornet too often about her silly parents. 'She's run away three times already because of their little tiffs,' she explained to the nun, who was looking at Hornet with deep sympathy. 'Her mother, who is my cousin, will get divorced soon, and until then I will take the girl in. Otherwise she'll probably run away again, and who knows where the police might find her then. Last time, they found her hiding somewhere in Burano. Imagine!'

Hornet was in seventh heaven as she listened to these lies. All the time she held on to Ida's hand as if she would never let it go. Ida's story sounded so true that, for a moment, Hornet herself almost believed in these quarelling parents.

The sister with the loud voice had tears in her eyes.

'Can I take Caterina with me right away?' Ida asked, as if it was the most natural question in the world.

'But of course, Signora Spavento,' the sister answered. 'We are so happy we could, for once, be of service to you. After all your generous donations. And the photographs you took of the children – I tell you they all treasure them.'

'Don't mention it.' Ida avoided Hornet's curious looks. 'Please give my regards to Sister Angela and Sister Lucia and also the Mother Superior. Just send any papers that need signing.'

'Of course!' the sister hurried to the door and held it for Ida. 'Have a nice day, Mr Lawyer.'

'Thank you,' said Victor, trying to look dignified.

Hornet's heart was beating wildly as they crossed the courtyard. Countless windows looked down at the pavement. Grey windows, empty except for a few Christmas stars stuck to the panes on the ground floor.

'So many windows,' Victor muttered sadly. 'So many windows, and so many children.'

'Yes, and nobody to take them in their arms and be grateful for them every day,' said Ida. 'What a waste.'

'*Arrivederci*, Signora Spavento – until next time!' called the sister who had run out of the porter's lodge to open the gate for them.

'Heavens!' Victor grunted, as they passed through the gate. 'They treat you like a saint!'

Hornet tore herself away from him. Suddenly, she was in a great hurry. She ran to the nearest canal, spat into the water, looked at the boats cruising on the Grand Canal, and took a deep breath. For a moment she just stood there, her lungs filled with the fresh, damp air.

Then she breathed out slowly, very slowly, and all the fear and the desperation that had crept into her since the police had brought her to the orphanage left her. But then she remembered Bo.

She turned around and looked at Victor and Ida. 'What about Bo?' she asked. 'And what about the others?'

Victor tugged the false beard from his chin. 'Mosca and Riccio are at Ida's,' he said. 'But Bo is still with his aunt.'

Hornet hung her head and kicked a cigarette butt angrily into the canal. 'And Prosper?' she asked.

'Riccio is looking for him,' Victor answered. 'Don't look so worried. He'll find him.'

38 Prosper

Riccio found Prosper in front of the Hotel Sandwirth. He was standing on the promenade as if frozen solid, oblivious to the crowds passing him by. There was always quite a crush on the Riva degli Schiavoni, even on a biting-cold day like this, since this was where some of the city's best hotels were to be found. Hundreds of boats called at the moorings along the canal and there were constant comings and goings. Prosper heard the wind pushing the boats against the piers, he heard the dull thud as they bumped against the wood. He was aware, somewhere, of people laughing and talking in many languages. But he just stood there, his collar turned up against the chill, and looked up at the windows of the Sandwirth. When Riccio put his hand on his shoulder, Prosper spun round.

'Hey, Prop, there you are!' Riccio said greatly relieved. 'I've been looking for you all day. I came here a few times, but I didn't see you.'

'I'm sorry,' Prosper apologised. He turned around again. 'I followed them the whole day, without being seen. I think Bo nearly spotted me a few times, but I quickly ducked out of the way. I was afraid he'd flip if he saw me. Prosper pushed the hair from his forehead. 'I followed them everywhere. They bought clothes for Bo. Esther even wanted to put a bow tie on him, but he chucked it into the next bin when they weren't looking. You probably wouldn't recognize him any more. He looks completely different now he's not in those huge jumpers Scipio used to bring back. They even insisted on taking him to a hairdresser's. There's not a trace of black left now. And then they took him from one café to another, but he never touched anything they ordered for him. He just kept staring past them. I think he saw me once through a window because he tried to run away. But my uncle quickly caught him again like a naughty puppy.

'They're in there now,' Prosper said, pointing up at the brightly lit windows. 'I even went and asked the porter which room Esther is in, but he just told me the Hartliebs won't see anybody.'

For a few moments the two boys just stood next to each other, gazing up at the windows. They were beautiful windows, glowing behind shimmering curtains. Which one was Bo behind?

'Come on!' Riccio said finally. He caught sight of a man swinging his camera around rather carelessly. 'You can't stand here all night. Don't you want to know where we're staying now? Ida took us in without batting an eyelid! We've even got our own room, in the attic. We couldn't take our old mattresses, but Ida had two old beds and so we've pushed them together for now. It's a bit cramped, but it's definitely better than sleeping outside. It's great! Come on, dinner will be ready soon. I tell you, that housekeeper can cook!' He took hold of Prosper's arm, but Prosper just shook his head.

'No!' he said, breaking free. 'I'm staying here.'

Riccio looked up at the sky and sighed with frustration. 'Prop!' he said pleadingly. 'What do you think the porter will do when he finds you skulking around here in the middle of the night? He'll call the *Carabinieri*. And what are you going to tell them? That your aunt has kidnapped your brother?'

Prosper ignored him. 'Go away, Riccio,' he said without taking his eyes off the windows. 'It's all over. We haven't got a hideout, Hornet's gone, and Bo is with Esther.'

'Hornet hasn't gone!' Riccio called out so loud that people turned their heads. He quickly lowered his voice again. 'She hasn't gone!' he whispered. 'Ida and the snoop got her out of the orphanage!'

'Ida and Victor?' Prosper looked at him in wonder.

'Yes, and they had a real laugh doing it! You should have seen them when they left, they had their arms linked like an old couple.' Riccio chuckled. 'The snoop's been behaving like a real gentleman. He opens doors for Ida and helps her into her coat. Only he won't light her cigarettes and keeps moaning about her smoking so much.'

'But how did they do it?'

To his satisfaction, Riccio noticed that Prosper had obviously forgotten about the hotel for a moment. 'Hornet was taken to the orphanage of the Merciful Sisters. Apparently that's where Ida was brought up,' he explained quietly. 'Anyway, she now gives them money every now and then. She collects toys, that sort of stuff as well ... Victor said the nuns treated her like the Madonna herself. They believed *everything* she said!'

'That's great news.' Prosper turned his attention back to the windows. 'Say hello to Hornet for me. Is she OK?'

'No, she isn't!' Riccio planted himself in front of Prosper so he would have to look at him. 'She's worried about you.

And about Bo, although *he's* probably not thinking about jumping into the lagoon like you!'

'She thinks I'm going to do that?' Prosper angrily pushed Riccio away. 'That's stupid. I hate water.'

'That's fine then! But could you tell her that yourself?' Riccio held out his hands imploringly. 'I just saw her for a couple of minutes when I went back to get something to eat. But she would hardly let me touch my food.' He altered his voice. *'Get out there, Riccio!'* he twittered, imitating Hornet. *'You've had enough to eat, Riccio! Go and find Prosper! Please! He might have thrown himself into some canal!* She even wanted to come with me, but Ida said she'd better stay in the house for a while, so she doesn't end up in the orphanage again. That was fine by me. Her nagging would have driven me crazy. And I knew you'd turn up here sooner or later.'

Riccio could make out a smile on Prosper's face, just a tiny one, but it was definitely there. 'Anyway,' he said, 'I've talked enough now. You can come back here tomorrow morning, but right now you're coming with me.'

Prosper didn't reply, but let himself be hustled along by Riccio, past the souvenir stands that lined the Riva degli Schiavoni. Most of the hawkers were already closing down their stalls, but you could still buy a few things at some of them: the plastic fans Bo liked so much – with black lace and the Rialto bridge printed on them, golden gondolas, coral necklaces, city guides, dried sea-horses.

Prosper followed Riccio through the crowd, but kept looking back towards the Sandwirth.

'Come on! If Ida and Victor managed to get Hornet back,' he said, 'then they'll work something out for getting Bo back too. You'll see.'

'They're flying home next week,' said Prosper. 'What can anyone do then?'

'That's plenty of time,' Riccio answered. He turned his collar up. He was shivering. 'And anyway, Bo's not in prison, or in the orphanage. Man, that's the Sandwirth. It's a really posh hotel.'

Prosper just nodded. He felt so empty. As empty as the big mussel-shells lying in those large baskets in front of the market.

Riccio stopped. 'Hang on, Prop.'

The sky above the lagoon had turned red. It was growing dark, although it was only four o'clock. A few tourists stood in wonder by the quay and saw how the setting sun glazed the dirty water with gold.

'What an opportunity,' Riccio whispered to Prosper. 'They wouldn't even notice if I stole their shoes. I only need a few seconds. You can check out the mussels until I get back.'

He turned around, already wearing his 'I am just a skinny boy who couldn't hurt a fly' expression. But Prosper grabbed him by the collar.

'Leave it, Riccio,' he said angrily, 'or do you think Ida Spavento will let you sleep in her house once the *Carabinieri* have caught you?'

'You don't understand!' Riccio pretending to be outraged, tried to free himself from Prosper's grip. 'I just don't want to get out of practice.'

But Prosper wouldn't let go, and so Riccio gave a shrug before walking on. The tourists continued to be enchanted by the sunset, without having to pay for it with their wallets.

39 All Lost

That evening Ida threw a party. Lucia, the housekeeper, had cooked, fried and baked all afternoon. She had whipped cream, scooped tiny cakes from the baking tin, made ravioli and stirred sauces. Different smells kept luring Victor into the kitchen, but every time he tried to sneak a taste he got his fingers rapped with a wooden spoon. Hornet and Prosper laid the table together in the dining room while Mosca and Riccio chased each other from one floor to the other, always followed by Lucia's yapping dogs.

The two of them were so happy and boisterous that they didn't even seem to mind any more that the Conte had duped them. When Victor asked them what they intended to do with all those wads of fake cash, Riccio said, quite openly: 'We can still spend it.' Victor told them off soundly and demanded that Riccio hand over the bag right away. But Riccio, grinning broadly, just shook his head and declared that he and Mosca had hidden it. In a safe place, he'd said. Not even Prosper and Hornet knew about it – not that they seemed to care particularly.

So Victor decided he'd better forget about the fake money

too. He sat down on Ida's sofa and started munching chocolates, telling himself he ought to go home. But each time he
got up with a big sigh to say goodbye, Ida had brought him
a glass of *grappa*, or a *caffè*, or asked him to put the tooth-
picks on the table. So Victor stayed.

While the sky outside darkened, Ida made her house glow
as brightly as a thousand stars. She lit countless candles and
the crystal shimmered so beautifully that Hornet could hardly
take her eyes off it.

'Pinch me!' she said to Prosper. 'This can't be real.'

Prosper obeyed. He very gently pinched her arm.

'It's real!' Hornet cried, laughing and dancing around him.

But not even her happiness could chase the sadness from
Prosper's face. They had all tried in their own way: Riccio
with his jokes, Mosca by showing Prosper all the strange
things hidden behind the dark doors in Ida's house. Nothing
helped. Not even Ida's sweets nor Victor's reassurances that
he would think of something to help Bo. Because if Bo wasn't
there, Prosper missed him like a lost arm or leg. He felt sorry
for spoiling the others' fun with his gloomy face. He began to
notice that Riccio had started to avoid him and even Mosca
busied himself with something or other whenever Prosper
moped by. But Hornet stuck by him, even though whenever
she tried to put her arm around him consolingly, he pushed
her away and adjusted the forks on the table, or sat in front
of a window and stared outside.

At dinner Mosca and Riccio messed around so much that
Victor grumbled that it would have been quieter with a bunch
of monkeys at the table. But Prosper never said a word.

After dinner, while the others played cards with Ida and
Victor, Prosper went upstairs. Ida had found a couple of air

mattresses so that they wouldn't be too crowded on the two beds, that Riccio had already pushed together. Hornet had put one of them by the wall and piled her books around it. Riccio and Mosca hadn't dared to leave even a single one of her precious stories behind in the cinema. Prosper dragged the second air mattress to the window so he could see Ida's garden and the canal behind it. The blankets from Lucia's linen cupboard smelled of lavender. Prosper curled up in them, but he couldn't fall asleep.

In fact, he was still awake when the others crept under their blankets. It was eleven o'clock when Victor finally said goodbye, swaying gently, driven home by his guilty conscience to his hungry tortoises. Prosper pretended to be asleep. He lay with his face to the wall and waited for his friends to doze off.

As soon as Riccio was giggling in his sleep, Mosca snoring beneath his blanket and Hornet finally sleeping with a happy smile between her books, Prosper got up. The well-worn floorboards creaked beneath his feet, but that didn't wake any of the others. They had never before felt as safe as this, secure in Ida's house.

Lucia had kept the door to the garden firmly bolted ever since Ida had told her how the children had crept into the house that night. The door squeaked gently as Prosper opened it. He stepped into the dark garden. There was a coating of white frost over everything.

At the point where Ida's garden bordered the canal there was a gate in the wall, just a few inches above the waterline. As he unlatched it, Prosper heard the canal water slosh against the base of the wall. Ida's boat swayed, tightly moored, between two painted wooden posts. Prosper carefully climbed into the boat, sat down on the cold wooden bench, and looked up at the moon.

What shall I do? he thought. Tell me, what shall I do?

But the moon did not answer.

In her stories about Venice, Prosper's mother had always talked about the moon – how it could make dreams come true. They called the moon *la bella luna* here, as if she was a beautiful lady. But ask as he might, Prosper knew that she wasn't going to help him get his brother back.

Prosper sat in Ida's boat and let the tears run down his face. He had believed that this was his city – his and Bo's. He used to believe that if they came here – the most beautiful city in the world – then they would be safe from Esther.

Esther despised Venice. She was an intruder. Why didn't the pigeons poo all over her? Why didn't the marble dragons bite her in the neck and the winged lions chase her out of their city? How wonderful they had seemed the first time he had seen them with his very own eyes, after learning so much about them from his mother. He had looked up and there they were, standing like sentinels among the stars on their pillars. He had felt they were the guardians not just of Venice's splendours – but of him, too.

He had felt as safe as a king in the centre of his realm, protected by lions and dragons – and by the water all around them. Esther hated the water. She was afraid to even board a ship. But still she had come here and taken Bo from him.

Prosper wiped the tears from his face with his sleeve. He heard a motorboat coming down the canal so he sank down in the boat and waited for it to pass. But it didn't. The engine cut-out, and Prosper heard someone cursing under his breath. Then something bumped hard against Ida's boat. Prosper carefully poked his head out.

It was Scipio! He smiled with such happiness that Prosper forgot for a moment why he had tears in his eyes.

'Look who's here!' said the Thief Lord. 'Well, if that's not a coincidence. I've come to pick you up!'

'Pick me up? And take me where?' Prosper scrambled to his feet. 'Where did you get the boat?' It was beautiful, built of dark wood and decorated with golden ornaments.

'It's my father's,' Scipio answered. He patted the boat as if it was a thoroughbred horse. 'It's his pride and joy. I've borrowed it – and just now it got its first scratch.

'How did you know we were here?' Prosper asked.

'Mosca called me.' Scipio looked up at the moon. 'He told me that the Conte tricked us. And Bo is with your aunt, is that right?'

Prosper nodded and wiped the back of his hand over his eyes. He didn't want Scipio to see that he'd been crying.

'I'm sorry.' Scipio said gently. 'It was stupid of us to leave him alone with Hornet, wasn't it?'

Prosper didn't reply, although he had had the same thought at least a hundred times.

'Prop?' Scipio cleared his throat. 'I'm driving out to the Isola Segreta. Will you come with me?'

Prosper stared at him, astounded.

'The Conte cheated us.' Scipio lowered his voice as if someone might be listening. 'He took us for a ride. Either he gives me the money, real money this time, or he lets me take a ride on the roundabout. It's on that island, I'm sure it is.'

Prosper shook his head. 'You don't really believe in that story, do you? Forget it – and forget the money. So we were cheated? Tough luck. Riccio's already working out how he can spend the fake money. And nobody wants to go back to that island. Not even for a whole bag full of real riches.'

Scipio fiddled with the string of his mask and looked at Prosper. 'I want to go there,' he said. 'With you. I want to ride that roundabout. And if the Conte won't let me then I'll take the wing back. Come with me, Prop. What have you got to lose, now that Bo has gone?'

Prosper stared at his hands. A child's hands. He thought of the condescending look he had received from the porter at the Sandwirth. He thought of his bulky uncle and how he had walked next to Bo, his hand possessively on his brother's thin shoulder. And suddenly Prosper wished that Scipio were right. He wished that out there, on that island, there really was something that could turn the small and weak into the big and strong. And suddenly he knew what he wanted to do. Without another word he jumped into Scipio's boat.

40 The Isola Segreta

It was a very dark night. The moon kept vanishing behind the scudding clouds. Although Scipio had stolen his father's sea chart, they still lost their way twice. The first time the sight of the island-cemetery had saved them. And when Murano appeared out of the darkness they knew they had gone too far west. Finally, when they were frozen so stiff they could hardly move their fingers any more, the wall of the Isola Segreta, pale and grey in the lamplight, appeared out of the night. The stone angels looked down at them as if they'd been expecting them.

Scipio throttled back the engine. The Conte's boat swayed with its furled sails by the jetty. Prosper heard the dogs barking.

'What now?' he whispered to Scipio. 'How are you going to get past the mastiffs?'

'Do you think I'm so stupid that I'd climb over the gate?' Scipio answered quietly. 'We'll try the back.'

Prosper said nothing, although he didn't think this was a particularly smart plan. Still, they had no choice if they wanted to get on to that island.

The dogs only fell silent once the boys had turned off the

boat lamps. Scipio steered the boat close to the shore. He was looking for a hole in the wall. In some places the wall rose straight out of the water and in others it stood behind a thicket of reeds. It seemed to surround the whole island. Finally, Scipio lost his patience.

'That's it. We're climbing over,' he whispered. He switched off the engine and dropped the anchor into the water.

'And how are we going to get ashore?' Prosper stared uneasily into the darkness. There was still quite a distance between the boat and the island. 'Are we going to swim?'

'No, of course not! Give me a hand here.' From a hatch by the steering wheel Scipio pulled out a dinghy and two oars. Prosper was amazed that a bit of rubber could be so heavy as he helped Scipio to heave it overboard.

Their breath hung in the air like white mist as they paddled towards the island. They hid the boat in the reeds growing at the base of the wall. From this close the wall seemed even higher. Prosper threw his head back and looked up. He began to wonder seriously whether the mastiffs only guarded the gate...

The boys were out of breath when they eventually sat next to each other on top of the rough ledge. Their hands were grazed, but they had done it. A huge overgrown garden lay in front of them. Hedges, bushes and paths, all were white with frost.

'Can you see it?' Scipio asked.

Prosper shook his head. No, he couldn't see the roundabout. All he could see was a big house rising gloomily between the trees.

Climbing down the wall was even harder than climbing up

it. The boys landed in dense, thorny scrub and when they finally managed to free themselves they hesitated, not sure in which direction to go.

'The roundabout's got to be behind the house,' Scipio whispered. 'Otherwise we would've seen it from up there.'

'Right,' Prosper whispered. He looked around.

A rustling sound came from the bushes and then something small and dark darted across the path. Prosper could see tracks in the snow. Bird tracks, and paw prints. Rather large paw prints.

'Let's try that path there!' Scipio walked ahead.

The path was lined with mossy statues. Some of them had almost been swallowed up by the thicket. At one stage Prosper thought he could hear footsteps behind them, but when he turned round it was just a bird, fluttering out of an overgrown hedge. It didn't take long for them to get lost. Soon they weren't even sure in which direction the boat lay or even the house they'd seen from the wall.

'Damn. Why don't you walk ahead, Prop?' Scipio suggested as they came across their own footprints. But Prosper didn't answer.

He had heard something. But this time it wasn't a bird they had startled from its sleep. This sounded like panting, short and sharp, followed by a growl, low and quiet and threatening, coming out of the darkness. Prosper forgot to breathe. He turned around very slowly – and there they were, hardly three steps away, as if they had risen right out of the snow. Two huge white mastiffs.

'Don't move, Scip!' Prosper whispered. 'If we run, they'll hunt us down.'

'Will they bite if I shake with fear?' Scipio whispered back.

The dogs were still snarling. They came closer, their heads lowered, the fur standing up on their necks, and their teeth bared. My legs are just going to start running whether I tell them to or not, Prosper thought.

'Bimba! Bella! *Basta* – enough!' a voice called from behind them.

The dogs immediately stopped growling and leaped past Prosper and Scipio. Confused, the boys turned around and found themselves staring into the beam of a torch. A girl of perhaps nine or ten years of age was standing behind them on the path. The black dress she was wearing completely swamped her. The dogs came up to her shoulders; she could have ridden on their backs.

'What have we here?' she said. 'How fortunate that I like to go for walks in the moonlight. What are you doing here?' The dogs cocked their ears as she raised her voice. 'Don't you know what happens to people who sneak on to the Isola Segreta?'

Scipio and Prosper looked at each other.

'We want to see the Conte,' Scipio answered. He sounded as if there was absolutely nothing remarkable about the fact that they were prowling around in someone else's garden in the middle of the night. Perhaps it was because the girl was smaller than him that Scipio sounded a little less frightened. Prosper, however, thought the mastiffs rather made up for that advantage. The dogs guarded her as if they'd tear to shreds anyone who came near her.

'The Conte? Well, well. So you like to pay visits at midnight?' The girl shone her torch into Scipio's face.

Then she pointed it at Prosper, who blinked uneasily into its light.

'We had a deal with the Conte,' Scipio shouted, 'but he cheated us. We might let the matter rest, though, if he lets us take a ride on the roundabout. The roundabout of the Merciful Sisters.'

'A roundabout?' The girl's eyes turned even more hostile. 'I know nothing about a roundabout.'

'We know it's here! Show it to us!' Scipio made a step towards her, but the dogs immediately bared their teeth. 'If the Conte doesn't let us take a ride on it, we'll go to the police.'

'What a generous offer!' The girl looked at him with amusement. 'And what makes you think he'd ever let you go again? This is the Isola Segreta. You must know the stories. Nobody who's ever visited this island has lived to tell the tale. Now move!' She pointed down a path to their left that wound into the bushes. 'That way. Don't try to run. Believe me, my dogs are faster than you.'

The boys hesitated.

'Do as I say!' the girl shouted angrily. 'Or you're dog food.'

'Come on, Scip!' Prosper grabbed Scipio's arm. Reluctantly, Scipio let himself be pulled along.

The dogs stayed so close behind the boys that they could feel their breath on their necks. From time to time, Scipio looked round as if to check whether it would be worth making a run for the bushes, but each time Prosper held on to his sleeve.

'Caught by a girl!' Scipio groaned. 'I'm just glad Mosca and Riccio aren't here.'

'If she really takes us to the Conte,' Prosper whispered, 'then you'd better not threaten him with the police. Who knows what he'll do to us?'

Scipio nodded. He turned around again to look at the dogs.

They soon found out where the girl was taking them. The house, which Prosper had seen from the wall, soon emerged between the trees. It was huge, even bigger than Scipio's. It looked abandoned and dilapidated, even in the usually flattering moonlight. The plaster was coming off the walls and the blinds hung crookedly in front of dark windows. The roof had enough holes for the moon to shine through it. A set of broad steps led up to the main entrance. Stone angels leaned down from the balustrade – the salty air had eaten away their features and they were now as fuzzy as the coat of arms above the door.

'Oh no. Not up there!' said the girl as Scipio walked towards the steps. 'The Conte will most certainly not talk to you tonight. You will spend the rest of the night in the old stables. Over there.' She made an impatient gesture towards a low building next to the house. Scipio, however, didn't move.

'No!' he said and folded his arms. 'You think you can order us around, just because you've got these dogs from hell with you? I want to see the Conte. *Now.*'

The girl clicked her tongue, and the dogs pushed their snouts into the boys' bellies. The boys slowly backed away towards the bottom of the steps.

'You won't be seeing anyone tonight,' the girl said to them in a sharp voice, 'apart, that is, from the rats in the stables. The Conte is sleeping. He will decide tomorrow morning what we will do with you. And think yourself lucky. At least you won't be thrown into the lagoon right away.'

Scipio angrily bit his lip, but the dogs began to growl again so Prosper quickly dragged him away.

'Better do what she says, Scip!' he urged as they walked

towards the stables, which looked just as decrepit as the main house. 'We've got all night to think about what to do next. And we can't do that if we end up as the dogs' dinner. And you won't be riding the roundabout then, either.'

'OK, OK.' Scipio flashed the girl a vicious look.

'Please enter, gentlemen!' she said, opening the stable doors. It was pitch black inside and they were greeted by a stench that made Scipio's face screw up in disgust.

'In there?' he called. 'Do you want to kill us?'

'Would you rather I left you the dogs for company?' the girl asked. She put her hands on the mastiffs' huge heads.

'Come on now, Scip!' Prosper pulled Scipio into the dark building. A few rats scurried away as the girl shone her torch after them.

'There should be some old sacks back there,' she said. 'They should do for the night. The rats are not very hungry. There's enough for them to eat around here, so they won't bother you tonight. You can forget about finding a way out of here – there isn't one. I will also leave the dogs outside. *Buona notte!*' With that she shut the door. Prosper heard her push a heavy bolt across it. The darkness was so complete that Prosper couldn't even see his own hands.

'Prop!' Scipio whispered next to him. 'Are you afraid of rats? I'm scared to death.'

'I've got used to them. We had lots in the cinema.' Prosper listened in the darkness. He heard the girl talking to the dogs outside. She spoke to them with a quiet, tender voice.

'How sweet,' Scipio muttered. Suddenly, there was a rustling noise behind him, and Scipio gave such a start that he nearly knocked Prosper over.

They heard the girl's steps receding and the dogs settling

down in front of the door. As soon as their eyes had got used to the dark, they searched for the sacks the girl had mentioned. But when a rat ran over Scipio's foot they decided not to sleep on the floor. Instead, they found two wooden barrels to lie on, and propped them against the wall.

'He'll just *have* to let us take a ride!' Scipio said after a while into the blackness. 'I mean, he was the one who cheated on us.'

'Hmmph,' Prosper grunted.

He could imagine only too well what else the Conte could do to them if he chose. And then all of a sudden he remembered Bo. It was the first time since he'd jumped into Scipio's boat. He wondered whether he would ever see his brother again.

It was past midnight when Victor heard the phone ring. He pulled the pillow over his head, but it kept ringing and ringing until he finally crept out of his warm bed and stumbled over the tortoise box into his office.

'Who the devil is that?' he growled into the receiver while he rubbed his aching toe.

'He's run away again!' Esther Hartlieb sounded so breathless that Victor didn't understand her at first. 'But I'm telling you: this time we won't take him back. No chance! The little devil pulled the tablecloth off the table, right in the middle of the best restaurant in town! And while we sat there with our pasta in our laps, he just ran away.' Victor heard her sob. 'My husband has always said that the boy wasn't right for us and that he's just like my sister. But he has such an angel-face... Anyway, they've thrown us out of the hotel, because he screamed so much they suspected us of beating him. Can you imagine? First he doesn't say a word and then he has a fit just because I try to put some clean socks on him. He even bit my husband! He cut holes in the curtain with his penknife and he poured the coffee from the balcony...' Esther Hartlieb gasped

261

for breath '…My husband and I are flying back home on Monday as we had planned. Should my nephews get picked up by the police then please have them put in an orphanage. There are supposed to be some good institutions here in this city. Did you hear me, Signor Getz? Signor Getz…'

Victor was carving patterns into his desk with his letter-opener. 'How long has that little boy been out there now, all on his own?' he asked coldly. 'When did he run away?'

'A few hours ago. We had to settle matters with the restaurant first. And then we had to find another hotel with all our luggage. All the decent places are booked up. Now we're in some awfully primitive place near the Rialto Bridge.'

A few hours. Victor ran his hand over his tired face and looked outside. The night crouched above the houses, dark and cold, like an animal that eats little boys.

'Did you call the police?' Victor asked. 'Is someone looking for Bo now? Your husband, perhaps?'

'What do you mean?' Esther's voice turned shrill. 'Do you seriously think one of us is going to go running about through those dark alleys? After all the boy has done to us tonight? We most certainly are not! We're at the end of our tether. I don't even want to hear his name mentioned ever again. I—'

Victor didn't put the phone down. He just dropped the receiver. Still numb with sleep, he started to get dressed.

When he stepped out of the door, the sharp cold air greeted him, bringing tears to his eyes. Well, at least it was better than bucketing rain, Victor thought as he pulled his hat down over his face. The previous winter the town had been under water several times, deep enough for a small boy like Bo to be washed away. The lagoon now flooded Venice more and more often, something that in the past only happened every five years or so. Victor didn't want to think about that right now. He felt miserable enough as it was.

His feet were like lead as he stumbled along the sparsely lit alleys and over the cobbles covered with silvery frost. There was only one place where Bo would hide. He didn't know, after all, that Prosper and his friends had found refuge with Ida Spavento. Victor snuffled and wiped his icy nose with his sleeve. The poor little kid didn't know a thing.

It was a long way from Victor's flat to the children's old hideout. He was frozen to the bone when he finally reached the cinema. I'll have to get myself a better coat, he thought as he fumbled for the right lock pick. Luckily, Dottor Massimo hadn't yet had the lock replaced. The lobby was also still full of rubbish – as if nothing had happened since the night when the children took Victor prisoner. When he entered the auditorium he heard faint crying.

'Bo?' he called out. 'Bo, it's me, Victor. Come here. Or do you want to play hide-and-seek again?'

'I'm not going back to her!' a tearful little voice said out of the darkness. 'I just want to be with Prosper.'

'You don't have to go back.' Victor let the beam of his torch wander across the seats until the light fell on blonde hair. Bo was crawling between the seats, as if he was looking for something.

'They've gone, Victor!' he sobbed. 'They've gone.'

'Who?' Victor bent down towards him and Bo turned his tear-stained face towards the detective. 'My kittens,' he snivelled, 'and Hornet.'

'Nobody's gone.' Victor helped Bo up and wiped the tears off his cheeks. 'They're all at Ida Spavento's house: Hornet, Prosper, Riccio, Mosca, and your kittens.' He sat down on a folding chair and pulled Bo on to his lap. 'I've heard some terrible things about you, mister,' he said. 'Pulling down tablecloths, screaming, running away. Do you know that your aunt and uncle have been thrown out of their posh hotel?'

'Really?' Bo sniffed loudly and buried his face into Victor's coat. 'I was angry,' he mumbled. 'Esther wouldn't tell me where Prosper was.'

'Well, well.' Victor pushed his handkerchief into Bo's dirty hands. 'Here. Blow your nose. Prosper's fine. He's probably lying in a soft bed dreaming of his little brother right now.'

'She wanted to make a parting in my hair,' Bo muttered. He ran his hands over his messy thatch as if wanting to make sure that Esther's efforts had been in vain. 'She wouldn't let me jump on the bed *and* she wanted to throw away the jumper Hornet gave me *and* she told me off because there was a little stain,' Bo indicated the size with his fingers, '*and* she kept wiping my face. *And* she said horrible things about Prosper.'

'Did she really?' Victor shook his head with deep sympathy.

Bo rubbed his eyes and yawned. 'I'm cold,' he said quietly. 'Can you take me to Prosper, Victor?'

Victor nodded. 'I will,' he said. But just as he was about to lift him up, Bo ducked between the seats.

'There's someone there!' he whispered.

Victor turned around.

A man was standing in the door to the lobby. He was shining a huge torch into the auditorium. 'What are you doing in there?' he called out with a rasping voice when the spotlight stopped on Victor.

Victor got up and put his arm on Bo's shoulder. 'The boy's kitten ran away,' he said calmly, as if he found nothing strange about being in a shut-down cinema in the middle of the night. 'He thought it came in here, through the emergency exit. The cinema is closed down, right?'

'Yes, but the owner, Dottor Massimo, has asked me to keep an eye on the place. Just the other day two street kids were picked up here. Behind you there...' the man waved with his torch, '...is that a child.'

'Well observed!' Victor stroked Bo's damp hair. 'But this one is no street kid. This is my son. As I said, he was just looking for his kitten.' Victor looked around. 'This is a beautiful cinema. Why was it closed?'

The man shrugged. 'Dottor Massimo wants to turn it into a supermarket, after all the trouble he's had with it. Could you please leave now. There are no kittens here, and even if there were, they'd be dead by now. I put down some rat poison.'

'We've gone already!' Victor pushed Bo towards the emergency exit.

'The curtain,' he said suddenly. 'Look, Victor, they pulled it down.'

The heavy fabric lay on the floor, crumpled and dirty.

'What are you going to do with the curtain?' Victor called to the guard who was about to disappear into the lobby.

The man turned around reluctantly. 'Listen, it's late!' he called. 'Why don't you just leave with your little one. Take the curtain, if you're so interested.'

'And how are we supposed to do that?' Victor grumbled.

Then he pulled a penknife from his pocket and cut a large piece out of the embroidered fabric. 'Here,' he said as he pushed it into Bo's hand. 'A souvenir.'

'Is Scipio at Ida's as well?' Bo asked, as they finally stepped through the emergency exit.

'No,' Victor replied, as he wrapped the boy in the blanket he'd wisely brought with him. Then he lifted Bo up in his arms. 'He's probably at home. I don't think he's very popular with your friends right now.'

'But his daddy's horrible,' Bo mumbled. He had trouble keeping his eyes open. 'You're much nicer.'

He wrapped his short arms around Victor's neck and squeezed his face against his shoulder. He was already fast asleep when they reached the Accademia Bridge. And so Victor carried him through the silent and empty alleys all the way to Ida Spavento's house.

42 Safety

Ida opened the door herself. She was wearing a bright red dressing gown and her eyes were bloodshot. Behind her stood Hornet, Mosca and Riccio. They all stared at Victor as if they had been expecting someone else.

'What's going on here?' he whispered as he pushed past them with the sleeping Bo in his arms.

'That's Bo!' Hornet cried out in surprise.

'Yes, this is Bo,' Victor grumbled, 'and he's quite heavy. Now would you please all get out of my way so I can put him down somewhere?'

They all drew back quickly and Ida walked ahead of Victor up the steep stairs to the room where she had put the children. With a sigh, Victor placed Bo on one of the beds, tucked him into another blanket, and then crept out of the room. Hornet, Mosca and Riccio were at the door. Only then did Victor realize that someone was missing.

'Where's Prosper?' he asked.

'That's why we're all up at this hour,' Ida answered in a

weary voice. 'Caterina woke me an hour ago because he wasn't in his bed. 'We searched everywhere,' she whispered. 'In the house, the courtyard, we even looked for him on the Campo. He's nowhere to be found.'

She looked at Victor expectantly, as if he could conjure Prosper up like he'd magicked Bo out of nowhere.

'Come on, let's not stand around here,' Ida said quietly. 'The little one doesn't have to find out till tomorrow that his brother has vanished. And Victor probably has a lot to tell us.'

The living room was cold. Ida usually only heated the bedrooms a little at night. So Victor lit a fire and as they all huddled together in front of the flames they soon felt warm. Bo's kittens climbed down from the wardrobe into the heat and rubbed against them with quiet purrs. Then Victor explained how Esther had woken him up and how he had found Bo. He found it hard to concentrate on his story as his thoughts kept returning to Prosper. Where could the boy be?

'What's that supposed to mean: she doesn't want him back?' Ida's voice startled him out of his worries. 'What on earth is she thinking of? The boy isn't like a shoe that she can try on and then throw away again because it doesn't fit her.' She angrily searched her dressing gown for cigarettes.

'How should I know what Esther Hartlieb thinks?' Victor growled. He rubbed his eyes. 'I only know that I was looking forward to seeing Prosper's face when I delivered his brother to him. And now I'm here and Prosper has gone. Damn it!'

He scolded the three children. 'Couldn't you have kept an eye on him? You all saw what a mess he was in.'

'What?' Mosca cried indignantly. 'So we should have tied Prosper to his bed, should we?'

Hornet began to sob. Her tears dripped on to the huge

nightshirt Ida had given her.

'There, there,' Ida said, taking Hornet into her arms. 'What shall we do? Where could we look for Prosper? Any ideas?'

'He's probably standing in front of the Sandwirth again!' Mosca said.

'And he doesn't even know that his aunt is no longer staying there,' grumbled Victor. 'I'll call the night porter and ask him if he's seen a boy hanging around the hotel.'

With a sigh he pulled his phone from his coat pocket and punched in the number of the Sandwirth. The night porter was just about to end his shift, but he did Victor a favour and looked out of the window. There was no boy on the empty Riva degli Schiavoni. Victor put his phone away again. He was at a loss.

'I need a nap,' he said, getting up from the sofa. 'Just a couple of hours, so I can think straight again. One brother is back, the other is gone,' he moaned. He massaged his forehead. 'What a night! I keep having nights like this lately. Is there an empty bed for me anywhere in this house?'

'I could offer you Prosper's air bed,' Ida replied.

Victor accepted.

They were all very tired, but none of them fell asleep quickly. And even when they did, the bad dreams were already lurking underneath their pillows. Only Bo slept as peacefully as an angel, as if all his worries had come to an end that night.

43 The Conte

Prosper and Scipio woke up with the sound of someone opening the door of the stable. Daylight flooded the room. For a moment they didn't know where they were. The girl leaning on the stable door, however, quickly brought it all back.

'*Buongiorno*, gentlemen', she said, holding back the mastiffs as they tried to run into the stable. 'I would have left you in here for a little while longer, but my brother insists on seeing you.'

'Brother?' Scipio whispered to Prosper as they stepped into the open. The big house looked even more run down in the light of the morning than it had at night.

The girl impatiently waved them up the steps, and hurried them past the stone angels with the lost faces. They stopped between the pillars in front of the main entrance. They felt the cold, musty air wafting towards them as the girl opened the door. The mastiffs pushed past them and vanished inside the house.

The height of the entrance hall made Prosper dizzy. He craned his head back and looked up at the ceiling. It was painted with beautiful pictures. They were darkened with soot and the colours had faded, but you could see how magnificent they had once been. There were horses rearing up and angels in flight in a summer-blue sky.

'Move!' the girl said. 'You were in a such a rush yesterday – in there!'

She pointed at an open door at the opposite end of the hall. The dogs padded ahead, their paws slipping on the stone floor. Scipio and Prosper followed them cautiously, walking over colourful mosaics of unicorns and mermaids.

The room into which the dogs had disappeared was dark, despite the daylight that came in through the tall windows. A fire was burning in a hearth shaped like the gaping mouth of a lion. The dogs had settled down in front of it. Toys lay between their paws. The whole floor was covered with toys: skittles, balls, swords, a whole herd of rocking horses, dolls in every shape and size lying about with their arms and legs twisted. Scattered among them were armies of tin soldiers, steam engines, and sailing ships with carved sailors – and in the middle of this chaos sat a boy. He looked rather bored as he put a tin soldier on a tiny horse.

'Here they are, Renzo,' the girl said as she pushed Prosper and Scipio through the open door. 'They smell of pigeon poo, but as you can see the rats didn't get to them.'

The boy lifted his head. His black hair was closely cropped and his clothes looked even more old-fashioned than Scipio's jacket.

'The Thief Lord!' he confirmed. 'Indeed, dear sister, you were right.' He carelessly dropped the tin soldier to the floor, got up, and walked towards Prosper and Scipio.

'You were also in the Basilica, weren't you?' he said to

Prosper. I apologize for the phoney money. It was Barbarossa's idea. I wouldn't have been able to pay you otherwise. You have probably noticed,' he pointed at the crumbling plaster on the walls, 'that I am not actually very rich, even though I do live in this palace.'

'Renzo!' the girl said impatiently. 'What are we going to do with them?'

The boy kicked aside a doll with his shoe.

'Just look how the two of them are staring at me!' he said to Morosina. 'Are you wondering how I know all this? Have you forgotten our meeting in the confessional? Or our night-time rendezvous on the Sacca della Misericordia?'

Prosper backed away. Next to him he heard Scipio breathe in sharply.

'The roundabout works!' Scipio whispered. 'You are the Conte?'

Renzo bowed with a smile. 'At your service, Thief Lord,' he said. 'Thanks to your help. Without the lion's wing it would have been just a merry-go-round, but now...'

'Ask them who told them about the roundabout,' his sister was leaning against the wall, her arms folded. 'Spit it out! Was it Barbarossa? I've always told Renzo, the redbeard cannot be trusted.'

'No!' Scipio exchanged a confused look with Prosper. 'No, Barbarossa had nothing to do with us being here. Ida Spavento, the lady who had the wing before, told us about the roundabout. But that's quite a long story...'

'Does she know you're here?' Morosina snapped. 'Does anyone know you're here?'

Scipio was about to answer, but Prosper got in first.

'Yes,' he said. 'Our friends know, and a detective, too. And they're going to come looking for us if we don't go back.'

Morosina flashed a dark glance at her brother.

'Did you hear that?' she asked. 'What are we going to do now? Why are you talking to them? How could you tell them about our secret? We could have lied to them and...'

Renzo bent down and picked up a mask from among the toy soldiers. 'They gave me the wing,' he said, 'and I didn't pay them. That's why I'm going to let them take a ride on the roundabout.' He looked at Prosper and Scipio.

'It spins quite slowly at first,' he said quietly, 'and you hardly feel a thing. But then it goes faster and faster. I nearly got off too late, but this' – he looked down at himself – 'is just how I wanted it. I got back what had been stolen from me. All those years ago. While the children of the Valaresso played with all this' – he pointed at the rocking horses and the toy-soldiers 'Morosina and I were forced to scrape the pigeon excrement from the dovecots. We had to weed and hack the moss from the faces of those stone angels in the garden, scrub the floors and polish the door handles. We got up before the master and went to bed when everybody else was fast asleep. But now the Valaresso are gone and Morosina and I are still here.' He paused. 'And now I find playing with all this quite boring. Strange, isn't it?'

'So you only called yourself Conte,' said Scipio. 'You're not a Valaresso.'

'No, he isn't,' Morosina answered for her brother. 'But you,' she looked at Scipio appraisingly, 'you're from a noble family, aren't you? I can tell from the way you talk, even the way you walk. Do *you* have a girl to pick up your dirty trousers when you throw them on the floor? Someone to polish your boots and make your bed? Someone barely older than you? You can't possibly have any reason for wanting to ride the roundabout, so what are you doing here? If it's the money you want, we haven't got it.'

Scipio hung his head. He traced the patterns on the floor with the tip of his boot.

'You're right, there is someone who picks up my things,' he said without lifting his head. 'And I do have my clothes laid out for me in the morning. But I hate it. My parents treat me like I'm too stupid even to put on my own trousers. *Scipio, wash your hands after you've touched the cat. Scipio, don't step into puddles. For goodness sake, Scipio, do you have to be quite so clumsy all the time? Scipio, just shut up, you don't know anything about it, you little flea, you useless weed.'*

Scipio looked Morosina in the eye. 'We read the story of *Peter Pan* at school. D'you know what? He's a stupid boy, and you and your brother are just like him. Turning yourselves into children so that adults can push you around and laugh at you again! Yes, I do want to ride the roundabout. That's why I came to this island. But I want to ride it in the other direction. I want to be grown up. Grown up! Grown up!' Scipio stamped his foot so forcefully that he crushed one of the little soldiers. 'Sorry!' he muttered, staring at the broken thing as if he had just done something truly terrible.

Renzo bent down and threw the pieces into the fire. Then he looked pensively at Scipio. A log crackled in the flames, sparks flew out and died down again between the scattered toys.

'I will show you the roundabout,' Renzo said. 'And if you really want to, you can ride it.'

44 The Roundabout

Prosper could feel Scipio shiver with anticipation and impatience as they followed Renzo through the large door into the garden. He wasn't sure himself whether he should feel excited. Ever since they had stepped on to this island everything had felt so unreal. Like in a dream. He couldn't even have said for sure whether it was a good dream or a bad one.

Morosina didn't come with them. She stood between the pillars with the dogs by her side.

Renzo led Scipio and Prosper to an arbour behind the house. Frozen leaves hung from the wooden trellis. The arbour led into a labyrinth. The hedges were overgrown and the labyrinth had turned into a dense thicket. But Renzo didn't hesitate for a moment as he led Scipio and Prosper through it. Suddenly, he stopped and listened.

'What is it?' Scipio asked.

The sound of a bell drifted through the cold air. It sounded as if someone was ringing it rather impatiently.

'That's the bell by the main gate,' said Renzo. 'Who could that be? The only person I'm expecting is Barbarossa and he wasn't due to come until tomorrow.' He looked worried.

'Barbarossa?' Prosper looked at him, surprised.

Renzo nodded. 'I told you it was his idea to pay you with fake cash. He even procured it for me. But of course the red-beard expects to be paid for his services. He wants to come tomorrow to pick up his reward – the old toys. He's had his eye on them for quite a while now.'

'That crook!' Prosper muttered angrily. 'So he knew all along that we would be given fake money for the job?'

'Don't worry about it! Barbarossa cheats everybody.' Renzo listened again, but the bell had stopped. The dogs were still barking, however. 'Probably some tourist boat,' he explained. 'Morosina keeps spreading terrible stories about this island whenever she's in town. But we still get the occasional boat coming here. The dogs soon chase away even the most curious visitors.'

Prosper and Scipio looked at each other. They could both understand that.

'I've been doing business with the redbeard for quite a while now,' Renzo told them as he struggled on through the overgrown hedges. 'He's the only antique dealer who doesn't ask too many questions. And he's the only one Morosina and I have ever allowed to come to this island. He thinks, of course, that he's dealing with the Conte Valaresso, who is so impoverished that he has to sell off some of his family's treasures every now and again. Morosina and I have lived for a long time off what the Valaresso left behind. However, there'll be no one to answer the door to Barbarossa when he comes to the gate tomorrow to pick up the toys. The Conte will have disappeared for good.'

'Barbarossa always pretended he didn't know what we were

supposed to steal for the Conte,' Prosper said.

'He didn't know,' Renzo answered.

'Does he know about the roundabout?' Scipio asked.

Renzo laughed. 'Good heavens, no! The redbeard is the last person I'd show it to. He'd immediately start selling tickets at a million lire apiece. No, he's never seen it. And luckily' – he pushed apart some thorny branches – 'it's quite well hidden.'

He squeezed between two bushes and seemed to disappear. Thorns scratched at Prosper and Scipio as they followed him. They emerged into a clearing surrounded by trees and hedges with their branches so densely intertwined they hid their treasure completely from the outside world.

The roundabout looked exactly as Ida Spavento had described it. Prosper may have imagined it a bit more colourful and magnificent – the paint had long faded, worn off by the wind, the rain and the salty air – but all this could not diminish the magic and gracefulness of its figures.

All five of them were there: the unicorn, the mermaid, the merman, the sea horse, and the lion, who now spread both his wings as if he'd never lost one. They each hung on their pole beneath the wooden canopy, and seemed to float. The merman held his trident in his wooden fist, the mermaid gazed into the distance out of pale green eyes, dreaming of the waters of the open sea. The sea horse with its fishtail was so beautiful, it made you forget that there were horses with four legs at all.

'Was it always here?' Scipio asked. He approached the roundabout cautiously.

'As long as I can remember,' Renzo answered. 'Morosina and I were still very little when our mother brought us to this island because the Valaresso were looking for a kitchen maid. Nobody told us about the roundabout. It was kept very secret, but we found out eventually. It was already standing here by then. I sometimes crept out here to watch the rich children as they rode on it. Morosina and I would lie in the bushes and dream of riding on it just once. But they always found us and chased us back to our work. Years went by and our childhood disappeared. Our mother died and we grew older and older. The Valaresso finally lost all their money and left the island. Morosina and I found work in the city. Then, one day in a bar, I heard the story of the beautiful roundabout of the Merciful Sisters. I knew immediately that it had to be this roundabout on our island. I suddenly understood why the Valaresso had kept it so secret – it had been stolen! I couldn't get the story out of my mind. I dreamt of finding the missing wing, of reviving the roundabout's magic, and of riding it with my sister. Morosina laughed at me, but when I decided to return to the island she came with me. The roundabout was still here, and I decided to search for the missing wing. Don't ask me how long it took me to find out where it was.' Renzo climbed on to the roundabout and leaned against the unicorn. 'It was worth it,' he said, stroking its wooden back. 'You brought me the wing and Morosina and I rode the roundabout.'

'Does it matter which figure you sit on?' Scipio jumped on to the platform and leaped on to the lion's back.

'Yes, it does.' For a moment, Renzo stood hunched, just like the old man he had once been. 'The lion was the right mount for me. You and your friend will have to sit on one of the water creatures – each animal works in a different way.'

'Come on, Prop!' Scipio called, waving at Prosper. 'Take

your pick. Which one do you want? The sea horse? Or the merman?' Prosper stepped curiously towards the roundabout. He could hear the dogs howling in the distance.

Renzo had obviously also heard them. Frowning, he walked to the edge of the platform. Then he said to Scipio: 'Get off. I think I'll have to go back to the house to check on Morosina...'

But Scipio had already skipped off the lion's back and was now climbing on to the sea horse. 'What are you waiting for, Prop?' he called out impatiently.

But Prosper didn't move. Even though he could picture himself, tall and grown up, striding into the Sandwirth and simply pushing Esther and his uncle out of the way, then marching out with Bo by his side, he still couldn't step on to the roundabout.

He looked up at the unicorn, at the merman with the pale green face, and at the lion, the winged lion. 'You go first, Scipio,' he finally said.

Disappointment clouded Scipio's face. 'If you say so,' he said. Then he turned to Renzo. 'You heard him. Let's go.'

'Hold on. You really can't wait, can you?' Renzo pulled a bundle from under his old-fashioned coat and threw it over to Scipio. 'You better put these on if you don't want to burst out of your clothes. They're some old things of mine, or I should say: of the Conte's.'

Scipio reluctantly climbed down from the sea horse again. Prosper nearly laughed out loud when he saw Scipio in Renzo's grown-up clothes.

'Don't laugh!' Scipio grinned, throwing his own things at him. Then he rolled up the long sleeves, pulled up the baggy trousers, and laboriously climbed back up on the wooden sea horse. 'These shoes are going to fly off my feet!' he complained.

'As long as you don't fly off yourself.' Renzo stepped up to Scipio and placed his hand on the sea horse's back. 'Hold on tight. Just one push and it's going to turn, faster and faster, until you decide at what age you jump off. Are you sure you won't change your mind?'

Scipio buttoned up the huge jacket. 'I've got to decide?' he asked. 'Hmm, I'm not saying I'd want to, but if I did want to, could I change back again, ride in the other direction?'

Renzo shrugged. 'As you can see, I haven't tried that yet.'

Scipio nodded. He looked at Prosper, who had taken a few steps back. He was nearly swallowed up by the shadow of the trees. 'Please come too, Prop.'

Scipio looked at Prosper so pleadingly that he didn't know where to look. But still he shook his head.

'Well, suit yourself!' Scipio sat up straight. The sleeves of the jacket slipped over his hands. 'Off we go!' he called. 'And I swear, I'll only jump off once I'm ready to have a shave!'

Renzo gave the sea horse a gentle shove.

The roundabout started to move with a slight jolt. The old wood groaned and creaked. Renzo walked back to stand next to Prosper.

'Whoopeeee!' they heard Scipio scream. Then he leaned down over the neck of the sea horse. The figures spun around faster and faster. It was as if time itself was pushing them along. Prosper got dizzy trying to follow Scipio with his eyes. He heard him laugh out loud, and then suddenly he too felt a strange surge of happiness spread through him. His heart felt lighter than it had in a long time as he saw the figures zoom past him. He closed his eyes and felt the magic as if he were turning into the winged lion himself. He spread his wings and flew away, higher and higher.

Renzo's voice brought him back to earth. 'Jump off!' Prosper heard him shout.

Startled, he opened his eyes. The roundabout was going slower now. The merman came around with his trident, now the mermaid, now the lion, and then the unicorn drifted into sight, even slower now. The roundabout stopped – and the sea horse's back was empty.

'Scipio?' Prosper called. He ran around the roundabout.

Renzo followed him.

It was quite dark on the other side. High, evergreen trees grew here, their branches reaching over the clearing. They were swaying gently in the wind. Something moved in their shade. A figure rose from the ground, tall and slim. Prosper stopped stock still.

'That was close,' said an unfamiliar voice. Prosper drew back, he couldn't help himself.

'Don't look at me like that.' The stranger laughed self-consciously. He seemed strangely familiar to Prosper. He looked like a younger version of Scipio's father. Only the smile was different, very different. Scipio reached out – how long his arms had become – and gave Prosper a bear hug.

'Prop, it worked!' he cried. 'Look! Just look at me!' He let go of Prosper and stroked his chin. 'Stubble! Incredible. Do you want to feel it?'

Laughing loudly, he spun around, his arms stretched out wide. Then he grabbed the protesting Renzo and lifted him into the air. 'As strong as Hercules!' he shouted, before putting Renzo back on the ground. Then he felt his face, traced his eyebrows and his nose with his fingers. 'If only I had a mirror!' he said. 'How do I look, Prop? Different?'

Prosper wanted to say, just like your father, but he quickly bit his tongue.

'Grown up!' Renzo answered.

'Grown up!' Scipio breathed. He looked at his hands. 'Yes, grown up. What do you think, Prop, am I bigger than my father? A bit at least?' He looked around. 'There's got to be some well, or a pond, where I can look at myself.'

'There's a mirror in the house,' Renzo answered, smiling. 'Come on. I've got to go back anyway.' But he stopped in the middle of the clearing. They heard a branch snap somewhere in the bushes, as if a large animal was creeping about.

'Where are you taking me, you little squirt?' they heard a voice say. 'I'm already as bristly as a cactus.'

'This is the way. We're nearly there,' they heard Morosina answer. Renzo looked at Prosper and Scipio, clearly afraid. He wanted to run in the direction of the voices, but Scipio dragged him back behind the roundabout.

'Duck!' he whispered to Prosper and Renzo. They all cowered behind the platform.

'You will pay for this!' they heard Morosina's shrill voice. 'You have no right to snoop around here. When the Conte finds out…'

'The Conte!' the deep voice sneered. Prosper thought the voice sounded somehow familiar. 'The Conte isn't here today! He told me so himself. No, you're here all by yourself, whoever you are. Why do you think Ernesto Barbarossa came to this island today of all days?'

Renzo gave a start. 'Barbarossa!' he whispered.

He wanted to jump up, but Scipio held him back. The three of them carefully crawled forward to peer over the top of the platform.

'Do you think I would have climbed over that wall otherwise?' They heard Barbarossa breathing heavily. 'I want to
find out once and for all what all this secrecy is about. And
I'm going to get quite unpleasant if I don't find out soon.'

A few more branches snapped loudly, and then Barbarossa
stomped into the clearing. He was panting, dragging Morosina
by her pigtails like a dog on a leash.

'What the devil is this?' the redbeard roared when he saw
the roundabout. 'Are you making fun of me? I'm looking for
something with diamonds, huge diamonds, and pearls. I knew
you were stringing me along. Right, well, the two of us are
going back to the house right now, and you'd better show me
what I'm looking for, or else!'

'Prosper!' Scipio whispered so quietly that Prosper could
hardly hear him. 'Do I look like my father? Tell me!'

Prosper paused, but then he nodded.

'Excellent!' Scipio straightened his jacket and licked his lips
like a lion anticipating a hunt. 'You wait here for now,' he
whispered. 'This, I think, is going to be fun. Great fun.'

Keeping low, he crept past Renzo and Prosper. He looked
around once more – then he stood up to his full height.

He was actually a few centimetres taller than his dad.
Sticking out his chin, just like his father always did, Scipio
walked towards Barbarossa.

The redbeard looked at him and gasped. He was still holding on to Morosina's pigtails.

'*Dottore*...Dottor Massimo!' he stammered. 'What...are
you doing here?'

'I wanted to ask you the same question, Signor Barbarossa,'
Scipio answered, giving a perfect imitation of his father's con-

descending tone. 'And what, for heaven's sake, are you doing with the Contessa?'

Barbarossa let go of the pigtails as if they had burnt him. 'Contessa? Valaresso?'

'Of course! The little Contessa often visits her grandfather. Isn't that right, Morosina?' Scipio smiled at her. 'But what brings you to this island, Signor Barbarossa? Business?'

'What? Oh . . . yes, yes.' Barbarossa nodded vigorously. 'Business.' He was still far too bewildered to notice that Morosina was looking at Scipio with just as much confusion.

'Indeed? Well, the Conte asked me to come here and take a look at this roundabout here.' Scipio turned his back on Barbarossa and tugged his earlobes, just like his father always did. 'The city may want to buy it. But I'm afraid it's in rather a sorry state. You do recognize it, of course, don't you?'

'Recognize it?' Barbarossa stood next to Scipio – and suddenly his eyes opened wide. 'Of course! Unicorn, mermaid, lion, merman' – he smacked his forehead – '...and there's the sea horse. The roundabout of the Merciful Sisters! Incredible!' He lowered his voice and gave Scipio a conspiratorial look. 'What about all the stories? What people say about it?'

Scipio shrugged. 'Do you want to have a go?' he asked with a smile that didn't look at all like Dottor Massimo. Luckily, Barbarossa didn't notice that either.

'Do you know how to start it?' the redbeard asked, already lumbering with some difficulty on to the platform.

'Oh, I have two young helpers with me,' Scipio replied. 'They must be back there somewhere. Probably trying to dodge work again.' He waved Prosper and Renzo out from behind the roundabout. 'Come on, you two. Signor Barbarossa wants to take a ride on the roundabout.'

When he saw Prosper, Barbarossa's eyes immediately narrowed. 'What's *he* doing here?' he growled. He stared suspiciously at Prosper. 'I know that boy. He works for—'

'I work for Dottor Massimo now,' Prosper interrupted him, as he stood next to Scipio. Morosina ran to her brother and whispered something in his ear. Renzo went pale.

'He gave the dogs poisoned meat!' Renzo shouted. He leapt on to the platform, but Barbarossa just pushed him down again.

'So what? They'll live,' he barked. 'Was I supposed to let myself be chased by those hounds of hell?'

'Go and give them some Ipecac*,' Renzo said to Morosina without taking his eyes off the redbeard. 'There should still be some in the stables somewhere.'

Morosina ran off. Barbarossa watched her, looking very self-satisfied.

'Those monsters deserved it, believe me, *Dottore*,' he said to Scipio. 'Do you know if it matters which animal one sits on?'

'Take the lion, redbeard!' Renzo stared with loathing at Barbarossa. 'That's probably the only one that will take your weight.'

Barbarossa looked at him with disdain, but he did waddle over to the lion. As he heaved his huge body on to the figure, the wood groaned as if the beast was coming alive.

'Excellent!' Barbarossa asserted. 'I'm ready for a little test-drive.'

Scipio placed his hands on Prosper's and Renzo's shoulders. 'You know what to do. Give Signor Barbarossa the ride he deserves.'

*Traditional Brazilian plant used to treat nausea in animals as well as humans.

'But just one round, to start with!' Barbarossa shifted his massive body forward a bit further and grabbed the pole with his be-ringed fingers. 'Who knows, if the stories are true ... I mean, I wouldn't like to turn into a little midget like that one there,' he said, pointing down at Renzo, 'but a few years...' stroking his bald head and laughing '...who wouldn't want to shed a few years, eh, Dottore?'

Scipio answered him with a thin smile.

'Renzo, Prosper, a good shove for Signor Barbarossa!' he ordered.

Prosper and Renzo stepped up to the roundabout. Renzo put his hand on the merman's back; Prosper braced himself against the unicorn.

'Hold on, redbeard!' shouted Renzo. 'This is going to be the ride of your life!'

The roundabout started with a big jolt. It looked as if the unicorn wanted to jump at the lion's neck. Looking worried, Barbarossa clung on to the pole. 'Hey, not so hard!' he screamed, but the roundabout spun around faster and faster.

'Stop!' Barbarossa cried. 'Stop! I'm going to be sick!'

But the figures kept spinning around in circles, round after round.

Barbarossa shouted, 'Damned contraption!' and it sounded to Prosper as if his voice was already higher-pitched.

'Jump off, redbeard!' Renzo mocked. 'Jump, if you dare.'

But Barbarossa didn't jump. He screamed, he cried, he hit the pole, and he kicked the lion, as if that could slow down this mad ride.

And then, suddenly, it happened.

In his desperate attempt to find a foothold, Barbarossa pushed his feet against the lion's wings. Scipio, Renzo and

Prosper all heard the old wood splinter. Then there was a terrible shattering sound, as if something alive was breaking apart.

'No!' Prosper heard Renzo scream. But there was nothing to be done.

The wing spun through the air, bounced off the merman, and landed with a loud thump on the platform. From there it slid down and hit Prosper's arm so violently that he doubled up in pain.

The roundabout lurched through one final round, and finally the figures juddered to a sickening halt.

'*Madonna!*' Prosper heard an unfamiliar voice moaning. 'What kind of a hellish ride was that?'

A boy slid down with shaking legs from the lion's back. Moaning, he tumbled towards the edge of the wooden platform. He stumbled over his trouser legs – and then stared in disbelief at his fingers: short, little fat fingers, dimpled with rosy fingernails.

45 A Few Rounds Too Many

'He's broken it!' Renzo screamed. He jumped on to the platform, pushed the mini Barbarossa aside so that he nearly fell over, and bent over the lion. Ida's wing was still firmly in its place, but only a stump remained of the other one. Renzo looked in desperation at Prosper and Scipio. Then, as if suddenly remembering the real culprit, he leapt at Barbarossa, who was still staring in shock at his fingers.

'You absolute idiot!' Renzo screamed. He gave Barbarossa a push that made him tumble backwards against the sea horse. 'You creep on to my island, you poison my dogs, you threaten my sister, and now you've just destroyed what I've spent half my life working for!'

'It wouldn't stop!' Barbarossa cried, holding his arms up protectively. Renzo kept flailing about blindly, until Prosper jumped on to the platform and held him back – with his one good hand. His other arm still hurt from its encounter with the wing. Renzo let his arms fall without resistance. Then he gazed at the mutilated lion.

Scipio was truly frightened. Slowly, as if he was afraid of what he might find, he walked towards the bush where the wing had landed. He pulled it from the branches.

'We'll have another wing made, Renzo!' he said as he stroked the splintered wood.

Renzo stepped up to the lion and rested his head against the wooden mane. 'No,' he said. 'Why do you think I spent so much time looking for the second wing? I learnt that after the thieves had lost the real wing the Conte Valaresso had more than thirty wings carved. But without the original, the roundabout is just that – a roundabout.'

'Rubbish, the other figures are still here!' Barbarossa called. 'So why the long faces?' He was standing in his bare feet, his shoes and socks having flown off during his wild ride. The sleeves of his coat hung down to the ground. Barbarossa was now even smaller than Bo. When nobody answered him, Barbarossa shook the coat off his shoulders, climbed out of his huge trousers, and stumbled towards the merman. But he couldn't reach up to its back, and so he tried the sea horse. All the figures were suddenly so big, far too big for a small fat boy, who was clumsy even before his transformation!

'You can save yourself the trouble, Barbarossa,' Prosper said sitting on the edge of the platform. 'You heard what Renzo said. It won't work any more.'

But Barbarossa screamed, 'Rubbish! Give it another shove! Dottor Massimo!' He ran back to the edge of the platform. 'Please, *Dottore*. Put an end to this childishness. Look at me. I am a respected man. I am known all over the city. People from all over the world come to my shop. Do you think I could serve them like this?'

Scipio was still looking at the shattered wing. He didn't even lift his head. 'Oh, leave me alone, Barbarossa,' he said. 'You don't understand. What were you doing here anyway? Now you've destroyed everything.'

'But *Dottore!*' Barbarossa pleaded.

'I am *not* Dottor Massimo!' Scipio yelled at him. 'I am the Thief Lord.' He wearily dropped the wing on the platform. 'But I'm a grown-up for ever now – I can never go back, you've ruined it for me. Damn it! I have to think.'

Barbarossa stared at Scipio as if he'd just been introduced to the devil himself.

'The Thief Lord?' he whispered. 'The honourable Dottor Massimo is the Thief Lord? Well, if that's not a surprise...' He lowered his voice threateningly, which from a five-year-old didn't sound frightening at all. 'Start the roundabout!' he said, clenching his little fists. 'Right away, or I'll tell the police who you are.'

Now Scipio had to laugh.

'Oh yes, you do that!' he said. 'Tell them that Dottor Massimo is the Thief Lord. What a pity you're such a little squirt that nobody will believe you.'

Barbarossa was lost for words. He was paralysed with anger, his tiny fists still bunched as he stared down at his bare toes.

'You despicable little blackmailer!' Renzo said behind him. 'I'm going to go and check on the dogs. If you've done as much damage to them as you have to the roundabout, then you'll wish you'd never stepped ashore on the Isola Segreta. Have I made myself clear?'

'You' – Barbarossa spun round – 'you dare to threaten me, you little—?'

'I am the Conte, Barbarossa!' Renzo cut him short. 'And you have no right to be on my island, so consider yourself my prisoner.'

He jumped off the roundabout and spoke to Prosper and

Scipio. 'Will you keep an eye on him? I have to check on Morosina and the dogs.'

Prosper nodded. He was still holding his aching arm.

'What's the matter?' Scipio asked anxiously when he saw Prosper's face was twisted with pain.

But Prosper just shook his head. 'The wing hit me. I'll be all right.'

'Morosina will have a look at your arm,' Renzo said. 'Bring the little redhead to the house.' Then he vanished through the bushes.

Barbarossa watched him go in utter confusion. 'That impertinent little twerp!' he muttered. He put his stubby hands on his hips. 'If he's the Conte, so what? His island, bah! I'm going home, and when I get there I'm going to employ the best carpenter in town, and make this devilish roundabout work again.'

'You'll do no such thing,' Scipio snapped. He planted himself in front of the redheaded boy. Although Barbarossa was standing on the platform, Scipio was still a lot taller than him. 'Are your parents still alive?'

Barbarossa shrugged. He was shivering. He sorely missed his coat. 'No. Why the hell are you asking?'

Prosper and Scipio exchanged a quick glance.

'Well, then, we'd better ask someone to take you to the Merciful Sisters,' Prosper answered him.

'You what?' Barbarossa recoiled in panic. 'You wouldn't dare! *You wouldn't dare!*'

Scipio jumped on to the roundabout and dragged the struggling little fellow from between the figures.

'The roundabout will never turn again, little redhead,' he said. 'All thanks to you. Nor will you be going back into town, at least for the time being. Who knows what other catastrophes you would cause there. No. You heard what Renzo said: you are now his prisoner. And to be honest: I don't envy you.'

Barbarossa kicked and struggled, but Scipio threw him over his shoulder like an old sack of potatoes and carried him all the way to the house.

They would never have found their way back through the labyrinth had Renzo's footprints not shown them the way. Scipio didn't say a word, although Barbarossa kept cursing and spitting and hitting his back. He kept looking at the sky and the trees, as if they were new and strange to him through his grown-up eyes. He seemed not to hear Barbarossa's screams. He just walked, as if deaf, his strides so long that Prosper struggled to keep up with him. Only when they had reached the house did Scipio turn to Prosper. He put the complaining Barbarossa back on his own feet and said: 'Everything has shrunk, Prop. The whole world is suddenly so small. I feel like I don't fit into it any more.'

He bent down towards Barbarossa. 'You probably see that quite differently, don't you, little redhead?' he asked mockingly. 'What's it like down there?'

Barbarossa paid him no attention. He looked around miserably, like a trapped animal searching for a way to escape. He struggled fiercely as Prosper started to haul him towards the steps.

'Let me go!' he screamed, his face as red as his hair. 'That boy ... the Conte, he's going to kill me! You have to let me go. We're business partners, after all. I'll give you all my money. My boat is lying by the gate. You could say I escaped.'

'Oh, *money*? It's OK – we still have a whole bag full of *fake money*,' Prosper answered. 'Ring any bells?'

For a moment Barbarossa was lost for words again. 'What fake money? I—I don't know anything about any—any fake money!' he said feebly, avoiding Prosper's and Scipio's eyes.

'You know absolutely everything about it,' said Scipio as he started up the steps. Barbarossa followed him, frowning darkly. But he stopped immediately when Renzo appeared between the pillars.

'Just look how angry he is!' Barbarossa whispered, holding on tightly to Prosper's arm. 'You have to protect me from him.'

At that moment the mastiffs appeared behind Renzo. Their eyes were still dull, but they were back on their feet. Morosina stepped between them and glared down at Barbarossa with pursed lips.

'You were very lucky, you little poisoner!' Renzo called. He came slowly down the steps.

'Yes, they're still alive,' he confirmed as he saw Barbarossa's relieved expression, 'but I think they could do with a bite to eat. Morosina's just suggested a little race. You against them. With, say, your boat as the finishing post.'

Barbarossa went pale.

Renzo stopped two steps above him,

'But I have another idea,' he said. 'Naturally, you will have to pay for what you've done. But this time you won't pay with your life, and you won't pass off any more bad money.'

'What then?' Barbarossa looked up at him suspiciously.

'Thanks to you, Morosina and I cannot undo what we have begun,' said Renzo. 'And neither can the Thief Lord, nor you. But I will let you go, if you give me all the cash you have in your shop. Not just in the register, but in your safe as well.'

Barbarossa backed away in shock – and nearly fell down the steps. Prosper grabbed him by the scruff of the neck at the last moment, but as soon as he was back on his feet Barbarossa pushed his hand away.

'Are you crazy?' he squawked at Renzo. 'And how will I live? I will hardly be able see over the shop-counter now. Why is it all my fault that rotten wing broke off?'

'Yes, why indeed?' Scipio sat down with a sigh on the cold steps and looked straight in to Barbarossa's eyes. 'I mean, it couldn't possibly be your fault that you crept on to this island with a bag of poisoned meat – or that you dragged Morosina by the hair…'

Barbarossa opened his mouth, but Renzo cut him off.

'We will go in to town together,' he said, 'and you'll give me the money. In return, I won't take revenge for the round-about or the dogs. Believe me, we could. We could draw the *Carabinieri*'s attention to the little orphaned boy who believes he is Ernesto Barbarossa. Or we could ask Scipio and Prosper to take you to the home of the Merciful Sisters. It's your choice, you can still buy yourself out of all this.'

Barbarossa stroked his chin and angrily dropped his hands when he realized it was bare and beardless.

'Blackmail,' he grumbled.

'Call it what you will,' Renzo replied. 'Though I could find a few choice words to describe what you've done on this island tonight.'

Barbarossa looked at him so pathetically that Prosper had to laugh.

'I'd take him up on his offer, little redhead,' he said. 'Otherwise Morosina will feed you to the dogs.'

Barbarossa clenched his chubby fists helplessly. 'Fine, I accept,' he said, looking up at the dogs who had settled on the top step. 'But it's still blackmail.'

46 Barbarossa's Punishment

It was early afternoon when they all returned to Venice. But
the sky was covered by such dark clouds that Prosper
thought that dusk must have already fallen.

He had completely lost all sense of time. The night before
– when he and Scipio had headed off for the Isola Segreta –
seemed like months ago, and now he felt like a traveller,
returning from a journey through strange and distant lands. It
began to rain as Scipio steered his father's boat on to the
Grand Canal. The wind drove cold raindrops into their faces
like hardened tears.

'How much longer do I have to be stuck in this hole?'
Prosper heard Barbarossa moaning.

Scipio had locked Barbarossa in the cabin to make sure he
didn't try any new tricks. Renzo was following them in
Barbarossa's boat, a big barge in which the redbeard had
probably intended to bring a few things back from the island.
Barbarossa had of course denied this. Morosina had stayed on
the island to look after the dogs. When Renzo had said goodbye to the mastiffs, they had wagged their tails so feebly that

he looked quite worried as he boarded Barbarossa's boat.

'How are you going to get back to the island?' Scipio asked him as they moored the boats by a jetty in a secluded canal.

'Oh, I think I'll borrow Signor Barbarossa's boat for a while,' Renzo answered. 'It's much handier than my sailing boat. And it will also stop him paying me any surprise visits.'

Barbarossa muttered something unfriendly before grumpily trudging ahead. Scipio had given him the clothes that he'd worn as a boy, but even they were too big for Barbarossa. The shoes kept slipping off his feet at every other step, and the more he tried to put on a dignified face, the more people kept turning around to laugh.

Scipio's grown-up figure also attracted a lot of curious attention. Renzo had given him his old cape as a present, making Scipio look as if he had just stepped out of an oil-painting. Prosper walked next to him, feeling very self-conscious. He missed Scipio's familiar features, which even with the mask had never seemed as strange as this. Scipio kept smiling at him, trying to reassure him, but it didn't help much.

The rain pelted down even harder on to the pavement, and when they finally reached Barbarossa's shop, the alley was practically deserted.

With a very glum expression, Barbarossa unlocked the door and switched on the light. He let the 'Closed' sign hang behind the glass, and locked the door as a precaution.

'You have to let me keep a third,' he complained as he led the way into his office. 'At least! What else am I going to live off? Do you want me to starve miserably?'

It was much easier for him, now he was smaller, to negotiate his way through his crammed shop, but he still tried to swagger past the shelves like he used to in the past. The attempt looked so strange that Scipio started to mimic him behind his back.

'What's the silly giggling about?' Barbarossa asked when Prosper and Renzo burst out laughing. Then he vanished through the beaded curtain with an indignant look on his face. The three followed him.

'Get out!' Barbarossa barked at them. 'You'll get the money, but the safe combination is none of your business.'

'We'll close our eyes,' Prosper said. He moved a chair underneath the poster of the Accademia Museum behind Barbarossa's desk.

'You spied on me!' Barbarossa hissed as he struggled to climb on to the chair. 'You and your hedgehog friend. Since when have you known that the safe is behind the poster?'

Prosper shrugged. 'We didn't know,' he answered, 'but Riccio always suspected that it was there.'

'You're just a bunch of cowards!' Barbarossa growled, while he awkwardly removed the poster from the wall. 'Robbing a little child. The pestilence and pox on you. Just you wait until I've grown back to a decent size...'

'That should take some time,' Renzo interrupted him. 'Now open it! I have to see a vet; you may remember why... Thinking about it, I'd say you were getting off more than lightly.'

Barbarossa stared at the safe.

'I've forgotten the combination!' he said. But Renzo gave him such an ominous look that it immediately came back to him.

'Is that it?' Renzo shouted, as Barbarossa held out two wads of banknotes towards him. 'That's what you've been moaning about all the time? It's hardly enough for the vet!' Without a further word, Renzo turned around and walked back into the shop.

'What's he doing now?' Barbarossa jumped off the chair and rushed after Renzo. 'Don't touch anything, do you understand?'

Renzo stood in the middle of the shop, underneath the chandelier with the coloured glass petals, and looked around. 'What would you take?' he asked Scipio. 'What would be a proper compensation for him smashing my lion wing?'

Scipio opened a glass cabinet and took something out of it. 'What about this?' he asked. He put the sugar tongs he'd stolen from his father's house into Renzo's hand.

Barbarossa, outraged, gasped for air. 'I paid for those, Thief Lord,' he screamed with his shrill child's voice. 'Ask your courier. I paid more than a fair price for them.'

Scipio stepped threateningly close to Barbarossa. The red-head barely reached up to his waist.

'The sum on the price tag is ten times what you gave Prosper,' he said. 'We've played to your rules long enough, redhead, now it's time for you to play to ours.'

'Like hell I will!' Barbarossa put his hands on his hips. Scipio, however, just turned away and looked at the other pieces in the cabinet.

Renzo stuffed the two wads of banknotes into his jacket and dropped the sugar tongs into his trouser pocket. Then he turned around.

'I wish you luck, Thief Lord,' he said. He opened the shop door. A gust of wind drove the rain inside. 'Should you ever wish to visit me again, just ring the bell by the gate and I'll open it for you.'

'But you, Barbarossa!' he said. 'You'd better give the Isola Segreta a wide berth in future. Our dogs will never forget your scent.'

'So what? Those monsters won't live for ever,' Prosper heard Barbarossa mutter. But Renzo had already turned around and stepped out into the alley. The rain poured off the roofs as if the sky had promised the sea to drown the city.

Scipio moved to the window and watched Renzo until he vanished between the houses.

'Prosper, you're probably going back to Ida Spavento's house now, aren't you?' he said, keeping his eyes on the alley. 'I'll take you there. All right?'

'Sure. You can sleep in our room – at least tonight,' Prosper answered. But Scipio shook his head.

'No,' he said staring out the window. 'I need to be alone tonight. I still have some money. I'll get a hotel room with a large mirror, so I can get used to my new face. Perhaps Mosca can give me some of that phoney money. For emergencies only of course! What hotel is your aunt staying in?'

'The Sandwirth,' Prosper answered. He wondered if he should go there first.

Scipio read Prosper's thoughts. 'Let's go to Ida's first,' he said, 'they're probably all worried about you.'

Barbarossa pushed between the two. 'And what about me? I can't be left alone!'

Scipio and Prosper had forgotten all about the redhead. How small he looked among all the valuable and worthless things he had greedily amassed. Now the counter reached up to his shoulders.

'You can sleep at my place,' Barbarossa said. 'I have a nice flat, very big, right above the shop.'

'No, thank you,' Scipio answered. He pulled the cape tighter around his shoulders. 'Come on, Prop. Let's go.'

'Hold on, not so fast. Wait!' Barbarossa stumbled past them and planted himself in front of the door. 'I'm coming with you!' he declared. 'I'm not staying here. It's out of the question. It may all look different tomorrow, but right now...' He cast an uneasy look out of the window. 'It's going to be dark soon. I mean, it's terribly dark already. The rain's washing away the whole city, and I won't even be able to reach my fridge, let alone my coffee pot. *Basta!*' He pushed Scipio's hands away as he tried to reach for the door handle. 'I'm coming with you. Only until tomorrow.'

Prosper and Scipio exchanged an amused look. Finally, Prosper shrugged. 'He can sleep in Bo's bed,' he said. 'Ida won't mind if it's only for one night.'

Relief spread over Barbarossa's still very round, but now completely beardless, face.

'I'll be right back,' he said, and he quickly fetched a huge umbrella. Protected by its wide canopy, the three of them embarked on the long trek to the Campo Santa Margherita.

Scipio left his father's boat where he had moored it. A police boat noticed it two days later, and Dottor Massimo was notified that the boat he had reported stolen had reappeared. His son, however, whom the *dottore* had also reported missing, was still lost without trace.

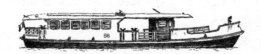

47 Strange Visitors

Scipio had been right: the others were worried about Prosper. Terribly worried.

They all remembered his desperate expression during their last meal together, and how not even Hornet had been able to cheer him up. They tried to hide their worries from Bo as well as they could. Hornet tried to convince him to stay with Lucia and the kittens instead of coming along with them to search for Prosper. But Bo just kept shaking his head and clinging to Victor's hand, and so they had to take him along.

First, they tried the Sandwirth again. Then they asked the *Carabinieri*, the hospitals, and the orphanages. Giaco took Ida's boat up and down all the canals and showed Prosper's picture to the gondoliers. Mosca and Riccio asked all the passengers on the *vaporetti*. But, as the rain came down and the sky turned black, they still could find no trace of Prosper.

Ida and Hornet were the first to return to the house. They didn't know where else they could look. On the Campo Santa Margherita they met Victor, a soaked and sleeping Bo on his back. Ida only had to look Victor in the eyes to see that he had been just as unsuccessful as she had.

302

'Where can that boy be?' she sighed as she unlocked her door. 'Lucia went to the old cinema again. She should be back soon, too.'

Hornet was so tired that she leaned her head against Ida's shoulder. 'Perhaps he stowed away on a ship,' she mumbled. 'And now he's far, far away already.'

But Victor shook his head.

'I don't believe that,' he said. 'I'll put Bo to bed now, then I'll eat a little, have a glass of Ida's port, then go over to Dottor Massimo's again. Perhaps Scipio has heard something. I've tried to call at least a dozen times, but nobody's answering the phone.'

Ida pushed the front door open. 'Yes, that's a possibility,' she said – and stopped stock still in the doorway.

'What is it?' Victor asked. But then he heard it too: voices, coming out of the kitchen.

'Giaco?' Victor asked, but Ida shook her head.

'He's gone to Murano.'

'I could go in and check,' Hornet whispered.

'No, that's my job!' Victor replied. He carefully put Bo down in a chair by the door. 'You two stay here with Bo, while I go and have a look at our visitors. If there's trouble,' he handed Ida his mobile, 'call the police.'

But Ida passed the telephone on to Hornet. 'I'm coming with you,' she hissed. 'They're sitting in my kitchen, after all.'

Victor sighed, but didn't try to stop her. Hornet looked after them anxiously, as they crept along the dark corridor.

The kitchen door stood open. Two boys and a tall man sat at the table on which Lucia rolled out her pasta dough. The tall man looked like a younger version of the honourable Dottor Massimo. The smaller of the two boys was not even

as old as Bo. He was just about to reach for a half-empty
bottle of port, which stood on the table, when the other boy
took it away from him.

'Damn it, Prosper!' Victor cried out. 'Have you any idea
how long we've been looking for you?'

'Hello, Victor!' Prosper pushed his chair back and looked
at him, shamefaced. His left arm was in a sling.

The other two quickly put down their glasses, like children
who have been caught doing something naughty. The young
man even tried to hide his glass under the table, and spilled
port all over his trousers.

'How did you get in here?' Ida asked Prosper, not taking
her eyes off his two companions.

'Lucia told me where she hides the spare key,' Prosper
answered in embarrassment.

'Well, well, and now you've brought even more people into
Ida's house.' Victor glared suspiciously at the young man. 'I
bet your name is Massimo,' he growled. 'And what about the
little midget there? Aren't there enough children in this house
already?'

The little redhead rose unsteadily. He eyed Victor from
head to toe and slurred drunkenly: 'Midget? I am Ernesto
Barbarossa. I am an important man in this city. And who the
devil, if I may ask, are you?'

Victor was astounded. He opened his mouth, but before he
could say anything, the young man pushed the redhead
roughly back into his seat.

'Shut up, Barbarossa, or should I say, baby Barbarino. If
you don't behave yourself we'll kick you out of the door. This
is Victor, a friend of ours. And the lady next to him is Ida
Spavento. This is her house.'

Victor and Ida exchanged a stunned look.

'I'm sorry we brought the redbeard here, Ida,' Prosper stammered. 'And that he drank your port, but he didn't want to stay in his shop by himself. It's only for one night...'

'In his shop?' Victor asked. 'Damn it, Prosper, could you please explain what's going on?'

'We've given our word not to tell anyone about it,' Prosper muttered, nervously tugging at the filthy cloth that was holding up his arm.

'Yes, we're really sorry, Victor,' the young man said. Victor couldn't remember ever having seen such an impertinent grin on a grown-up's face. 'But perhaps you'd like to guess who you're talking to. You've already had quite a good shot at the name.'

Victor was spared having to answer. Somebody tugged at his sleeve, and when he looked over his shoulder, Hornet was standing behind him.

'What's going on?' she asked in a low voice while trying to peer inside the kitchen. She spotted Prosper and immediately pushed past Victor and Ida. She didn't even look at the boy with the red curls, or for that matter the young man leaning against Ida's table. She only had eyes for Prosper's injured arm.

'Where have you been?' she cried, anger and relief both ringing through her voice at the same time. 'Where have you been, for god's sake? Have you any idea how worried we've been? You just disappear in the middle of the night...' She had tears in her eyes.

Prosper opened his mouth and tried to say something, but Hornet wouldn't let him.

'We've been searching for you all over town. Mosca and

Riccio are still out there!' she shouted. 'And Lucia and Giaco.
And Bo has been crying his eyes out. Not even Victor could
calm him down...'

'Bo?' Prosper had been avoiding Hornet's eyes, but now he
looked at her incredulously, as if he couldn't believe his ears.
'B-Bo?' he stammered. 'But Bo's with Esther!'

'No, he isn't!' Hornet shouted. 'But how would *you* know
– going off and vanishing like that? And what happened to
your arm?'

Prosper didn't reply. He just looked at Victor.

'Don't look at me like that. Yes, your little brother ran
away from Esther again,' Victor said to him. 'But not before
he misbehaved so thoroughly that your aunt no longer thinks
he's an angel. She doesn't want to see him again. Ever. Not
him, and definitely not you. Those were her words. I'm supposed to find a decent Italian children's home for the two of
you, should you ever reappear again. But *she* won't have anything to do with either of you any more.'

Prosper shook his head. 'It's not possible!' he whispered.

'I found your brother in the cinema,' Victor continued. 'I
thought if I brought him here you'd throw yourself at me with
gratitude, but you weren't even here.'

Prosper shook his head again, as if he still couldn't believe
what Victor was saying.

'Did you hear that, Scip?' he muttered.

'Well, if that's not cause for a party,' the young Signor
Massimo said, putting his arm around Prosper's shoulders.
'Maybe we should spend a bit of our fake money.'

'Who the hell *is* that, Prosper?' Victor asked.

'Scipio, of course!' Prosper answered. 'And now, please, tell
me where Bo is.'

306

But Victor was lost for words. He opened his mouth, and closed it again. But not a single sound passed his lips. Finally, Ida took Prosper's hand.

'Come with me,' she said, leading Prosper into the corridor.

Bo was still sleeping in the chair, right where Victor had put him. He had curled up like one of his kittens underneath the jumper Hornet had spread over him. His hair was still wet from the rain, and his eye lids were red from crying. Prosper bent over him and pulled the jumper up to his chin.

'Yes, Bo took matters into his own hands,' Ida said quietly, guessing the truth, 'while his brother took off to the Isola Segreta.'

Prosper looked ashamed.

'I'm not allowed to talk about it,' he said. 'It's someone else's secret, and...'

'...and the Isola Segreta may keep its secret,' Ida completed the sentence. She sat down on the arm of the chair. 'At least the wing seems to be back in its proper place,' she said. 'And Bo will be very happy that you didn't ride on what we're not allowed to speak about.'

'Yes, I think so, too.' Prosper stretched himself. 'What did he do to Esther?'

'Your aunt has been kicked out of the hotel,' Ida answered. 'And I seem to recall something about pasta and tomato sauce.'

Prosper smiled.

'It was just as beautiful as you told us,' he said suddenly. 'But now it's broken. It was Barbarossa's fault. And I think it will never ever work its magic again.'

Ida said nothing. She leaned forward and stroked a wet

strand of hair out of Bo's face. 'You should wake your brother now,' she said. 'And then I'll have a look at your arm.'

'It's not so bad,' Prosper answered. 'But maybe you could find a vet who'd dare to go out to the Isola Segreta to treat a couple of dogs?'

'Sure,' Ida answered. Then she went back into the kitchen. And Prosper woke Bo.

48 A Crazy Idea

That evening Hornet put ten plates on Ida's dining table. When Ida had told Lucia that the little redhead and the very strange young man would also be staying for dinner, the housekeeper had just shaken her head, mumbling something about 'all these mouths eating Signora out of house and home,' and went off to the kitchen to cook a fantastic amount of spaghetti. Nearly all of them were already sitting at the table when Lucia finally brought in the steaming bowls. Only Ida and Barbarossa were missing.

Prosper saw Riccio, Mosca and Hornet surreptitiously looking at Scipio, who had seated himself and his long legs at the top of the table. They were all looking for something familiar, but there wasn't much to find. From time to time Scipio ran his hand flat over his hair, just like he used to; and he still arched his eyebrows the same way as ever. Other than that he was a stranger, even to Prosper. Scipio seemed to feel it himself, although he gave his friends a smile whenever he noticed their uneasy glances.

'Now, Signor Massimo, when are you going to see your

parents?' Victor asked, after Lucia had also sat down with an exhausted sigh. 'Today?'

'Why should I?' Scipio ran a finger over the prongs of his fork. 'They probably won't miss me. But I may sneak into the house to see my cat.'

'But you can't just leave your parents in the dark like this,' Victor told him. He was already eating his second helping of pasta, a fact Lucia acknowledged with a deep frown. 'It doesn't matter what you think of your father, you can't leave him with the constant worry that his son might have fallen into a canal, or been kidnapped.

Scipio ran his fork over the tablecloth and said nothing.

'But he doesn't want to, Victor!' Bo said. 'And anyway, he's grown up now.'

Scipio smiled at him.

'Grown up? So what!' Victor was just about to announce what he thought of Scipio's growing up when the door opened and Ida walked in. She held Barbarossa firmly by the hand, and when everybody turned to look at him, he just stared moodily at the ceiling.

'From now on your friend here will not be allowed to move around the house unsupervised,' Ida said angrily. 'He's been snooping around my dark room, going through my things, and eating my chocolates.'

Barbarossa turned as red as a cocktail cherry.

'I was hungry!' he snapped at Ida. 'I'll buy you some nicer ones, once I've got some money again. How often do I have to tell you that my wallet is still on that godforsaken island? As soon as the banks open tomorrow morning, I'll withdraw some money and replace your chocolates – and I'll get some decent clothes. It's a disgrace that a man like me should...' he wrinkled his nose and tugged at the jumper Bo had lent him '…should have to walk around in silly clothes like these.'

'Well, that's just great!' Ida shoved him roughly on to the last remaining empty chair, between Riccio and Mosca. Then she pulled up a stool for herself and sat down next to Victor.

'I thought you begged Prosper and Scipio to bring you here?' Hornet asked from across the table. 'So why don't you at least try to behave?'

'The little devil is not only stealing chocolates,' Lucia confirmed grimly. 'I caught him with our silver spoons. And he had a camera stuffed under his jacket.'

Riccio giggled, and Prosper caught him looking almost admiringly at Barbarossa. Bo, meanwhile, took his plate and sat down with it on Ida's carpet. 'I don't want to sit next to him,' he declared. 'He's going to steal my pasta as well.' Barbarossa threw an olive at him, which immediately earned him a resounding slap from Hornet.

'Now stop it, all of you!' Victor shouted. 'What's the matter with you? Has the little dwarf driven you all mad?'

Lucia got up, uttering another one of her deepest sighs.

'Signora, I'm going home,' she said, folding up her napkin. 'Perhaps you should lock the little one in the broom cupboard, if he really has to stay here tonight.'

'Any more of your cheek,' Scipio said to Barbarossa, after Lucia had closed the door behind her, 'and you can sleep in your shop. And what a cosy night that would be: with the dark alley outside, the rain drumming against the windows, and baby Barbarino all alone, with his little teeth chattering all night.'

Barbarossa stared into his plate, his lips tightly pressed together. Hornet, Mosca, Riccio and Prosper – none of them

311

had a a kind word to say to him. Ida and Victor were whispering to each other and weren't paying him any attention either.

'Maybe we should put an advertisement in the paper, Barbarino.' Scipio leaned back in his chair and put his hands behind his head. 'Unbearable little fellow, four or five years old, seeks mother. Or are you planning on looking after yourself? I don't think Ida wants to be your foster mum.'

'Definitely not!' Ida said, popping an olive into her mouth. 'But I think for an important man like you we should be able to find a bed at the Merciful Sisters.'

'No, thank you!' Barbarossa wrinkled his nose. 'No need. And should I really have any need for a foster mother, then it would definitely not be someone who wastes her silver cutlery on a bunch of orphans and who doesn't comb her hair.'

Ida gasped.

'You seem to know quite well, what you want, Barbarino,' Victor growled. 'Considering that you will barely be able to see over your shop-counter at the moment. But don't worry, the nuns in the orphanage are always immaculately groomed!'

Riccio giggled, until Barbarossa kicked him in the shin so hard that the tears welled up in his eyes.

'I'll cope,' the redhead retorted. 'I have more than enough money in the bank.'

'Yes?' Victor and Ida exchanged amused glances. 'And you think the bank is just going to hand out Ernesto Barbarossa's money to some five-year-old boy?'

Barbarossa's face went blank. He poured himself another glass of red wine.

'Once I'm big again,' he mumbled, glowering at Scipio and Prosper, 'I'll take revenge on everybody who didn't stop me from getting on to that cursed roundabout. I'll—'

Prosper interrupted him: 'Shut up, Barbarino! You have, just like us, given your word not to talk about it. And anyway, I know two dogs who probably can't wait for you to pay another visit to the island.'

'Don't listen to him, Prop,' Scipio crossed his long legs. 'Nobody cares what the midget has to say.'

'Well, Barbarino,' Riccio said, giving the miniature Barbarossa's shoulder a hard slap, 'welcome to the land of the small folk!'

'Get your hands off me!' Barbarossa growled. 'Who do you think you are? I'm not one of your silly little friends, you louse. And you?' Barbarossa stared down at Bo, who was still lying on the carpet. 'What are you looking at? Stop staring at me with your big puppy eyes.'

Bo didn't answer. He was lying on his belly, his chin resting on his hands, looking at Barbarossa as if he was some strange animal who had just crawled out of the canal and crept into Ida's house.

'I think Esther would like the way he talks, don't you, Prop?' Bo finally said. 'He talks posher than Scipio. And he's even smaller than me. But she probably wouldn't like the swearing.'

'Smaller? I'm not smaller, you woodlouse!' Barbarossa barked. 'We're worlds apart, do you understand? I am smart, I went to university, and you haven't been to kindergarten yet.'

Bo rolled nonchalantly on to his back. 'And he doesn't spill his food,' he observed. 'I think Esther would like that best. Don't you, Prop?'

Prosper dropped his fork and looked closely at Barbarossa.

'You're right,' he said, 'there's not even a tiny speck. She would be stunned. And just look how neatly he has brushed his hair. Did you do that, Ida?'

Ida shook her head. 'You've heard him: I can't even brush my own hair. What about you, Victor? Did you brush the redhead's hair?'

'Not guilty,' Victor answered.

'Who is this Esther these airheads keep talking about?' Barbarossa turned to Riccio.

'Prosper and Bo's aunt,' Riccio replied with his mouth full. 'She was crazy about Bo, but doesn't want him any more.'

'Very smart of her.' Barbarossa ran his hand through his thick curls. His new head of hair seemed to console him for the loss of his beard.

Scipio looked at him thoughtfully.

'You know what? I've just had a crazy idea,' he said slowly. 'It's still a bit hazy, but it's completely brilliant...'

'Brilliant?' Barbarossa reached for the wine again, but Victor grabbed the bottle and put it next to his own plate.

Barbarossa gave him a sinister look. 'You know, Thief Lord,' he growled in Scipio's direction, 'you can't possibly hatch any brilliant plans, because you're nothing more than a clone of your father.'

Scipio shot up as if something had bitten him. 'Say that again, you little squirt...'

Prosper and Hornet had to use their combined strength to stop Scipio from jumping on Barbarossa.

'Don't let that little rat get to you, Scip!' Hornet whispered to him, while Barbarossa smugly inspected his rosy fingernails.

Scipio dropped back into his chair. 'Fine,' he muttered, not taking his eyes off Barbarossa. 'I'll stay calm. Maybe I'll send a postcard to Signor Barbarossa at the orphanage one day. That's where he'll end up, if he doesn't starve to death in his shop. I won't waste another thought on him, let alone a brilliant one.' He got up, pretending to be offended, and looked out into the night.

Riccio and Mosca nudged each other, and Prosper couldn't hold back a grin. Yes, that was definitely the Scipio they knew, still the gifted actor.

And Barbarossa swallowed the bait.

'OK, OK,' he squawked, 'what about your brilliant idea, Thief Lord? Heavens, that man is touchier than a dog with a bone.

But Scipio kept his back turned. He stood by the window and looked out at the Campo Santa Margherita as if he was completely alone.

'Spit it out, for heaven's sake!' Barbarossa shouted, as the others began to chuckle. Scipio didn't move.

Barbarossa slurped the remaining wine from his glass and slammed it on the table so hard that it nearly broke. 'Do I have to go down on my knees?'

'Prosper and Bo's aunt,' Scipio said without turning around, 'is looking for a sweet little boy who has good table manners and can behave like an adult. You are looking for shelter, and a home for the future. And someone who puts food in front of you and who sleeps next door when it's dark...'

Barbarossa's eyebrows shot up. 'Is she rich?' he asked, brushing a stray lock from his forehead.

'Oh yes!' Scipio answered. 'Right, Prop?'

Prosper nodded. 'That's really quite a crazy idea, Scip,' he said. 'It's never going to work.'

49 What Now?

Barbarossa refused to sleep in the same room as the other children. Instead, he camped on the sofa in the living room. Ida let him please himself, but she locked him in as a precaution. Luckily Barbarossa didn't notice. Then she saw Victor to the door before going to bed herself.

Scipio had long gone. He had asked Mosca for some of the money they had left from the deal with Barbarossa, and then he had vanished into the night. Where he intended to go he hadn't said.

'Just like old times,' Hornet murmured, as they watched him from Ida's balcony.

They all knew what they couldn't forget – a door in a narrow alley, a curtain full of stars, mattresses on the floor, the moth-eaten chairs, and the gold and silver from the Thief Lord's satchel. All lost.

'Come on, let's go inside,' Hornet said finally. 'It's starting to rain again.'

They went up into their room. The piece of curtain Victor

had cut off was hanging on the wall. Ida had put a rug on the bare floor. The walls were decorated with whatever they had managed to salvage from the cinema. But many of their favourite pictures and photographs were still hanging on that cinema wall, above the empty mattresses, along with their homely scrawls and scribbles.

They all crept wearily under the covers. However, none of them could get to sleep, not even Bo, who usually dropped off as soon as his head touched the pillow.

'It would be quite something if Barbarossa managed to move in with your aunt,' Mosca said into the dark after a bit. 'But what are we going to do? Now that Prop is back, and Bo too. Has anyone got any ideas?'

'Nope,' Riccio mumbled into his pillow. 'We'll never find anything like the Star-Palace again. Definitely not with a bag full of fake money. And there's not much left of the other cash either. Maybe we'll find something over in Castello. There are lots of empty houses over there.'

'Why?' Bo sat up so abruptly that he pulled the blanket off Prosper. 'I don't want a new hideout. I want to stay here, with Ida!'

'Oh, Bo!' Hornet switched on the lamp, which Ida had put by her bedside so she could read in the evenings.

'Listen to him,' Riccio laughed. He was leaning against the wall and wrapping his blanket around his scrawny chest. 'What does Ida know about honour among thieves? No, I'll have a look around in Castello tomorrow. What about you lot?'

Mosca nodded. 'Count me in,' he agreed. He was staring out of the window as if he was trying to stare a hole in the night.

Hornet avoided the question and grabbed one of the books she had taken from Ida's shelf and started to leaf through it.

'I'm staying here!' Bo insisted. He stubbornly folded his arms. 'Yes, sir!'

'You go to sleep now,' Prosper said to him, pushing him back down on to his pillow. 'We'll talk about it tomorrow.'

'We can talk about it for a hundred years, a thousand years,' Bo shouted, kicking the blanket off him again, 'I'm staying here. My kittens like it here. They like teasing Lucia's dogs. And Victor picks me and Ida up and we go and have ice-cream, and Lucia cooks my favourite pasta for me and...'

'And what?' Riccio cut him off. 'And soon they'll tell you that you have to go to school, and what you have to eat, and that you should wash more often. No, way! Jeez, we've been on our own for so long, I'm not going to let anyone tell me that I'm too young to go out, or that my fingernails need cleaning. No way, josé! Not Riccio.'

The others fell silent for a few moments. Then Mosca said with great deliberation: 'Boy, Riccio, that was a real speech!'

Hornet put aside her book and walked slowly on her bare feet to the window to look outside.

'I'd like to stay here as well,' she said so quietly that the others could hardly hear her. 'This is much better than I ever imagined.'

'You're mad,' Riccio yawned, crawling back under his blanket. 'I'll ask Scipio what he's going to do now. *If* he comes back. Perhaps he'll have another one of his brilliant ideas.'

'I wonder what he's doing now,' Mosca said. 'Have you any idea, Prop?'

Hornet returned to her bed and switched off the light.

'Maybe,' Prosper answered. He stared into the darkness

and tried to imagine Scipio as he walked through the alleys, looking at his reflection in the dark shop windows, stepping into the glow of a street light to inspect his long shadow. Perhaps he would go into one of the bars where the grown-ups sat well into the night. Once he got tired he might check into a hotel room, like he had said, one with a big mirror, and shave for the first time.

'Is he OK?' Bo asked, laying his head on Prosper's chest.

'I think so,' Prosper answered. 'Yes, I'm sure he's fine.'

50 The Bait

Victor returned to the *Casa Spavento* the next morning with a newspaper with Scipio's picture on the front page. Nearly all of the city's papers ran the picture, together with an appeal by the police to all citizens of Venice to help the honourable Dottor Massimo find his missing son.

Ida was in the dark room, developing the photos she had taken of the city's stone lions. They were hanging on the walls all around her, sitting, roaring, grim-faced, along with peaceful lions with and without wings. Ida read Dottor Massimo's appeal and sighed. 'Do you know where Scipio is?' she asked Hornet, who had been watching her work.

But Hornet shook her head. None of us know,' she said, 'not even Prosper.'

'We should get a message to the *dottore*,' Victor muttered. 'Even if the Thief Lord doesn't want to.'

'I agree. I'll be right back,' Ida said to Hornet, and went with Victor into the living room where Barbarossa was hanging about on the sofa, looking rather bored as he leafed through a book on Venice's art treasures.

'I haven't touched anything,' he said guiltily, when Ida and Victor entered the room. He had woken the whole house at dawn, screaming after he had realized that Ida had locked him into the room.

'Just as well, redlocks,' Victor growled.

Ida sat down at her bureau and wrote on a card. Then she handed it to Victor.

'Dear Dottor Massimo!' he read. *'I would like you to know that your son is fine. He does, however, not want to come home right now, and I am afraid he is not planning on doing so in the near future. He is well and has a place where he can sleep, and he wants for nothing. I am sorry I can't tell you more at the moment. Kind regards. A friend.'*

'Could you drop this into the Massimo's letter-box?' Ida asked Victor. 'I would normally have Giaco do it for me, but ever since Prosper told me it was him who sold the ground plan of the house to the Conte I'm not sure I can trust him any more.'

'No problem.' Victor put the card in his pocket. 'Is there anything else I can do for you?'

'What about the aunt?' Barbarossa slipped off the sofa and stood with folded arms in front of Ida. 'It's already past ten. I suggest you call her now and tell her to come here, so that I can have a look at her.'

Victor was ready with a curt reply, when Hornet put her head round the door.

'I hung the photos up to dry, Ida,' she said, 'is there anything else I can do?'

'Yes, you can call Prosper and Bo down for me,' Ida replied, glaring at Barbarossa, 'I'm going to call their aunt and maybe they should be here when I do.'

Prosper and Bo were on the Campo playing football with Riccio. When Hornet came out to tell them that Ida really wanted to see if Scipio's crazy idea would work, they couldn't wait to get back to the house.

Ida was sitting next to the telephone when the four of them tumbled into the room. They all squatted down eagerly on the carpet. Prosper and Hornet sat on each side of Bo, so that they could hold his mouth shut, in case he started to giggle. Barbarossa was enthroned in Ida's best armchair like a king forced to watch a bunch of mediocre actors perform.

'I don't know why you're making such an effort for that brat,' Victor whispered to Ida. 'Just look at him, how he's sitting there...'

'That's exactly why I have to try this: so I can spare the Merciful Sisters from having to look after him,' Ida whispered back. 'It might also help Prosper and Bo. I think Prosper is still worried his aunt could change her mind about Bo. So let's give her' – she smiled at Barbarossa who was watching her and Victor suspiciously – 'our little redlocks.'

'If you think so,' Victor grudgingly agreed. 'She speaks Italian.'

'Even better,' Ida replied. She reached for the telephone and dialled the number of the hotel where the Hartliebs had ended up.

'*Buongiorno!*' Ida said with a firm voice after the receptionist had answered. 'This is Sister Ida, from the Order of the Merciful Sisters. Could I please speak to Signora Esther Hartlieb?'

It took some time before Esther's voice came through the receiver.

'Ah, good morning Signora Hartlieb,' Ida said. 'The reception told you who I am? Good. The reason I'm calling is that last night the police delivered two boys to our orphanage. One of the sisters immediately recognized the boys as your nephews, the ones on those posters all over town.' Ida paused and listened. 'Oh. Really? No, how unfortunate. Well. Pardon? What do you mean, you don't want the boys any more?' She listened again. Bo started to chew his fingernails nervously, until Hornet wrapped her arms around him.

'But aren't you their legal guardian?' Ida continued. 'I understand. Yes, the children have told me a similar story. That is sad, *Signora*, very sad. Of course we will look after your nephews, that is our mission, after all. But we still need you to come in to settle all the formalities…Yes, I'm afraid that it is absolutely necessary, Signora.'

Ida put on a stern face, as if Esther could see her. 'Yes, absolutely, I'm afraid. When did you say you were leaving?…So soon? Well, then I will arrange an appointment for you tomorrow afternoon. Hold on, let me just check my diary.' Ida rustled with the newspaper on the sofa. 'Hello, Signora?' she said into the receiver. 'I could see you at three o'clock…No, I'm afraid your presence is required. I will meet you in our town office, in the Casa Spavento, Campo Santa Margherita, number 423. Ask for Sister Ida. Yes. Thank you, Signora Hartlieb. Until tomorrow.'

Ida took a deep breath as she put down the phone.

'Excellent!' Victor said to her. 'I couldn't have done it better myself.'

'And I didn't laugh,' Bo said, pushing away Hornet's arm.

'She's really coming?' Prosper looked at Ida in disbelief.

Ida nodded.

'Incredible!' Barbarossa pushed away one of Bo's kittens that had tried to climb on his lap. 'Some people are really incredibly gullible.'

Ida took a cigarette and shrugged. 'I've laid out the bait,' she said, 'and now it's up to you whether Signora Hartlieb goes for it.'

Barbarossa stroked his thick curls. 'That shouldn't be a problem.'

'I don't want to be here when Esther comes,' Bo muttered, rubbing his nose uneasily.

Prosper got up and walked to the window. 'Me neither,' he said.

'There's no need for you to be.' Victor went and stood next to him. 'You see that café over there? I suggest you all go there tomorrow and have yourselves some nice helpings of ice-cream, while Sister Ida talks to Signora Hartlieb. I'll give you some money, so you don't have to pay with your fake notes.'

'I hope you do well tomorrow, Barbarino!' Mosca growled. 'So we can finally be rid of you.'

'Little redhead, Barbarino – I strongly object to these names!' Barbarossa complained. He had trouble getting out of the big chair. 'I just hope your aunt really has as much money as you say. Otherwise I'll tell her about the tricks you have been playing on her.'

'At least Esther is always perfectly groomed,' Prosper answered sarcastically.

'Very funny!' Barbarossa said, and with a look of disgust picked a cat hair off the trousers Bo had given him. 'What if she's really stingy? Her money won't be of any use. And she definitely won't be allowed to send me to school. Ernesto Barbarossa is not going to sit among a bunch of screaming, snotty-nosed brats who can't tell A from B. What if aunt Esther doesn't understand that?'

'Then,' Hornet said, with a sweet-as-honey smile, 'we will

have to find a bed for you with the Merciful Sisters.'

'You can go and ask them,' said Ida, 'because I would like you and Prosper to pick something up for me from the sisters.'

'Pick something up? What?' Barbarossa asked, now deeply suspicious.

But Ida put a finger to her lips. 'That is a secret,' she said. 'But you'll find out soon enough, Barbarino.'

51 Esther

Esther came alone. She walked straight past the café where Prosper was sitting with the others, and had no idea who was watching her through window. Victor had chased all the children out of the house as soon as the hand on Ida's kitchen clock had struck three. All except for Barbarossa.

'Who are you looking at?' Hornet asked Prosper when she noticed him staring through the window.

'She really came,' Prosper answered without taking his eyes off Esther.

'Your aunt?' Full of curiosity, Hornet leaned over Prosper's shoulder. 'That's her?' Prosper nodded.

'Who?' asked Bo, his mouth full of ice-cream. He was having the same sundae as Riccio, only he was already finishing his second.

'Nobody,' Prosper muttered. He watched Esther walk towards Ida's house. She was wearing Wellington boots and her umbrella dripped with rain.

'I imagined her to be completely different,' Hornet whispered into Prosper's ear. 'Taller – and sort of more sinister.'

'Hey, don't you like your ice-cream, Prop?' Riccio asked.

He licked some chocolate ice-cream from his nose. 'Shall I eat it?'

'Leave him alone Riccio,' Hornet answered for him.

When Esther rang the bell to Ida's house, a round, surly-looking nun opened the door and silently signalled Esther to follow her. Ida had begged Lucia for nearly an hour until her housekeeper finally put on the nun's habit, and now she looked very impressive. Lucia marched the visitor towards what was usually the store and laundry room. Lucia's ironing board, the water bottles, and the large stock of flour had all been moved. Instead, there was now a desk – which Victor had dragged down from the attic with a great deal of cursing and swearing – together with a few simple chairs and a large candelabra. The whitewashed walls were adorned with a picture of the Madonna and Child that usually hung in Ida's kitchen.

'Signora Hartlieb, I presume?' Ida rose from behind her desk as Lucia showed Esther into the room.

Next to Ida stood Victor, no beard, no disguise, simply the Victor Esther knew. Ida, however, was wearing the dark habit of the Merciful Sisters like Lucia. 'Please tell Signora Spavento that the habits have to be back before tonight,' the nun had whispered to Prosper after she had passed the clothes through a hatch in the orphanage's gate. She had looked guilty, as if she was committing a serious crime. But she would do anything for the kind and generous Signora Spavento.

'Please have a seat, Signora Hartlieb,' Ida said, pointing sternly at the dusty chairs as Esther came in. 'Your husband couldn't come?'

'No, he is unavoidably detained on business. After all, we are leaving the day after tomorrow.'

Victor watched Esther sit down. She straightened her skirt over her knees, and looked uneasily around the bare room. When she noticed him, Victor gave a polite nod.

'You already know Signor Getz,' Ida said after sitting down behind her desk again. 'I asked him to come since the police informed me that he had been in charge of the search for your nephews. He has also been a loyal friend to the convent for quite some time.'

Esther looked at Victor as if she wasn't sure whether his being there was good or bad for her. Then she turned back towards Ida.

'Why did you ask me here?' she asked, straightening her skirt again.

'Well, that should be perfectly obvious,' Ida answered with exaggerated patience. 'We have to look after many children, whereas the money at our disposal is limited, very limited. So if, as in the case of your nephews, we do find out that there are relatives...'

'I am not prepared to look after them again!' Esther interrupted her brusquely. 'I *was* prepared to, but the little one...' she fiddled nervously with her earlobes, '...I'm sure Signor Getz has already told you what we've been through with Bo. He might have fooled you with his angelic face, but I've been cured – thoroughly. He is stubborn, moody, and bites like a little dog. Anyway...' she took a deep breath '...I am sorry, but not even for the sake of my late sister would I be ready to take him in again. And there is nobody else in our family who would take one of the boys. So if you could keep them both here ... after all, they so desperately wanted to come to this city ... the family would agree to give what little money their mother left behind to the orphanage.'

Ida nodded. With a deep breath she folded her hands on the desk. 'This is all very unfortunate, Signora Hartlieb.' Suddenly, Ida glanced at the door.

Victor had of course also heard it: steps approaching down the corridor, perfectly according to plan. There was a knock. Esther Hartlieb turned around.

'Yes?' Ida called.

The door opened, and Lucia pushed Barbarossa into the room.

'The new boy is having problems again, Sister!' Lucia announced. She looked at the redhead as if she was handling a hairy spider or some other distasteful animal.

'I will deal with it,' Ida answered, and Lucia gruffly left the room.

Barbarossa stood by the door, looking very small and forlorn. Noticing Esther's curious look, he gave her a timid smile.

'Please excuse me, Signora Hartlieb,' said Ida, 'but this boy has only come to us recently and he is having a lot of trouble with the other children. So they teased you again, Ernesto?'

Barbarossa nodded, casting a quick sideways glance at Esther. Then he started to sob, quietly at first, and then more and more violently. 'Do you have a handkerchief for me, Mother Ida?' he snivelled. 'They took my books away from me.'

'Oh no!' Ida reached into her black habit, but Esther was quicker. Smiling shyly, she handed Barbarossa her lace-embroidered handkerchief.

'*Grazie, Signora*,' he replied, dabbing the tears from his long lashes.

Victor looked sideways at Esther, noticing that she couldn't take her eyes off the little redhead.

'Go and see Sister Caterina, Ernesto,' Ida instructed him, 'and tell her from me to take the books back from the boys. She should also send them to their rooms as a punishment.'

Barbarossa nodded and sniffed delicately into Esther's handkerchief. Then he walked hesitantly towards the door.

'Mother Ida?' he queried as he put his hand on the door-knob. 'May I ask when we will finally go on that excursion to the Accademia Museum? I would so much like to see Titian's paintings again.'

Lord, Victor thought. The redbeard is really laying it on rather thick. Esther's enraptured look, however, quickly put him right.

'Titian?' Esther asked, smiling at the little one. 'You like Titian's paintings?'

Barbarossa nodded.

'I like them a great deal myself,' Esther continued. Her voice was suddenly very soft, completely different from the way Victor had heard her shout before. 'Titian is my favourite painter.'

'Oh really, *Signora*?' Barbarossa pushed the red locks from his face. 'Then you have probably seen his grave in the Frari Church. I like his self portrait best, where he pleads with the Madonna to spare his favourite son from the plague. Have you seen it?'

Esther shook her head.

'His son still died of the Black Death,' Barbarossa went on. 'And Titian died of it as well. If I may say so, *Signora*, you look a bit like the Madonna in that painting. I would love to show it to you some time.'

By all the winged lions in Venice, Victor thought, now he's got schmaltz literally dripping from his mouth, the little flatterer. However, if Victor remembered rightly, the Madonna in the painting did look rather stern, perhaps she did resemble Esther Hartlieb a little. In any case, the compliment had its desired effect.

Pointy-nosed Esther had turned as red as a poppy. She sat on the edge of her chair and looked at the tips of her shoes like a little girl. Suddenly, she turned to Ida.

'Would that be possible?' she stammered. 'I mean, you know, my husband and I will only be in the city until tomorrow, so could I maybe take the little one here...'

'Ernesto,' Ida interrupted her with a dry smile, 'his name is Ernesto.'

'Ernesto.' Esther repeated the name as if she was sucking at a sweet. 'I know that this request may be a little unusual, but would it be possible for me to take Ernesto on a little excursion? He could show me the Frari Church, we could have some ice-cream, or go on a boat... I would carefully bring him back on time tonight.'

Sister Ida raised her eyebrows. To Victor her surprise looked convincingly real.

'This is indeed an unusual request,' Ida said, turning to Barbarossa. The redhead was still standing there with the most innocent expression, his hands folded neatly behind his back. He had brushed his hair himself until it shone. 'What do you say to Signora Hartlieb's offer, Ernesto?' Ida asked. 'Would you like to go on an excursion with the Signora?'

Go on, say yes, redhead, Victor prayed. Think about those beds in the orphanage. Barbarossa glared at Victor as if he had guessed his thoughts. Then he looked at Esther again. Not even a dog could have managed such a trusting look.

'An excursion like that would be wonderful, Signora!' he said, giving Esther a smile that was as sweet as one of Lucia's puddings.

'That is really very nice of you, Signora Hartlieb,' Ida said. She rang the little silver bell on the desk in front of her. 'Ernesto is not having an easy time settling in here. Concerning your nephews, however,' she added as Lucia entered the room, 'I regret to have to tell you that they don't want to see you. Shall I ask Sister Lucia to bring them here nevertheless?'

The smile on Esther's lips disappeared in an instant.

'No, no,' she answered quickly. 'I will visit them later, sometime, when I come back to Venice.'

'As you wish,' Ida replied. She turned to Lucia, who was waiting by the door. 'Please get Ernesto ready to go out, Sister. Signora Hartlieb has invited him on an excursion.'

'How charming,' Lucia grumbled. She grabbed Barbarossa's hand. 'So let's quickly wash the little one's ears and neck.'

'They're clean!' Barbarossa hissed at her. For a moment his voice sounded neither very nice nor very shy. But Esther hadn't noticed anything. She sat, lost in thought, on the hard chair in front of Ida's desk, and looked up at the picture of the Madonna. Victor would have happily given three of his favourite false beards to read her thoughts.

'Has the boy got any parents?' Esther asked after Barbarossa had left with Lucia.

Ida shook her head and shrugged. 'No. Ernesto is the son of a wealthy antiques dealer who vanished last week under mysterious circumstances. The police suspect a boat accident at night on the lagoon, maybe during a fishing trip. The boy has been with us since then. His mother left his father years ago and she is not willing to take the boy in. Quite astonishing, isn't it? He's such a delightful little child.'

'Indeed.' Esther looked at the door as if Barbarossa was still there. 'He's so – different from my nephews.'

'Being related is not a guarantee of love,' Victor reminded her. 'Even though we would all like it to be that way.'

'How true, how true!' Esther laughed a tiny, cheerless laugh. 'I would really like to have a child, you know, but…' she looked up at the ceiling before looking at them both '…I haven't yet found one who would like me as a mother. My nephews, for example, seem to think I'm some sort of witch.' She looked at the ceiling again. 'No, they probably consider me too boring even for that,' she said. And again she laughed her small, sad laugh. 'I really wish there was a child somewhere that I was suited to.'

Ida and Victor looked at each other conspiratorially.

Esther returned Barbarossa quite late that evening. Prosper and Bo watched from the living room window as they walked across the square. Barbarossa was licking a huge cone of ice-cream without getting a single drop on himself. Bo would really have loved to know how he did that. Esther was laden with big overstuffed shopping bags, but her left hand held on to Barbarossa's and on her lips was a blissful smile.

'Just look how she worships him!' Riccio leaned over Bo's shoulder. 'And all those packages! I bet they're all for him. And you're still not sorry you put her off so badly that she doesn't want you back?'

Bo shook his head vigorously. Prosper, meanwhile, was thinking of someone else, someone who had looked a little like Esther. He was glad when Victor startled him out of his thoughts.

'Well? Aren't those two the perfect match?' he whispered into Prosper's ear. 'They were made for each other, don't you think?'

Prosper nodded.

'Go on, put away that worried face for a bit,' Victor said, giving him a gentle nudge in his back. 'Two more days, and your aunt is flying home. And Bo won't be sitting next to her on the plane.'

'I'll believe that once she's in the air,' Prosper grumbled back.

And as he watched Esther wipe the ice-cream off Barbarossa's mouth he asked himself for the hundredth time where Scipio was. He wanted to tell him that his crazy idea was working.

52 Everything Will Work Out Fine – or Will It?

Esther Hartlieb did not fly home as scheduled. Her husband boarded the plane alone, while she was visiting The Doge's Palace with Barbarossa. The day after that she picked up Ernesto again – for a trip to the glassblowers on Murano. First, however, she took him shopping, and when Barbarossa returned to the *Casa Spavento* that evening, he was wearing the most expensive clothes one could buy in Venice for a child of his age.

He strutted into the living room, as proud as a peacock. The others were all squatting on the carpet and playing cards with Ida. 'You really are a pair of extraordinary idiots,' Barbarossa said to Prosper and Bo. 'You have the amazing luck to have such a rich aunt and you run away from her as if the devil himself was after you. Your brains must be the size of a pea.'

'And you, Ernesto,' Ida replied, 'probably have a wallet where other people have a heart.'

Barbarossa just shrugged impassively and reached into his smart new jacket. 'Speaking of wallets,' he said, producing a well-filled purse, 'I would like to ask one of you to regularly check on my shop over the next few months, in return for an appropriate fee, of course. You know, keep an eye on it, and clean it – that sort of thing. And I also urgently need a saleswoman who knows her job and hasn't got her fingers in the till all the time. That won't be easy, but I have complete confidence in you.'

They all looked at him in total surprise.

'You think we're all your servants now?' Riccio replied angrily. 'Why don't you do it yourself?'

Barbarossa's mouth screwed into a very pompous expression.

'Because, you spiky airhead, tomorrow I will be boarding a plane with Signora Hartlieb,' he replied with a swagger. 'And my place of residence will be outside this country. My future foster mother will call Sister Ida tonight and ask for her approval of my adoption by the Hartliebs. A lawyer has also been hired, who will remove any remaining legal obstacles. My future parents don't know about my shop, and I would like it to stay that way. I will try to open an account into which the earnings may be deposited. After all, I do not intend to live off pocket money alone.'

Riccio was so startled he dropped his cards. Mosca took the opportunity to quickly check Riccio's hand.

'Congratulations, Barbarino,' said Hornet. 'Seems like you've got quite a pleasant life ahead of you.'

Barbarossa just shrugged disdainfully.

'Well,' he said, casting a disgusted glance around Ida's living room, 'more comfortable than yours, that's for sure.' Then he turned on his heels and strutted out of the room. Bo stuck his tongue out as he left. The others gazed thoughtfully at their cards. 'Ida,' Mosca said finally, 'Riccio and I are leaving as well, probably at the end of next week or so. Riccio has found an empty warehouse, over in Castello. It's right by the water, and there are even moorings for my boat.'

Ida fiddled with her earrings. This time they were tiny golden fish with eyes of red glass.

'How are you going to get by?' she asked. 'Life in Venice is quite expensive. The Thief Lord won't be looking after you any more. Are you going to start stealing again?'

Riccio fiddled with his cards, pretending not to have heard Ida's question. Mosca, however, shook his head.

'No way. We've still got some money to start with from our last deal with Barbarossa. If that's not fake money as well.'

Ida nodded. Then she turned to the other three, Prosper, Bo and Hornet.

'What about you?' she asked. 'You're not going to leave me all at once too, are you? Who's going to eat all the food Lucia has bought? Who's going to tease her dogs, read my books, and play cards with me?'

Hornet smiled. Bo knelt down next to Ida. 'We'll stay with you,' he said, placing one of his kittens on her lap. 'Hornet told me she wants to live here for ever.'

'Bo!' Hornet went bright red with embarrassment.

Ida, however, let out a big sigh. 'Well, I'm relieved!' she said. Then she leaned over towards Bo and whispered: 'What about your brother?'

Prosper looked at them sheepishly.

'He wants to stay too,' Bo whispered back. 'But he's too shy to ask you.'

With a groan, Prosper buried his face in his hands.

'Well, it's just as well that he has a brother who can do the talking for him,' Ida smiled. 'So, Ida and Hornet, Prosper and Bo. That makes four!' she said. 'A good number, especially for playing cards. But we may have to explain to Bo again that he can't keep making up his own rules.'

The next day, Barbarossa got on to a plane, just as he had planned. Of course Ida had promptly approved of the adoption and Esther Hartlieb's lawyer had sorted out the rest.

On the boat-taxi to the airport Barbarossa was very quiet, and when Venice disappeared behind the horizon he let out a deep sigh. But when Esther asked him apprehensively whether there was anything wrong he just shook his head and claimed that he had never really liked boat trips. That was how Barbarossa said farewell to Venice, but inside his stubbornly greedy heart, he resolved to return one day in his brand new life.

Two days and two nights later, as the sun was already disappearing behind the roofs, Mosca and Riccio packed the few belongings they had managed to salvage from the cinema into Mosca's boat. They said goodbye to Prosper, Bo, Hornet, Ida and Lucia, who also gave them two plastic bags full of provisions. Then they cast off towards Castello, the poorest part of Venice, but not before giving a promise to get in touch as soon as they had found a place to stay.

The other three children missed the two boys badly. Bo cried his eyes out even though Hornet tried to tell him that they were, after all, staying in the same city. To take Bo's mind off things, Victor took him to St Mark's Square to feed the pigeons. Ida showed Hornet the school she and Prosper would be going to in the spring. But every evening before going to bed, Prosper stared out of the window, wondering what Scipio was up to.

But Prosper wasn't the first one to see Scipio again. One

evening, as he returned from shadowing someone, Victor went past Barbarossa's shop to put up a sign Ida had written:

Salesperson required, experience preferred. Applications to:
Ida Spavento, Campo Santa Margherita 423

The sticky tape kept wrapping itself around his thumbnail and Victor was cursing quietly to himself, when suddenly a tall figure approached him.

'Hi, Victor,' the stranger said. 'How are you? And how are the others?'

Victor stared at him quite dumbfounded. 'Heavens, Scipio! Did you have to creep up on me like that?' he spluttered. 'Appearing here like some ghost – I nearly didn't recognize you in that hat.'

'Yes, I know. This hat was the first thing I bought.' Scipio lifted it off his black hair. 'Since then I've only been greeted *three* times a day as Dottor Massimo.'

'Ida wrote a card to your father.' Victor tried once more to stick the note to the shop's door. This time it worked. 'She wrote that you are fine and that you won't be coming home for the time being. Did you see your father's appeal in the newspaper?'

Scipio nodded. 'Yes, yes,' he muttered. 'Having a son is really quite a nuisance. And now, on top of everything, he's also gone missing. I went home last night to fetch my cat. Luckily, nobody saw me.'

They both stood silent for a while and gazed up at the moon. Finally, Victor said: 'Your idea . . . you know, the one about Barbarossa . . . it worked.'

'Really?' Scipio put his hat on again and pulled its brim

down over his face. 'Well, I knew it was brilliant. Are the others still at Ida's?'

'Prosper, Bo and Hornet are,' Victor answered. 'Mosca and Riccio are now living in an empty warehouse in Castello. But how are you?'

He looked into Scipio's face carefully. As far as Victor could make out in the dark, the Thief Lord did not really look very happy. He looked rather tired.

'If you're not doing anything right now,' Victor continued when Scipio didn't answer immediately, 'you could walk with me a little and tell me on the way what you've been doing. It's too cold to be standing around here and I've got to get home. I've been on my feet all day, and I'm starving.'

Scipio shrugged. 'I'm not doing anything special at the moment,' he answered. 'And my hotel room is not so cosy that I'd want to get back there in a hurry.'

So they set off together towards Victor's flat. The air that night was not as icy as it had been on previous evenings; the sky above the old city was so full of stars that the alleys between St Mark's Square and the Grand Canal were still crowded with people enjoying the sights.

Scipio broke the silence only when they reached the Rialto Bridge.

'I haven't been doing much at all, really,' he said as they walked next to each other up the stairs.

A thousand lights twinkled on the water – the lights of the restaurants along the canal, the lights of the gondolas, of the *vaporetti* weaving their way along the broad waterway. It was hard to tear your eyes from it all. Victor leaned over the parapet. Scipio spat into the canal.

'Victor,' he asked, 'what do adults do all day?'

'Work,' Victor answered, 'eat, shop, pay bills, use the phone, read newspapers, drink coffee, sleep.'

Scipio sighed. 'Not really very exciting,' he muttered, resting his arms on the cold stone of the parapet.

'Well,' Victor grunted. But he couldn't think of anything else to say.

They sauntered on, slowly, across the bridge and into the maze of alleys in which every visitor to Venice gets lost at least once.

'I'll think of something,' Scipio said, determination ringing in his voice. 'Something exciting and adventurous. Maybe I should go to the airport and get on a plane. Or maybe I could become a treasure hunter. I read about that somewhere. I could learn to dive...'

Victor had to grin and Scipio noticed it.

'You're making fun of me,' he said angrily.

'No way!' Victor smiled. Treasure hunter, diver – he had never wanted to be anything like that!.

'Go on, admit it, you also like a bit of adventure,' Scipio continued more calmly. 'After all, you're a detective.'

Victor didn't reply. His feet ached, he was tired, and he would have loved to be just sitting next to Ida on the couch. Why the hell hadn't he done just that? Instead he had gone traipsing through the night.

They were already crossing the bridge near Victor's house. 'You should look in on your old friends sometime,' Victor said.

'I will, I will,' Scipio said absent-mindedly – as if his thoughts were elsewhere all of a sudden. He stopped abruptly. 'Victor!' he said. 'I think I've just had another brilliant idea.'

'Oh dear,' Victor muttered. He stepped wearily towards his front door. 'You can tell me about it tomorrow, OK? Why don't you come to Ida's for breakfast? I'll be there, I'm there nearly every day now.'

'No, no!' Scipio shook his head vigorously. 'I'll tell you right now.'

The young man took a deep breath, and for a moment he looked just like the boy he had been, not so long ago. 'Listen. You're not really that young any more...'

'What do you mean?' Victor spun around indignantly. 'If you're saying that I'm not a child in a grown-up body, then you're damn right...'

'No, don't be silly!' Scipio interrupted impatiently. 'But you've been doing detective work for years now. Don't your feet sometimes ache after you've followed someone for hours? Just think how difficult it was to keep up with us...'

Victor gave him a suspicious look. 'I'd rather not,' he growled. He was already unlocking the door.

'OK, OK. Fine!' Scipio pushed past him. 'But imagine this...' he skipped so nimbly up the stairs that he had Victor completely out of breath just trying to follow him.' Imagine having someone who would do all the running around, the shadowing at night, and everything else that makes your feet ache. Someone...' Scipio stopped in front of Victor's door and spread out his arms triumphantly '...someone like me!'

'What?' Victor, panting heavily, stood in front of him. 'What do you mean? You want to work for *me*?'

'Of course! Isn't that a wonderful idea?' Scipio pointed at Victor's sign, which looked like it needed a good clean. 'It could still say Getz at the top and my name would go underneath...'

Victor was just about to answer when the door opposite opened and his aged neighbour, Signora Grimani, popped her head around the door.

'Signor Getz,' she whispered with a curious sideways glance at Scipio. 'I'm so glad I caught you. Would you be so good as to get me a loaf of bread when you're going to the baker's tomorrow? Climbing these stairs is becoming such a burden for me, especially on damp days like these.'

'Of course, Signora Grimani,' Victor answered, rubbing his nameplate with his sleeve. 'Is there anything else I can get you?'

'No, no!' Signora Grimani shook her head. She eyed Scipio furtively, as if he was someone whose name she couldn't recall.

'Dottor Massimo!' she called out suddenly, clinging on to the doorknob. 'I saw your picture in the newspaper. And you were on television too. I am really sorry about your son. Has he been found yet?'

'Unfortunately not, Signora,' Scipio answered with a grave face. 'That is why I am here. Signor Getz has offered to help me with the search.'

'Oh, that is good. *Benissimo!* Signor Getz is the most wonderful detective in the whole city! You'll see.' Signora Grimani beamed at Victor as if he had just grown a pair of angel's wings.

Victor muttered, '*Buonanotte!* Good-night, Signora Grimani!' and pulled Scipio into his flat before he could start any more rumours.

'Great!' he grumbled while struggling out of his coat. 'Soon the whole of Venice will know that Victor Getz is looking for Dottor Massimo's son. What the hell were you thinking?'

'It was a sort of intuition.' Scipio hung his hat on Victor's coat rack and looked around. 'It's quite cramped,' he observed.

'Well, not everyone has their own fountain or ceilings as high as those in The Doge's Palace,' Victor grunted back. 'It's good enough for me and my tortoises.'

'Your tortoises, of course!' Scipio wandered into Victor's office and sat down on one of the visitor's chairs. Victor went into the kitchen to fetch some lettuce for his pets.

'Weren't you surprised when I appeared so suddenly in front of Barbarossa's shop?' Scipio called after him. 'You walked past me on the Accademia Bridge. Only you were so lost in your own thoughts that you didn't see me. So I decided to shadow you, just for the fun of it. Admit it, you didn't notice a thing. That proves what a first rate detective I would be.'

'It proves nothing,' Victor grumbled as he squatted down next to the tortoises' box. 'It only proves that you seem to think the job of a detective is jam-packed with all sorts of excitement. The truth is, it's mostly boring.'

Victor flung the lettuce at his tortoises and stood up. 'And anyway, I can't pay you much.'

'Doesn't matter. I don't need much.'

'You'll soon get bored.'

'We'll see.'

With a sigh Victor dropped into his desk chair. 'I'm not having your name on the sign.'

Scipio shrugged. 'I'll need a new name anyway. You don't really think I'm going to run around Venice as Scipio Massimo?'

'Fine. Here's one last condition.' Victor fished a sweet out of his desk drawer and popped it into his mouth. 'You will tell your father.'

Scipio's face darkened. 'What am I going to say to him?'

Victor shrugged. 'That you're all right. That you're going to go to America. That you'll look in on them in ten years or so. You'll think of something.'

'Damn!' Scipio spluttered. 'OK, I'll do it. If you teach me how to be a detective.'

Sighing, Victor folded his hands behind his head. 'Are you sure you wouldn't rather take over Barbarossa's shop?' he asked hopefully. 'Ida and I are looking for someone. You would get half of the earnings. The other half you would have to send to Barbarossa in his new home. That's what we agreed.'

Scipio wrinkled his nose at the prospect.

'What? Stand around in a shop all day and sell Barbarossa's junk? No, thanks! I like my idea much better. I'm going to be a detective, a famous detective, and you're going to help me become one.'

What could Victor say? 'Fine. Then you'll start tomorrow morning, straightaway, while I'm off having breakfast with Ida.'

345

53 And then...

Half a year later, Victor did put Scipio's name on his door, although he put it in slightly smaller letters.

Nobody, not even Prosper, ever asked Scipio whether he regretted having gone on the roundabout. However, maybe the new name he had given himself, the one he put on Victor's door, already gave the answer: Scipio Fortunato, the fortunate one.

Every now and then, just as he had promised Victor, Scipio wrote a postcard to his father. Signor Massimo never suspected that his son was living only a few alleys away from him in a flat that was hardly bigger than his own study, and where Scipio was happier than he had ever been in the *Casa Massimo*. Sometimes he visited Riccio and Mosca in their new hideout. He usually gave them some money, although they seemed to be coping quite well by themselves. They wouldn't tell Scipio how much was left of the counterfeit cash since, as Riccio put it: 'You're a detective now, after all.' Mosca had found work with a fisherman on the lagoon. Riccio, however – well, Scipio suspected that he had gone back to pickpocketing.

Scipio saw Hornet, Prosper and Bo more often. He and Victor visited Ida at least twice a week.

One night, as autumn approached again, Scipio and Prosper decided to go back to the Isola Segreta. Ida lent them her boat and this time Scipio found his way immediately. The island looked unchanged. The angels were still standing watch up on the wall. But this time there was no boat at the jetty and no dogs barked as Prosper and Scipio vaulted over the gate. They called out in vain for Renzo and Morosina in the stables and in the old house. Even the pigeons seemed to have disappeared. When the two had finally fought their way through the labyrinth of brambles and reached the clearing beyond, they found nothing but a small stone lion, almost hidden beneath the fallen autumn leaves.

Prosper and Scipio never found out whether Renzo and his sister disappeared the same night the roundabout was ruined. During the following years they would keep asking themselves if perhaps Renzo did find a way to repair the roundabout and if, somewhere, they were doing their rounds again: the lion, the merman, the mermaid, the sea horse, and the unicorn.

Anything else? Ah, yes – Barbarossa...

Esther carried on believing for quite a while that he was the most wonderful child she had ever met – until she caught him stuffing her most precious earrings into his trouser pockets and then discovered in his room an entire collection of valuable items that had mysteriously disappeared. Tearfully Esther sent him off to an expensive boarding school where Ernesto became the terror of his teachers and fellow pupils. Dreadful things were said about him: that he forced other children to do his homework and to clean his shoes, that he even encouraged them to steal things, and that he had given himself a name that everyone had to call him.

It was 'The Thief Lord'.

Glossary

Some of the Italian words used in The Thief Lord

Accademia, Galleria dell'   Academy of Fine Arts (grandest
   gallery and museum in Venice)

angelo   angel

arrivederci   goodbye

avanti   let's go; forward

basilica, the; as in Basilica San Marco Private chapel of the
   doges until 1807 when it became St Marks Cathedral.

basta   enough; that will do

benissimo   excellent; very good

bricola/bricole   wooden post/s that mark shallow areas in
   the lagoon to prevent craft from running aground.

buongiorno   good morning; good afternoon (a greeting)

buonritorno   have a good return trip

buonanotte   good-night

buonasera   good evening

calle   alley or street

campo   an open square

Campo Santa Margherita   St Margaret's Square

cara   my dear

carabiniere carabinieri   Italian policeman/police

casa   house

chiuso   closed

conte; contessa   count; countess

dottore   doctor

fondamenta   paved quay or walkway beside a canal

doge   chief magistrate

gondola   famous flat-bottomed 'taxi' boats of Venice, they are each punted along by a gondolier (oarsman).

grazie   thank you

isola   island

lira   Italian monetary unit (replaced by euros, January, 2002)

palazzo   palace or grand building

Palazzo Ducale   Palace of the Doges

pazienza   patience

piazza   square

Piazza San Marco   St Marks Square

ponte   bridge

pronto   ready; hello (only when answering the telephone)

Rialto   Market district by the Grand Canal in Venice.

sacca   bag

salotto   sitting room or reception room

salve   hi; or hello

scusi   excuse me

si   yes

signora / signore   Mrs, madam / Mr, sir

va bene   all right; fine; OK

vaporetto / vaporetti   (little steamer) waterbus/es

vietato ingresso   no entry; no admission

For everyone who loves books...
For everyone who dares to imagine...

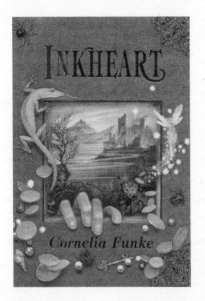

Meggie loves books. So does her father, Mo, a bookbinder, although he's never read aloud to her since her mother mysteriously disappeared. They live quietly until the night a stranger knocks at their door. He has come with a warning that forces Mo to reveal an extraordinary secret – a secret that will change their lives forever.

INKHEART is the thrilling new adventure from Cornelia Funke. It's a story within a story, where the imaginary becomes real.

Dare to read it aloud...

Read an extract:

www.doublecluck.com